15 July 2010

...nks for picking up this Little ...
of the great new titles from our series of fun, page-turning
romance novels. Lucky you – you're about to have a fantastic
romantic read that we know you won't be able to put down!

Why don't you make your Little Black Dress experience
even better by logging on to

www.littleblackdressbooks.com

where you can:

- ♥ Enter our **monthly competitions** to win
  gorgeous prizes
- ♥ Get **hot-off-the-press** news about our latest titles
- ♥ Read **exclusive** preview chapters both from
  your **favourite** authors and from brilliant new
  writing talent
- ♥ Buy **up-and-coming** books online
- ♥ Sign up for an essential slice of romance via
  our **fortnightly email** newsletter

We love nothing more than to curl up and indulge in an
addictive romance, and so we're delighted to welcome you
into the Little Black Dress club!

With love from,

The *little black dress* team

Five interesting things about Allie Spencer:

1. Four years at university gave me the skills necessary to roll a Hula Hoop across the floor of the college bar with my nose.

2. I have a secret ambition to be a stand-up comedian.

3. The first rule of life is: if you love it – buy it. I'm still thinking about the orange silk fifties cocktail dress I saw in a vintage shop ten years ago . . . sigh.

4. I have a total soft spot for men in glasses (and I keep nagging my husband to wear his more often).

5. I once had a cat that used to eat chillies covered in vindaloo curry sauce.

Tug of Love

Allie Spencer

HEADLINE PUBLISHING GROUP
An Hachette UK Company
338 Euston Road
London NW1 3BH

little
black
dress

First published in 2009 by
LITTLE BLACK DRESS
An imprint of HEADLINE PUBLISHING GROUP

A LITTLE BLACK DRESS paperback

1

ISBN 978 0 7553 5293 7

Typeset in Transit511BT by Avon DataSet Ltd,
Bidford-on-Avon, Warwickshire

Printed and bound in Great Britain by
Clays Ltd, St Ives plc

Headl͏   ͏ and
recyclabl   forests.
The loggin   m to the

To Chris; I couldn't have done it without you!

Acknowledgements

Firstly, I'd like to thank Claire, Sara and all the team at Little Black Dress for the phenomenal amount of work they have put in turning this from a manuscript into a real (live?) book. I also owe my agent Teresa Chris an enormous debt of gratitude: she has been truly superb throughout and I can't thank her enough. There have been many, many people involved in the development of this novel but my special thanks go out to: Chris, Sarah-Jane, Lucie, Nancy, Jane, Sam, Claire, the Julies G and W-J, Karen, Grace, Clive, Isla, Noëlly, Vicky, who generously donated her line about weasels in Armani, and, for allowing me to run legal things past her, that star of the Manchester Bar: Pauline McHugh. I would also like to acknowledge the tremendous support I've received from the Romantic Novelists' Association and all my friends there – and wish the RNA a happy fiftieth birthday for 2010!

'Of course,' I said, ignoring the bustle of the busy restaurant behind me and pouring myself another glass of San Pellegrino, 'the thing to remember is that in a divorce, there are never any winners.'

The woman from *Marie Claire* who was interviewing me leant forward over the table and nodded earnestly.

'Now that's interesting.'

'Unless, of course, you're Zsa Zsa Gabor,' I quipped.

My interviewer and the photographer both laughed gratifyingly.

'Seriously, though,' I pulled the interview back on track, 'what I cannot overemphasise is that one of the primary duties of a legal team is to make sure that cases are worked out in a friendly, conciliatory atmosphere – especially when there are children involved.'

The *Marie Claire* lady nodded again in enthusiastic agreement.

'I'm sure our readers out there will be pleased to know that someone as influential as you holds that view.'

I smiled modestly.

'And what about your feelings on relationships? I mean, given the job you do, it must be easy to become a bit cynical.'

'Well,' I began carefully, 'I think the thing to remember is that people change, relationships *do* go wrong; but that doesn't mean we should shy away from love altogether. People need to forgive themselves and move on.'

Actually, that wasn't strictly true, but I wasn't going to get into a discussion with the *Marie Claire* lady about it. I'd always been a bit sceptical about love, commitment and that sort of thing – and with good reason. Not only did my divorced parents still fight like cat and dog, but on the one occasion that I thought I'd found the real deal, I ended up getting my fingers very badly burned. The fact that I now sorted out other people's marital differences for a living (in itself an unbelievably bad cosmic joke) had done little to help matters.

'Okay,' said the photographer, 'let's get a few pics for the feature.'

A make-up girl leaped forward, brandishing a brush so huge that the Scottish curling team were probably out looking for it, and swiftly covered my face in some sort of expensive powder. I rearranged my features for the camera to make sure I had a serious yet caring expression.

'Right – to me – that's it.' CLICK! 'And again – super!' CLICK! 'Now – looking out the window – sort of dreamy – wonderful!' CLICK! 'How about one with the briefcase? Yup! Excellent.' CLICK! 'And let's have a close-up so we can make those blue eyes really stand out against that dark hair. Lovely.' CLICK!

How fabulous was this?

I turned back to the *Marie Claire* lady, who was waiting with her pen poised.

'You see,' I continued, 'very often people have this idea that lawyers are just out to rack up the fees as high as they can – but when you're dealing with people's happiness, you can't afford to do that.'

There was a smattering of applause from the people at the next table, who had been listening in on our conversation.

'Hear, hear!' said my interviewer, smiling broadly.

'Exactly the sort of thing our readership will feel strongly about. Now, I think that's just about all I wanted to cover. I'll put in something about your Lawyer of the Year Award, of course – and the fact that you've currently got a six-month waiting list for new clients.' She paused, before continuing thoughtfully, 'You know, that's longer than for the new Chanel handbag.'

'Got some cracking shots here,' cut in the photographer. 'We'll probably put you on the cover – you won't mind, will you?'

Mind? Of course I won't mind!

My interviewer switched off her tape recorder, then leaned in towards me and whispered: 'Lucy, is it true you are currently advising three big-name film stars, four Premier League footballers and a member of the royal family?'

I met her eyes without a flicker of expression.

'I couldn't possibly comment.'

God, I was *so* professional!

Still, it was all in a day's work for me: head of my own chambers, big-name cases, masses of respect and recognition for my overwhelming achievements ... what's not to like? Just then, however, a phone rang.

Ka-*bloo*-ie!

My daydream crashed to smithereens on the perennially untidy floor of my office. I brought myself back to the real world with a shake of my head – and found myself groaning involuntarily as I picked up and a thin, weasely voice came on the line.

It was Hugo. Yuck.

'I need the latest *Family Law Notes* for court on Monday, Looby-Lou, and I think you're hiding them in that pit you call an office.' His voice became even oilier. 'Oh, and I could hear you talking to yourself again. You need to be careful about that – or Guy will start thinking you're a couple of papers short of a brief!' He rang off, sniggering.

Damn. *That* was what not to like.

The fact was that, in real life, rather than schmoozing my way through a glittering existence, I spent my days in a cramped, dingy basement room with horrible Hugo Spade on the other side of a thin partition wall. Don't get me wrong – I loved my job. I was – am – a barrister, good with my clients and hardworking. But my fantasy of legal fame and fortune was light years away from reality.

Unenthusiastically, I fished the journal he had requested off the floor (where I tended to keep most of my important documents in little piles) and sloped off next door to deliver it. I paused for a few seconds before turning the handle in order to prepare myself for the challenge that was Dealing with Hugo: he was unbelievably hard work. A couple of weeks ago, after he had spent a full two hours telling me how much money he had and how he didn't actually *need* to work at all, Henrietta ('Hez'), my best friend and flatmate, offered to hire someone to put him out of my misery. I'd told her that being sent down as an accomplice in a contract killing might not be the best way to enhance my legal career; although when I came to think about it now, bumping off Hugo might just get me into *Marie Claire*, so perhaps I shouldn't have dismissed it out of hand . . .

'Well then, Looby-Lou,' Hugo slimed as I handed over *Family Law Notes*, 'got any big plans for the weekend?'

'Don't call me that,' I muttered, 'and yes, actually I do. I'm going to a party tomorrow night.'

'Gosh, that'll be exciting for you,' he replied as patronisingly as possible. 'And which one of your legions of admirers will be chosen to accompany you?'

'The one who reminds me least of you.' I smiled sweetly whilst suppressing the urge to deck him. How did he always know when I was dateless?

'Well, I'd have to decline anyway. You know how it is – dinner at the Ivy, a couple of drinks with the boys before winding the evening up at Annabel's. Unless of course that Henrietta friend of yours is free. I could always manage to squeeze her in. Or even just squeeze her.' He snorted unpleasantly through his nose.

I chose not to tell him that Hez would rather munch her way through a kitten kebab at an animal rights meeting than spend time alone with him, and went to leave the room.

'No, seriously, Lou, I hope you have a really good time.'

I almost tugged my ears to make sure they were still in place. Surely Hugo hadn't managed to utter an entire sentence that was not rude or condescending in any way? Surely he wasn't being *nice*?

I needn't have worried.

'The last thing I would want is for you to spend any time fretting over this e-mail from Guy,' he drawled.

I froze. Guy Horatio Jennings QC was our head of chambers. To describe him as 'well known and well liked' would have been the understatement of the century, as he engendered the sort of acclaim that a minor deity would have been pleased to receive. He could barely move for the hordes of grateful clients swooning at his feet, and his spare time was spent parading his stunning wife and two apple-cheeked children at public events and charming the pants off the media. The one thing he didn't do, though, was waste time on anybody who wasn't important.

Like me.

I was right at the bottom of the chambers' food chain, and on the one occasion he had deigned to speak to me, he'd mistaken me for the cleaner and told me to give the loos another going-over.

So, basically, an e-mail from Guy wasn't going to be good news . . . unless it was all a hoax and Hugo was just trying to frighten me.

'This isn't some kind of wind-up, is it, Spade?' I

asked, putting on my scariest courtroom voice. Sadly, Hugo was not intimidated.

'See for yourself,' he said and, with a 'ping', the e-mail in question sprang on to the screen of his laptop.

> To: lucystephens@3templebuildings.co.uk;
> hugospade@3templebuildings.co.uk
> Cc: clerks@3templebuildings.co.uk
> Subject: Tenancy
>
> Hi, chaps!
> Just a quickie to let you know that I have arranged for a meeting to be held on the 3rd of next month to settle who gets a permanent place in chambers. I'm afraid that the provisional view of the tenancy committee is that only one of you can be taken on, although who that will be is undecided at present. I wish you both good luck – and may the best man win.
> Yours,
> Guy
>
> PS If either of you happened to record my performance on Question Time last Thursday, I'd be interested in a copy. Cheers.

'Is this for real?' I asked.

'Go and look on your own machine if you don't believe me,' replied Spade. 'Or ask the clerks.'

Now, here's the thing: even though Hugo and I had both qualified aeons ago, neither of us had been formally taken on by chambers. We were what are known, in elegant legal parlance, as 'squatters'. But in five weeks' time, that was all going to change. One of us would get the glittering prize of a tenancy at 3 Temple Buildings – name on the board outside, the works – whilst the other was going to be booted out. It felt like being a contestant on *Big Brother* but without the hot tub or the trendy furniture.

Or the on-screen snogging, thank goodness.

I shot a look at Hugo. He had pressed a couple of keys on his computer and pulled up some sort of game that seemed to consist entirely of drive-by shootings. This was vintage Spade. He was tall, fair-haired and actually rather bright; but even though I heard rumours in chambers that he was good with his clients, he seemed to spend a disproportionate amount of his time playing on his laptop, reading *Loaded* and chatting to his mates on the phone. So much so that it niggled me that there had to be any sort of competition for the stupid tenancy – under all normal rules of the universe, I should have walked it. However, in addition to a trust fund the size of Jupiter, Hugo's father was a judge in the Court of Appeal, and no doubt every conceivable string was being pulled vigorously on his behalf.

Still, there was a month to go before eviction day, and anything could happen in a month. Maybe I'd get some amazing case and become the toast of legal London; maybe I'd win the lottery and never need to work again; or maybe Spade would trip over his own ego and fall under a tube train.

Hope, as they say, springs eternal.

'Thanks for letting me know, Hugo,' I called over my shoulder as I left. 'And whatever you get up to this weekend, make sure you have a horrible time.'

'And you,' he replied cheerfully.

I stomped back into my own room, filed on the floor the brief I'd spent the afternoon reading and shoved my laptop in its bag prior to heading off home for the weekend. A memo sheet slithered off my desk and on to the chair; one of the clerks must have dropped it in whilst I was closeted with Hugo.

Was it good news? Was it a big-name case with a wealthy client? My ticket to gainful employment at the family law Bar? I snatched it up and pulled a face. Sadly, none of the above: my dad had rung. *Tell your mother,* the note said, *that if she doesn't agree to a reduction in her maintenance payments I'll take the whole thing back to court.* I dropped it in the bin and made a mental note not to mention anything of the sort to my mother. I was sick of this. Whenever they fell out (which was pretty much all the time) they would try to rope me in to take sides, and it drove me nuts. Why couldn't they just keep their disagreements to themselves?

As I put my coat on, I did a quick inventory of Things Not Going My Way. It was quite impressive: my mum and dad were gearing up for another bout of fisticuffs; I was facing a fight to the death over my job; and to cap it all, it sounded as if Hugo, a.k.a. the Weasel in Armani, had a better social life than me.

But life, as always, had a few little surprises up its sleeve . . . like the fact that Mark was about to turn up.

Or, to be accurate, Mark was about to turn up and Jonathan was about to reappear.

Or, to be even *more* accurate, Mark was about to turn up, Jonathan was about to reappear *and* the Prime Minister was going to get divorced.

And it all started at the party I'd mentioned to Hugo.

The party was at my friend Jo's. Unlike Hez, who had been my bosom buddy since university, I'd met Jo at Bar school; and in the ensuing three and a bit years she had been the only one of us who had managed to get herself a proper life. She now owned the first two floors of a lovingly restored Victorian house in Vauxhall, had built up an enviable practice doing clever things with inheritance tax and reeled in a sweetie of a husband in the form of Devoted Dave. However, despite this extreme provocation, Hez and I still loved her to bits.

The party in question was a sort of massed return invite for Dave's banking colleagues. I arrived chez Williams at about eight thirty, just as things were getting going. Jo was dashing about with a bottle of cava, topping up people's glasses, but as soon as she saw me, she wasted no time in elbowing her way through the throng to give me a hug and thrust a glass of fizz into my hand.

'Lou,' she beamed, 'brilliant to see you! I'll just make sure everyone's got a drink, and then we can catch up properly. Pippa's here,' she nodded towards a red-headed girl over in the corner, 'and Nancy and Rob are about somewhere; but I'm afraid most of them are from Dave's work.' She pulled a face. 'Still, grab yourself a canapé or three and I'll come and find you in a mo.'

I helped myself to a cunning little thing that looked

like a mini crispy duck pancake and scoured the room for Pippa. I couldn't see her, but I did notice Dave making a beeline for me through the crowd.

One of the many good things about Jo and Dave was that they normally had the decency not to lure their single friends (i.e. *me*) over for the evening with the promise of 'Someone I'd Like You To Meet'. In my experience, these heavily hyped assignations – 'He's just *wonderful*; you'll *love* him' – usually meant an evening of me feigning interest as the someone in question droned on about the finer points of 1960s diesel locomotives or the digestive system of the bumble bee. But, as I said, they weren't like that, which was why – just as I was opening my mouth to say hello to Dave – I was amazed to hear that he was uttering the dreaded words: 'Lou, there's someone I want you to meet.'

My heart sank as he guided me over to the other side of the living room. This was the last thing I wanted. I was after an evening spent in the company of a bottle of wine and a few friends, not one where I was followed round the house by an unwanted man-limpet. I decided that I'd smile sweetly while Dave did the introductions and then immediately leg it to the drinks table muttering something about a chronic alcohol addiction.

But as the person he was about to introduce me to swung into view through the throng of bodies, I decided against it.

You know that thing that happens in cartoons when your eyes grow really huge and jump out of your face on wobbly stalks? Well, I wouldn't swear to it, but I'm pretty sure that's what mine did right then. My tongue was probably dragging along the floor as well, but thankfully Dave and his companion pretended not to notice. You see, standing in front of me was a tall, broad-shouldered man, fidgeting a little nervously with the stem of his wine glass. His face could probably be described as pleasant rather than rugged, and his light brown hair was cut flatteringly short to disguise, I suspected, a tendency towards waviness.

In summary, he was exactly my type; although I hadn't had a type up until the moment I clapped eyes on him.

'This is Lucy, one of Jo's closest friends,' said Dave.

'Hi. I'm Lucy, one of Jo's closest friends,' I repeated moronically, hoping that the *zing, zing, zing* of my heartstrings wouldn't be audible above the background chatter of the party.

'I'm Mark,' the Handsome One replied, smiling at me. 'Dave and I were at school together. I've, um, just started a new job in London and Dave asked me along so that I could get to know a few people.'

I nodded, my voice box temporarily out of order.

'Right. I'll leave you to get to know each other,' said our Host with the Most. His mission accomplished, he buzzed off to help Jo with the topping-up.

'So—' we said simultaneously.

'You first.'

'No, you.'

Actually, I was desperate for him to go first. The words 'You're totally gorgeous – can I snog you now, please?' were running on a loop-tape round my brain, and I didn't trust myself not to say them out loud.

'How do you know Jo?' he asked.

'Bar school. We used to sit next to each other in lectures writing notes and eating Maltesers.'

As soon as the words left my lips, I could have kicked myself. The man was probably some sort of high-flying *über*-achiever with a million degrees. The announcement that my education had been spent skiving and scoffing chocolate was not going to go down well.

'Sounds like me and Dave,' he grinned, 'except it was St Peter's Grammar School and we ate Fruit Pastilles. They make less of a mess in your pocket.'

Phew! I risked a grin as well.

'Do you know many people here?' I asked.

He glanced round the room. 'Not a soul – apart from Dave and Jo, of course. I'm an engineer, so all this finance stuff Dave does is a bit beyond me.'

Ah. An engineer. Maybe my luck wasn't in after all and he'd soon be steering the conversation on to the boiling point of helicopters or the world record for setting concrete. But – no!

'And you?' he continued. 'What do you do?'

KER-CHING! Had I hit the jackpot?

'I'm a barrister, like Jo.'

'What type of law?'

'Divorce mainly,' I said, a little sheepishly.

It's awkward having to say that. It seems to make people feel uncomfortable; especially when you introduce yourself at weddings.

'Drink?' I asked, saving him the trouble of changing the subject, as a tray of liquid refreshment wafted past us attached to Jo.

'Yes, please,' he said.

Helping myself to two, I passed one to him. As he took it, his hand grazed mine.

Oh. My. *Life!* It was as if I'd just licked my fingers and plugged myself into the mains. What was happening? I downed my wine in one to help me think more clearly. It didn't, of course, but it *did* make me feel a bit more confident, and I risked a full-on ogle.

Yup, he was still gorgeous, and (my tummy did a pleasing little wobble) blessed with the most amazing blue eyes. I luxuriated in the view for a couple of seconds, until he began to stare back; then I quickly pulled my gaze away and focused hard for a moment on a pot plant in the corner. The last thing I wanted was for him to decide I was a total looper and make a break for the door.

'Between you and me,' I said, lowering my voice, 'I'm

here mainly because Jo said she needed some moral support.'

'Same here,' he replied, leaning in towards me. 'Dave said if there wasn't at least one real human being present, he'd go mad. Do you think,' he went on, almost whispering as he indicated a few of Dave's colleagues, 'this is the result of some genetic breeding programme to clone people with no chins?'

'And hideous laughs?' I added as a resounding 'Hwah-hwah-hwah!' echoed round the room.

We cringed in unison.

'Listen,' Mark's fabulous eyes looked straight into mine, 'have you eaten?'

I decided that the Marmite sandwich I'd had before I came out didn't count.

'No.'

'Shall we do a bunk? I saw a Chinese place round the corner – we could slip out and slip back again before they notice.'

'Done,' I said. 'Time and sweet and sour chicken wait for no man. Or something.'

'I couldn't have put it better myself,' he agreed.

Two hours, a set meal for two and a bottle of red wine later, things were feeling decidedly mellow.

And they would have felt even mellower if, when I dared to look across the table, my stomach hadn't felt as if it had climbed inside a washing machine set on the fast spin cycle. Each time my eyes focused on anything other than my chopsticks, they seemed to crash straight into his. Surely this wasn't the product of my feverish imagination? Was there a chance that he might – just – perhaps – be finding me as attractive as I found him? Sure, it was a long shot, but considering there are daily sightings of both Elvis and Lord Lucan alive, well and working in chip shops, perhaps it wasn't beyond the bounds of possibility.

And it wasn't just the smouldering glances across the

crispy seaweed that put me on red alert. We had spent the last couple of hours having one of those 'me too!' conversations, and it was amazing how much common ground we'd discovered between us, including some really important stuff like 'Waterloo' being altogether a superior composition to 'Knowing Me, Knowing You', and the fact that fizzy cola bottle sweets deserved recognition as one of the culinary masterpieces of the twentieth century.

But it wasn't until we were waiting for the waiter to take our order for coffee that IT happened: The Point Of No Return. His knee brushed mine and there was a repeat performance of the fingers-in-the-socket moment I'd experienced at Jo and Dave's. At the same time, our eyes met – only briefly, but enough for me to think the knee thing may have been more experimental than accidental. However, I thought it would be a good idea to check that I hadn't imagined it; I mean, how often do you meet amazing fellas who happen to be just hanging around at your mate's house?

Okay, how often does that happen when you are *awake*?

Anyway, I moved my knee so it touched his.

He looked at me.

I looked at him.

He nudged his knee in between my legs.

I slid my foot round his ankle.

Quite a promising game of Under-The-Table Twister was developing when Mark raised the stakes and ran his fingers along the back of my hand.

Once, one snowy night at university, I had a heavy evening in the pub down the road. When I got home, I reckoned that the best way to thaw out my frozen fingers would be to plunge my hands into the toaster. Luckily, Hez intervened before I'd managed to work out how to switch it on. Had she not, the result would probably have been similar to what I experienced just then.

Minus the smell of singed hair, perhaps.

Mark glanced at me with a 'Was that what you wanted me to do?' look.

I gave him a 'Yes! Yes! Yes!' look.

His hand homed in on mine again. This time I wasn't taking any chances and grabbed it.

He grinned at me and my heart joined my stomach in its loop-the-loop extravaganza.

I nudged my knee up the inside of his thigh as far as I could reach, which, given that he was sitting on the other side of a restaurant table, was sadly not very far. Even so, there was a sharp intake of breath and momentary closure of those blue eyes. That had to be a good sign.

'We were only supposed to be slipping out for a quick bite to eat,' he murmured, glancing at a clock on the restaurant wall and frowning slightly.

'Mmmm,' I said non-committally, repeating the knee massage and hoping this wasn't going to be the cue for us to scarper back to the party. I wanted to keep him all to myself.

The question was – how? Could I say something? Suggest a hot beverage made from ground, roasted beans back at my flat and hope that Hez had gone out?

'Whatchagonnadoaboutit?' yelled my brain.

I didn't know. This sort of thing wasn't my forte. In fact, the only time previously I had pursued a man (as opposed to simply giving in when one pursued me – my usual method of finding a boyfriend), the chap in question had been Jonathan, and look how badly that had worked out. But on the other hand, if I did nothing, the moment would pass and Mark might drift out of my life just as easily as he'd drifted into it . . .

'Um, we haven't ordered our coffee yet,' I said tentatively. 'What if we get some back at my place – coffee, I mean – some coffee – back at mine?'

I'd done it! Hoorah for me!

Mark's expression brightened considerably.

'Really?' he said, signalling for the bill.

'Yes.' I nodded vigorously as he helped me into my coat.

'Jo and Dave'll kill us,' he continued, opening the restaurant door.

'What's life without a few risks?' I replied, hailing a cab. 'Muswell Hill, please.'

'No,' interrupted Mark, taking my hand to help me into the taxi, 'Kentish Town.' He paused. 'It's nearer. And I live there,' he added as an afterthought, in case I assumed he was just calling out the names of random parts of north London.

We sat in the back as the cab zoomed across the river and up Tottenham Court Road. There was something about being alone together in the dark of the back seat that seemed to fast-forward our need to be in physical contact with each other. Any worries about Mark not reciprocating the magnetic pull I felt towards him were long gone. First our legs met, then our hands, then as much of our bodies as we could manage given the fact that we'd both been conscientious enough to put our seat belts on. Then his right hand, which had been round my shoulders, crept under my coat, inside my dress, and began a gentle but determined exploration of my underwear.

Frankly, he was lucky I didn't spontaneously combust and leave him with a lot of explaining to do to the taxi driver (who, before you ask, had no idea what was going on).

Not to be outdone, I eased my hand in under Mark's jacket and ran it round the top of his thigh. I took the fact that he then forgot to breathe for at least ten seconds as a good sign: he wanted to be in Kentish Town as much as I did.

The cab swung into Dartmouth Park Road and as we bundled out Mark thrust a fifty-pound note at the astonished cabbie and told him to keep the change. Together we pounded up the steps to his flat, Mark fumbling with his keys, before we almost fell through the front door in our eagerness to be inside.

Even though the pair of us were by now as randy as a couple of rabbits in a pheromone factory, we hadn't actually kissed – but boy, it was worth the wait. None of this quick peck on the lips stuff first. As soon as the heavy black-glossed door closed, leaving us more or less in total darkness, I threw my arms round his neck and snogged him as if my life depended on it. The kiss he gave by way of return literally took my breath away, and left me in no doubt that a mug of Gold Blend was not going to be top of his list of priorities for a while.

Next he planted equally ravenous kisses on my neck and round my ear, before unhooking my hands from the back of his neck and removing my coat. I did the same for him, kicking my shoes off as I did so. Leaving our outer garments in the hall, we snogged our way through the blackness of the hall and into the living room, by which time he'd undone the zip at the back of my dress and loosened my hair out of its customary twist. While he was thus engaged, I used the shafts of orange street light filtering through a window at the far end of the room to locate his buttons and remove his shirt. I left it lying in the doorway and, with mouth on hungry mouth, he steered me into the middle of the room, bumping into an armchair and the corner of a rolltop desk as we went.

But bruises were the least of my worries. As he eased my dress down to the waist and wriggled his hand inside the cup of my bra, a moment of doubt flashed through me.

Did I really want to be doing this with a man I'd only just met?

True, it was the sort of thing Hez got up to occasionally, but we were very different people. She was tall, stunning and confident; whereas I was, well, me. I didn't *do* one-night stands, just like I didn't *do* stunning. (And as for tall, let's not even go there.)

I was suddenly heart-poundingly, palm-sweatingly nervous. It wasn't that I actively tried to keep the physical side of things at bay, but if I *did* meet someone I liked, it generally took quite a few drinks, dinners and movies before it got to this point. However, for some reason I seemed to have bypassed my normal safety checks with Mark.

'Is this what you want?' murmured a voice next to my ear, bringing me sharply back to the here and now. 'I'll stop if you ask me to.'

Mark's hand was hovering over the clasp of my bra and his mouth was covering my ear in tiny kisses and bites.

Make-or-break time, then.

I laid my face against his chest and inhaled. The feel of his skin on my lips and the smell of his body made my heart start pounding again, but this time with a tingly sort of anticipation: I wanted this man very badly indeed. And I wanted him now – to hell with the rest of it.

'I don't want you to stop,' I said firmly and decisively. 'It's just I don't normally go around doing this sort of thing, that's all.'

'Me neither,' he said, grazing my right breast with his lips and making my knees go all wobbly. 'In fact, I'm probably a bit out of practice.'

Out of practice? Blimey, if he'd been on top form, I don't think I'd have been able to cope. Anyway, putting my moment of doubt behind me, I resealed his mouth with mine and we were pretty much back on course; so much so, in fact, that we never even made it into the bedroom. Mark broke off again momentarily to rummage through his wallet and produce a small, foil-wrapped packet. Then he put his hands on my hips, pulled me towards him and his kisses became more ravenous than before. The atmosphere changed from passionate to urgent, and I was aware of him guiding me down on to the floor. Then – well, do you really need me to go into detail? Suffice to say, I couldn't tell you whether the earth did actually move, because I *was* rather pre-occupied, but I wouldn't have been surprised if it had.

It took me quite a while to come back down afterwards, and it was even longer before Mark eventually found his voice.

'So,' he said solemnly, stroking my well-tousled hair away from my face, 'black or white?'

'I'm sorry?' I queried, struggling to hoick myself up on to one elbow and peering at his face through the gloom. What was this? A riddle? An offer of a game of chess?

'The coffee,' he explained. 'I won't have it said that I got you round here under false pretences.'

I smiled and tried to wriggle my dress down a bit. 'Bad joke,' I said, 'but I'm willing to forgive you.'

I snuggled up to him and doodled a finger round on his chest in what was meant to be an alluring, seductive manner.

'In fact,' I continued, 'if you can live without a caffeine boost for a while, we could always adjourn to your bedroom and, um . . .'

'. . . you could show me how forgiving you really are?'

'Something like that.'

When I arrived home in Muswell Hill at lunchtime the next day, I was treated to the sight of Hez in her dressing gown, pacing round our cluttered kitchen clutching a cigarette in one hand and her mobile in the other.

'Everything all right?' I asked, pointing at the ciggie. 'I thought you'd packed them in?'

'I had,' she growled. 'See what you've driven me to?'

'Me?'

'I've been worried sick about you – no phone call, no text, no nothing. I rang Jo to see if you'd crashed at hers but she didn't know where you were either, so now she's panicking too. Oh, and your mother's rung four times. She's freaking out because your dad wants to cut her maintenance money and she's hoping you'll ring him and tell him he can't.'

I groaned.

'You didn't tell Mum I stayed out last night, did you?'

Hez shook her head and dragged deeply on the cigarette.

'No. I said you'd just popped down the road to get some milk, but it's been so long since her first call she's now asking whether you're hand-rearing the cow yourself. Do you want me to deal with her?'

Hez had much experience in fobbing off my olds.

'I'll love you for ever. I'm just not up to either of them this morning,' I replied.

The house phone leapt into life from its habitual position on top of the bread bin. Hez made a dive for it.

'Yes, she's here. Just come in. No, she seems fine. I'll put her on.'

I was making wild 'I don't want to speak to her' type gestures, but Hez handed it over nevertheless. I reluctantly took the receiver and prepared to deflect a tirade from my mum about my father's meanness, but it was Jo's voice that came on the line.

'Are you okay?' she said. 'I've been having kittens about you.'

Obviously she and Hez were employing the same scriptwriter. (Either that, or I needed to get out more.)

'I'm fine,' I said, in what I hoped was a reassuring voice.

Jo paused, before asking innocently. 'Um, you don't happen to know what became of Mark, do you?'

'Well,' I began slowly, savouring the news, 'Mark and I did pop out for a bite to eat last night.'

'Mark? Who's Mark?' Hez barked, thrusting her head

as near to the handset as she could in a bid to turn it into a three-way conversation.

Jo was still fishing away like a North Sea trawlerman: 'And afterwards . . . ? You didn't come back to the party, did you?'

'I said, *who's Mark*?' Hez demanded loudly, in case the people in the upstairs flat hadn't heard properly the first time.

'Dave's friend from school,' Jo yelled, virtually bursting my eardrum in the process before asking me, 'So, what happened after dinner?'

'We went back to his flat for coffee.'

Hez raised an eyebrow and Jo giggled.

'And?' they squawked in unison.

I shrugged. 'I sort of forgot to come home.'

Jo cheered and Hez slapped me on the back; I felt more like an Olympic champion than a dirty stop-out. I must have been smiling a rather goofy smile, because Hez winked at me.

'You're in love,' she said.

'I don't think so,' I replied. 'Lust, perhaps, but nothing serious.'

Hez smirked but said nothing.

'Well, whatever it is, good for you,' said Jo, re-entering the conversation after relaying the news to Dave that I'd spent the night with his best mate and not dead in a ditch near the North Circular. 'He's a real sweetie, isn't he?'

'Sweetie – schmeetie. What I want to know is, how good looking is he?' probed Hez, getting down to brass tacks. 'Out of ten, please.'

This was Hez's method of assessment for anything you cared to mention.

I considered. 'About seventeen and a half, I should think.'

Massed cheering from all sides – including Dave, whose voice suddenly come on the phone, adding cryptically: 'It's about time the poor bugger had a bit of luck.'

'When are you seeing him again?' asked Jo.

'This afternoon. In fact, the sooner the better.'

Hez was jumping up and down with excitement and dropping ash everywhere in the process.

'Cool,' said Jo, 'Oh – and don't forget, I want to be bridesmaid for introducing the two of you.'

Honestly!

'You know my views on marriage,' I said firmly. 'And even if I changed my mind, it should be Dave who's the bridesmaid, seeing as he did the actual introduction.'

'Yeah, well, he doesn't have the figure for it. Anyway, take care and I'll catch you later. Say hi to Mark for me. Byeeee!'

And she hung up, leaving me to the tender mercies of a full-on Hez interrogation. The afternoon with Mark couldn't come soon enough.

Thankfully, Mark survived Hez's rigorous vetting procedure. I texted her as he was driving us over to Muzzy Hill on Sunday evening in the vain hope that she'd make herself scarce, but she refused to take the hint and was on the doorstep to welcome us, waving a pizza delivery menu and a bottle of wine. It only took five minutes in the company of the Blessed Mark before she was grinning and nodding like a maniac behind his back and giving me an unequivocal thumbs-up. Then she tactfully slid off to the pub and left us to it.

The next twelve hours passed with Mark and me cocooned in the sort of single-minded absorption of each other that I'd thought only happened in the fluffiest of chick flicks. If I'd had the mental capacity for anything that didn't touch directly on Mark and his general amazingness, I might well have found this headlong rush into intimacy rather scary. Instead, however, the fact that I could not now comprehend how my life had limped along without him *in situ* felt like a complete no-brainer: d'uh – this was *Mark*, stupid. How else was I going to feel?

We parted at Highgate tube station on Monday morning with much kissing and promises to meet up after work, which (after a day of stolen texts and sneaky e-mails) we duly did and sat up talking until four thirty the next morning. We then passed Tuesday night in a similar fashion (by which time I felt I could have gone on *Mastermind* with 'Mark Landsdown' as my specialist subject); and I had high hopes for Wednesday too – until Mark told me he needed to fly out to Dublin after lunch to meet a client and wouldn't be back till Thursday morning.

'I'm sorry, Lou,' he said as he dropped me off at the tube station on Wednesday morning. 'I really wish I could get out of this one, but I can't. Can I meet you from work tomorrow and we'll go out somewhere to make up for it?'

'Or even just stay in and make up for it?' I suggested, privately wondering how on earth I was physically going to survive a whole thirty-six hours without him. I'd have preferred to spend a day and a half without one of my lungs – or possibly lose one of my legs.

'Whatever you say.' He smiled at me and kissed the tip of my nose. 'I'll be counting the minutes till I see you again.'

Awwwwww!

Then I wafted on a raft of pink fluffy clouds down the Northern Line and into the clerks' room at my chambers.

The clerks' room in any set of chambers is where the real power lies; and it's not just that the clack of the keyboards and the lure of the pigeonholes make it an automatic focal point. All bookings, fees and pretty much anything else that gets your average barrister to heave themselves out of bed in the morning are handled by the clerks, although where *they* come from remains one of life's great unsolved mysteries. As far as I know, there are no qualifications you need before you can become a barrister's clerk; you just have to be born to it – a bit like being the heir to the throne, really. The checklist of essential skills seems to be:

1. a talent for hard work
2. devastating negotiating abilities, and
3. a life-long devotion to West Ham FC.

Our clerks Stan, Jane, Ben and their junior, Danny, were no exception to any of this – and you crossed them on peril of your professional life.

In my chambers, the clerks commanded the second largest room in the building; daylight flooded in through three huge sash windows and was supplemented, less attractively in my mind, by two fluorescent strip lights overhead. In the centre of this vast space was an enormous mahogany conference table, round which their computer terminals were located at seemingly random intervals. A floor-to-ceiling rack of pigeonholes dominated the near side of the room and three huge piles of briefs tied up with trailing ribbons of pink string (incoming, current and outgoing) were located on another monster table at the far end.

'No need to ask if you had a good night.' Jane, who was about my age but probably earned twice what I did, grinned at me over the top of her screen and clocked my ear-to-ear smile. 'Does he have a brother?'

'Two older sisters. Sorry.'

'Never mind. If there's a nice cousin lurking away in the woodwork, don't forget to earmark him for me.'

'Consider it done. Anything in my diary for today?'

Jane pulled a face. 'Don't hate me . . .'

'But?'

'But Mr Watson's ill.'

'So?'

She lowered her voice to a conspiratorial whisper. 'He had a morning hearing with Ms Woodford. I need you to pick up the brief.'

It felt as if someone had just hoovered up my fluffy pink clouds, leaving me to fall to earth with a resounding crash. Jennifer Woodford was the scourge of chambers. She was in her late thirties and did something impressive in the City. However, she had already sacked about half of the London Bar in her search for a legal team who 'shared her vision' of the case. In English, this translated to 'would mindlessly do her bidding', and she'd managed to alienate some of the biggest names in family law during her campaign through the courts.

I'd rather have chewed my own arm off than represent the maddest client in Christendom, but I couldn't conjure up a decent reason to refuse.

Jane read my thoughts with a spooky accuracy. 'It's not Legal Aid,' she cajoled, dangling the cash-carrot for all it was worth. 'So you'll get paid decent money. Plus, it's only listed for an hour. The district judge simply wants to know if the new arrangements for the little boy are working out.'

'Okay,' I said gamely. 'Where are the papers?'

'At home with Mr Watson – but don't worry, I got Ms Woodford's solicitors to fax over a crib sheet of everything you need to know. It'll be a piece of cake.' Jane was doing her best to sound convincing.

Great. Bonkers client; no brief. Could it get worse?

'Who's on the other side?' I asked, running my eye down the sheet of A4 I had in lieu of proper instructions.

'Mr Spade,' mumbled Jane into the pages of her diary.

Of course it could get worse.

I looked at my watch. According to the piece of paper Jane had just given me, the solicitors were expecting me to meet the client at court for half past nine. If I was going to make it on time, I would need to get a wriggle on.

'If I'm not back in three hours,' I yelled to Jane as I legged it out the door, 'send out the search parties.'

Grabbing my bag, I power-walked my way up Chancery Lane, reading the background info as I went and trying not to fall off the pavement or bump into a lamppost.

Client: Jennifer Woodford. Senior fund manager with Hyams Oliver. Child: four-year-old Joshua – at Tiny Toes Day Nursery; likes Pingu *and*

Fireman Sam. *Nub of the case: father left when child was six months old. Mother has previously tried to stop contact between him and Joshua. Animosity levels between the parents running high, but things have improved in the last year. The current arrangements for father to see Josh seem to be working well. Visits every other Saturday for two hours.*

The father's name wasn't given, but that wasn't a problem. I could get it from the solicitor at court.

Okay, I thought, planning it all out in my head, we'll be looking for more of the same where the visits are concerned and a further review back at court to monitor the situation in, say, three months. Easy-peasy. And – bonus – it shouldn't take the full hour, either. I'd be out of there in thirty minutes and I could skive off for a coffee and daydream about Mark for a bit. Result!

Jennifer Woodford and her solicitor, Mandy, a girl I knew well, were in the waiting room when I arrived. Flawlessly elegant in what could only have been a designer suit and with her glossy black hair straightened to within an inch of its life, Ms Woodford gave me a look that could melt steel girders at thirty paces and pointedly glanced at the clock on the wall: I was two minutes late.

Just hang on in there and think of the money.

I stapled my friendliest smile on to my face and marched towards them, hand outstretched. Mandy shook it warmly but Ms Woodford declined.

'You're not Mr Watson,' she said, frowning at me.

'That's right,' I explained, keeping the smile fastened determinedly to my face. 'He's unwell this morning. I'm Lucy Stephens, one of his colleagues.'

I tried extending the hand again, but Jennifer sniffed and looked away.

'Jenny's a bit upset,' explained Mandy. 'She says there was a bit of an – um – development over the weekend.'

'He's appalling,' spat Jennifer. 'I don't know what I ever saw in him. I won't allow Joshie to spend time with a man like that.'

Mandy and I exchanged worried glances. It sounded serious.

'Why don't you tell me all about it?' I said soothingly, slipping into the worn-out-looking chair opposite hers and opening my notebook.

'He turned his mobile off,' she growled.

'Right,' I said, making a note of this. 'And when did you try to ring him?'

'Sunday,' replied Jennifer slowly, as if she were speaking to a bear of very little brain. 'I rang forty-two times on Sunday and it was off all day. In fact, it's been turned off for the past two nights as well.'

'And why did you need to contact him so urgently on Sunday?' I asked, choosing not to tell her that if one of my exes rang forty-two times in one day, I might start screening my calls too. 'Was there a problem with Joshua?'

'Don't be ridiculous,' she snapped. 'The point is that he didn't pick up the phone. If I *had* needed to get in touch with him, I wouldn't have been able to. He's an unfit father and I want contact between him and Joshie stopped right now.'

Riiiight.

Mandy was discreetly rolling her eyes in despair. She looked as if she'd been here before.

'And are there any other problems?' I asked.

The client raised her eyebrows. 'Apart from the fact that he's a lousy father?'

I stuck to my guns. 'Are there any specific issues with the way the visits are working out?'

'No, I suppose not.'

'And does Joshua enjoy the time with his father?'

Jennifer shifted in her seat. 'Yes,' she muttered sulkily.

'Okay,' I said, taking a deep breath before giving her the news she almost certainly wouldn't want to hear. 'The district judge will really only be interested in how well things are going between Joshua and his father. If you want, I will mention the phone, but so long as you can get a message to him in an emergency, it's unlikely to be seen as a problem.'

'Here,' she demanded loudly, 'whose side are you on? He's got his own lawyers, thank you very much, without you standing up for him!'

'Miss Stephens *is* on your side,' Mandy intervened as calmly as she could. 'She's only explaining how the judge may view it.'

'I suppose so,' Jennifer agreed grudgingly. 'All right – he can still see Joshie, but we keep it to two hours per visit. Now, if that's all, I'm going to get a coffee.'

And she stalked over the nasty patterned carpet to the vending machine on the other side of the room. Mandy flopped back in her seat and ran a harassed hand through her hair.

'I am *so* sorry about that,' she whispered. 'If I'd known what the "problem" was, I'd have tried to knock it on the head before you got here.'

'Has the case always been this conflicted?' I asked.

Mandy sighed. 'To be honest, this is a good day. You should have seen her when Joshua's father found someone else. She took it really badly – suicide threats, the works. In the end, he broke it off with the new woman, but it's taken us for ever to get the visits established again.'

'So you're saying her ex is the wronged party in all of this?'

Mandy regarded her shoes for a moment. 'For professional reasons I couldn't possibly say.'

That would be a resounding 'yes', then.

'Anyway,' said Mandy, changing the subject, 'what have you been up to recently?'

A bashful grin spread across my face, and I picked self-consciously at the foam stuffing oozing out of my battered chair.

'Oooh!' she squealed, as loudly as she dared. 'What's he like? Tell me all!'

'Mand, he is sooooo nice. I met him on Saturday and the whole thing – him, me, *us* – it's awesome. We've spent every night since the weekend together.'

Mandy clapped her hands gleefully. 'Well, it's about time!'

I wish people wouldn't keep saying that.

'What does he look like?' Mandy continued.

'About six foot, fairish hair, blue eyes and a body to *die* for.'

'Sounds scrummy. Something nice to look forward to after a morning with our mate Jennifer,' she added wistfully.

But Jennifer wasn't the only blot on the landscape of my Wednesday morning. A shadow loomed over us.

'Morning, ladies,' drawled Hugo Spade. 'Sorry to break up the party, but I think a little chat is in order. How about it, Looby-Lou?'

Picking up my notebook, I retreated to a quiet corner with Hugo. If we could get the case agreed before we went in, it would reduce the length of the hearing still further . . . which meant I could spend even more time at the nearest Starbucks staring out of the window with a ridiculous smile on my face.

'Basically, it's all pretty straightforward, Loobs—'

'*Don't* call me that.'

'I do beg your pardon, *Lucy*,' he said with all the false sincerity he could muster. 'Or would you prefer Miss Stephens?'

What I actually wanted was to be treated like an educated professional, but I decided to stick to attainable goals.

'Lucy will be fine.'

'Just had a word with my chap on the phone – he's stuck in traffic but should be here any minute. He's happy not to push for any extra time with Josh at the moment, but he does want the current arrangement to continue. What are your client's views on that?' He gave a particularly horrible smirk. 'From what I could hear just now, it doesn't sound likely that we'll be singing from the same hymn sheet.'

The evil little toad – he'd been earwigging in on the confidential chat I'd just had with Jennifer. Choosing not to remind him that this was against the rules of professional conduct, I decided to take the wind out of his sails another way.

'Actually, Hugo, it's fine by her.'

He looked quite deflated. Ha! One–nil to me. Encouraged, I went on.

'However, she does have some minor concerns over contacting your client by phone,' I said.

'Really?' Hugo raised a supercilious eyebrow. 'I hope she hasn't been up to her old telephone-stalker tricks. If she has, my instructions will be to get another injunction against her. If she needs to contact my chap – about Joshua *only* – we agreed she can leave one message on his mobile and one on his landline. In return, he'll ring her back as soon as he can. A bit of a non-issue, I'm afraid.'

Damn! One–all. Still, it wasn't a deal-breaker. Just then, however, I noticed the court usher striding in our direction, her black gown flapping out behind her.

'Ah, good,' said Hugo, 'they're calling us in.'

'But your client's not here yet,' I protested.

'Oh yes he is,' responded Spade, in the manner of a pantomime villain. 'He's right over there.'

I followed Hugo's finger, which was pointing towards the door.

I dropped my notebook.

I wobbled a bit.

I forgot to breathe for quite a long time.

The man who had rushed into the waiting area, looking as if he'd just run the hundred metres in record time, was Mark.

Or, rather, he was MARK!!!!!!!

'Are you sure that's him?' I asked Hugo as soon as I could speak.

But Hugo was already halfway across the room and cheerfully shaking Mark by the hand.

Mid-handshake, Mark's eyes met mine. It was only for the nano-est of nano-seconds, but he went whiter than an albino polar bear in a tank of bleach, and I knew he understood the situation. I suddenly felt horribly, horribly sick. My gorgeous, enchanting, captivating, I've-never-felt-this-close-to-anyone-before man was none other than The Other Side. And not only was there a long-running court case he'd forgotten to mention as we'd murmured sweet nothings to each other, but a four-year-old child and a vindictive ex as well. Quite a nasty little case of amnesia.

Paralysing levels of fear were rising within me. I had (quite literally) been sleeping with the enemy, and aside from the hideous personal fallout, this was serious stuff professionally. A lawyer can never act in a case in which they are personally involved – and the excruciatingly intimate nature of my time with Mark meant that I was involved in <u>Landsdown v Woodford</u> up to my eyeballs. Buggerfuck. I would certainly have to back out of the case, but could I lose my job over it? And even if I wasn't booted out immediately, Guy was so obsessed with the reputation of his precious chambers that there was a real risk this would be the death knell to any hopes I had of winning the tenancy competition.

Oh God, what on earth was I going to do?

I ran through the possibilities. Killing myself or emigrating to Australia were hot contenders, but they weren't going to solve the immediate problem of me having to stand up in front of a district judge *right now* and make coherent words come out of my mouth. If I could just get out of doing the hearing without announcing our relationship to the entire world, something might be salvaged from this mess – even if it was just my personal dignity.

Sprinting for the double doors that led through to the district judge's room, I managed to grab Mandy's coat just before she disappeared through them with Jennifer.

'Two seconds,' I told the court usher. 'Bit of a problem.'

I dragged Mandy out of earshot.

'What's up?' she hissed. 'Are you ill or something?'

'No – it's the father. He's called Mark.'

She blinked at me, uncomprehending. 'Yes, I know,' she said. 'Mark Landsdown.'

'You didn't tell me what he was called.' I was almost on my knees with panic.

'Why? Is it important?'

'Yes!' I whispered. 'You see, Mark – this Mark – is, um, *my* Mark. The guy I was telling you about. I had no idea!'

Mandy clapped her hand to her forehead. 'Oh my God,' she hissed. 'You spent the past four days shagging *the other side*?'

'Well, just Mark,' I clarified hastily. 'I wouldn't touch Spade with a disinfected bargepole.'

'What are you going to do?'

'I'll have to ask for an adjournment and get someone else up here to take over.'

'Okay,' Mandy hissed back. 'Leave Jennifer to me – but for God's sake don't tell her *why* you've got to withdraw from the case. She'll go into orbit.'

'Don't worry; I don't fancy being chucked over Vauxhall Bridge with rocks in my pockets. Right, Mand, let's do it.'

Head held high, I strode through the doors and took

my seat next to Jennifer at the large table in the middle
of the room, trying not to look up in case I caught the eye
of either Mark or Hugo, who were sitting opposite us.
The district judge, sitting in a high-backed chair at his
own, smaller table adjoining ours, had his head buried in
the six lever-arch files of paperwork that constituted the
case.

'Yes, Mr Spade,' he said jovially when he had finished
reading. 'What are you looking for today?'

But before Hugo could open his mouth, I leapt to my
feet. Even though I had successfully avoided looking at
Mark, the bravado with which I had entered the room
hadn't lasted. The blood was pounding in my head and
my legs seemed to have turned into a pair of those red
liquorice shoelace things.

'Before we start, sir, I am afraid I am going to have to
ask for an adjournment.'

The district judge put down his pen and frowned at
me. 'I am well acquainted with the history of this case,
Miss Stephens, and your client needs to understand that
I will only accept further delays in *exceptional* circumstances.'

I took a deep breath.

'A matter came to light as the parties were entering
your room, sir, and I find myself in professional
difficulties. I cannot continue to represent the mother
and I ask that the case is put back so I can arrange for
someone else to act for her.'

The DJ sighed. 'Very well, Miss Stephens; if you can't
do it, you can't do it. I'll put the case back for an hour.
But there must be no more adjournments – do you all
understand?'

We nodded fervently, bowed to the DJ and then
trooped out. When we were back in the waiting area,
Hugo caught me by the lapel of my jacket and pulled me
to one side.

'What's all this about?' he asked. 'You're not

chickening out of a tough case, are you?'

'Shut up, Spade,' I snapped, pushing him away with one hand and dialling chambers with the other. 'Hi? Jane? Look, there's a real mess here. It turns out I can't represent Ms Woodford after all. I'll tell you why later,' I added for the benefit of Hugo, who was hovering around with his ears flapping like windsocks in a stiff breeze. 'Let's just say it's a conflict of interest.'

There was a pause while Jane rang round to find a replacement for me.

'Guy's on his way,' I called over to Hugo and snapped my phone shut. 'He'll be here in ten.'

I girded my loins and went over to try and make my peace with Jennifer, but to my surprise found she was neither foaming at the mouth nor chewing the furniture. In fact, she looked relatively calm and serene.

'Guy Jennings?' she asked sweetly. 'He's good, isn't he?'

'The best,' I said encouragingly.

'Excellent.' She rubbed her hands together in the manner of Cruella de Vil spotting a puppy shop. 'It will be nice to be represented by someone who knows what they're talking about.'

I could have been offended.

I could have been hurt.

But I wasn't.

And you know why? Because all I had to do now was take the twenty or so steps that lay between me and the door: *I was going to get away with it.*

I picked up my bag and strode out across the hideous carpet to freedom.

You know those dreams you have when you're running and running but never get anywhere? Well, it felt exactly like that. Each step was an eternity, and it seemed that all eyes in the waiting area were trained upon me . . .

. . . which they may well have been, because Mark

suddenly decided that right then would be a really good time for us to have a chat.

He sprinted over from where he and Hugo had been huddled by the coffee machine and grabbed my arm before I could escape.

'What do you think you're doing?' I hissed.

'I can't let you just disappear like this,' he whispered back. 'Meet me. At the Fleet Street Café Rouge at one o'clock. We can sort this out.'

'Right now, I don't know if we can,' I replied as calmly and as quietly as I could. 'I need some time to work out what to do for the best. And you need to go to Dublin.'

'Dublin cancelled. Listen.' A hint of panic entered his voice and its volume started to rise worryingly. 'I'm sorry. I should have mentioned something. I just didn't think . . .'

There was fear in my eyes as I looked around the waiting room. Even if we did have some sort of future together, now was not the time to have that discussion. Not with Jennifer's beady eyes measuring me up for my body bag.

'I have to go,' I said firmly, marching for the door.

'Lucy – darling – *please*!' he cried.

Nooo! Not that! Not *out loud*!

The entire waiting room fell silent – apart, of course, from the resounding noise of my career being flushed down the toilet, and the voice of my erstwhile client in full snarl.

'What did I tell you? He's a total shit. And as for you . . . don't think you're getting away with this!'

The last bit was presumably meant for my personal edification.

I legged it; and the last thing I saw as the doors closed behind me was Hugo, with the world's biggest smirk plastered over his face.

I pounded down the street away from court feeling utterly, utterly wretched. Why hadn't Mark told me about Joshua and Jennifer? Even though we'd only been together for a few days, I felt as though I had known him all my life – and possibly for quite a few other lives preceding this one. For the past two nights we had sat up into the wee small hours and discussed everything under the sun, from religion and politics right down to the occasion when I was seven and stuffed a bit of Lego up my nose (it turned out he'd done the same thing with a frozen pea). I'd assumed he'd told me everything of importance about himself: the obvious (such as him having two older sisters) right through to the more obscure snippets of information, like the fact that his mother had an enormous crush on George Clooney. He'd even spoken candidly about the loss of his father in a car accident when he was five years old and we'd both ended up in tears – so the fact that he had somehow forgotten to tell me that he had a *son* left me feeling betrayed and bewildered.

As soon as I got my breath back, I ducked down a side street away from the roar of the traffic and rang Hez.

'Hey!' she said. 'What's up?'

After qualifying as a barrister, Hez had got a job with a firm of trendy solicitors in the West End. She loved her job but detested her bullying, slave-driving boss, Henry

Spiggott, who had joined Sheppertons three months previously. I could hear him in the background barking orders at Estelle, his overworked secretary.

'Oh, you know,' I said, trying to stay calm and coherent. 'Same old, same old – Mark's got a son and he's spent the past four years caught up in a vicious legal battle over contact rights. That sort of thing.'

'*What!*' shrieked Hez. 'A *son*? When did he tell you this?'

'He didn't,' I replied, wiping my face with the back of my hand and wishing I'd put on waterproof mascara. 'I found out in court this morning when I was there representing his ex-girlfriend.'

'Bloody hell! How are you – out of ten?' she hissed.

'Minus five hundred and sixty-three,' I replied. 'Can you get away? I need to talk.'

'I'm sorry, Lou; I'd love to but I'm really tied up here. I'll be home as early as I can, though. Look, I've gotta go,' Hez whispered as the sound of Spiggott being loud and obnoxious wafted down the line. 'He's shouting at poor Estelle because she did my typing before his. I'll try and call you in chambers, and if I can't, we'll talk tonight.'

She hung up and I checked my watch. It was still only ten thirty and the whole hideous day stretched out before me. I simply couldn't face going back into work, so in the end I rang the clerks and left a feeble excuse for my absence on Jane's voicemail. Then I headed to the calm of the National Portrait Gallery in an attempt to collect my thoughts.

It was about six when I arrived home in Muswell Hill, feeling a bit better. After lunch I'd crept back into work and hidden out in my room, refusing to answer the phone or the door, and sloped off home as soon as it was acceptable to do so. I kicked my shoes off into the random collection of footwear that lurked under the hall table and was getting myself a glass of wine when the front door burst open and Hez tornadoed into the flat, dragging her supersized briefcase behind her. 'Guess what?' she yelled.

I checked my watch. She wasn't normally home this early.

'Er, Spiggott died from overwork and everybody on the staff was allowed out before midnight as a special treat?'

'No. Better than that.'

'Is it about work?'

'Yup.'

'A client?'

'Uh-huh.'

'A rich client who wants to buy you a yacht as a thank-you present?'

She paused. 'Not *that* good.'

'Famous client?'

She nodded enthusiastically.

'Really famous?'

'Give up?' she asked, almost wetting herself in her excitement.

'Go on then.'

'Swear you won't tell anyone?'

'Cross my heart.'

She paused dramatically. 'Llew Jones. He's getting divorced.'

My jaw clanged on to the kitchen floor.

'Llewellyn Jones? The Prime Minister? But he's always going on about family values and the sanctity of marriage.'

She nodded. 'That's the reason why it's so hush-hush – it will be political suicide if the news isn't handled properly.'

'And he's *your* client?'

She contorted her pixie-like features into a grimace. 'Well, he didn't actually make an appointment to see *me*, of course. He's Spiggott's client really, but I'm going to help out. I've had to sign the Official Secrets Act and everything.'

'Well, they chose the right person there, didn't they? You've managed to keep it to yourself for all of, ooh, forty-five minutes.'

'Hey!' Hez took off her jacket and helped herself to my glass of wine. 'If I didn't tell someone, I'd explode. And anyway, I'm not really breaking any rules, because guess who's getting the brief?'

Unless the Prime Minister had lost his mind along with his marriage, it wasn't going to be me.

'It's Guy! The papers went out to him tonight.'

She sounded as if she'd just won the lottery.

'So?'

'Well . . .' said Hez in a sort of teasing voice, 'he'll need a junior, won't he?'

'Yes,' I replied, 'and there are at least ten other people in my chambers who would get the job over me.'

'Ah-*ha*,' she went on, in the manner of Hercule Poirot solving a particularly knotty little murder, 'I did take the liberty in the covering letter of mentioning you as a possible contender – well, the only contender really.'

I boggled at her. Hez breezed on regardless.

'I dictated a PS at the bottom to say that the PM specifically wanted you as Guy's second in command. Come on, Lou, think about it – you're doing a big, important piece of work that is probably going to finish long after the tenancy meeting happens, and Hugo is just—'

'A hopeless skiver.'

'Exactly! Who are your chambers going to ask to stay on?'

'Oh Hez, you're a genius!' I screeched, throwing my arms round her neck.

'Careful,' she cried, trying not to slop wine on to the kitchen floor. 'And better than that . . .'

'How can it possibly get better? Do I win a night out with David Tennant? Get a case of Moët every Friday?'

'It gets better,' said Hez, 'because this is going to make us. Not only will your chambers give you the tenancy over Hugo the Weasel; not only will I be treated like a human being by Spiggott, but both of us will have a *name*.'

She said it as if we were about to alight upon the Holy Grail or the Elixir of Life – except this was *even more* amazing.

Because a good reputation meant more work, and more work meant I'd finally be able to pay off the thousands of pounds of debt I'd acquired in order to qualify. If her scheme succeeded and Guy did select me as his junior, it would, quite literally, change my life.

'Okay,' continued Hez, the beneficent smile of a fairy godmother on her face, 'so I've sorted out your career and your bank balance. What's next? Ah, Mark the Magnificent. Has he called?'

'Probably. I haven't actually listened to my messages yet.'

Hez raised an eyebrow at me.

'I don't know if I still want to go out with him, okay?' I admitted, getting another glass out of the cupboard and sloshing it full of vino.

'Please don't do anything you'll regret, Lou,' she said gently.

'You mean like getting involved with a big fat liar who might just have ruined my career?'

'From what you've told me, he's *not* a liar.' She waggled her wine glass in my direction to emphasise her point. 'In fact, he's really sweet. And more to the point, he's hotter than a jalapeño. *Of course* he should have told you about Josh, that goes without saying; but maybe the right moment hadn't arrived yet?'

'He told me everything else,' I grumbled. 'Look, can we talk about this another time? I need a bit of head space to come to terms with it all.'

Hez narrowed her eyes at me over the top of her glass.

'You can't avoid him for ever, you know. You'll have to sort it out sooner or later.'

'Well, I don't like confrontation,' I replied.

Hez flung her arms heavenwards.

'You're a lawyer, for God's sake. You're *paid* to be confrontational.'

'Yes, but I'm confrontational for other people,' I said. 'It's completely different.'

Hez made a funny growling noise in the back of her throat.

'What you mean is you don't like putting yourself in a position where you might become vulnerable. Look, I know Jonathan hurt you, but that was six years ago; it's time to move on.'

I studied the label on the bottle of wine and said nothing.

'All right,' she said, relaxing slightly, 'I won't make you ring him now.'

I looked up, hopefully.

'But we'll sort it out after we've both had something to eat,' Hez continued, selecting a takeaway menu from the cluster on the fridge and delving in her bag for her specs. 'I didn't get any lunch and I could eat a scabby horse on toast.'

The next time I looked at the clock it was half past ten. The pair of us had eaten our own body weights in tikka masala and naan bread, polished off another bottle of wine and were lying on the floor of the living room in the flickering light of our feeble flame-effect gas fire, planning our futures as the goliaths of the family law world.

'Well, obviously,' Hez was saying, 'I'll make sure that all my briefs come to you, and all the briefs from my whole firm; because I'll be in charge and able to do whatever I want.'

'What about Spiggott?'

She rolled over and looked murderously at me. 'This

is *my* firm, not Spiggott's. When I'm famous, he won't be allowed over the threshold. In fact, I'll have special anti-Spiggott devices everywhere to stop him sneaking into the building.'

She paused.

'Do you know what he did today? He's reworked the contracts for all the secretaries in the matrimonial department and abolished their right to overtime pay – so not only is poor Estelle expected to stay till at least half six every night and come in on weekends if there's an emergency, she's got to do it for free. *And* her husband was made redundant three months ago, and I know they need that money to stop the bank foreclosing on them. She was in tears all afternoon. Bastard.'

Hez took another swig of wine.

'You could always give Spiggott a job in your fantasy firm,' I suggested.

Hez snorted. 'Why would I want to do that?'

'Payback, of course – you could make him do something like sorting out the post or cleaning the toilets. And get him to make Estelle lots of cups of tea.'

She smiled, flipped back over and stared at the ceiling.

'Cool. I could be, like, "Spiggott, I want those toilets so clean I could eat my dinner off them."'

'Urgh! That's gross!'

'True. I wouldn't eat my dinner off anything Spiggott had touched.'

We howled with laughter. God, we were hilarious.

'And all my clients will love me and follow my advice to the letter,' Hez continued, soaring from the realms of the barely possible into the totally unlikely.

Obedient clients immediately made me think of Jennifer, and the small, dark corner of my mind into which I'd managed to squash the ugliness of that morning's encounter with Mark sprang unbidden into life. Feeling a bit sick, I pushed away the poppadom I'd been nibbling on. Hez shot me a look.

'You know you *are* going to have to speak to him at some point,' she said.

I rubbed my tired face with my hand.

'And tell him what, exactly? That he has the most conflicted personal life since Oedipus and he almost killed my career?'

'Look,' she said, 'for what it's worth, you and Mark . . . I don't know quite how to explain it, but you've got this – this *vibe* going on.'

I groaned. The last thing I needed was Hez and her undying faith in happy-ever-afterness; the situation was complicated enough already.

'It's a mess,' I explained patiently, in case she didn't already know. 'It's a fucking awful mess. He needs UN peacekeeping troops in his life, not a girlfriend. I don't know if I want to deal with all that aggro; it'll be like Mum and Dad, only worse.'

'No it won't. You need to be a bit more rational about the whole thing. Now, what's the worst that could happen?' asked Hez, undeterred. 'I bet we can find a way through it.'

'Well, if I carry on seeing Mark, Jennifer will make his life hell – like she did when he started seeing someone else last year. Then she'll make my life hell too. Then she'll try and stop Mark and Josh seeing each other. Then she'll—'

'Slow down!' Hez ordered. 'Let's take this one bit at a time. Look, mad ex: not good, but we can handle it. There's nothing you can do if she's foul to Mark – that's his problem – but if she starts freaking *you* out, *I'll* take her on, and believe me, I can out-weird anyone.'

She could too, I knew.

'And then there's Josh,' I said, turning to possibly my biggest concern of the lot. 'I don't know anything about children. I sometimes even wonder if I was one myself. How on earth am I going to cope with being a quasi-stepmother to a four-year-old boy?'

There was a short pause while Hez attempted to pour wine from the empty bottle into her glass.

'Well,' she replied, giving the bottle a final shake before putting it upside down in the waste-paper bin. 'Josh lives most of the time with Jennifer, and from the sounds of things, that's not going to be changing any time soon. I reckon all you have to do is learn how to kick a football for a couple of hours on a Saturday afternoon and maybe cook the odd fish finger here and there. Meanwhile, you'll get exclusive access to the man of your dreams.'

Put like that, it sounded so simple, even I could manage it. It would require no parenting skills; no healthy, functional upbringing; no maternal instinct: just the ability to run around like a lunatic shouting 'Goal!' from time to time.

'I suppose so. But what if Guy sacks me for inappropriate whatevers with a client? What if the solicitors who brief me think I acted unprofessionally and I never work again?'

'Oh, that,' she replied, as if we were discussing some minor technicality. 'Firstly, Mark wasn't your client; secondly, you knew nothing about the fact that he had a court case going on; and thirdly, by tomorrow morning, Guy'll think you're the PM's favourite lawyer and soon everyone else will too. You are untouchable.'

If only I had her confidence in the ability of things to work out for the best.

'Come on, Lou,' Hez continued, 'you can't deny that the man is gorgeous – and he's crazy about you. Blimey, if I had a bloke like Mark begging me to be with him, wild horses wouldn't be able to stop me.'

'You have guys falling over themselves to ask you out,' I protested.

Hez pulled a face.

'Oh, *please*,' she said. 'A third of them are morons, another third dump me after the first date and the rest just want to be seen out with a girl who's got a rich dad.'

Hez's father ran several large companies from the golf courses of Hertfordshire. The term 'loaded' could have been invented especially for him.

'I'm telling you, I would *kill* for a good-looking, solvent, intelligent man like Mark to be beating a path to my door.' She gave an enormous sigh.

'You're drunk and maudlin,' I reasoned, trying to pull the conversation away from Mark.

'Hmmph!' she said, 'and tomorrow I'll be hungover and maudlin – but I'll still be right!'

'Go on then,' I said, trying to get her on to her favourite subject so that she would forget all about me and my disaster-strewn love life. 'Tell me about this ideal man of yours. What's he like?'

There was no reply. Glancing across at her, I saw that her head was resting on a cushion, her eyes were closed and her mouth was lolling open. Ignoring the temptation to take a photo of her in such a ladylike position, I removed her shoes and her specs, covered her up with a throw and left a large glass of water on the table near her head. Then, after downing a pint of the stuff myself, plus two Nurofens (guaranteed to stop a hangover before it starts), I crawled in under my own duvet.

My spare pillow still had lingering vestiges of eau de Mark, and I snuggled up to it, inhaling as deeply as I could. I *did* miss him; I *did* want to be with him: but was the price of playing unhappy families with him simply going to be too high?

I yawned. Whatever the answer was, half-eleven on a Wednesday night wasn't going to be the best time to sort it out.

I turned over and closed my eyes: I'd make a decision about him tomorrow.

No, really I would.

5

Thankfully, the big news in chambers the next morning wasn't my interlude with Mark but the Prime Minister's impending divorce. Gossip in chambers travelled notoriously fast, and today was to be no exception. Considering that Guy hadn't even opened the brief yet, let alone read it, everybody seemed to be remarkably well informed about its contents. A small but vociferous group had gathered by the pigeonholes and were clucking away like a bunch of mother hens on amphetamines.

'Well, *I* heard it was his wife who ended it,' boomed Gerald Masters QC. 'Decided after thirty years of marriage that she should really be playing for the other side, if you know what I mean, and ran off with her personal shopper.'

'No, I'm sorry, Gerry, but you're way out on your facts,' Phillip Kingston butted in.

'What's new?' threw in some wag, and the group (minus Masters, who looked as if he might burst a blood vessel) roared with laughter.

'And what are the facts, then?' Masters raised a superior and very bushy eyebrow.

'I have it on good authority that her personal shopper is called Quentin and is as camp as a row of pink tents,' retorted Kingston. 'My wife's hairdresser's boyfriend knows him.'

'Oooooh!' This impressed everyone.

'No, you're both wrong.' Rob Staunton, a young high-flyer, stuck his oar in. 'The case is that Mr and Mrs PM don't even sleep in the same room any more, let alone the same bed, and it's a bit awkward when they're off on foreign trips – especially in Washington. I hear the President and his wife are at it like a pair of randy gerbils.'

Massed tittering.

'And he needs the whole thing sorted out now, so that it's all blown over by the next general election.'

'And your source is?'

'This girl I met at Ronnie Scott's last week who runs the housekeeping department at Number Ten.'

With an educated elite like this, who needs a tabloid press?

Gerald Masters was just about to wade back into the discussion when Guy entered the room. You could have cut the silence with a plastic airline knife.

'What's my fee going to be then, Stan?' he asked our head clerk.

Stan pushed a slip of paper over to him.

Guy grinned and whistled under his breath.

'Well done,' he said to Stan. 'I bet you're pleased you're still on a percentage.'

Stan nodded happily. He was the only one of the clerks still to get paid the old-fashioned way on a cut of our fees. I dreaded to think what he earned per year.

'Henry Spiggott's been on at me all morning to confirm who you're going to have as your junior on this case, sir,' Stan said. 'Let me know when you've made the decision.'

There was a lot of murmuring and clearing of throats amongst the gossipmongers, who were obviously hoping for a slice of the action themselves, but Guy turned on his immaculately shod heel and walked back to his room.

'Just remember, Stan, if Mr Jennings asks for me,

there is nothing in my diary that can't be given to someone more junior,' said Kingston, casting a meaningful
glance in Rob Staunton's direction.

'Hey,' said Staunton defensively, 'not so much of this
"junior" business. What Guy needs is fresh blood, a
young pair of eyes—'

'You're making it sound less like a divorce case and
more like a multiple organ transplant, Mr Staunton,' said
Stan, a wry smile on his face. 'I'm sure Mr Jennings
will let us know when he's good and ready. Now, aren't
all three of you supposed to be in the High Court for half
past nine?'

That did it. They snatched up their briefs and legged
it out the door, leaving me alone with the clerks.

'Anything come in for me?' I asked tentatively. My
pigeonhole was empty, and I feared my diary for the next
few days was going to be barer than a builder's bum-
cleavage.

Stan scanned his computer screen and rubbed his
bald head thoughtfully. 'Possibility of a twenty-minute
hearing next Thursday, but it looks as if it might settle.
Don't panic,' he said, catching sight of my worried face,
'it'll pick up. Last week was good, and I'm trying to get a
cheque in from Sheppertons for that case you did back in
October. That'll keep the wolf from the door.'

Perhaps.

But what I really needed was enough money to pay
for a whole new door, complete with razor wire and
machine-gun nests, so the wolf was kept out once and for
all.

As I turned to go down to my room, Hugo whizzed
past the clerks' room, muttering that he was going to the
library. There were two libraries Hugo frequented:
the one more usually known as the Odeon in Leicester
Square, and the one with the pool table that was actually
the Inner Temple Common Room. I watched as he happily
trotted along King's Bench Walk and disappeared down

into the basement where the latter was situated. At least it meant that he was at a loose end too.

I went downstairs and had opened up the latest *Family Law Report*, intending to put Hugo to shame and catch up on some recent cases, when there was a knock at my door, a pause, and a large bunch of flowers walked into the room. It was huge – not so much a bouquet as a tropical wilderness. I swear I could hear the screech of parakeets and the rustle of monkeys swinging through the greenery on vines.

'These came for you, Miss Stephens.' Jane's voice was muffled by the plant life, although it couldn't hide the girlie giggle that all women get when flowers are involved. 'And if they're anything to do with that client of Mr Spade's, then you have my undying jealousy.' She lowered her voice and stuck her head round the side of the blooms. 'I wouldn't kick him out of bed for leaving biscuit crumbs, I tell you.'

Bloody hell, Mark – flowers at work! Didn't yesterday teach you anything about how precarious my position is?

'Jane – did anyone else see these arrive?'

Thankfully she shook her head, and despite my wrath, I relieved her of the blooms. As I delved around near the bottom of the stems for the card, I noticed that my hands were trembling: for good or ill, Mark had well and truly got to me.

'Whatdoesitsaywhatdoesitsay?' asked Jane peering over the desk.

'Um, hold on a moment.' I fumbled with the doll-sized envelope. ' "To my Waterloo. Mark xxx." '

My stomach churned and I could feel myself blushing. Anxiety, infatuation or annoyance?

Probably all three.

In contrast, Jane was practically jumping up and down with excitement.

'It's soooo romantic.' Then she paused, thoughtfully.

'But why Waterloo? Does he commute in on the Northern Line?'

'Something like that,' I said, choosing not to cut a swathe through her Abba ignorance for the time being. 'Anyway, let's find a vase to put these in – and if anyone asks, they are from Mrs Meredith for the injunction I got her last week.'

'Roger, wilco,' promised Jane. 'But I wouldn't worry too much – the rest of chambers are too obsessed with the PM to show any interest in a bunch of flowers.'

Which was probably true, thank goodness.

After much searching, Jane and I found a chipped jug, an old milk bottle and a plastic bucket. While none of them was going to wow the punters at Heal's, they would fill a gap for now. Then, once she'd disappeared back off upstairs, I turned my mind back to the main problem of Mark: i.e. what I was actually going to do about him. Despite the double fat-headedness of announcing our relationship at court and then sending a mobile florist's shop to me at work, I had no doubt he really did care deeply about me. Maybe Hez was right after all – men like that didn't come along very often, and perhaps the wise thing to do would be to point out his stupidity to him in words of one syllable and then put the whole episode behind us.

However, on the other hand—

The phone rang and my heart missed a beat: was this Mark following up his floral extravaganza with a plea for clemency and get-back-togetherness? What was I going to tell him?

'Lucy Stephens? Is that you?'

It was Guy. Oh no!

'Are you there?' Guy demanded, sounding slightly nonplussed at my lack of response. 'We need a bit of a chat.'

I pulled a face. He obviously wanted to talk about the

debacle at court yesterday. I just hoped I still had a job at the end of it.

'I'll be right up,' I said, and began the long walk up from my basement lair to what I was personally convinced was the scaffold.

Guy's room was one of the best in the building and the one traditionally inhabited by the reigning head of chambers. It was on the ground floor and had enormous eighteenth-century sash windows that looked out on to a small garden and, not quite as attractively, the car park beyond. The walls were decorated with expensive wallpaper and elegant portraits of long-forgotten lawyers; the curtains were made of a sumptuous, if sun-damaged, velvet; and the carpet was red – presumably so you couldn't see the blood on it after our periodic leadership struggles. On the far side of the room, dwarfed by the scale and grandeur of the decor that surrounded him, sat my boss, Guy Jennings QC, at his Chippendale desk.

Guy was reading as I entered and didn't look up, but there was a tray of coffee things on his desk. Hope surged through me: maybe he wasn't going to talk about the Woodford case after all; perhaps we would just have a cosy chat, munch bourbons and he would ask me about my five-year plan. However, Jane followed me into the room, grabbed the tray and took it away, along with my hopes of an easy ride.

I sat down in one of the antique chairs that faced Guy's desk in a little horseshoe and took a deep breath. He looked up and, slightly guiltily, shoved the magazine he had been poring over into a desk drawer. It seemed to be a copy of *Time Out*.

'Right, Stephens,' he began, and then stopped and squinted at me. He removed his trendy and obviously expensive glasses and peered again. 'You *are* Lucy Stephens, aren't you?'

I nodded.

'You, er, look rather like one of the domestic staff, that's all. Anyway, you may be aware that we've got a bit of a problem on our hands.'

My heart sank into my boots. Jennifer had obviously spent some of the time at court with him yesterday making sure she put some actual conflict into the phrase 'conflict of interest'.

'Yes,' Guy continued, 'a definite problem. And to be frank, I don't quite know how we're going to handle it.'

My heart sank even further, down to about the level of the floor joists: I was for it big time.

'I have in front of me a piece of paper concerning the intimate lives of two people that could, at any moment, be transformed into front-page news . . .'

Shit! Jennifer wasn't threatening to go to the papers, was she? I didn't know whether my parents had guessed I was no longer pure and virginal or believed I spent my evenings reading novels about true love and looking forward wistfully to my wedding night. But whatever their delusions, I certainly didn't want them to find out via the pages of the *Daily Stoat* or its stablemates that I'd spent the week in bed with a man I'd only just met.

'. . . and so what I am about to tell you is in the utmost confidence.'

Aaah! The penny dropped and the plot thickened. (And the metaphors got hopelessly mixed into the bargain.)

'You mean Llewellyn Jones and his divorce?' I asked brightly, the weight of anxiety rolling off my shoulders.

'Correct,' he said. 'Our revered leader has decided to join the ranks of the previously married.'

'And how can I help?' I asked.

Guy produced five huge lever-arch files from under the desk and plonked them in front of me: he was going to ask me to do the photocopying. But – no!

'Mr Jones appears to have requested that you act as

the junior on this case, and whilst I confess you would not have been my first choice for the job, I am not going to question his judgement.'

'Um,' I said with great eloquence, my gob feeling well and truly smacked.

Sure, Hez had been going on last night about some sort of postscript to the brief, but I hadn't thought for one moment anyone would take it seriously.

Guy knitted his fingers together and leaned forward over the desk.

'You do *want* the job, don't you?' he asked, frowning slightly.

'Yes, yes, I do,' I said, unable to stifle the enormous grin that was spreading across my face.

'Good.' He smiled back at me. 'Just checking. Now, your first job is to get the paperwork organised. We have a conference with the client tomorrow afternoon, and I'd like a chronology of the significant dates in the marriage, a schedule of matrimonial assets, a summary of the correspondence and a proposal for a financial settlement.' He paused for a moment. 'Actually, perhaps you and I had better have a preliminary meeting tomorrow morning so that I can – ah – familiarise myself with the facts. Shall we say eight o'clock?'

I looked at the mound of files. To achieve Guy's early-morning target was going to mean me working flat out between now and then, probably even counting the hours between eleven and seven, which I would normally spend packing the zeds in.

But I didn't care. I was Llew Jones's barrister and I could handle anything!

I was so overwhelmed by the idea of having the PM as my client that it took a moment or two for me to realise that the atmosphere in the room had changed. The smile had gone from Guy's face and he was regarding me with serious eyes.

'However,' he said, folding his arms and sitting back

in his chair, 'if you are going to be my junior, there's something else we need to discuss.'

There was something almost cutting in his tone of voice. I bit my lip and waited for him to continue.

'Poor Jennifer,' he said, shaking his head. 'She was exceedingly upset about the incident at court yesterday. I managed to smooth her ruffled feathers a bit and get the visits between Josh and the father back on course – but it was touch and go there for a while.'

He leaned forward over his desk and fixed me with a penetrating stare.

'What happened yesterday was unprofessional in the extreme, Stephens. It is a basic rule of conduct that a lawyer does not act in any case where he or she already has a personal interest.'

'I know that, really I do,' I said. 'And I would never have accepted the brief if I'd known about Mr Landsdown's involvement.'

'Indeed?' Guy raised a disbelieving eyebrow at me. 'I find that hard to believe, Miss Stephens, given the – shall we say "intimate"? – nature of your relationship with Mr Landsdown.'

The horrible, sick feeling I'd had last night was starting to come back. I needed to convince him of my innocence – if not, I had an awful feeling that he would relieve me of my duties as Llew Jones's lawyer before I'd even begun.

'I only met Mr Landsdown on Saturday,' I stammered. 'We hadn't got round to talking about his personal life in any great detail.'

Guy frowned as he considered this possibility.

'Well, Amanda French did say that she hadn't put Mr Landsdown's name in the paperwork . . .'

Thank goodness for that – *I love you, Mandy!*

'. . . but even so,' Guy continued, 'look upon this as a warning. Any other mistakes of this kind – in fact, any other mistakes full stop – and there will be no more second chances. I will not have the reputation of my chambers being dragged through the mud. Do you understand?'

I nodded dumbly.

'As my junior, you will be handling a very sensitive case for the next few weeks. I think that under the circumstances it would be best if you gave Mr Landsdown a very wide berth indeed.'

My ears boggled. Was he telling me to dump Mark?

'When the news about Llew Jones breaks, there's a risk that the papers will come snooping round us, as the PM's legal team,' Guy went on. 'I'll back you in your story that you were unaware of Mr Landsdown's connection with Jennifer Woodford – but only if you draw a line under him now. Is that clear?'

He bloody was, you know.

'So,' I said, needing to get it clear in my own head, 'Mr Landsdown and I are to finish?'

Guy gave me a humourless smile.

'That's correct,' he confirmed. '*If* you intend to accept the Jones brief. Are you telling me you don't want to be my junior?'

'Of course I do!' I replied.

'Right. That's settled then. Well, what are you waiting for?' chivvied Guy. 'Off you go, and close the door on your way out.'

My heart pounding, I gathered up the lever-arches and staggered out of the room in an ungainly manner.

Back in my basement lair, I dumped the files unceremoniously in the corner and shut the door. In the space of the last half-hour, two momentous events had occurred: I had been offered the job of legal adviser to the most powerful man in the country; but if I wanted to fill the above vacancy, it would preclude me getting back with Mark.

I fell into my chair and rested my forehead on the desk. Words alone could not describe how much I wanted to be Guy's junior in the Jones divorce. It was the ultimate vindication of all the exams I'd sweated over, the debts I'd accrued and the heartache I'd endured to worm my way into the exclusive gentlemen's club that was the Bar. Moreover, if I played my cards right, it would land me on a lifelong gravy train full of juicy briefs with fees to match.

The one thing, however, that it would take away from me was the chance to be with Mark.

Bugger, bugger, *bugger*!

This was much worse than having to decide if Mark was worth the hassle his high-octane personal life would invariably bring with it. What was I going to do?

Did the Jones case mean more to me than my own happiness?

No.

Was I so sure my future lay with Mark that he was worth jacking in my hard-won career for?

Of course not.

I looked guiltily at the swathes of flowers littering my room: there was no doubt Mark was keen to pick up where we had left off. Wouldn't there be other briefs? Even other tenancies? Supposing the worst happened and Hugo the Slimeball got taken on; I knew I'd still get a cracking reference – plus I had a good clutch of solicitors who instructed me on a regular basis and would continue to do so whichever set of chambers I happened to be in. It would be fine: I could have Mark *and* do my job.

But I would never get another shot at being the Prime Minister's lawyer. And I wanted that so badly it hurt.

There just didn't seem any way round the problem.

I lifted my head and rubbed my eyes. At least I had time on my side: it wasn't as if Mark was standing next to me demanding an answer. What I needed to do was calm down (very important), then weigh up the pros (lovely, lovely Mark) against the cons (money; professional reputation; getting the sack if I went against Guy's wishes; the fact that Mark and I were bound to break up at some point *anyway*) and thus come to a rational decision. The problem was, the whole dilemma had me feeling far from cool, collected and capable of determining my future. Then my eye caught the stack of files by the door . . . Ah, that was how I'd do it! I'd lose myself in the Jones papers for a bit.

I grabbed the first of the lever-arch files, booted up my laptop and prepared to do battle with the Joneses' bank statements. My spirits rose quite considerably: I enjoyed getting to grips with the nitty-gritty of complicated cases. Understanding the financial nuts and bolts of other people's lives and then reconstructing them into a fair and workable divorce settlement was a strangely satisfying occupation; plus, with this particular case, I had the added interest of finding out all sorts of weird and wonderful things about our PM. Would he be a McDonald's or a Burger King man? Would he buy his underwear at M&S like Mrs Thatcher? And how often did they have Chinese takeaways at Number Ten? The answer to all these glittering questions lay in the paperwork before me . . .

Just as I was flicking through Mrs Jones's credit-card statements (*a hundred pounds in Fortnum and Mason? Every month? On cheese!*), the phone rang.

It was Jane.

'It's him,' she hissed. 'Mr You-Know-Who. Shall I send him down?'

Panic gripped me. What on earth was Mark doing here? Shouldn't he be out on a building site somewhere wearing an unattractive fluorescent jacket and discussing load-bearing walls with a bunch of men in wellies?

'No! Don't!' I cried. 'Someone might see him! Tell him to go away and I'll call him. Tell him to go away *quickly*.'

'He says it won't take long,' Jane replied in her stage whisper. 'He had a meeting about the renovations they're doing at Mitre Court and called in on his way back to the office. You can make a bit of time for him, surely?'

I didn't know if I could – I had not yet managed to feel calm *or* rational and was thus light years away from actually making a decision about him.

'Come on!' Jane was almost pleading with me. 'You can't just leave him cluttering up the waiting room. Guy's got a big meeting in half an hour and there won't be enough seats once they all start arriving.'

That focused me. The waiting room was directly opposite Guy's office. The last thing I wanted was for Guy to open his door, clock Mark reading a back copy of *Country Life* and give me my notice.

'Any of the conference rooms free?' I asked.

'Number three. I'll reserve it for you.'

'Tell him I'm on my way.'

I stomped up the staircase to the ground floor with a feeling of doom hanging over me: what was it with the man – did he have some sort of perverse wish to get me fired?

However, as I entered our tiny waiting room, Mark stood up and grinned at me, and my stomach did its loop-the-loop thing and my knees went wobbly. He was so lovely – I would be mad to end it when what I actually wanted was to have my body glued on to his, wouldn't I?

But 'yes' to Mark meant a 'no' to Llew Jones.

Arrggh!

Mark walked over to me. 'Did you get the flowers?' he asked hopefully.

'Mr Landsdown,' I said, forcing myself to sound professional and shaking him by the hand to put any potential onlookers off the scent. 'This way, please.'

We set off down the corridor, and I was about to usher him into Conference Room Three, thanking my lucky stars that no one had bumped into us, when Hugo slimed past on his way back from pool practice. He acknowledged Mark with a cheery hello, before remarking to me sotto voce:

'Using chambers facilities for nefarious liaisons, Looby? Just the sort of thing I think Guy ought to know about.'

Shoving Mark unceremoniously through the door and shutting it behind him, I advanced on Hugo with a murderous expression on my face.

'Listen, you little shit,' I began, drawing myself up to my full height of five foot four (*in* heels), 'I've had just about enough of you. Any more of your crap and I'll—'

Hugo was unrepentant.

'You'll what?' he asked, half curious, half threatening.

I gave him my best withering stare.

'I'll tell Guy you've been using the chambers' computer to download the women's swimwear section from the Next Directory.'

He blanched.

'How did you know it was me?'

'You saved it in a folder with your name on, you moron. Now piss off and mind your own business.'

Like an arrow from a bow, he dashed down the stairs to our basement, where the communal computer was located. There was a gratifying thud and a howl of anguish as he missed the bottom step and (I hoped) fell flat on his face. What a shame I wasn't in the right frame of mind to enjoy a really good gloat.

I turned my attention back to the main event in the conference room.

One bloke down (literally); one to go.

Mark was on the far side of the oval table that took up most of the room. He had his back to the door, and was staring through a grubby window covered by an even grubbier net curtain out on to the rows of BMWs and Mercs in the car park beyond. He turned round and gave me a rueful smile as I entered. I chose not to return it.

'You shouldn't have come,' I snapped. 'After what happened yesterday, turning up here is a hideously bad idea.'

His face dropped a bit.

'I'm sorry,' he replied, 'but I had to see if there was any chance we could rescue something from this awful mess.'

Oh God, this was going to be tough. Even though I was spitting feathers, the sound of his voice made me go meltier than a bar of Dairy Milk left out in the sun. How was I going to stop myself from simply caving in and telling him to come over after work tonight?

Remember what happened yesterday, a shadowy section of my brain suggested slyly. *Think how angry you were.*

'Plus,' I said to Mark, 'there are a whole lot of other issues we need to deal with.'

A lot of nasty, confrontational issues, my brain reminded me.

'Of course.' His smile faded. 'It can't be easy taking on someone with a kid – but Josh is great. And I do only see him occasionally.'

But Josh is just one small part of it, my brain whispered. *Imagine how hideous the professional fallout might have been. How could Mark have laid you open to so much public humiliation?*

'I fully admit the idea of Josh is rather scary,' I replied, 'but what really concerns me is the fact that you didn't *tell* me about him, or about Jennifer, or the court case. Then, to make matters a million times worse, you go and announce our relationship to the whole world. I was made to look a fool in front of my client, my solicitor and most of the people I depend upon for a living. I'm the laughing stock of the family law profession, and if Guy hadn't believed me when I said I knew nothing about your involvement in Jennifer's case prior to the hearing, I could have lost my job. Do you understand how serious this is?'

He blanched. Obviously none of this had occurred to him.

'I was going to mention the case,' he said, 'but you and me – it just felt so, I don't know, *right* somehow. I was afraid that telling you about Jennifer and Josh would spoil things.'

I knew what he was talking about: I'd felt that rightness too.

Noooooo! scolded my brain. *Think negative! Focus on the whole shame and anger thing! Make him suffer too!*

'I'm afraid it doesn't end there. What if Guy had walked out of his room just now and seen you? Or he'd been in reception when the flowers arrived? You're an intelligent man, Mark; don't you realise how close you've come to tanking my career?'

Mark went very, very pale and then very, very red.

'I'm sorry,' he stuttered. 'Of course you're right – I know you're right. It's just . . . well, you, me, us – the whole thing – has been so totally overwhelming that all I've been able to think about is not losing you. I didn't really compute any of the other consequences.'

He ran a harassed hand through his hair.

'I know we only met at the weekend, Lucy, but I feel a hell of a lot for you; and if I could turn the clock back and stop you from having to go through that farce at court yesterday, I would. Instead, all I can do is admit I've made some horrible mistakes and apologise profusely for them. Nothing like this will ever happen again.'

You've got him now – go on, ratchet his guilt up just one more notch.

'No more children tucked away ready to come out of the woodwork, then?' The words were out of my mouth before I could stop them, and I saw him wince as the sarcasm hit home.

He reddened again. 'No. And whilst we're busy raking over my past, neither do I have any more exes like Jenny.'

I had the decency to feel ashamed: I had overstepped the mark. There was no way he could have foreseen the muck-up at court. If Roger Watson hadn't had the misfortune to be ill, none of this would have happened. I did my best to grapple the shadowy bit of my psyche back under control.

'I'm sorry,' I said, 'that was out of order. Look, I'll be straight with you, Mark: things have got a tad more complicated since yesterday.'

He shook his head. 'Whatever it is, Lucy, we can work through it. I know we can.'

Not a chance. My shadow mind sprang free and

recommenced its siren song. *If you so much as go for a drink with Mark, either Hugo, Jennifer or some other busybody will find out and grass you up. There is no way you can make it work – forget about him and move on.*

Mark was waiting expectantly for me to continue.

'I have something I need to discuss with you,' I said, twisting my hands awkwardly in front of me. 'There's a problem. A big problem. You see, Guy spoke to me about the incident yesterday, and—'

Before I knew what was happening, Mark had taken another step forward and was holding my fidgety hands in his.

'Guy shouldn't be blaming you for what happened yesterday,' he said softly. 'Like I said, I should have told you about Josh. It's up to me to take full responsibility for not doing so.'

Rather bravely, I met his gaze. It was like staring at one of those snakes that mesmerise their prey before eating it.

But in a good way.

I shook myself to break the spell.

'No, Mark,' I clarified, 'he's not trying to make me feel bad.'

'Pleased to hear it,' he replied. 'So what's up? Is it us? Lou, if I could do anything, *anything* to make up for yesterday, you know I would, don't you?'

Mark sounded so sorry, so genuine, so, well, *caring*, dammit, that for a moment I was sorely tempted to jack in Mr Jones and run off into the sunset with him. Maybe I had found the man of my dreams. Maybe our mutual love of cheesy seventies disco would see us through the rough times that lay ahead. Maybe Jennifer would want to be my best mate rather than kill me in a slow and painful way . . .

Stop! yelled my brain. *Apart from the fact that you'd be mad to pack in the Jones case, have you learned nothing over the years? The relationship is doomed and*

*you might as well get the breaking-up bit over and done
with now. Go on, you can use the Guy thing to make
it look as if the decision has been taken out of your
hands.*

'Look,' I said, 'the problem is this case Guy's got me
on. The client is, um, quite famous and it's going to raise
my profile substantially. In fact, if I play my cards right,
I'll not only win the tenancy, but it's the nearest I'll ever
get to guaranteeing my future.'

Mark stared down me. 'But that's wonderful, Lucy.
It's the best news I've heard in ages.'

Once again I risked meeting his gaze. He was
positively beaming, so chuffed was he on my behalf.
Then his eyes closed and he dipped his head towards
mine, brushing my lips with his. This was presumably an
oral reconnaissance exercise to see if I was up for a full-
on kiss. I couldn't help it, honest: my lips parted, and
before I knew it, his mouth was on mine. For a minute I
put my brain on hold as I relished the taste of him, the
movement of his body against mine and the rather
determined way in which his hands were making their
way down my back, around my rib cage and in between
the buttons on my shirt.

But somehow I couldn't shake off the feeling that it
was all futile. My brain was right: it would all grind to a
bloody but unspecified end at some point in the future.
It was much better to finish it now and save myself the
hassle I'd get from Guy, Jennifer et al. Using reserves of
self-control I never knew I possessed, I disentangled my
tonsils from his.

'No,' I stuttered. 'You don't understand! It's not good
– not good at all.'

'Yes it is,' he contradicted. 'You are my fabulous,
clever, sexy girl and you've landed the case of a lifetime.
Even if it means you'll be a bit tied up here and there, we
can deal with that.'

And he went to kiss me again.

Tell him! Tell him!

'If I take the case,' I blurted, pulling away out of his arms, 'it's so sensitive, Guy says we have to stop seeing each other.'

Mark froze. It was as if someone had just pressed the 'pause' button on a cosmic remote control. I couldn't even tell if he was breathing.

'*Huh?*' he managed at last.

'In case the papers get hold of it,' I explained. 'There's going to be enough fuss about the Pri— about the divorce I'm dealing with as it is, and if anyone finds out that a member of the legal team was caught in public in a compromising position, it could be a PR disaster.'

Mark looked at me for a long time before speaking, and when he did so, his voice was scarily calm.

'Let me get this straight: your *boss* told you we were not allowed to see each other?'

I nodded. 'If I take the job, yes.'

'And you told him where to go, didn't you?' he asked.

I bit my lip by way of reply, and there was one of those silences when all you're aware of is the blood thumping round your temples. Mark shook his head disbelievingly.

'Lucy, I reckoned we had something amazing here, and I – I, well, I thought you felt the same.'

'I *did*, but—'

'Then tell Guy where to stick his interfering attitude!'

'I can't – I need this case.' I found myself pleading with him not to hate me. 'Mark, please, this is work: it's not personal.'

'Well, it feels bloody personal from where I'm standing.' His gaze crashed into mine and I swear there were sparks coming from his eyes. 'Look, I acknowledge that what happened yesterday put you in a difficult position – and that I shouldn't have come here today either – but surely the bottom line has to be that we are together, Guy or no Guy!'

I hadn't bargained on Mark feeling this strongly about losing me. What made it worse was that a mirror-image of his pain was busy sloshing around inside me and I found myself close to tears.

But I'd come too far down the road to backtrack now.

'No, the bottom line is that I need this case,' I said, trying to mask the catch in my voice, 'and if I take it, I have to do so on Guy's terms. I'm sorry, Mark, but you're going to have to deal with it.'

'And what if I don't want to deal with it?'

'Then you'll just have to get over yourself. Or even better, get over *me*!' I cried, hammering the last nail into the coffin of our fledgling relationship.

Poor Mark. I couldn't bear to look at his face; the crumpled sound of his voice was bad enough.

'This shouldn't be happening, Lucy,' he said quietly.

He was right; it shouldn't have been happening. We stood in silence for a moment, both of us hoping for some sort of death-row reprieve.

But of course it never came.

Instead, I opened the door and the pair of us stepped out into the corridor. Mark turned to face me, to say goodbye, but I didn't trust myself to open my mouth without blubbing all over him like a big girl's blouse. So I did the best possible thing under the circumstances, which was to leg it down the stairs to my own room, leaving him to figure his own way out.

I pounded along the corridor in the basement, wiping my eyes angrily on the sleeve of my jacket. Oh, how could Mark Landsdown have this much of an effect on me? I'd only known him five minutes – it was ridiculous. I reached my room and slammed my door out of sheer frustration, prompting a muffled 'Keep your hair on, Looby!' from Hugo's room.

I sat down at my desk and buried my head in my hands. For two pins I could have dissolved into a soggy mass there and then, but with a superhuman effort, I pulled myself together. Crying didn't get you anywhere; you had to pick yourself up and get on with your life. Didn't I have better things to do than anguish over Mark? (Go, girl!) Wasn't I the legal adviser to the Leader of the Free World? (Well, one of the leaders, anyway.) And wasn't that much, *much* more important than one crappy bloke? (Of course it was.)

I'd done exactly the right thing, I told myself firmly; and at least I had Mr Jones to take my mind off Mark . . . Speaking of which, I had work to do. So I blew my nose loudly, switched my computer on again and tried to turn my attention back to the lever-arch files.

But it was no good.

I found that my concentration levels were languishing at about one and a half on the Hez Irving Scale for Everything: Hester Jones and her cheese simply couldn't hold my attention any more.

At one o'clock I surrendered to the inevitable and headed off to Selfridges, where I blew fifty quid I couldn't afford on lipstick and mascara. Next, in case you are in any doubt as to the seriousness of the situation, I bought a pair of frivolous high-heeled foxtress-type shoes. Then, before I could console myself any more, I forced myself to return to work.

All this time, the row with Mark was running over and over again in my brain on a sort of neural loop-tape, and each time I viewed it, I found something new to cringe over. Had I made the right decision? Had I done the right thing in telling him about Guy's injunction against us? Or should I simply accept that I had as much chance of enjoying a functional relationship as I did of captaining the next England World Cup squad.

The bottom line was that Mark had somehow managed to break through my usual defences. Somewhere deep inside me, a small glimmer of hope had emerged that he might be one of the good guys; that our relationship might not simply be a one-way street to misery and accusation; and I felt horribly let down. It was like putting your faith in a holiday brochure that promised you a luxury hotel room overlooking the beach, and instead you found yourself in a cockroach-infested hovel with a first-class view of the bins.

Finally, at five o'clock, after a further three hours of non-progress on the Jones case, I decided I would get on better if I worked from home. So I got Jane to order a cab and bill it to Hez's firm before heading off to Muswell Hill.

For the second time in twenty-four hours, I felt enormous relief as my front door shut behind me. Shoving a stack of old Sunday papers to one side, I put the files down in a space on the living-room floor and went into the kitchen to get a glass of wine. However, as I tripped over the two empty bottles from yesterday, I told myself that it would be only *one* glass. This evening, the fate of the country, the future of our democracy, the very foundations of Parliament itself were in my hands. It was a time for sobriety; not for getting shedded and writing bad poetry about might-have-beens called Mark.

Anyway, I poured my wine, put a stopper purposefully back in the top of the bottle and returned to the living room.

The files hadn't moved.

I glanced at the clock. Wow – only half past five. It was amazing how much quicker it was to get a cab home than to stagger up the Northern Line. Normally I didn't get in until about a quarter to seven – if I was lucky.

Hmmm. Half past five. *Neighbours* time.

You know, I thought, a bit of telly would help me chill out properly and put all thoughts of Mark firmly to one side; plus, if I got cracking with the Jones stuff at six, I would still be starting earlier than if I'd got the tube home.

It sounded like a plan.

Hez, Jo and I had been avid soap fans whilst at Bar school, but my habit had lapsed a bit since entering the world of work. I squinted at the opening titles. They seemed to have replaced almost the whole cast since I'd last seen it, but it only took about twenty milliseconds to get right back into the plot: someone was having an affair; a geeky teenager fancied his teacher; and someone else thought they might be adopted – all top stuff.

I settled down and slurped away at my wine. Bonzer!

As the credits rolled, I was quite surprised to notice that my glass was empty; but I was feeling fairly relaxed and hadn't considered the Mark Issue for at least three minutes, so my cunning idea was obviously working.

Then I looked at the files.

Instantly, the image of Guy telling me that I had to jack Mark in swam before my consciousness.

Maybe I should go and change before I started work?

Yes – get out of my office clothes and put the day behind me. So off I went to my bedroom.

Half an hour later, I had showered and put on a nice comfy pair of jeans and a linen shirt that sort of knotted round my waist. Plus, I'd had no thoughts of Mark for at least five minutes – excellent.

I went back into the living room. The files were, unsurprisingly, still in the corner. I reached for my calculator, determined to block Mark out for even longer; but as I did so, my tummy gave an ominous little rumble. I hadn't been able to face lunch, and suddenly I realised I was starving. I looked guiltily at the files. To hell with it, I thought. I couldn't work on an empty stomach; my concentration span would be zero and I might go mad through hunger and start trying to advise the Prime Minister about fraud or armed robbery or something by mistake.

I wandered back into the kitchen and opened the fridge. Mmm . . . some of those grapes . . . and Kettle Chips and hummus . . . and maybe a bit of chocolate . . .

I piled my little feast on to a plate and looked at it. I needed something to wash it down. What about a glass of Coke? Good idea – non-alcoholic *and* it would keep me awake till three in the morning so I could get my work done.

Then I saw the Coke bottle standing empty and forlorn beside the bin. Damn! Hez must have drunk it all to fend off her hangover that morning. So before I knew what was happening, I had refilled my wine glass.

I went back into the living room again. This time I didn't even bother to glance at the files. Even though they didn't have eyes or faces they were still managing to give me funny looks, and there were strange rustling mutterings coming from their corner.

I turned the telly back on to drown them out – *and* to exorcise the thought that by letting them into my life I had effectively evicted Mr Landsdown.

There was a game show called *That's My Bollard!* or something equally tedious, but as an accompaniment to snack-munching/Shiraz-slurping/Mark-banishing it was bang on. In fact, I even stayed glued for the next show (*Strictly St Vitus' Dance*, broadcast from one of London's major teaching hospitals) while I polished off a chocolate mousse. As the credits rolled, I checked my watch. Shiiiiiiiit! Eight o'clock. If I didn't crack on, like, *now*, I was going to be watching the sun rise over a lever-arch file.

I sat on the sofa surrounded by files, laptop and calculator: Mark or no Mark, I'd accepted the brief and I had to get this done. I opened the first file. It contained the correspondence relating to the divorce petition, and I noticed a letter with Hez's reference at the top that seemed to be outlining a disagreement of some kind. I read three more sentences before my eyes jumped out of my head and stayed there, dangling over the page:

He did what with a water melon? No – two water melons!

Good grief! What else would I find buried amongst the correspondence? A kumquat coming forward with a kiss-and-tell story for the Sunday rags? A kiwi fruit love child?

I read on and a sense of relief crept over me. Hez's letter gave a plausible explanation of the incident; apparently it related to something he'd got up to at university – a Hattie Jacques impersonation or something. I flipped over the page to the next piece of correspondence, eager to find out how the matter resolved itself. Did Hester Jones's solicitors accept Hez's explanation, or was the PM going to have to answer some tricky questions about his agricultural policy ... ? No, Hester was retracting the allegation. Phew! At least I wasn't going to have to stand up in a court of law and explain melon fetishism to a senile old judge.

Even so, it had given me a nasty turn. My poor beleaguered brain needed soothing, so I logged on to the net, intending to play around on Google for five minutes *only*. I typed in Hez's name first and got on to the Sheppertons website.

Henrietta Irving, barrister. Fee-earner in the family law department at Sheppertons for the past three years. Specialisms include divorce and financial settlements, private Children Act work, international child abduction cases and paternity issues.

Yawn. Made her sound as dull as mince. They obviously felt that the time she turned up to the office Christmas party dressed as a go-go dancer wouldn't help pull the punters in. Personally, I thought they were wrong, but still . . .

My fingers hovered over the keys: an idea had just struck me. This might not be a good idea, but it was absolutely guaranteed to take my mind off Mark. Checking to make sure Hez had not snuck into the room when I wasn't looking, I typed in the name: Jonathan Hodges.

Ping! Sites 1–10 of 146,900 for Jonathan Hodges.
Blimey! I clicked on one at random.

Leading research scientist Dr Jonathan Hodges revealed today to a packed conference at the Institute of Physical and Earth Sciences, University of Salisbury, that the eagerly awaited results of his investigation into sustainable energy were even more impressive than had previously been thought. Dr Hodges, famous for presenting the iconic TV programme How Green Is Your Valley? *and one of the world's leading authorities on . . .*

Grrrrr! Even six years later, he still had the power to make me angry. Why did he have to be the world's leading authority on *anything*? Couldn't the gods have taken pity on me and let me discover he'd cocked up somewhere along the line? I could feel my heart pumping and my blood seething. Now I needed to be distracted from my distraction.

The fingers hovered again. I shouldn't, I really shouldn't. This was a monumentally bad idea . . . Hadn't I spent most of the evening trying to put him firmly out of my mind?

Mark Landsdown. Click.
Sites 1–10 of 1,587 for Mark Landsdown
Click.

And there he was, grinning up at me from the screen with one of those yellow Bob the Builder hats on and a speck of mud on his nose.

> *Mark is a very recent addition to the team here at Historical Construction and has already proved an invaluable addition to our expertise. A structural engineer with ten years' experience in the field, he has a particular interest in pre-eighteenth-century buildings, especially those with timber frames. After graduating from King's College, London . . .*

Yet again I had to stop reading, but this time it was not out of annoyance with the subject of the piece, but because a huge fat tear had just rolled down my nose and splashed on to the keyboard. It was joined by another and another, until eventually the picture went all blurry and I couldn't see it. I put the laptop on the floor and ran to the bathroom to get a tissue, but the flood tide of misery that had been building up since that morning burst through and completely overwhelmed me.

Stop this now! I told myself, as the tears coursed down my cheeks. How long, exactly, have you known him? Five days! For goodness' sake, you've waited longer than that for other blokes to call you after a date! There is no way – repeat, *no way* – that Mark bloody Landsdown justifies this amount of angst.

But it was useless. The time when my heart was prepared to accept orders from my head on matters concerning Mark was long gone. Even as I berated myself for being so weak and shallow as to allow a man to affect me in this way, further waves of hurt and disappointment were washing over me. Finally I dissolved into a soggy heap on the bathroom floor, my arms round the pedestal of the toilet, my head resting on the lid.

And that was how Hez found me half an hour later.

At nine o'clock the next morning, I strode into Guy's room and presented him with fresh, crisp photocopies of the paperwork he'd asked me to prepare. I was in kick-ass mode: I was having a good hair day; I looked pretty hot in my new black suit; and I'd even managed to crawl out of bed in time to iron my shirt.

Divorce of the century? Easy-peasy.

Client one of the most powerful men in the world? Do I look worried?

Fight on our hands? Bring it on!

Surely it was only a matter of time before *Marie Claire* was on the phone, inviting me to give an exclusive interview . . .

Guy scanned the papers, nodded, said 'Good girl' a couple of times and then made me a cup of coffee.

After that, Llewellyn Jones arrived and told me how delighted he was to meet one of the rising stars of the legal world. He was astounded by my breathtaking analysis of his financial position, and even Guy kept his trap shut long enough for me to do some of the talking at the conference. Hez and Spiggott stared admiringly at me, dazzled by my insightful comments and forthright advice, and *nobody* asked me to do any photocopying.

At the end of the conference, the Prime Minister took my hand and, in a voice dripping with gratitude, thanked me for my time. He invited me and Hez to the next party

at Number Ten and went on to say that he would call the
Richard and Judy office immediately in order to
recommend me for a slot on the show: in his vision of
Britain, all people should have access to the quality of
advice I had just delivered. After he'd gone, my mother
rang and announced that she and my dad were getting
back together; and finally, on my way to Pret A Manger
for a tuna buttie, I found a fifty-pound note on the
pavement and treated Hez and myself to lunch and a
bottle of wine at El Vino instead.

Er, no, actually.

Apart from the bit about Guy calling me a good girl,
which made me feel like one of the canine contestants on
One Man and His Dog.

When Hez found me the previous evening (after she
had ascertained that I had not joined a religious cult that
promoted simultaneous weeping and toilet-hugging),
she prised me away from the loo and manhandled me
back into the living room.

'Look,' she said, holding me with one hand and a
glass of water with the other, 'try and drink this – you'll
feel better.'

I shook my head. 'I'm not going to feel better.
Ever.'

'Yes you will,' she replied. 'One of two things is going
to happen: either it will somehow work out for you and
Mark; or you're destined to meet someone better.'

'You're forgetting the third option,' I said, 'that I give
up men once and for all and become the first nun in
history with a thriving divorce practice.'

'Don't be daft,' Hez admonished, 'and it's not as if you
haven't got anything to distract you in the meantime.'

I looked at the pile of lever-arch files on the floor.
There seemed to be about twice as many as I had
originally brought home with me, and I suspected they
had been breeding.

I let out a heavy sigh.

'Lucy . . .' said Hez in a warning voice.

'I know, I know,' I said quickly. 'I'm not thinking of throwing in the towel. The consequences are just too awful: Guy would think I'm a girlie lightweight; Hugo would get the tenancy; and you would be forced to kill me with your bare hands for passing up the opportunity of a lifetime. I've got to stop wussing around and get on with it.'

It was the truth, the whole truth and nothing but the truth. I'd accepted the brief and it was more than my life was worth not to see it through. I could cry about Mark another time.

'Good,' said Hez, delving into her vast briefcase. She produced a sheaf of papers and a CD-ROM and handed them over. 'Then you'll be wanting these: a schedule of assets, debts and income; chronology of major events in the marriage; and a list of important matrimonial cases. I did them all for Spiggott last week and there's no point in you going over the same ground again for Guy. You'll need to update them from the past couple of days' correspondence, but basically you're there. Now put that Landsdown boy out of your mind for a while and get on with the job in hand!'

I loved her. In fact, if I'd been into that sort of thing I would probably have asked her to marry me there and then.

I was even in bed before midnight.

At one forty-five the next day, Spig the Pig and Hez arrived at the biggest, plushest conference room my chambers could provide, miles better than the dingy little place where Mark and I had had our row. Spiggott was empty-handed but Hez, trailing along in his wake, was juggling two briefcases, a laptop and some law reports. She spent the next ten minutes scurrying round plugging in computers, setting out paper and pens on the polished surface of the conference table and fetching glasses of water, whilst Spiggott sat in an armchair and read the newspaper. Honestly, it was like witnessing some sort of bonded servitude.

Our revered Prime Minister arrived at two o'clock on the dot. I'd always thought of him as youngish and a bit fanciable but was dismayed to find he looked much older, shorter and fatter than he did on the telly, with a nasty mullet-like haircut that made me want to leap at him with a pair of scissors and give it a trim. After him came a seemingly endless stream of security men, civil servants and accountants, until I found myself awash in a sea of suits. As far as I could see, Hez and I were the only representatives of the female sex in the room. It was all rather unnerving.

Predictably, Guy told me to go and make the coffee (three million bazillion cups for the assembled multitude), and by the time I'd finished doing that and sat down again (in a corner by the window, miles away from where the main players were seated), he had already started to give his advice.

From here on in, I knew I wasn't going to have much to do apart from take notes. Guy had made it quite clear that the conference was to be his chance to shine and that he expected me just to sit quietly and smile sweetly. I could have been put out, but after the high emotion of the previous couple of days, I was quite looking forward to taking it easy. So I grabbed what looked like a bundle of paperwork to lean my notebook on and tried to look intelligent.

Guy kicked off by explaining to Llew Jones the implications of some recent divorce cases. I'd compiled the information myself the night before, so I didn't bother taking a verbatim note. Instead, I wrote the words 'Conference with the PM', the date and 'see list of cases' underneath it and waited, pen poised. Guy, however, glanced over the top of his trendy specs at me and I decided it would be politic to at least *look* busy, so I wrote my name very quickly six times. Then I got bored with that and tried my name with the letters *QC* after it. Next, I added the words *Lord Justice* to the front, and I was just about to work the title *Lord Chancellor* in there somewhere when I became aware that Guy was no longer speaking and that everyone in the room was looking at me expectantly.

I smiled what I hoped was a winning smile.

'Sorry about that,' I said. 'Just a tiny delay between what's being said and taking the notes.'

'The papers,' said Guy, probably for the second time. 'If you don't mind.'

I didn't mind at all. I simply had no idea which papers he might be referring to: I'd given him all the paperwork that morning.

Then I removed my left hand from underneath the pile of stuff I'd been leaning my notebook on. It was covered in newsprint.

Ah – he meant *those* papers.

I handed them over to Guy, who spread them on the table.

My eye was drawn immediately to a copy of the *Daily Stoat*. Whilst the *Guardian* was leading with 'Civil Service Typos: The Government's Secret Sandal' and the *Mail* had gone with 'Shock Rise in OAP ASBOs', right across the front page of the *Stoat* ran the banner headline:

'HAS PM BEEN GETTING FRUITY?'

Below, in slightly smaller letters, it read:

Downing Street sources today refused to confirm or deny a rumour that the Prime Minister wanted to bring the fruit bowl into the bedroom. Whether or not this will turn out to be the core of the ongoing marital disharmony between him and Mrs Jones remains to be seen. Full story on pages 2,3,4 and 7. Nutritional experts agree that this is not the way to get the most out of your five a day, page 11.

Underneath there was a picture of a weeping Mrs Jones, one of a smug-looking Mr Jones and another of a lonely looking cantaloupe.

Mmm . . . not good.

I cast my eye round the assembled throng. Hez was stifling a giggle; Spiggott looked as if he was about to burst a blood vessel and the Prime Minister had his head in his hands. I glanced at Guy. Normally he was more chilled than a Mr Whippy at the North Pole, but even he bit his lip and started to tap his Montblanc on the table in an agitated fashion.

For a moment there was an uneasy silence as everyone cleared their throats and looked at their feet. Then, with a low growl that made me jump, someone spoke.

'It's disgrrrraceful,' said the Prime Minister's press secretary, Cameron Macdonald. 'The woman's a liability – trrrying to get the public on her side before we've even announced a divorrrrce is in the offing.'

Throughout his time at Number Ten, Macdonald had made no secret of his antipathy towards Hester Jones. In fact, last summer she was alleged to have thrown a clotted cream scone at him after he made a remark about the shortness of her skirt at a Buckingham Palace garden party. She was always going to be his number one suspect in a situation like this. Mr Jones, however, did not react well at all to the suggestion that his wife was the architect of this unfortunate revelation. He went very white and Hez pushed a glass of water towards him.

'This is a disaster,' he muttered. 'I don't know how I'll ever live it down.'

'I've alrready got the focus groups worrrking on it,' consoled Macdonald, 'We'll turrrn it to our advantage with the voters somehow.'

'Damn the electorate,' cried his boss. 'It's my mother I'm worried about – she's never going to let me forget this.'

Hez and I glanced at each other. Was this really the alpha male, the Lion of Britain, we saw on the news footage?

'Now, Mr Macdonald,' said Spiggott, in an uncharacteristically calm tone of voice, 'we don't actually know that the story *was* leaked by Mrs Jones. Her solicitors are vociferously denying it.'

'And I'm afraid,' added Guy, 'that a one-off leak is not uncommon in a high-profile divorce. What we need to do is find out the source of the story and make sure the incident isn't repeated. Any ideas who it might be, Macdonald?'

'I can assurrrrre you that inforrrmation is cirrrrrculated on a strrrictly need-to-know basis,' he rumbled. 'Only a chosen few are prrrivy to it.'

I looked disbelievingly round the packed conference room: the chosen few what – hundred?

'Even so,' Guy concluded, 'we all need to raise our game and make sure that no one has the opportunity to sneak any more nuggets of information out to the press.'

His mention of possible further revelations had an unhappy effect on the PM, who was now mopping his face with a flamboyant silk handkerchief.

'I couldn't agree more,' he said. 'But leaving that aside for one minute, can we please decide what we are going to do about the leak that has already occurred. It's bad enough I'm getting divorced, let alone the fact that everyone now thinks I'm a fruit-fixated pervert.'

I couldn't help feeling sorry for him – although I *did* make a mental note to record the next session of Prime Minister's Questions. It looked as if it might be rather entertaining.

'We need to knock the rrrumour on the head right now,' growled Macdonald. 'Make the *Stoat* look rrrridiculous forr even suggesting it.'

A flicker of movement outside the window caught my eye. Shit! It was Mark, walking across the car park. He was carrying a hard hat and a spirit level and talking animatedly to a man with a clipboard. He looked relaxed, chilled and even – dare I say it – reasonably happy.

A lump the size of a small planet lodged itself in my throat and made breathing rather difficult. I *had* to do something to take my mind off him – and quickly. It was a toss-up whether I would ruin my tenancy chances more by bursting into tears in front of the PM or by joining in the discussion round the table. In the end, hoping Guy would find it in his heart to forgive me, I pitched headlong into the fray.

'I think we have to be open about the fact that there is a divorce in the pipeline,' I said, conscious of the slight wobble in my voice. 'That much is now unavoidable – but we need to stop all the melon rubbish here and now.'

The PM nodded his head in agreement.

'And just how are you proposing we do that?' asked Spiggott with a nasty sneer. 'When I spoke to Mrs Jones's solicitor this morning, they refused to issue a joint statement denying it.'

Bugger. Obviously I hadn't been aware of *that*.

'All right then,' I said, casting my mind back to the figures that I had spent three quarters of an hour rejigging last night. 'If she won't do it willingly, we'll just have to *make* her agree. If you look at her schedule of expenditure, she says she spends twenty thousand pounds a year in Fortnum and Mason, quite a lot of it on cheese. Plus a thousand a month for the hairdresser and the same again for Botox – and that's before we get into clothes, personal shopper, astrologer, pet psychic and the like. Why don't we tell her lawyers that if they don't come in with us on a joint denial, we will be doing a reply to her divorce petition citing her misuse of public money? Then, if there are any more leaks, her spending habits will be splashed all over the front pages. How does that sound?'

I glanced at the window. Mark and his companion

had moved out of my line of vision: the crisis was over. And I wasn't the only one in the room breathing a sigh of relief. The PM smiled for the first time since he'd walked into the room.

'Good thinking,' he said. 'Although it needs to be stressed that I had *absolutely no idea* that she was spending that much.'

'Naturally,' I said, making a careful and accurate note of all this. 'Mr Spiggott will write the letter this afternoon, won't you, Mr Spiggott?'

'Er, ah, yes. It will be a priority,' he sputtered.

'Good,' said Guy, wresting back control of the conference. 'The matter appears to be settled, then.'

I rocked! I rocked!

'Right, well I think that just about wraps it all up for now,' Guy continued. 'It was a pleasure to see you again, Llew.'

'Likewise, Guy,' replied the PM, stuffing his hankie back into his trouser pocket and offering his hand first to Guy and then to me. *Me!* Shaking hands with Llew Jones!

Then everybody shuffled out. I was about to follow them, but Guy caught me by the arm.

'Just a minute, Lucy,' he said.

My heart sank. He was going to haul me over the coals for speaking out of turn.

'That was good thinking of yours to, er, persuade Hester Jones to come on side,' he said grudgingly. 'Well done. I was just about to suggest something very similar.'

I could hardly believe my ears: Guy was cool with the fact that I had stolen his thunder?

'I'd like you to type up a full note of the conference, please. Can you make sure that everybody here today gets a copy faxed to them by close of play tonight?'

'Of course.'

I tried to leave again, but Guy was there before me and closed the door.

'Have you spoken to Mr – er . . . ?' he asked.

'Landsdown,' I supplied. 'Yes. It's off.'

Guy's expression changed and became almost apologetic. 'You do understand why that was for the best, don't you, Stephens?'

I glowered at him.

'Well, as I said, notes typed and faxed by five thirty.' He hastily changed the subject before flipping his mobile open and punching in a number. 'Yes, it's Guy Jennings. I'd like my usual table for eight thirty, please . . . for two.' He turned back to me. 'Are you still here? Chop, chop, let's get this show on the road.'

I picked up my notebook and walked off to the basement to get chopping.

Guy needn't have had any concerns about my chop-ability. Anxious to keep thoughts of Mark at bay, I went into overdrive, and by five o'clock I had not only placed a typed note of the conference on his desk and faxed a copy to everyone else, but I'd prepared for a hearing of my own in Oxford that had come into the diary for next week. I had only just put my biro down when the phone rang. It was Jo.

'Hi!' she chirruped. 'Been trying to get you for a couple of days, but you're always busy. How's things? And when I say "things", I of course mean Mark.'

'Um, not so good,' I replied. 'Big case, no boyfriend.'

'No!' she cried. 'What happened?'

My mind skipped back over the various hellish scenarios that had been played out between Mark and myself over the past few days: so much to choose from, so little time . . .

'Well, it was mainly this big case of mine: mega-client, all very hush-hush. Guy said that if I wanted to be his junior on it, I had to finish things with Mark.'

Jo made a sound like someone who needed the Heimlich Manoeuvre administered as a matter of urgency.

'Guy can't do that!' she squawked as soon as she had recovered the power of speech. 'What's Mark got to do with a mega-client? Tell Guy it's none of his business –

and then tell him some intimate places where he can go and stick his meddling attitude.'

'Sadly, it isn't as simple as that. You see, I had a bit of a disaster at court on Wednesday when I got landed with representing Jennifer. At the point I accepted the brief, I had no idea there was any connection between her and Mark. Anyhow, the balloon went up and Guy is terrified the press will get hold of the story and chambers will be portrayed in a bad light and—'

Jo cut me off. 'You're kidding! You mean Mark didn't mention *anything* to you about him and Jennifer? Or Josh?'

I replied in the affirmative.

There was the sound of Jo whistling through her teeth.

'Silly, *silly* boy. Of course, I'd heard something on the grapevine about a conflict of interest and things getting nasty at court, but I had no idea it was you and Mark. Oh God, Lou, I feel awful. I should have mentioned the whole Josh debacle to you on Sunday.'

I gave a heavy sigh.

'Mark's grown-up; I would have expected him to tell me himself.'

'Look,' Jo continued, obviously anxious to make amends, 'I know things have gone majorly pear-shaped, but do you want me to get Dave to talk to Mark? There must be some way round this – perhaps you and he can just cool off for a bit while this big case is ongoing and hook up again later. Anyway, he and Dave are going to the pub this evening. Well, actually, they're playing squash, but they always spend twice as long drinking as they do on the squash court, so there will be ample opportunity for Dave to—'

I was out of it and I'd be better off keeping it that way.

'Thanks but no thanks, Jo,' I said hurriedly. 'It's probably for the best in the long run. Now, what can I do for you?'

'Would you like to come to the theatre with me tonight? I can officially confirm that this is not the month I get pregnant, so I need cheering up too. I've got tickets off eBay for *A Midsummer Night's Dream* – interested?'

Of course I was. Despite the fact that *MND*'s plot line of marital bust-ups, warring lovers and mind-altering drugs was more or less what I dealt with at work on a daily basis, going to the theatre was a brilliant excuse to dress up, get out and lose myself for a couple of hours.

I dashed home in record time, put on *The Best Chill-Out Album for Girls Who Live in Muswell Hill – Ever*, shoved a peanut butter sandwich in my gob and set about selecting a suitable going-to-the-theatre-type outfit from Hez's wardrobe. I eventually settled on a floaty skirt, a low-cut fitted top and a pair of black suede knee-high boots with kitten heels. I nodded approvingly at myself in the mirror: I looked good. Mark would be sobbing into his beer because I was no longer his. Then I shook myself – Mark wasn't going to be there; and what was more, I was better off without him and his hideously complicated private life.

Holding that thought, I applied some of my newly acquired cosmetics and sallied forth to theatreland for an evening of culture and edification with my mate Jo.

We found each other (predictably) in the bar, and ordered gin and tonics. As she paid, I had a bizarre feeling that there was somebody else close by that I knew. I'd never had myself down as Mystic Lou before, but couldn't deny the weird prickly feeling that had just run up the back of my neck and made me shiver slightly. My immediate thought was that Jo had invited Mark along, intending to slope off and leave us to it, and I looked round to try and pinpoint where he was.

'It's all right, this isn't a set-up,' Jo said, swishing ice round her glass. 'I had a text from Dave five minutes before you arrived – the pair of them are halfway through their first pint.'

I blushed slightly. Of *course* Mark wasn't going to be there; I was just being silly.

'I know,' I said, taking a large mouthful of G and T and trying not to be jostled off my feet by the heaving mass of bodies around me.

'Oh, Lou,' said Jo, reaching over and stroking my arm solicitously, 'I can't help but feel responsible for all this; after all, Dave and I did set you up together. I was sure you'd hit it off.'

'The "hitting it off" part wasn't the problem,' I replied. 'It was the "having a horrible boss who forced us to split up" bit we had trouble with. Look, there was nothing you could have done. Mark has things he needs to sort out, so I guess that even without Guy it was pretty much doomed.'

'I still think you could have been good together,' said Jo sadly. 'But your call, I suppose.'

'And whilst we're on the subject of disappointing news,' I said, 'I'm so sorry to hear about the un-baby.'

'Oh, that.' Jo shrugged. 'After two years, I'm beginning to think it's never going to happen. I'm off to the quack in a couple of weeks to get prodded and poked again, and Dave's got another check-up next Thursday. I hate it; it's all so clinical.'

'But it can't be all bad,' I consoled. 'There's all that sex, for a start.'

'Except I can't remember the last time we actually did it because we wanted to, rather than because the stupid ovulation kit told us we had to. There's no romance any more; it's just "let's get it over and done with now so we can watch *Spooks* later".'

For a split second, a seriously indecent image of Mark invaded my brain; surely there was no way on earth I'd *ever* find sex with him clinical? But I drove the picture from my mind. This sort of thinking had to stop.

'Shall we go and sit down?' I suggested. 'They're doing the one-minute-to-curtain announcement.'

'Good idea. We're in the front row of the gallery, so we should have a good view.'

As we were getting comfy (and Jo was announcing loudly that if she heard any mobiles going off during the performance she would personally flush them down the toilet during the interval), I gazed down on to the stalls and thought that I recognised the person on the far end of the fourth row.

But I couldn't be sure.

I squinted over the edge of the gallery, trying to get a better look; but as I did so, the house lights went down, putting paid to any further investigation. Just like the feeling I'd had in the bar, it was all a bit unnerving: I was pretty certain I hadn't been able to make out a face – it was more a feeling, the sort of *essence* of a person that had jogged my memory.

Hmm . . . I'd probably just caught a glimpse of one of my clients. It wasn't a thought that filled me with joy, because bumping into punters out of hours is always a bit awkward. Small talk is tricky, because you don't know much about them other than the excruciatingly personal details that made them your client in the first place. And: 'So, Mrs Green, is your husband still sleeping with the woman at number fifty-four or did the fact that you threw a brick through her window on Tuesday do the trick and lure him back?' is not really acceptable as a topic of general conversation. But as there was nothing I could do about the familiar stranger right then, I dismissed the whole thing from my mind and settled back to watch the play.

It was a naturalistic interpretation and the set tried very hard to imitate a native broad-leafed woodland. Everywhere had been decked out with greenery, and there were real rabbits hopping around. To my joy, one of them bit Oberon just as he was squeezing the love potion on to Titania's eyes and made him swear loudly: it was the best thing that had happened to me all week. The interval was upon us before I knew it, and as Jo joined the queue for the toilets (thankfully *sans* other people's mobiles), I went down to the bar to get the drinks in.

Just as I was giving up hope of ever being served, a man pushed in next to me and ordered a pint of Fuller's, a dry white wine and a Glenfiddich. I turned round, ready to tear him off a strip for jumping my place in the queue; but when I saw who it was, all the little hairs on the back of my neck sprang to attention and my mouth went dry.

Even though I had spent years honing feelings of righteous anger where this person was concerned, I found my immediate reaction was one of pure panic. Instinctively I turned to scarper, but found myself pinned up against the bar by a crowd of thirsty theatregoers. Escape having eluded me, I then tried to hide, but the best I could manage was covering the left side of my face with my programme. Needless to say, it didn't work. There was a tap on my shoulder and the queue-jumper shot me a smile so dazzling they could probably see it from space.

'Well, well, well.' Jonathan's soft Edinburgh accent wafted over the hubbub of the bar. 'Talk about coincidence – I was going to try and track you down this week.'

At the familiar sound of his voice, my stomach gave a violent lurch and I could feel my heart rate more than double. It was a few moments before I could find my voice to reply.

'Why on earth would you want to see me?' I asked at last.

The mental and physical turmoil currently overtaking my being was obviously not shared by Jonathan, and he grinned affably, running a hand through his dark, foppish hair.

'Since you ask, I'm up in the smoke for a term's sabbatical so I thought I'd look up some old friends.'

Friends? Er, no, I don't think so.

My fear and confusion fled and were replaced by anger. Now I knew where I was. I decided to forgo the usual social pleasantries (e.g. 'How are you?'; 'Super to see you'; 'So, what have you been up to since I told you to go to hell?') and waste no time in disabusing him of this 'friends' business. Hez was my friend, Jo was my friend; even (on a *very* good day and on the condition she returned all the clothes she'd nicked off me) my sister Lisa was my friend.

Jonathan was not.

Not even close.

Not even have another go and try again.

Unfortunately, I had just opened my mouth to let him have it with both barrels when there was a tug at my elbow and Jo appeared.

'Well, he-*llo*!' Jonathan flashed another supernova of a smile in her direction.

I cringed: he was so *obvious*! Jo, however, seemed to like it. In fact she did a sort of mini-blush and fluttered her eyelashes as if she was being introduced to a particularly luscious male specimen. I dug her in the ribs to snap her out of it and announced through gritted teeth:

'Jo, this is Jonathan Hodges. Jonathan, Joanna Williams.'

I hoped she would get the message and we could leave; but instead she gave a tiny, girlie gasp.

'You don't have to tell me! Wow! Jonathan Hodges! The alternative energy' – she paused for effect – 'guru?'

Yeah, yeah, yeah, like he'd had his own telly programme *two years ago* and everybody was still going on about it.

'You were voted Most Fanciable . . .'

Jonathan finished her sentence. '. . . TV Personality last year. Yes, that's right.'

That was all I needed! Doubtless his ego would now have swelled from huge to totally unmanageable.

'So, how do you know each other?' Jo went on, her eyes fixed on the man whose devotion to the wind turbine knew no bounds.

'We went out with each other,' Jonathan replied.

'Really?' Jo seemed genuinely surprised. 'I never knew that!'

It was true that it had all ground to an unhappy halt before I'd met Jo, but she'd heard me and Hez dissing him often enough, surely?

'Yes you did,' I hissed. 'You know – *Jonathan*. Now say goodbye and we can go back to our seats.'

But Jo wasn't having any of it. Her eyes widened in astonishment. 'You mean *that* Jonathan?' she hissed back.

I nodded.

'I'd always assumed you were talking about *another* Jonathan Hodges.'

I shuddered. The idea of two of them let loose on humanity was a little too much to bear.

Jonathan, meanwhile, was oblivious to this little exchange. He had handed the whisky and the glass of wine to another guy a few feet away, whilst keeping the pint for himself.

'So, Lou.' As he spoke, he flashed another smile at Jo, who simpered slightly in return. 'How are things at the Bar?'

'Fantastic,' I said, stretching the truth just a tad. 'More clients than you can shake a stick at.'

'Good for you.' Jonathan beamed. 'I never thought you'd make it as a lawyer; I always said you were too short.'

That was true, he always had. Jo stopped mid-simper and frowned slightly.

'But I'm glad to see you proved me wrong,' he continued. 'I also have to say that you're looking rather lovely on it.'

Then he held my gaze for slightly longer than necessary and *didn't* smile. That normally meant he was being serious. It was now my turn to do a mini-blush, and boy, didn't I hate myself for it.

'How are your mum and dad?' he asked, sipping his beer. 'Still in line for the Nobel Prize for Marital Disharmony?'

'Divorced for four years. Although you'd never know it the way they're still at each other's throats,' I replied.

Jonathan shook his head sympathetically and Jo, with a final bat of her eyelashes, said she needed to make a phone call and disappeared, leaving us on our own. I tried to follow her lead and plunge off into the crowd, but Jonathan pulled me back.

'Stay and chat for a bit,' he said. 'There's loads we need to catch up on. Where are you living, by the way?'

'Muswell Hill. The flat above the deli on the Broadway.'

I hadn't wanted to tell him but Jonathan has this sort of hold over people (I call it the Hodges Effect), and I knew from experience that I was particularly susceptible. With each breath, I could feel the fight trickling out of me.

'Nice part of town,' he replied, as if he'd designed and built it himself. 'I'm in Islington. I bought a garden flat I use whenever I come up to London.'

Islington? Blimey! Not even Jo and Dave could afford Islington. He was obviously doing all right.

Then Jonathan put his pint down on the bar and lowered his voice. As he dipped his head in closer to mine, I couldn't help but do the same. I could feel his breath on my ear and it wasn't an entirely unpleasant experience.

'I know it's going to sound odd, but I've wanted to get in touch with you for a while now,' he admitted.

'So what's wrong with a message on Friends Reunited?' I asked warily.

He gave a bit of a sigh. 'Look, Lucy, this isn't easy for me to say, but I want you to know I'm not proud of what happened. You deserved so much better, and while I'm not expecting us to kiss and make up . . .'

Thank goodness for that!

'. . . I would like to spend a bit of time with you while I'm in London.'

Huh?

'If that's okay with you, I mean,' he added hastily, obviously clocking the astonished expression on my face.

This was so *not* the Jonathan I loved to hate. The old Jonathan would never have bothered to check my feelings on the matter.

I was dumbstruck.

Then suspicious.

And then worried.

'Are you all right?' I asked, seeking a rational explanation for both his transformation and his eagerness to get in touch. 'You haven't been told you've got three weeks to live or something?'

He laughed again. 'No. But I regret how it ended between us and I'd like to patch things up a bit. How about a drink sometime?'

I stared hard at him, trying to read his features for some sign that this was a Hugo Spade-like wind-up. But no, he seemed completely serious and even – heaven forbid – slightly *humble* about the whole thing.

Don't do it, cautioned the Jonathan-damaged part of my psyche. *He cannot be trusted. Run fast and run far*.

But an out-and-out refusal was beyond me: the Hodges Effect was too strong. So I did the best I could under the circumstances.

'I don't know,' I said, trying to sound vague. 'Maybe. Perhaps. I'll need to think about it.'

Jonathan beamed at me again and kissed me lightly on the cheek.

'Great,' he said, as if I'd actually agreed to his loony scheme. 'I'll catch you later.'

As if by magic, Jo materialised back at my side.

'We ought to go and sit down,' she said. 'Thirty seconds till curtain.'

'Good idea,' I said. 'See you, Jonathan.'

He grinned. 'Not if I see you first!' And he plunged into the sea of bodies surrounding us to find his other friends.

'That was a turn-up for the books,' I remarked to Jo, using phenomenal levels of understatement.

Jo, not yet fully clear of the Hodges Effect herself, did a bit more simpering.

'I had no idea he was, well – you know – so nice. You've always made him sound like he had horns and went round carrying a big pointy fork.'

'Watch it!' I warned her. 'Any more of this kind of talk, Mrs Williams, and I'm phoning Dave to tell him you're lusting after other men.'

'Am not!' She nudged me coyly with her elbow. 'But it's not every day I get to bump into a gorgeous celeb on a girlie night out. And his *voice*! I've always had a bit of a soft spot for Scottish men. How long did you see each other for?'

'About four years in total – although there was a break in the middle when he went to the States.'

'That's a long time when you're young.'

We squeezed our way down the row to our seats.

'What went wrong?' asked Jo.

I blushed a deep, deep red from the roots of my hair down to my décolletage.

'Oh, you know, the usual. He thought he was God's gift and I was too love-struck to tell him where to get off.'

We paused for a moment to watch a stagehand chase an escaped rabbit round the set.

'And I dumped him after he slept with someone else,' I added.

'He did *what*?'

We turned our attention back to the rabbit, which, after Oberon in Act Two, had obviously developed a taste for human blood: it sank its teeth into the stage hand's finger and almost got dropped into the orchestra pit.

'Have you forgiven him?' asked Jo.

'Are you kidding? Of course not.' I examined my fingernails in a sheepish fashion. 'Although I have an awful feeling I may have agreed to go for a drink with him.'

'But you're not – I mean, you don't – with him again?' Jo hissed as the house lights dimmed.

'I'm not about to start dating him, if that's what you're worried about,' I whispered. 'Once bitten, twice as likely to avoid self-satisfied, two-timing boyfriends, I always say. Anyway, it'll probably come to nothing. He doesn't have my phone number and I don't see him trudging all the way up to Muswell Hill on the off chance.'

'Glad to hear it,' Jo replied loudly – and was 'SSSSSHed' by almost the entire theatre.

Despite recent excitements, the weekend passed uneventfully. I escaped London and the one-week anniversary of my meeting with Mark by spending Saturday and most of Sunday with my student sister Lisa in Manchester. Then, as the working week began once again, I got up early to put the finishing touches to my case in Oxford. At six forty-five I was having a quick cup of coffee before catching the bus to the tube station when Hez rolled in from a date with a devastatingly handsome young partner in the litigation department at Sheppertons. She'd made me check out his mugshot on the firm's website and I could confirm he was very much her type, all dark, brooding eyes and Oswald Boateng shirts. Hez had had her eye on him since he'd started, and I'd hoped it would be a match made in heaven.

'Good night, was it?'

She wobbled her hand equivocally.

'Nice guy; reasonable food.'

'But?'

'But he lives in Bethnal Green, for goodness' sake. It took me nearly an hour to get home this morning.'

'So? It takes you nearly an hour to get into work *every day*.'

'Yes, but not because I'm walking barefoot to the tube in case I need my spike heels to defend myself from attackers.'

Hez was so not one of life's Urban Warriors.

'So you're not seeing him again, then?'

She shook her head and helped herself to my coffee. 'There wasn't any spark between us – you know, like you have with Mark. Talking of which, I know you've avoided doing so all weekend, but are you going to ring him today?'

'Please stop speaking about Mark and me in the present tense,' I said, picking up my bag and checking I had everything I needed for my hearing. 'And no, I am not. We are over. Even without Guy poking his oar in, I've made a rational, adult decision that Mark and I are better off apart.'

'Based on what?'

'The fact that our relationship ended in complete disaster.'

'Er, I don't think so,' Hez contradicted. 'I think you're not going to ring him because you know he's something special, and you're frightened you'll make yourself vulnerable and end up getting hurt.'

'All right, I made a rational, adult decision that I didn't want to get hurt. What's wrong with that?' I replied defiantly.

'Sometimes,' she said, fixing me with her best probing stare, 'you meet someone worth taking a risk for. And no matter how crap your family is, or how cynical your job has made you, or – yes – how much of a shit Jonathan was, you need to go for it. I would if it was me and Mark,' she added, opening the biscuit tin and shoving a chocolate digestive into her gob. 'He's gorge.'

'Well good for you,' I said, my throat tightening ominously at the thought of Mr Landsdown. 'I'll see you later – have fun with Spiggott.'

I picked up my coat and bag and headed for the door. A look of panic suddenly filled Hez's eyes.

'Where are you going?' she mumbled through a mouthful of beige biscuity mush.

'Oxford. Don't worry, it's quite safe – unlike Bethnal Green.'

Hez swallowed hard and choked on a crumb. 'No, I mean, you can't. Haven't you seen the papers?'

She burrowed in her bag, pulled something out and slid it down the counter towards me. It was a copy of that morning's *Daily Stoat*. The headline read:

'WORLD EXCLUSIVE: Is Mystery Woman involved in PM's Fruity Flight of Fancy?'

After I had climbed down from the ceiling and my nervous system had stopped twanging, I read the article underneath the headline. Actually, the word *article* gives the impression there was journalistic integrity involved. I think 'wild speculation and unsubstantiated rumour' would probably be a better description.

> *With Downing Street sources last night denying allegations that the Prime Minister's divorce petition will make reference to unusual practices involving fruit, we think Mrs Jones might like to consider adding the charge of adultery to the paperwork. Our eagle-eyed camera team snapped this lady sneaking out of the back entrance to 10 Downing Street the day before yesterday. As yet, the PM's private office and legal team are declining to comment but what the Stoat wants to know is – does it take two to tango? And if so, is that tango orange or apple flavour? See pages 2,3,4,5,7 and 9. For readers' top foxy food tips, see 'Dear Elsie' on page 20.*

Underneath, there was a grainy picture which may have been of a woman in sunglasses stepping out of a door but equally could have been a still from the Roswell Autopsy. My heart sank.

'Oh, shit,' I said, staring first at the paper and then at Hez.

'Oh and indeed shit,' she agreed. 'I've already had Spiggott on the phone twice this morning and there's an emergency meeting in your chambers at half-eight. I don't think you'll be going to Oxford.'

'No,' I agreed, getting out my phone and punching in a number, 'and I think I need to ring Guy.'

An hour and a half later, myself, a freshly showered Hez and a pale-looking Guy were assembled in the posh conference room in chambers. Just as I'd finished setting out the coffee cups and sugar bowl, there was a knock at the door and the PM and Cameron Macdonald were ushered in by Jane, followed by Spiggott.

'Well,' hissed Spiggott to Guy in a poorly disguised stage whisper, 'fat lot of good your injunction did us.'

Guy ignored him. 'Good morning, everyone, and thank you for making it in early,' he said.

'Wouldn't need to be here at all if you'd done your job properly,' growled Spiggott into his coffee cup.

Guy bared his teeth in a sort of smile.

'As Mr Spiggott is so diligently reminding us, the first matter we need to discuss this morning is the latest offering from the *Stoat*. As you will be aware, on the instructions of Mr Spiggott I made an emergency telephone application to a High Court judge at midnight last night to stop the story.'

'A failed application,' Spiggott pointed out.

'A failed application,' continued Guy, 'due to the fact that I was only instructed to make it *after* the first editions had been printed and distributed. I must emphasise, Mr Jones, that despite this, and despite the fact that the judge was not happy at being woken at midnight to hear the case, we did succeed in stopping later editions of the paper from running the story.'

'Thank you for achieving what you did,' said the PM graciously.

'It was my pleasure,' Guy replied, equally graciously.

Spiggott grunted, in a bad-tempered sort of a way.

'Our task this morning is to formulate a statement in time to catch the lunchtime news bulletins,' Guy continued. 'Now, what are everybody's thoughts?'

'Well, what I want to know,' Llew Jones cut straight to the chase, 'is who this woman actually *is*. I hate to disappoint you all, but I've never seen her before in my life.'

Guy went even paler than he had been previously: probably lack of sleep, I reasoned.

'If it is a woman,' Cameron Macdonald added.

'Indeed,' said Guy, winning the fight to regain his composure. 'It *is* hard to tell, isn't it? Presumably the subject of the photo was one of the guests at the party on Saturday – thank you for the invitation, by the way, Llew.'

'Yes, thanks,' said Spiggott.

Party? Hez and I glanced at each other. There had been a party and *we* hadn't been invited.

'One thing, though, is clear,' said Guy firmly. 'Whoever it is in the photo did not want their identity known. The fact that she chose to leave—'

'Orrrr *he*,' put in Macdonald.

'Of course,' Guy corrected himself. 'The fact that she *or* he chose to leave through a back exit means they wanted their attendance kept secret, and we must respect that. After all, there were some pretty big names there.'

My eyes met Hez's for the second time. Bugger! Big names were just the sort of people we wanted to mix with.

'Okay,' the PM conceded, 'so we let whoever-it-is have their anonymity, but who tipped the papers off in the first place? Do we think it was the person responsible for last week's leak coming back for a second pop at me? Miss Stephens – what do you think?'

I reread the story, hoping for inspiration. As my eye slid over the accompanying photograph, I had a momentary flicker of recognition – *was* it someone I knew? However, the flicker disappeared as quickly as it had ignited, and I put it down to some sort of brain fever brought on by the overexcitement of the case.

'Well,' I began, 'as the party took place the day before yesterday, the picture could just have been one of the *Stoat's* tame paparazzi getting lucky and the weekly editor fighting off his Sunday counterpart for the privilege of dragging the divorce story into another week. It doesn't have to be a leak.'

'Good point,' said Guy, pouring himself another cup of coffee.

'Well, that's something, I suppose,' said the PM. 'I don't know if my ratings can take another hit like the one they experienced over those wretched melons.' He closed his eyes and shuddered slightly.

'You sound very confident that the source of this picture was not the same person responsible for last week's leak, Miss Stephens,' said Spiggott, looking across the table at me accusingly. 'How can you be so sure?'

'I can't,' I replied with as much politeness as I could muster, 'but it is a logical possibility. However, I think none of us should be resting on our laurels where this is concerned. As Mr Jennings said at our last conference, we all need to raise our game and make sure nothing further is fed to the press, inadvertently or not.'

Spiggott made a sort of 'hmph-ing' noise. 'Well, Miss Stephens, I can categorically state that the leak did not originate from my office.'

Guy raised an eyebrow. 'That is very reassuring, Mr Spiggott. May I enquire how you can be so certain?'

Spiggott went very red in the face and glared at him.

'Are you suggesting my staff sell secret information to the gutter press?' he spat. 'We have a very strict confidentiality clause in all staff contracts.'

'But therrre could always be the odd disgrrruntled employee who could spill the beans given the rrrright motive,' interjected Cameron Macdonald.

'On the contrary, I have a happy, productive work-force who are all entirely satisfied with their conditions of employment,' said Spiggott sanctimoniously.

Hez, who was taking a sip of coffee, choked at this point and had to be patted on the back by the PM.

'And if there was even a *hint* that any of them were singing away like a canary,' Spiggott continued, 'I personally would see to it that their lives were not worth living.'

As he spoke, he gave Hez a particularly nasty look.

'Getting back to the press statement,' said Guy, who looked as if he had been enjoying Spiggott's discomfort, 'I propose we say something to the effect of 'Mr and Mrs Jones confirm that there are no plans to base their forthcoming divorce on the grounds of adultery or to cite any improper conduct in the particulars thereof.' How about that?'

Llew Jones nodded his agreement.

'Right, we'll fax a draft over to Mrs Jones's solicitors and get their agreement. While we're waiting for them to get back to us, let's have a look at their latest proposal for a financial settlement . . .'

The meeting dragged on for what felt like millennia as we worked our way through each point of Mrs Jones's latest letter and agreed our counteroffer. We were pretty close to an agreement: in the absence of any more salacious revelations, we'd probably be there in a couple of weeks.

It was almost a shame I didn't have a big reunion with Mark to look forward to.

When the meeting finally broke up at lunchtime, Macdonald and the PM headed off to the press conference, whilst Spiggott went back to the office to draft a letter to Mrs Jones's solicitors containing our counteroffer. Hez wanted to postpone returning to work for as long as possible, so she stayed to have a sarnie with me. Like everyone else at the meeting, she was beginning to look a bit frayed round the edges.

'You all right?' I asked through a mouthful of chicken tikka bagel.

'I s'pose.' She shrugged. 'Spiggott has been an unbearable pig since the leak happened. Actually,' she corrected herself, 'that should be *more* of an unbearable pig, shouldn't it? All my e-mails are being checked and he hovers around when I'm on the phone. It's awful.'

I was incredulous: despite the way Hez had been treated since Spiggott arrived at the firm, she was still unbelievably loyal. She'd even worn a Sheppertons baseball hat out in public *without needing to be threatened with her P45 first*.

'But he can't possibly think it's you, can he?' I replied. 'After what he said in the conference about Sheppertons' staff being above selling stories to the gutter press.'

'He probably just came out with all that guff to try and keep Llew's faith in our firm,' she said. 'In private he's been horrible – and not just to me; he's giving both Estelle and Laura the trainee a hard time, plus he's made a number of remarks about you as well. The only reason I haven't killed him yet is because we're on the fifth floor and there's nowhere for me to hide the body.'

'Central-heating duct?' I volunteered, eager to help.

She shook her head. 'Nah, not wide enough to accommodate all Spiggott's spare tyres.'

'Have you had any thoughts on who *could* be blabbing to the *Stoat*?'

Hez shrugged and fiddled with a piece of lettuce.

'I dunno, but I wish it would *just stop*. We should be a team, Lou, we should be focused on getting a good deal for the client and instead we're all watching our own backs.' She glanced at her watch. 'Shit! I didn't realise it was so late. I ought to be getting back to the labour camp – I mean office.'

We threw our sandwich wrappers (and in Hez's case, most of her sandwich as well) into the bin. Hez picked up her coat and briefcase and we walked out of my room towards the stairs. Just then, a cold draught blew down the corridor and the lights flickered momentarily.

'Hello, Looby,' said Hugo, sliming his way towards us. 'Not on your way to closet any more of my clients in a conference room, I hope.'

Then he stopped and hastily rearranged his features as he caught sight of Hez.

'Although even if you did, what business could it possibly be of mine?' he added in a conciliatory tone.

'No sign of that brain donor yet, Spade?' Hez said airily.

'Ah, yes; very amusing. Ha ha!' he said, his voice trailing away into a nervous-sounding cough.

By now, he was so close that I was afraid I might touch him by accident, which would probably result in my hand withering away with a hissing sound.

Hez fixed her eyes firmly on me and ignored Hugo.

'So I'll catch you later?' she said.

'Yup.' I nodded.

And with a flick of her dark corkscrew curls, she barged past Spade, letting her briefcase catch him a heavy blow on the shin. He grimaced, pleasingly; then turned to watch the retreating figure of Hez with what can only be described as a wistful gaze.

I tried to make the most of this diversion to get back to my room but found I was being followed by a limping man.

'Still there, Spade?' I asked.

'The thing is, Looby . . .'

'Don't call me that.'

'Sorry. I'm really sorry. The thing is, *Lucy*, I think you've got the chambers copy of the Red Book and I need it to check a point of law for a case I've got tomorrow. Can I have it, please?'

I don't think Hugo had ever previously uttered the words 'please' or 'sorry' in my presence, but before I had time to come up with a pithy reply, I remembered I'd left my laptop in Guy's room and he had a meeting there in five minutes.

'Yeah, whatever,' I replied, legging it up the corridor. 'It's somewhere down by my desk.'

By the time I returned, my room was empty. There was no sign of either Hugo or the Red Book. I breathed a sigh of relief: life was complicated enough without having him sliming around the place trying to chat up my friends – or worse, trying to be nice to me.

But Hugo Spade's weirdness was the least of my worries. Of far greater concern was the fact that for some reason Spiggott had Hez – and possibly me too – down as suspects for the Jones leaks. This was seriously bad news. The matrimonial side of the legal profession is a fairly tight-knit community, and whilst news travels fast, gossip travels faster. All we needed was for him to air his suspicions in public and it might be curtains for both of us professionally, especially given that the tenancy meeting was looming on the horizon. It was a dangerous position to be in, and I hoped and prayed for both our sakes that there were no more revelations in the *Stoat* for him to get hot under the collar about.

Things did not improve for Llew Jones over the next few days. Every morning there was wild press speculation about Grainy Woman, and the longer it went on, the wilder that speculation became. Not that it was anything more than speculation, mind you – no journalist was foolish enough to risk a libel case – but the effect was like water drip, drip, dripping away on to a stone: slowly but surely the latter is worn away.

To begin with, news that he might be enjoying a bit of a fling did the PM's popularity no end of good; but after seven days of relentless media pressure, things were not quite so rosy. His poll ratings were down and he was subject to constant 'nudge nudge/wink wink'-type questioning everywhere he went. Mrs Jones didn't help matters by having herself papped frequently looking sad and wistful. The only saving grace was that no fresh information had found its way into the public domain. If we could just ride out the storm, in a week or so the press (and hopefully Henry Spiggott too) would be focusing on other things.

For Hez and myself, though, times were tough. We were both flat out with our normal caseloads as well as with the Jones Saga, and if we made it home before eleven we counted it a good day. I was so busy that I barely had time to breathe, let alone attend to the other basics of life like eating, sleeping and watching

Coronation Street. Every day, just as I seemed to be nearing the end of Jones-related paperwork, Jane would trudge down the stairs to my basement room with a fresh load from Guy for me to plough through.

Still, Guy himself seemed pleased with my efforts, and as the day of the tenancy meeting edged ever nearer, I comforted myself with the thought that I was doing all I could to snatch the job away from Hugo.

Finally, on the Friday following our emergency meeting with Mr Jones, I gingerly stuck my head above the parapet at six o'clock and asked Guy if there was anything else for me or whether I could, in fact, go home. Apparently there wasn't, and I could.

Yay!

I didn't even have a case to prepare for Monday – which meant I had a whole weekend to chill out. I felt great as I virtually skipped through Middle Temple on my way to the tube. The sun was shining, tulips were tentatively putting in an appearance in the herbaceous borders and there was a pale green fuzz covering the trees: spring was on its way. I took a deep breath of the evening air, which smelt only partially of traffic fumes, and contemplated my options for the next two days. I might see if Jo wanted to go for a drink tomorrow night; or maybe Hez and I could go to the cinema. Or perhaps I would just spend most of the weekend in bed, eating takeaway food and luxuriating in the fact that I had nothing better to do.

As soon as I got home, I slung my jacket over a chair, made myself a cuppa and (after I'd carried last night's pizza box into the kitchen to make room for it) booted up the laptop on the dining table so that I could catch up on all the personal e-mails I hadn't had time to look at in the past few days.

You have 64 new e-mails.

Blimey! And about ten of them seemed to be from my mum.

110

To: juicy.lucy@yahoo.co.uk
Sender: yummymummy578@ntlworld.com
Subject: Your Father

*Why haven't you rung me? Your father seems hell-bent
on leaving me penniless and I need you to tell me how to
stop him. How can he do this to me, the mother of his
children? I gave him the best years . . .*

I couldn't bring myself to read any more, and sent
my standard reply telling her to go and see Gill, her
long-suffering solicitor. There was one from my father
too, and judging by the subject heading, he was
mithering on about the same thing. I deleted it without
even opening it. God! You know, if you could divorce
your own parents, I'd be straight in there *begging* for
a decree absolute.

Then I turned my attention to the rest of the inbox.
There seemed to be quite a few from Jo. I selected the
two most recent ones.

To: juicy.lucy@yahoo.co.uk
Sender: lawchick5@hotmail.com
Subject: Bite to Eat

*Hi Lou! Given what you said about work, I thought I'd
mail rather than text. Why don't you and Hez come to
dinner on Friday? Let me know. Jx*

Oh, hell – it was Friday now. Was I too late? What did
the next one say?

To: juicy.lucy@yahoo.co.uk
Sender: lawchick5@hotmail.com
Subject: Bite to Eat

Actually, better make that Saturday. Dave has a corporate thingy at Twickenham on Friday. Yuck. J

Right, so there was dinner at Jo's tonight, only it had been changed to tomorrow. I was up for it and I knew Hez would be too, so I rang Jo and left an affirmative answer on her voicemail. Then the doorbell went. Damn and blast! If it was Jehovah's Witnesses, they were going to get short shrift for disturbing my only evening in for ten days. However, as I struggled to my feet to answer it, a slightly scary thought struck me – what if it was Mark?

Temporarily forgetting that I'd made up my mind never to speak to him again, I smoothed my hair down (with some success), followed by my crumpled shirt (not quite so much success); then, just for good measure, I wiped my suddenly sweaty paws on my trousers. I opened the door – and almost fell over in shock.

It wasn't Mark Landsdown, the rare-building specialist with the amazing eyes.

It was Dr 'Carbon Neutral' Hodges.

If I had been in a movie, I would no doubt have slammed the door shut, gawped bug-eyed into camera for five seconds then cautiously reopened the door, all to hilarious comic effect.

But I wasn't.

So I just stood there like a lemon, staring at him standing on my front door mat, with my heart pounding and my mind racing.

'Hi, Lou,' he said, adding (just in case I'd been wondering), 'it's me.'

I gave a small squeak, similar to the one my pet hamster had once made when my mum sucked him up into the vacuum cleaner. I'd been so busy, I'd forgotten about Jonathan and his threat of wanting to be my friend.

'I didn't take your number at the theatre so I thought I'd just pop up. Hope you don't mind.'

He beamed at me and, interpreting my

speechlessness as consent, took a step towards the open door. Before I knew what I was doing, I had moved aside to let him pass and he strode down the hall and into the living room.

'Nice,' he said, obviously not noticing the stacks of newspapers and magazines that littered the floor or the extensive collection of unwashed mugs that were crowding together on the mantelpiece. Next, he walked off in the direction of the kitchen.

'Not bad.' The nodding approval continued. 'Yeah, I've got one of those,' he said, indicating Hez's state-of-the-art espresso-maker that jostled for space between the recycling bin and the empty fruit bowl. 'Aren't they the best?'

'The best,' I echoed, my brain still refusing to pass on any meaningful signals to my mouth.

'Bathroom down here?'

'Uh-huh.'

And off he went, with me trotting meekly in his wake.

'Lovely.' He even peeked into the shower; I mean, what's *that* all about? 'And the bedroom's in here? Oh yes, very nice.'

I hoped to God I wasn't blushing. Somehow, the fact that I had slept with him once upon a time in a galaxy far, far away was enough to make me feel rather embarrassed: as if merely juxtaposing the ideas of 'Jonathan' and 'bed' would be enough to raise the ghosts of long-forgotten passions.

And it wasn't even my bedroom.

'Er,' I said, finding my tongue at last, 'that's not my room.'

'But this is your flat, isn't it?'

'Yes.'

'I see, you have a *lodger*.' He made it sound as if it was a quaint olde-worlde custom that we up here in Muswell Hill sometimes indulged in.

'No, a flatmate. I share with Hez.'

The actual reaction was even better than I had hoped for. He went white and mouthed the word 'Hez' at me a couple of times.

I nodded, rather enjoying the moment.

'Henrietta *Irving*?'

'Yes, *the* Henrietta Irving,' I said, shamelessly rubbing it in. 'The one you were at college with. Her.'

He looked around him wildly, as if he was checking the place out for emergency exits.

'Amazing thing, friendship,' he said at last, a slightly manic look in his eyes.

'You bet,' I confirmed, shepherding him back into the living room and sitting down on the sofa.

'Like I said,' he snapped out of his reverie and parked himself next to me, 'I forgot to take your number when we bumped into each other last week. I thought I'd risk turning up to see if you were free to go for that drink we talked about – if you still want to, that is.'

I took a deep breath, ready to turn him down once and for all; but to my surprise I found myself holding fire. There was a slight hesitation – almost a deference – in his tone and it intrigued me. Could it really be true that this particular leopard had rejigged his spots? Or was it just a cunning ploy designed to lure me into a false sense of security?

Then he smiled, the same really nice smile I remembered from years back, and I felt some of the grudges I'd worked so hard to maintain soften and relax a bit.

It was only a drink, the smile said to me; what harm could it possibly do? And somewhere, deep down inside me, the answering ghost of a smile began to stir, and I thawed a little bit more.

'Give me five minutes for make-up and a change of clothes, and you're on.'

Four and a half minutes later, I was back in the living room, putting my expensive new lipstick in my bag, when I heard a key in the door.

'Guess what,' I called as Hez clattered into the hall. 'We've got a surprise visitor!'

'Brilliant!' Hez yelled back. 'Male or female?'

'Male.'

'For you or me?'

I looked at Jonathan. He'd gone a bit quiet; not to mention a bit pale.

'Me,' I said. 'He's taking me out for a drink to make amends.'

'Oh, that's so cool!' Hez hotfooted it into the living room. 'I am sooooo pleased for you. You make a brilliant couple. Doesn't "Mark and Lucy" just sound so right? Hi, Mark – how are things . . . and . . . oh . . .'

And she trailed off, arms open wide in pre-hug mode.

'Not Mark,' she croaked.

I shook my head. I didn't need my tightening stomach to tell me this wasn't going to end well.

Hez suddenly unfroze and shot her cuffs in an alpha-male sort of a way.

'I thought you were Lou's boyfriend,' she remarked casually, with the air of one playing the winning hand. 'He's totally gorgeous, completely solvent, fantastic company and,' she added, fixing Jonathan with a stare that would have turned a lesser man to jelly, 'treats Lucy like royalty.'

'Yes, but—' I began, anxious to remind her of the disaster area that had constituted my relationship with Mark.

But Hez was on such a roll that not even a Chieftain tank could have stopped her. Not, that is, unless it was full of rich, good-looking soldiers waving at her, in which case she might have paused for a moment to admire the view before continuing.

'What was it you were saying last week, Lou? Something about the fact that you'd never met anybody like him before?'

I blushed and stammered, but could not deny the undeniable.

'And that he had the most perfect body you'd ever clapped eyes on?'

Again, guilty as charged.

'And that you now realise that all the relationships you had before you met him were just rubbishy, puerile—'

'Yes, yes, yes,' I said sulkily. 'Jonathan and I were only going to the pub, not jetting off to the Little White Wedding Chapel in Vegas.'

I'm not sure if Hez dusted off her hands at this point; it wouldn't have surprised me if she had. Her expression clearly read 'mission accomplished'. She folded her arms and smiled at us both.

'I know,' she said. 'I just thought that Jonathan should be fully aware of the facts.'

Jonathan, meanwhile, was now standing up. The ghostly pallor that had covered his face the moment he heard Hez's voice was starting to disappear.

'Hello,' he said. 'Er, long time no see.'

'That'll be about right,' Hez retorted.

'Job going well?'

'Fabulous, thanks. I just don't have time to spend what I earn – shame, isn't it?'

That was a tiny lie there from Hez: her credit-card bill was almost as scary as mine. The difference was, my parents didn't sigh heavily and then pay it off for me twice a year.

'So,' she went on, 'how's your hot-air problem?'

'You mean global warming,' corrected Jonathan automatically.

Out of the corner of my eye I was aware of Hez muttering the words 'not necessarily' while Jonathan gave us a précis of the latest developments ozone-wise.

'Oooh, super,' Hez said as he finished. She was almost – but not quite – in full sneer mode.

I couldn't bear it any longer: it was like watching my parents.

'Enough!' I cried. 'Jonathan – let's go.'

'Can I just use your bathroom before we do?'

'Of course,' I said. 'You know where it is.'

I shut the living-room door behind him. Hez's face was a study in incredulity and rage.

'You are not seriously going for a drink with *him*?' she spat. 'He's a lying, back-stabbing, amoral ...' Words failed her '... *thing*,' she articulated at last.

Crikey! Even given what had occurred in our last year at uni, this was way over the top. Whilst her concern for my welfare was laudable, there had to come a point where she shrugged and said: 'I think you're mad, but it's your call and – hey, it's only a drink.'

I told her this. It didn't help.

'The man has no scruples whatsoever – remember Susan Geoffreys?' she hissed. 'He'll cheat on you then rip your heart out. Oh, I'm sorry; didn't he already do that?'

'Oh, for heaven's sake,' I snapped, not caring for the reminder about Jonathan's appalling track record – which, by the way, was especially rich coming from Hez. 'Stop going on as if he's some sort of cross between Macbeth and Dick Dastardly. All I am doing is having a pint with him for old times' sake; I am *not* going to sleep with him. In fact, I don't even fancy him.'

Actually, the last bit wasn't strictly true. At no point had I stopped fancying Jonathan. I just fancied other people (well, Mark) more, which was progress of a sort.

Hez looked a bit upset and started studying the wallpaper intently.

'Look,' I said, reining my temper in as best I could, 'we are going to the Alexandra. We may go for a pizza afterwards or we may not, but I will see you back here *without* Jonathan by eleven at the latest.'

'Ready?' Jonathan was back.

'What if Mark rings?' cried Hez, in a last-ditch attempt to scupper my evening out.

'He won't,' I said firmly. 'But in case he does, I promise to keep my mobile on.'

I turned to Jonathan. 'The Alexandra?'

'The Alexandra,' he echoed.

And off we went, leaving Hez standing in the middle of the living room, staring bleakly after us.

Despite Hez's obvious fear that Jonathan was going to cajole me into bed through a combination of black arts and bottled beer, I arrived home with my virtue intact, at ten to eleven. I allowed him to see me safely to the front door of our building but, not wanting to subject him to another tirade from Hez, bade him farewell there.

As I climbed the stairs to my flat, I reflected on what had been an unexpectedly pleasant few hours. Rather than the self-centred guy I remembered from university, Jonathan seemed to have discovered the meaning of the words 'charming', 'interesting' and 'attentive' and put them to good use during the course of the evening. We chatted about my job, his job and how, after he'd done his telly bit, it was impossible for him to buy a super-market ready-meal without the checkout lady giving him grief about overpackaging. I even told him about Mark and how we'd fallen out over Guy's ultimatum. Jonathan reckoned he sounded like a decent bloke; not good boyfriend material perhaps, but a decent bloke even so.

See, Hez? No problem!

When he was up at the bar getting in our second round of drinks, I took the opportunity to have good look at him and try to work out what it was that had changed. It wasn't simply that his Inspiral Carpets T-shirt had been replaced with something by Thomas Pink and he'd ditched the studenty baseball boots; it went deeper than that. For a start, he looked different. He'd always been a bit on the skinny side at uni, all gangly legs and big feet; but he'd grown into his body in the intervening years. As he stood with his back to me, I couldn't help tracing the line of this improved body up through his thighs, his (nicely toned) bum, slim torso and broad shoulders, all topped off with his trademark mop of sleek dark hair. It was a very pleasant experience; a sort of mildly lustful 'spot-the-difference' exercise.

But it wasn't until he turned round to face me that I knew what had happened: he'd gone and *grown up*. The boy I'd known was now a man with a mortgage, a job and the sort of chest that, if it had been anyone other than Jonathan, I would have wanted to nuzzle up against on a cold winter evening.

It was all very bizarre.

After the pub, we went to Pizza Express and he insisted on paying – something else he would never have dreamed of doing all those years ago. Despite the news that he had shelled out for a flat in one of the most expensive parts of London, I would have been willing to bet he was still as tight as Tom Jones's trousers where money was concerned. However, to my utter amazement, my offer of going Dutch was brushed aside with an airy 'That's okay, Lou, this one's on me.'

'So,' I said, as we picked at the garlic bread, 'why did you decide to look me up now? I mean, you must spend loads of time in London or you wouldn't have bought a flat here. Or,' I narrowed my eyes, 'was it just something to say when you bumped into me unexpectedly?'

Jonathan diverted his gaze to the pink gerbera in the middle of our table.

'Oh,' I said, feeling slightly deflated and not understanding why. 'That *was* it, wasn't it?'

'Not exactly,' he replied, 'I have been meaning to ring.'

'Really? For how long?'

'About four years, actually.'

My drink went down the wrong way and I coughed a bit.

'Four *years*?' I echoed. 'What was stopping you?'

He shrugged. 'To be honest, I was nervous. You were pretty definite I was never to darken your door again.'

I could see where he might have got that idea. I think the exact words I had used when I finally dumped him were: 'If I ever see you again, I will shove your teeth so far down your cheating throat that you will need to stick your toothbrush up your arse to clean them.'

'Lucy,' he went on, this time staring into the flame of a tea light the waiting staff had thoughtfully placed on the table, rather than meeting my eye, 'I behaved badly, mea totally culpa; and I'm not naïve enough to be asking you for another chance. But I miss having you in my life – in whatever capacity that might be – and I'd like it if we could see each other sometimes, the odd cup of coffee, trip to the pub and so on. What do you say?'

My mouth went dry and for a moment I couldn't say anything at all. This was a conversation I'd had over and over again in my head: the one where Jonathan turned up out of the blue, apologised profusely for his behaviour and begged me to take him back. In my imagination I had always spurned his advances, turned on my heel and left him weeping into his beer. Only now that it was for real, I didn't know if that was how I actually wanted to play it.

'I'm not sure,' I said slowly. 'The things that happened – I took a long time to recover from them.'

Actually, that was a bit of an understatement. Mark, six years later, had been the first man whom I hadn't constantly compared to Jonathan.

We regarded each other through the flickering glow of the tea light for a moment.

'Me too, believe it or not.' Jonathan reached over and

took my hand in his, but I wriggled it free again. That certainly didn't feel right. Not yet, anyway.

'About Hez this evening—' I began before Jonathan cut me off.

'I'm guessing she hasn't forgiven me,' he said.

'No. I think you're probably right.'

We sat in silence for a while. I fiddled with the stem of my wine glass whilst Jonathan pressed his fingertips together thoughtfully and rested his forehead against them. I looked at his hands: large and capable with long, elegant fingers – the total opposite of my short, stubby digits. But then we'd always been like that: where he was tall and slender, I was small and curvy; where he was rational and analytical, I was instinctive and heartfelt. Call it yin and yang or opposites attracting or whatever you like, but the first moment we met, I had felt us slot together like pieces from a two-part jigsaw; and much as I hated to admit it, I'd felt his absence from my life like the loss of a limb.

'If we did go for the odd drink now and again, you'd probably have to put up with bumping into Hez from time to time . . .' I grinned, hoping to lighten the atmosphere. 'Do you think you'd be up to the challenge?'

'Well, if that's what it takes . . .'

Blimey. He *was* keen.

Jonathan poured me another glass of wine and gave me a smile that seemed to radiate more from his eyes than his mouth. I smiled back and tucked a strand of hair in behind my ear. Where would be the harm in going out every so often? So long as we kept it all light, fluffy and strictly platonic, I'd be all right, wouldn't I? Even though I was trying very hard, I couldn't entirely ignore the little thrills of pleasure I was getting simply from being in his company once again.

'Okay,' I said at last. 'As long as your intentions are honourable.'

'As honourable as they come,' he replied, and we clinked our glasses together in a toast.

When I got back to the flat, I hesitated slightly before I put my key in the door. I sincerely hoped that Hez was in a better mood than when I'd left her. Softly I opened the door and called her name, but there was no reply. In fact, the entire place was in darkness. I tiptoed my way into the kitchen and, switching the light on, found a note magneted on to the fridge: *Gone to bed*, it said. *See you tomorrow*.

A wave of relief that I wasn't coming home to another row swept over me and I suddenly felt exhausted. Peace, quiet and a good night's kip seemed an excellent idea, and I decided to take a leaf out of Hez's book and turn in. However, an hour and a half later, I was still awake. Spending time with Jonathan after all these years had brought back many memories – not all of them good – and they were batting round my brain like moths in a lampshade. I tried tossing and turning, counting sheep and even switching on my light for a bit of bedtime reading, but to no avail.

One incident in particular kept raising its ugly head, despite my very best efforts to beat it back down into the hinterland of my consciousness. I lay in bed, my eyes fixed on the ceiling, willing it to go away and leave me alone.

But it refused.

It was the final term all of us spent in Bristol. Hez and I were doing the first year of our legal training, whilst Jonathan was studying for a masters before going on to Cambridge to do his doctorate.

One Saturday night in early April, I'd come back to Bristol after spending the day with my family. It had been a particularly miserable twenty-four hours. Even though my parents had been separated for over a year at this point and my father had hooked up with the unspeakably awful Suzanne (who looked for all the world like an ageing feral glamour model), they still managed to make any occasion they were forced to attend together a living hell. The happy event this time had been my cousin's wedding, to which, as her godparents, both of my olds had been invited. The consequences had not been pretty, and rather than stay Saturday night with my mother as I'd arranged, I decided to cut my losses and go home.

As the train pulled out of Leeds station, I sank back into my seat and soothed my nerves with a Mars bar, telling myself that in a few hours I would be back home and able to cry on Jonathan's capable shoulder. For all his faults, the one thing he was spectacularly good at was handling my mum and dad. The first time he had witnessed the full horror of the Stephens *en famille* was when I'd taken him to meet my parents about four months into our relationship. He had been truly appalled at what he found. They were still living under the same roof, but spent the weekend subjecting me, my sister Lisa and yes, even Jonathan, to a constant barrage of barbed comments about each other.

'How dare you accuse me of being selfish,' my mother screamed during dinner on the last night of his stay. 'I have devoted my life to this family! It's you – going off on ridiculous conferences all the time – that's what causes the problems.'

'If I hadn't gone on any of those ridiculous conferences, I wouldn't have been promoted and we wouldn't have half the salary I get now. Were you this argumentative when I married you, or have you been practising especially?'

My mother then chucked a framed wedding photo at the wall, narrowly missing my father's head, and I dissolved into tears for the fourth time that day. Suddenly Jonathan pushed back his chair and stood up, holding his arms out like Moses parting the Red Sea.

'Enough!' he thundered.

For a nineteen year old he had a pretty impressive voice. Mum and Dad looked at him, their mouths slightly open. I gulped tearfully and blew my nose on a napkin.

'I fully acknowledge that it's none of my business what you do or say to each other when I am not here,' he said, 'but when I am, please do me the common courtesy of behaving like civilised human beings. And furthermore,' he was warming to his theme, 'I will not sit by and allow Lucy to be upset like this. For goodness' sake, she's your *daughter*! Don't you care who else you hurt by carrying on like this?'

He paused. Then reached over and took my hand.

'If you'll excuse us, I think we'll leave you to cool off for a bit. Come on, Lou.'

And that was the moment when I allowed myself to fall hopelessly and irretrievably in love with him.

Things between my parents were never quite as bad again when Jonathan was around; although when he wasn't, it could still get quite vicious. So his last-minute decision to stay in Bristol over the weekend of the wedding because he wanted to run an experiment was not what I'd wanted to hear – in fact, we'd a blazing row over it and I'd told him to go to hell. As for the wedding, let's just say it lived up to expectations.

So anyway, there I was, counting down the minutes until I could throw myself into Jonathan's arms and do a bit of kissing and making up. I was one of the first passengers off the train, got a cab round to his place and hoped to God that he was in. However, just as I raised my hand to ring the bell of the run-down terraced house he lived in, the door opened and Peter, Jonathan's best friend and Hez's (recent) ex, grinned at me.

'Hiya,' he said, looking rather drawn despite his smile. 'I think Jon's around but I'm not sure; I just popped back for my car keys. If he is here, he'll be in his room.'

Rats! I should have rung from the station – it was quite a walk from Jon and Peter's back to my own place and it had just started to rain. Still, if Jonathan wasn't in, he probably hadn't gone far. I'd hang around for a bit and have a cup of tea while I waited for him to come back.

'See you!' called Peter cheerfully as he exited the house and closed the front door behind him. I dumped my bag next to the inevitable student bike propped up against the hall wall and began to make my way up the stairs.

At first I thought I might be alone in the house. There was a damp, musty smell that spoke of emptiness, and even though it was dark outside, the only light on in the entire place was the one in the hallway that Peter had presumably switched on to look for his keys. Also, the curtains on the landing window were open – something that Mr Energy Saving Hodges would never normally have countenanced. ('The best way to keep the heat in, Lucy, is to use simple, everyday measures like closing the curtains once it gets dark.') But as I climbed the stairs, I heard what sounded like a squeak – and then another one – and then the sound of low, muffled human voices. At first they were so quiet that I couldn't make out where they were coming from, let alone what they were saying, but after a while, the sound grew louder.

Almost against my will, I followed the noise to the end of the landing. I couldn't help it; my legs were moving by themselves, as if I was being reeled in by some sort of gigantic fishing rod.

By now, the squeaking had begun to adhere to a regular rhythm and the voices were semi-audible. I could tell that one of the participants in the exchange was male and the other was female. And whilst I couldn't hear what they were saying, I knew it wasn't conversation they were having: it was sex.

I couldn't move; I was frozen to the spot. I wasn't even aware of being inside my body any more; the only thing I was conscious of was the drama being acted out behind the darkened door in front of me. The squeaking of the bedsprings was increasing in both volume and tempo.

I could hear the woman's voice rising above the cacophony of the springs and I put my hands over my ears in a vain attempt to block out the sound. *Why* couldn't I run away? It was purgatory; hideous, hideous purgatory and there was nothing I could do.

The noise was getting louder and louder, and as in a nightmare, I was immobile; panic and disbelief fighting for control of my brain. With each squeak and moan, my throat tightened further, until simply drawing breath was painful. And then:

'Oh, *Jonathan!*' the woman cried, leaving me in no doubt as to her identity.

The spell was broken. With a howl of anguish as I felt the entire fabric of my world shatter around me, I ran along the landing, down the stairs and out of the front door into the rain.

It was a sunny Saturday morning back in Muswell Hill, and Hez was up and out before I surfaced. Wandering through the flat and finding no sign of her, I found myself breathing a huge sigh of relief. I didn't think I could stand a repeat of her performance the night before, plus I wanted some thinking time to work out how I would stop her from foaming at the mouth the next time she coincided with Jonathan; not that I was planning on making it a regular occurrence, you understand, but I'd like to feel I could invite him round if I wanted to without World War Three breaking out.

For a moment, I considered sitting her down and talking to her, but as that would mean touching on a few issues that were best left alone, I dismissed the idea. No, the thing to do would be to let her get to know this new, improved Jonathan herself; then she would see how much he had changed and begin to mellow towards him. Realistically, though, the chances of her agreeing to talk to him of her own free will were less than zero.

Hmmm . . . I needed an occasion where she would be constrained by the rules of social engagement to be polite to him, like – the dinner party at Jo's house! That was it! I'd speak to Jo and check that she didn't object to feeding another hungry mouth, then invite Jonathan to the bun-fight that evening. H and J would spend a civilised couple of hours together, and bingo! Hez would be converted. Then if, in the fullness of time, Jonathan and I happened to go to the pub again, all would be sweetness and light.

I was sure Jo wouldn't object to Jonathan's presence. She thought he was the bee's knees, the cat's pyjamas and the dog's whatnots all rolled into one and hadn't stopped talking about him since that night at the theatre – it was a total win-win situation.

I ambled into the kitchen, located the phone under half a loaf of sliced white and dialled Vauxhall.

'Ah, Mrs Williams,' I said, 'can I bring an extra body along with me tonight? Someone Hez could do with getting acquainted with.'

'Ooh! Who is it?' Jo salivated at the prospect of a juicy piece of gossip. 'Anyone I know?'

'Sort of,' I replied warily. I didn't trust her not to blab to Hez, and that would ruin my finely honed plans.

'Come on, you have to tell me,' she wheedled. 'It's my party.'

'And you can cry if you want to,' I countered, 'but you'll still have to wait till tonight to see. Nice bit of arm candy, though,' I added as a sweetener.

'All right, then.' She ungraciously conceded defeat. 'I don't mind if you're sure he's good looking.'

Next I rang Jonathan and arranged to meet him outside Angel tube station at seven. I found myself looking forward to seeing him again rather more than I'd anticipated, but I decided to put that down to a sense of achievement at my cunning little ploy coming together. Then I spent the rest of the day pottering around the flat. Eventually, when I'd almost given up hope of ever seeing her again, Hez arrived home.

'In here!' I called from my room as I heard her key in the lock and the front door open. I listened as footsteps came down the hall and she put her head round my bedroom door.

'Hi,' she said.

'Hi,' I replied. 'Are you all right?'

She looked okay – not her normal level of fabulousness – just okay.

'I'm sorry about yesterday,' she said. 'I was hideous. I think work is getting to me.'

'You mean Spiggott is getting to you?' I asked.

She nodded. 'Estelle and I have been in since stupid o'clock doing stupid affidavits on the stupid Jones case. It's taken for ever because every semicolon has to be approved by the client first and then that arsehole Macdonald. Honestly, as if anyone is going to give a stuff about what breakfast cereal the PM eats.'

Indeed.

'And why wasn't your beloved boss doing them if they were that big a deal?'

'Oh, he's on a golf weekend in Portugal, which is *much* more important. Anyway,' she went on, managing a thin smile, 'let's get ready for the main event. What are you wearing?'

I shrugged. 'Jeans probably.'

Hez stared at me as if I'd suggested turning up dressed as the back half of a pantomime cow.

'You can't do that!' she cried.

'Why on earth not? It's only Jo and Dave.'

'Because – because we've both been working like stink and it'll do us good to get glammed up.'

'Fine. What do you suggest?'

An hour later and we were ready to go. Hez had decked me out in her new clingy wine-red wrap dress with a plunging neckline and the highest of strappy high heels, and put herself in a slinky little black number. Apart from the fact that I could barely walk, I had to admit she'd come up trumps: we looked fab.

'Right!' said Hez. 'Let's go. Cab or tube?'

Oh, bugger! I had to get to Islington to rendezvous with Jonathan – on my own. If Hez saw him, she'd throw another wobbler.

Think! *Fast!*

'Er, Jo said she needed me to bring a bottle of fizz,' I lied. 'I'm just popping to Marksies – see you in Vauxhall.'

And I raced out of the flat as fast as my heels would let me before she suggested we went wine shopping together en route.

As I tottered off the bus at Angel and made my way along the pavement in the dusky half-light of the spring evening, I could see Jonathan waiting outside the tube station: tall, dark and undeniably handsome. I gave a little shiver of excitement: I was about to travel across London with a man who had been voted Most Fanciable TV Personality last year. People were bound to recognise him and maybe ask for his autograph. My God – I might even find myself in the next issue of *Hello!*. I could almost get used to this . . .

'Hi there!' He grinned, kissing me on the cheek. 'Will I do?'

'You look fab,' I said, returning the kiss. 'How about me?'

Even though I had been dressed, exfoliated and made-up to within an inch of my life, I wasn't quite expecting the enthusiastic Leslie Phillips-style 'Ding-*dong!*' that issued from his lips.

'Er, right!' I said, brandishing my Oyster card. 'Let's go!'

Jonathan made his way over to the edge of the pavement and hailed a black cab.

'No tube?' I asked. After the amount of money I'd spent on comforting myself recently, I was flat broke.

'No tube,' he replied firmly, ushering me into the taxi. 'Firstly, I'm paying, and secondly,' he nodded at my four-inch heels, 'if you try to get down an escalator wearing those, you're going to break your ankle, and I'm not spending my evening in A and E while they strap you up. Now, where are we going?'

I gave the address to the cabbie and filled Jon in on

who else was going to be present. Although he seemed pleased at the idea of dinner with Jo and Dave, he was rather disconcerted when I mentioned that Hez was also going to be in attendance.

'Look,' I soothed, 'it's perfect! She can have a civilised chat with you in familiar surroundings and be reassured that you are a nice bloke.'

'Perhaps.' But he didn't sound convinced and spent the next moment or two frowning out of the cab window.

Just then, however, a bus zoomed by with an ad for the National Gallery emblazoned across it. Jonathan had an insatiable appetite for art and we had often visited galleries together in the old days.

'Lou,' he said, cheering up slightly, 'would you like to go and see the new Turner exhibition next week?'

'Well, I don't know . . .' I began.

My plans for spending time with Jonathan involved an occasional beer and an even more occasional meal out to ensure I didn't succumb to his all-too-obvious charms once again; three dates in less than a week was not something I felt comfortable with. Not wanting to seem ungracious, however, I went for the oldest excuse in the book (which thankfully also happened to be true).

'I've got a lot on at work at the moment.'

My companion gave me one of his supersmiles.

'Oh, forget about work! You've got to have a life as well. Listen, we'll do the exhibition and then I'll take you to this little restaurant I know just off Leicester Square.'

'I'd love to,' I half lied, 'only it really is tricky at the moment, and—'

'Shall we say Thursday, then? And if that proves impossible, then we'll reschedule for Friday.'

Before I could put him straight, the taxi pulled up at Jo and Dave's and we bundled out. While Jon was sorting out the cabbie, I went and rang the bell. Jo's face appeared round the door with eyes like saucers.

'So? Who've you brought?' she hissed.

I jerked my head in the direction of her front gate and watched her goggle a bit more as Jonathan made his way up the path.

'You remember Jon,' I said casually as we entered and Jo took our coats.

'Of course!'

He smiled at her, and she instantly beamed back; it was the Hodges Effect again, and I was beginning to think that Jo was as susceptible as me.

'I want Hez to see how much he's changed,' I whispered by way of explanation. 'He's not my date or anything.'

'Oh – er – good,' she muttered mysteriously, and ushered us through into the large, sleekly decorated reception room that doubled up as both a living and dining area.

'Hi, Lou!' said Dave as we entered. 'Red, white or – bloody hell, you're that wind-turbine bloke, aren't you?'

'I've been called worse things!' Jonathan grinned his award-winning grin and shook Dave's hand. 'Jonathan Hodges.'

'Of course! I'm Dave Williams and you've already met Jo, my wife, haven't you? Now, red or—'

'Red for me, and Lucy always likes to start off on white, don't you?'

I had been planning on a glass of the fizz I'd been conscientious enough to actually go and buy – but it could probably do with a rest. The route our cabbie had taken seemed to involve every single speed bump known to man, and I didn't want to cause an explosion in Jo's living room.

'Hez not here yet?' I asked, looking round the room.

'No.' Jo shook her head. 'I just had a call from her. She had to pop into the office on the way here to fax an affidavit and said to start without her.'

Jonathan went to hand me my wine and I realised I was still clutching my bottle of cava.

'Would you like to pop that in the fridge?' said Jo, the hint of a smile playing round her lips. 'You know where it is. Now, Jonathan, tell me what you thought of the play the other night.'

And I scurried off in the direction of a very enticing savoury smell that was emanating from behind the kitchen door, leaving Jo and Jonathan deep in conversation about A *Midsummer Night's Dream*.

When I walked into the kitchen, I don't think I'm kidding when I tell you that everything seemed to run in slow motion for a few seconds. Whatever the laws of the universe are that determine time and how we perceive it, they were momentarily suspended as my mind adjusted to what I found there.

Or should that be 'whom'?

Because standing on the far side of the room, calmly chopping coriander, was none other than Mark.

He smiled, put down his knife (always a good sign) and walked over to where I'd ground to a halt by the kitchen table.

'Hello, stranger,' he said, taking the bottle out of my hands.

I was so flabbergasted I couldn't actually reply; but I felt my face growing hotter by the second and the backs of my knees went a bit sweaty. Mark put the wine down on the table.

'Does Guy know you're here?' His voice was almost, but not quite, teasing.

I shook my head, my eyes welded on to his.

'Good!' He grinned before rearranging his features into a more serious expression. 'I should have rung, Lucy, and tried to see if there was some way through it all. I can't apologise enough for losing my rag with you. I – I've missed you dreadfully.'

Oh, God – he *missed me*!

'I know it was a bit underhand getting you round here under false pretences, but I'd like the chance to talk a bit; maybe after dinner? I really hope we can work something out. Even if it means ducking under Guy's radar till your case is finished, I'd like to give us another try.'

I was just about to grab him and tell him I was sorry too, and there was nothing I would like better in the world than to kiss and make up, when a thought struck me. Yes, that was what I *wanted*, but was it actually the best idea in the long run – I mean, hadn't I suffered enough where Mark was concerned? Shouldn't I be saying 'thanks for the memories but I'll see you around'?

Just to confirm this was the right thing to do, I looked into his face, and at that exact moment his gaze met mine. And there I was: floating away from the real world and bound once again for Planet Mark. I simply couldn't help it.

However, right at the crucial moment, when I was sure he was going to close his eyes and start moving his mouth in towards mine, the kitchen door burst open and Hez stalked in with a face like thunder.

'Jo said you'd be in here,' she growled at me.

Noticing Mark, however, she went through a rapid personality change, elbowed me out of the way and gave him a big hug.

'How wonderful to see you!' she cooed. 'What a lovely surprise – it's been ages since we coincided!'

'Two weeks,' Mark replied, looking slightly bemused.

'Well, it's felt like a lifetime,' continued Hez. 'Now, Mark, can you be an angel and find the corkscrew? Dave thinks he left it in here and I'm dying for a drink.'

Mark shrugged and smiled at me. 'We'll catch up later,' he whispered and slid his hand round my waist as he walked past.

As soon as his back was turned, Hez flipped back into 'bad cop' mode and scowled at me.

'What the hell's going on?' she whispered.

'What does it look like? Mark was trying to convince

me to give things another go – till you walked in, that is,' I hissed back.

'Not Mark, you wazzock.' She cut me off. '*Jonathan*. Did Jo invite him?'

'At my suggestion,' I said. 'I thought it would help.'

'Help who?' Hez was incredulous.

'You. To know Jonathan better.'

'But I don't want to know him better.'

'That's only because you don't know him!' I replied, impressed by my own display of inescapable logic.

Hez scowled at me and put her hands on her hips.

'The only reason why I am not walking out of here right now is that I assume you have had some sort of mental breakdown and Jo will need help restraining you when the men in white coats turn up.'

Emboldened by having Mark (and hopefully some sort of reconciliation) in close proximity, I decided to tell it like was. No way was I going through a repeat performance of her diva moment yesterday over Jonathan,

'Now you listen to me, Henrietta Irving,' I said, 'he has changed and you need to get over yourself and give him a chance – you never know, you might enjoy yourself.'

Hez snorted indelicately through her nose.

'The only way I'll only enjoy myself is if I get to fill his pockets with concrete and throw him into the river on the way home!'

God, she was impossible!

'Well, seeing as you're stuck with him,' I whispered, 'you might want to try behaving like a grown-up for a change. You're going to be seeing quite a bit of him over the next few months, and I've had just about enough of you and your infantile behaviour where he's concerned.'

I manhandled her back into the living room before she could respond. Mark followed with a puzzled expression on his face.

'Jonathan!' Hez said through obviously gritted teeth. 'How *lovely* to see you again.' The she turned her back on him and sidled up to Mark. 'Mark, did I mention that you're looking good.' She paused. *'Really* good.'

'No,' frowned Mark, 'but, er, thanks.'

She shook her dark, glossy tresses in a 'don't mention it' sort of a way, and pressed on. 'Dave tells me you're up in Scotland next week.'

Mark nodded. 'Yes. Nairn and Inverness. Couple of castles that have seen better days.'

Hez shook her head admiringly. 'How wonderful that you do a job that makes a real difference to the world. You are very clever, you know.'

She had always liked him, but this was totally over the top.

I shook myself and went to try and strike up conversation again with Mark; but this time I was foiled by Jonathan, who walked up to me, put his hand on the small of my back and manoeuvred me over to the sofa.

Mark watched this with his mouth ever so slightly open and his eyebrows ever so slightly raised.

'This is Jonathan,' Jo explained, noticing Mark's quizzical expression. 'He's Lucy's um, er, friend.'

'Lucy's um, er, friend' beamed at Mark and, after depositing me on the sofa, offered him his hand. But the Hodges Effect failed to register with Mark and I saw him frown slightly as he gave Jonathan a less than hearty shake.

'So, you're Mark Landsdown, then,' Jonathan continued, oblivious to Mark's reserve.

'I was when I last checked,' Mark replied.

'Lucy was telling me about you.'

'Was she?' Mark's frown deepened.

'Yes, when we were together last night.'

'Really?' Mark was now managing to look worried and surprised at the same time.

I leapt off the sofa, intending to explain the platonic nature of our evening together, but Jo plonked a large blue casserole dish down on the dining table and announced: 'Food's ready, so you can all come and put your nosebags on.'

I made a mental note to set Mark straight as soon as possible.

Seeing as I needed to talk to Mark and Hez needed to get to know Jonathan, seating was vital. Luck, however, was momentarily on my side, and I not only managed to grab the seat next to Mark, but made sure that Hez was sitting next to Dr Hodges.

Ha! It was all coming together nicely . . .

I watched as she took her place, scowling; then I settled down and glanced at Mark, who was being handed a steaming vat-sized plate of braised lamb and root vegetables by Jo.

You know, sometimes when you don't see a person for a while, your memory of them can be more flattering than they actually are in real life. However, this was categorically *not* the case with Mark. In fact, in contrast to the rather drawn individual with whom I had had a stand-up row almost two weeks ago, he was looking even more scrummy than I remembered him.

Scrummy, perhaps, but not relaxed or happy. As I watched, I saw him casting suspicious looks in Jonathan's direction. Fortunately, Jonathan was busy regaling Jo with an amusing anecdote from his TV show and was unaware that he was under surveillance. Obviously the last thing I wanted was any more interruptions, so waiting until Dave and Hez were engrossed in conversation, I turned to Mark, intending to pick up where we'd left off in the kitchen. Seeing him again had left me feeling as if I'd just been run over by a tube train. Even without being under the influence of his amazing eyes, I was beginning to think that maybe – perhaps, possibly – I shouldn't have finished it between us; and he at least deserved the opportunity to plead his case and tell me how life with Jennifer and Josh in the background could still be a romantic idyll.

'I'm glad you're here tonight,' I said quietly. 'And you're right, we need to talk.'

He nodded. 'I owe you an apology.'

'Apology accepted; and I owe you one too.'

'I was going to get in touch, but I was terrified I'd get you into trouble at work if we met up; and it wasn't a conversation I wanted to have over the phone. Then I had to go to the States for a couple of days on business and—'

'Look, it doesn't matter any more, Mark,' I said. 'What's done is done. Maybe it's time to forget about it and move on.'

To my surprise, he didn't grin and try and slip his hand into mine under the table. Instead, he shot another look at Jonathan and furrowed his brow.

What was wrong? What had I said?

I examined his exquisite features for a clue. Mark must have felt me looking at him, because he raised his eyes and met my gaze. However, rather than giving me another of the intense, desirous glances he'd been throwing my way in the kitchen, there was a questioning, slightly bewildered expression on his face.

I opened my mouth to say: 'Mark, maybe we can sort this out'; but I only got as far as the 'Mark' bit before Jo piped up.

'Jonathan was just telling me he's in talks over a new TV show,' she announced. 'One about art and the environment. Isn't that exciting?'

'That's right,' Jon enthused to the table at large. 'Lucy and I were always going to galleries in the good old days. Paintings have always been a passion of ours.'

He grinned at me.

'It's great we're going to be able to get back into that habit again. I've really missed it.'

'Is that a fact?' said Mark, glowering into his plate. 'Pass me the spuds, please, Dave.'

'You know,' Jonathan continued, as if he were doing Mark the most enormous favour, 'you really ought to look at getting into television. The heritage thing is a hot topic at the moment and the exposure could really help your career.'

'Oh, he doesn't need to worry about career exposure,' purred Hez, batting her eyelashes at Mark vigorously. 'He's already one of the leading men in his field. I assume you got that promotion, Mark?'

Promotion? He hadn't mentioned anything about a promotion to me.

Mark shrugged modestly. 'Yes, the partnership came through.'

'To Mark!' said Hez, holding her wine glass aloft. 'And his dazzling future.'

I was just about to ask him for some details – and suggest we celebrated his success at some point in the future – when Jonathan's voice boomed out once more:

'Lucy, I was just telling Jo that you'll let her have the details of that place I'm taking you to on Thursday.'

'Oh?' Dave sounded interested.

'Brilliant restaurant,' enthused Jonathan, 'tucked away down one of those little roads behind Chinatown. Very intimate, all small tables and candles and stuff, and it's Moroccan – Lucy loves Moroccan food.'

'I didn't know that, Lucy,' said Jo, her mouth full.

'There you go, Lou!' Jonathan winked across the table at me. 'Nobody knows you quite as well as me.'

'Obviously not,' muttered Mark.

I turned to Mark, to try and put him straight about Jonathan and me and our nights out, but he had pushed back his chair and was giving Dave a hand clearing the plates. All but snatching the dirty cutlery off the latter, I hoofed it into the kitchen after him.

'Mark,' I began, 'I need to explain about me and Jon.'

He shrugged and turned his back on me as he dumped the dirty dishes in the sink.

'Nothing to do with me,' he said.

'Jonathan and I,' I gabbled, 'we used to be together – when we were students – but he hurt me. Very badly.'

Mark turned to face me, his expression impassive.

'I know who he is, Lucy; you told me all about him when we first met.'

'Then you'll understand how important it is to me that I've been able to get past all that pain and recrimination. I'm at peace with myself for the first time in ages.'

Mark nodded, and for a second I felt relief.

But only for a second.

'Fair enough,' he replied, turning back to the sink. 'I hope you both enjoy your new-found peace.'

'It's not like that!' I replied. 'It's nothing serious – for old times' sake, really.'

'Well, whatever floats your boat,' said Mark coldly, picking up a bottle of wine and walking towards the kitchen door.

'Mark, listen!' I wailed. 'I mean it – I haven't even said I *will* go to this wretched exhibition.'

'He certainly seems to think so.'

I followed Mark back into the dining room, my face flushed and my heart thudding.

'You all right there, Lou?' asked Jonathan. 'Hey! If I can seduce you away from that workload of yours, we could go and see the new Ang Lee movie too. Jo here was telling me how brilliant it is.'

I shot a look at Mark, who now looked as though he was trying to disembowel the bottle of wine rather than merely uncork it.

'No. I. Don't. Think. So,' I said in a firm and emphatic tone meant to convey the message that Jonathan should stop talking right there and then.

He didn't take the hint.

'We could go next Saturday. I'll pick you up round about eight – unless you want to come for a bite to eat at mine first. And whilst I'm thinking about it, if you're not doing anything on the Sunday after, I was wondering if you'd fancy a trip—'

'Oh, fucking hell!' Mark shouted.

All eyes turned to look at him. My heart leapt into my mouth – was he going to roll up his sleeves and tell Jonathan to meet him outside?

'Bloody useless corkscrew,' he muttered, throwing the offending utensil on to the table and going back into the kitchen. I trailed along behind him.

'Mark, *please!*' I hissed. 'This has all got over-complicated.'

'Has it?' he asked. 'It seems perfectly straightforward from where I'm standing.'

Impassively he selected a large knife from the drawer and went back into the dining room, hopefully to rescue the wine rather than continue his disembowelling practice.

I leant my face against the cool of Jo's stainless-steel fridge, closed my eyes and told myself not to panic. All was not yet lost; it was merely a case of crossed wires. Mark thought Jonathan and I were an item when we weren't, and all I had to do was to convince him of that and it would be sorted – simple!

The kitchen door burst open noisily. Thinking that it was probably Mark returning to look for a bigger knife, I jerked my face away from the comforting chill of the fridge and prepared to explain myself.

But it wasn't Mark.

It was an extremely pissed-off Dave, followed by a livid-looking Jo.

'You're being ridiculous,' she hissed. 'Of *course* he doesn't fancy me.'

'Well from what I've seen, he certainly seems to be under that impression – and it's not as if you've been discouraging him; you've hardly spoken to anyone else all evening.'

'I'm only being polite. He's our guest and he doesn't know anyone.'

'He knows two out of the other five people here; and even if he didn't, nothing would excuse the way you keep batting your eyelids at him.'

Jo rounded on him, hands on hips. 'You've gone mad, David Williams. You've gone stark, staring, raving *mad* and – oh, hello, Lucy; didn't see you there.'

I had been trying to exit the kitchen as unobtrusively as possible. I raised a hand in a 'carry on as if I'm not here' sort of a manner and left them to it.

The mood round the table was even more discordant than when I had exited. Jonathan was still trying to offload career advice on to a glowering Mark, and Hez was providing a running commentary of the latter's manifold achievements. They looked up expectantly at me as I entered, but without armed back-up from a crack platoon of Special Forces personnel, I was unequal to the challenge of bringing peace to the dining room.

'Nice weather we've been having,' I offered lamely.

Jo and Dave burst back through the kitchen door carrying bowls and some sort of fragile meringue concoction. She elbowed him hard in the ribs and hissed the word 'Smile!' Dave failed to obey orders and they placed the dishes on the table in angry unison. Then Jo clapped a hand to her mouth.

'Oh, damn! I forgot the dessert wine,' she exclaimed.

Eager to escape, I leapt up and made my way towards the kitchen.

'There wasn't any room in the fridge, so I asked Mark to put it outside to chill,' Jo called after me. 'Mark, would you mind . . .'

Right! This was my chance to get him on his own. I stepped outside and, momentarily blinded by the darkness, listened as heavy male footsteps came up behind me and then stopped. There was a weighty, pregnant silence as I took a deep breath of icy-cold night air and prepared my words carefully. I was conscious of just how important the next twenty seconds would be if we were to have any chance of a relationship in the future.

'I know it didn't go smoothly for us last time,' I said as calmly as I could, 'and things have got a bit, well, confused this evening. But you mean a lot to me and I'd really like it if we could work something out. Please tell me you'll think about it.'

The pause that followed seemed to go on for ever, and my heart was in my mouth as I waited for him to speak.

'I'll think about it if you want me to,' came the reply, 'but I reckon you already know I'd be happy to move things on to the next stage.'

My stomach clenched nauseatingly; how could something as simple as two people having a conversation go so totally wrong? I turned round and stared open-mouthed at the man in front of me.

It was Jonathan, complete with a smug-looking grin on his face. I stamped my foot on the floor in sheer frustration.

'What the hell do you think you're doing, creeping around the garden and pretending to be Mark?' I cried. 'What if he heard my little speech – and yours? He's already convinced—'

Jonathan's face fell and then crumpled itself into a frown.

'He'd disappeared off somewhere, so I made myself useful and came out with you.' He sounded a bit pissed off. 'Look, what's all this about me pretending to be Mark? You told me last night that you and he were over, so naturally I assumed—'

'Oh, just forget it!' I said ungraciously, and stormed back into the warmth of the kitchen, leaving Jonathan in mid-protest back in the yard.

Right! This was it. I had to find Mark and tell him straight: no more ambiguity, no more double meanings, and hope for the best. If he didn't believe me, well, that was tough; but I had to have one last shot at convincing him.

Back in the dining room, Jo and Dave were sitting at opposite ends of the table, looking daggers at one another, but there was no sign of Mark. Or Hez, for that matter.

I stalked through the living area and out into the hall, thinking that he'd probably slipped out to the bathroom and I could catch him on his way back.

What I saw in the hall, however, was enough to knock the breath out of me and bring me grinding to a halt: in front of me, next to the row of coat hooks on the wall, was Hez. And vigorously trying to disentangle himself from her clutches was Mark. My legs suddenly seemed to get bored of their primary function of keeping me upright and I had to grab hold of one of the banister spindles for support.

'I don't know what's got into you,' Mark hissed, 'but there is no way there is ever going to be anything between us, so you might as well forget it.'

A wave of pure, cold fear sliced through me like a blade: Hez was after him.

What other explanation could there possibly be? She'd been acting weird all evening, but I'd put that down to some sort of brain fever brought on by a severe allergic reaction to Jonathan. I'd never thought she might be serious.

That was the moment I lost it.

I hated her. I absolutely, one hundred per cent, swear-to-God hated her. And if my limbs had been capable of receiving orders from my brain, I think I would probably have walked over to her and hit her: every fibre of my being was yelling at me to return some of the pain she was dishing out to me. She *knew* how deeply Mark had affected me; she even knew, for goodness' sake, that I'd been within a hair's breadth of kissing him in the kitchen not two hours previously.

Before I could stop them, the memories of that night in Bristol ran screaming through my brain; the feeling of claustrophobic, airless blackness – of being lost and totally alone – that I'd experienced as I rushed out of Jonathan's house swept over me once again.

Only more so.

Because this time it was Mark, and for reasons I didn't understand, the twist of the knife went much, much deeper.

With enormous effort, I forced my vocal cords back into life.

'What the hell do you think you're doing?' I yelled, my heart pounding and stomach churning.

Mark obviously saw this as his moment to escape and legged it into the safety of the living room. Hez stared up at me, a horrified expression on her face.

'I can explain,' she stammered.

'Just get back in there,' I shouted, indicating the door through which Mark had vanished. 'Now!'

I followed her into the living room and was greeted by the sight of Mark making his hurried farewells.

'Don't you dare leave,' I growled at him, and he stood, rooted to the spot, his coat half on and a nervous look on his face.

'Right!' I said, striding over to the table and pounding my fist down on to it so loudly that the cutlery rattled and Jo jumped a good two feet into the air. 'I have had enough, so all of you – pay attention!'

They stared at me, open-mouthed.

'She,' I pointed at Jo, 'is not in love with him.' I pointed at Jonathan. 'So you,' I pointed at Dave, 'can stop worrying. Although you,' I pointed at Jo again, 'could have done with toning it down a little.'

'Sorry, Dave,' said Jo. Dave forced a half-smile and nodded.

'Now I,' I indicated myself, 'am not romantically involved with him.' I pointed at Jonathan. 'Whereas you . . .' I pointed at Mark and took a deep breath. 'How can I put this? Maybe somewhere in an alternative universe we could make it work; but here – now – all that happens is that I end up getting hurt. I think it's best if we don't see each other again.'

Mark sat down heavily on the arm of the sofa, and I paused and collected my thoughts: ironically, that had been the easy bit.

'You,' I looked at Hez, my voice catching as I spoke, 'how could you do this to me? Boyfriends, well, you expect them to fuck up and hurt you, you know? But my *best friend* – I should be able to trust you with my life.'

'No.' She shook her head violently. 'It wasn't like that.'

I gave her the cuttingest of cutting stares.

'Which time?' I asked. 'Now – or in Bristol with him?' I glanced towards Jonathan.

Hez went unbelievably pale and clapped her hand across her mouth.

'I'll start looking for another flat,' I went on. 'With any luck it shouldn't take long. In the meantime, I'd be grateful if you'd keep out of my way as much as possible. Now, has anyone got any questions? No? Good.'

And, to the sound of their collective stunned silence, I picked up my coat and walked out into the night.

I pounded two hundred yards down the road in my tottery heels before giving up and sinking into a despondent huddle on a garden wall. It was as though someone (well, Hez, actually) had cut my heart up into little pieces and jumped on them: I felt physically bruised and totally exhausted. I'd been in quite a few relationships that had ended badly, but, either as the dumper or the dumpee, I had never experienced such pain as I did now.

Hez had been my best mate; the person who, in the absence of a normal, sane family, had been a surrogate sister to me and for whom in return I would gladly have walked across burning coals if she'd ever needed me to. I'd assumed we would always be there for each other. But, as I'd just had the misfortune to find out, the more you love someone, the harder it hurts when they do the dirty on you.

And this hurt very, very much. About sixteen million out of ten, if you're interested, Hez.

I shivered and put my coat round my shoulders. Even though I felt like crumpling into a little heap and letting the scene around me fade to black, the chill of the April night and the discomfort of perching on a lumpy brick wall brought me back to the immediate problem of What I Was Going To Do Next. This was a tricky one, because although yelling a lot and then making a dramatic exit had been good things to do at the time, it meant that I was now faced with a limited number of options. I could:

1. Wander aimlessly round central London for a bit on my own, or
2. Go home to Muswell Hill and risk bumping into Hez sometime in the not too distant future, or
3. Get unbelievably drunk so that I didn't care *who* I met back at the flat.

Finding a bar somewhere and drinking myself into alcoholic oblivion did have its attractions, but I decided against it. Instead I would go home, lock my bedroom door and hope that Hez had the sense to stay the night with Jo and Dave.

I reached down for my bag, ready to fish out my Oyster card – and realised I was in an even worse fix than before. My bag, containing my purse, Oyster card and house keys, was currently hanging from a peg on the hatstand in Jo's hall. If I wanted to go home – or anywhere else for that matter – I was going to have to turn tail and shuffle back up the road to get it.

I groaned. I couldn't imagine anything worse; but what choice did I have? I couldn't kip out on the pavements of Vauxhall all night. Reluctantly, I slid off my wall and started to walk back from whence I had come.

After I had taken about two steps, I heard a shout and looked up to see a figure running towards me through the gloom. Oh, great, I thought, after everything else that's happened tonight, I'm going to get mugged. Or raped. Or both. Mugged *and* raped: what a fabulous way to round off an evening of arguments, betrayal and general misery.

Then the mugger yelled again; and this time I could make out the word 'Lucy!' Weird, I thought, was this some sort of personalised robbery service?

'Hello, my name is Darren and I will be your mugger

for this evening. We are offering three different levels of service today: the basic, where we nick your phone; the deluxe, where we threaten you with a knife and take your handbag; and the super-deluxe, where we beat you up and steal everything you've ever owned, but call an ambulance before we run off and leave you bleeding in the gutter.'

Well, there was no point trying to run in these heels, I was just going to have to stand my ground and accept my fate ... Wait: these *heels*! Remembering my erstwhile best friend and her shoe-based self-defence tactics on the mean streets of Bethnal Green, I slipped one off and waited for the Shouting Man to appear round the corner.

'If you try anything, I shall stick this shoe right through your lousy skull!' I cried as he ran into view. 'I am armed and dangerous and totally insane – and I advise you to go and pick on someone else!'

The man skidded to a halt in front of me.

'What are you on about? It's me – Jonathan!' he panted.

'Jonathan? Oh, er, hello.'

'Are you all right?' he asked, looking about him. 'Has someone been threatening you? Where are they? I'll—'

'No, no; it's fine,' I said, fumbling with the shoe as I tried to put it back on. 'I overreacted a bit and thought you might be a mugger. It's been a bit of a weird evening.'

'You're telling me,' he said, putting his arm round my waist so I could lean against him as I battled with the strap on my shoe. 'Are you sure you're all right?'

'No,' I replied. 'I fact I don't think I've ever been so *not* all right in my entire life. I hate her, Jonathan, I really hate her.'

'Then why don't you hate me too?'

I pulled away from him and regarded him for a moment, standing before me bathed in the sodium orange of a street lamp.

'I did,' I said at last, 'and you know that's why I finished with you. But I couldn't face losing both of you over it.'

'So you dumped me and kept her?'

I nodded. 'I didn't even tell her I knew; up until tonight, she thought I chucked you because I caught you with Susan Geoffreys again. Oh, Jonathan, how could I be so stupid? I let her have the benefit of the doubt, and now this, *this* happens.'

I could feel tears pricking the corners of my eyes. I finished fiddling with my shoe and wiped them away with the back of my hand. Jonathan put an arm round my shoulder. It felt a bit awkward to begin with, but I allowed myself to be pulled in towards him and rested my head on his chest. The familiar feel of his arms round me, the smell of his body, was comforting beyond belief. Jonathan rested his chin on the top of my head as had been his wont all those years ago.

'For what it's worth, I didn't get the impression she was, well, *after* him,' he said thoughtfully.

'Then why was she acting like it? Why did Mark think she was?'

Jonathan shrugged. 'God knows. But I didn't pick up on anything between them.'

I wanted very much to believe him, but the wound Hez had reopened was too deep to be staunched by Jonathan's words. In the disaster zone that constituted my important relationships, the one that had stood out as proof positive that I *could* interact with other human beings in a normal way had been my friendship with Hez.

That night in Bristol had spelled the end of the line for Jonathan and me, but *Hez* . . . Well, I felt there had to be an explanation for her actions lurking around somewhere. Jonathan revelled in this sort of rakish behaviour (in fact, I was surprised I hadn't caught him at it before), but I knew it wasn't anything Hez would get up to under normal circs. And although I never found my explanation, I somehow moved on with her as my friend – and sure enough, it had never happened again.

Until now.

'You can't do it, can you?' I said half to myself and half to Jonathan.

'Can't do what?' he replied.

'Guarantee any happy-ever-afters, even if you think what you have is indestructible. The question is, does that mean we shouldn't even try?'

I pulled away from him and stuffed my hands into my coat pockets to keep warm.

'I don't know,' replied Jonathan, 'but whatever the answer, now's not the time to get all philosophical. To which purpose, by the way, I think you'll be wanting this.'

He handed over my bag; I clutched it to me like a lifebelt.

'Thanks,' I said, trying to summon up a smile, 'and sorry for the crappy evening, by the way. My friends aren't normally this bonkers.'

He grinned. 'Don't worry. I'm just glad I caught up with you. Are you heading back to Muswell Hill?'

I pulled a face. 'I suppose so. I don't fancy having to face Hez over the coffee-maker tomorrow morning, though.'

'Look, Lou, whatever the rights and wrongs of the situation, the pair of you probably need a bit of time apart to get your heads together. I was thinking that you could, er, you *could* stay at my flat tonight if you liked,' Jonathan went on, adding hastily, 'the bed in the spare room is made up and things might seem less fraught after a good night's sleep.'

I considered this: as rocks and hard places went, both Islington and Muswell Hill were looking pretty uncomfortable, but Jonathan's had the distinct advantage that there was no way Hez would pop round hoping for a chat . . .

'Okay, then – thanks.'

And improbable as it seemed, Jonathan and I set off down the road together.

I was woken from my slumber at about half past nine the next morning by Jonathan throwing a copy of the *Stoat on Sunday* at my head.

'Sorry,' he said. 'I was aiming for your legs.'

'That doesn't make it all right,' I growled, struggling to sit up in Jonathan's spare bed.

'I was out for a run and saw the headline. It looks like we're heading for some sort of constitutional crisis. Anyway, coffee's on, so come through when you're ready.'

I rubbed the sleep out of my eyes and stared in horror at the banner headline right across the front page:

'PM LEFT ME UNLOVED AND ALONE.'

Beneath it was a picture of Mr Jones standing next to a dirty-looking train. He was carrying a suitcase and had a huge – nay, obscene – grin on his face. I groaned, slung my legs over the side of the bed and staggered into the kitchen.

Jonathan's flat was unbelievably posh. Whereas Mark's place had been nice in a beech-effect-IKEA sort of a way, Jonathan's simply breathed large pay cheques. For someone who didn't own one pair of jeans without holes during his entire student career, it was rather impressive. The kitchen was a rhapsody in chrome, and so high-tech it resembled the bridge of the Starship *Enterprise* rather than a food preparation area; whilst the rest of the place was all stripped floorboards, kilim rugs and antique furniture. It must have cost a bomb, if not several. I ran my hand along an old but expensive-looking dresser.

'Shame you couldn't afford anything new,' I said.

'Watch it,' replied Jonathan, pushing a double espresso in my direction. 'No eggy bread for girls who decry my humble abode.'

Wow, eggy bread! I hadn't had it for years. In fact, not since Jonathan and I . . . Well, enough said. I climbed up on to a breakfast stool and spread the newspaper out on the counter in front of me. I was going to have to ring Guy in a minute and see if it was all hands on deck, but I wanted to read the story first.

It related to the latest offer for settlement we had received from Mrs Jones. In their most recent letter to Sheppertons, her solicitors had been carping on about how isolated she'd felt, due to the fact that Llew had spent long periods of time away from her on official business. They claimed she'd bought her pack of yappy little dogs to help her make it through the long, lonely nights and they were asking for an extra ten thousand a year in her maintenance payments for the upkeep of the said pooches. We had responded that, rather than hand over ten grand in cash, we'd pay for pet insurance. And it was our brisk and businesslike letter that the Powers of Evil (a.k.a. the news desk at the *Stoat on Sunday*) had splashed all over the front page, making it sound as if we were heartlessly denying her feelings of abandonment and loneliness.

'What do you reckon?' asked Jonathan, busy breaking eggs into a bowl. 'As a divorce professional you must have an opinion on how his legal team is handling this.'

I froze. And then unfroze and choked on my coffee. That was all the evidence Jonathan needed.

'Oh my God.' He stared at me, mid-egg-break. 'You *are* Llew Jones's legal team, aren't you?'

I'd taken another sip of coffee and I practically spat it back out again.

'You mustn't tell anyone, Jon, do you promise? Somebody is leaking stuff left, right and centre to the press. Hez is working on it too, and her boss already suspects her; and I'd be for the high jump if it got out I was gossiping to all and sundry.' I put my head in my hands. 'The tenancy committee in my chambers meets in two weeks, and if there is so much as a whiff of guilt from my direction, my rival Hugo will get the job.'

'Even if there's no proof it's you doing the leaking?'

'Yup.'

'That's outrageous!' Jonathan dunked a couple of slices of bread into the egg mixture and then threw them into a frying pan, where they spat and hissed angrily. 'Have you any idea who it could be? Then you could shop them before they do any more damage.'

'I wish. The list of suspects is huge and I have no way of narrowing it down. If I could even *see* copies of the leaked documents it would be a start – there might be some clue in there that would help.'

Jonathan nodded thoughtfully. 'It doesn't sound like a fun situation to be in; I wish there was something I could do to make things easier for you.'

I shrugged. 'I suppose I'll just have to ride out the storm.'

'Even so, if I have any bright ideas, I'll let you know. Now, the next item on the agenda . . . Hez.'

'Oh, no,' I said confidently, my mind half on the Jones's case and half on my breakfast, which Jonathan was just about to take out of the pan. 'She might not be my favourite person at the moment, but she's not the mole either. She's honest, reliable and loyal.'

Jonathan raised his eyebrows.

'At work, Jon, at work. If there was a good-looking man around, obviously she wouldn't hesitate to trample over me to get her claws into him.'

Jonathan put a plate of eggy bread in front of me.

'We need to talk about that,' he said.

'No we don't,' I replied hurriedly, sawing off a large chunk and stuffing it in my mouth. 'It all happened years ago.'

Even though I'd been under his roof now for twelve hours, the subject of Henrietta Irving had not been mentioned, and I wanted to keep it that way.

Jonathan pulled up the stool next to mine and sat down. 'However long ago it was, it obviously still has the power to upset you and cause you to break up with your best friend of ten years.'

'She is not my best friend. I do not *have* a best friend,' I muttered, my mouth full of food.

'If you say so.' He shrugged and turned his attention to his plate.

I was outraged. 'Excuse me!' I cried. 'She is the one who slept with you while we were together and spent yesterday evening hitting on Mark. I am the innocent party in all this. Are you seriously suggesting I go round and apologise to her for the fact that she's a raving nympho?'

'That night. In Bristol. You said she never found out you knew.'

'Oh? And that makes it all right, does it? So long as your best mate never finds out, it's quite acceptable to shag her fella?'

'No, of course not. But I happen to know she felt dreadful about it afterwards. As I did too, I might add.'

I put down my cutlery and stared at him.

'You mean you actually got together afterwards and *talked* about it?' I said at last. 'Did you meet up for a drink and a bit of a debrief; or was this some sort of post-coital pillow talk about poor Lucy and how she'd been deceived?'

I got off my stool and stood there, quivering with rage and dressed in not much more than one of Jonathan's shirts and a pair of hiking socks.

'You know what, Jonathan Hodges,' I continued, 'you're sick. I was mad to take you up on your offer of a spare bed; mad to even talk to you at the theatre. In fact, what I should have done was empty the ice bucket from the Old Vic bar over your head while I had my chance.'

By now I was ready to storm out of the room, but then Jonathan stood up too. And he was a good foot taller than I was.

'Sit down,' he said quietly but with an unbelievable amount of authority.

To my astonishment, I did.

'Now listen. For starters, you know that Peter dumped Hez about a week before it happened? Well, she'd come round to try and make it up with him, but they had another row and he left. I found her in tears, and, in an admittedly clichéd manner, one thing led to another. My only defence, which doesn't get me off the hook, I know, was that I was pretty pissed off with you. When you left to go to that wedding, you'd been pretty forthright in your opinion that I was a selfish, uncaring rat who was ruining your life, and that didn't go down very well with me. However, for what it's worth, I shouldn't have done it and I'm sorry. You made me pay for it, though, didn't you?'

'What did you expect? Of course I wasn't going to carry on our relationship once I finally had proof of what you were up to on a regular basis,' I retorted.

Now it was Jonathan's turn to look incredulous.

'What do you mean, "regular basis"?'

'Oh, come on. You had girls falling over themselves to get to you. The carpet outside your room was practically threadbare with them constantly beating a path to your door.'

'Are you talking about Susan Geoffreys?'

'Amongst others.'

'I cannot believe we are having this row after – what – six years? For the umpteenth time, I did *not* hit on her.

She was pissed, she tried to snog me and you walked in at the wrong moment.'

'Yeah, right!' This didn't impress me one little bit. 'And as for Hez – how do I know you weren't out to pull her? You can't be blind to the fact that she despises you. Why would she feel that way if you hadn't tried it on – probably over and over again – till she gave in?'

The pain was still as raw, still as real, as it had been at the time. The fact that Jonathan had fancied another woman enough to seduce her still filled me with an unattractive cocktail of anger and insecurity.

'Oh, for God's sake, Lucy; is this what they teach you at Bar school – concoct a ridiculous theory and then run with it despite all the evidence to the contrary? Well, try this one on for size: maybe – just maybe – she hates herself for what happened and uses me as a handy lightning conductor for her own guilt. Have you considered that?'

I hadn't, actually.

'And as for the others. Well,' he sat down heavily on his stool, 'of course I haven't been living like a monk since we split up; but whilst we were students, I only saw one other girl.'

'I knew it,' I growled. 'Who was she?'

'When we broke up the first time and I went on that exchange programme to Yale. There was a girl I dated while I was over there.'

I frowned. 'You've never mentioned her before.'

'And do you know why? Because you and I weren't together and it was none of your damn business.'

'And that was it? In the whole time we knew each other?'

'Yes.'

He sounded convincing, and I paused for a moment to compute this new information.

'This American girl; it didn't last, did it? Did you finish with her before we got back together?'

'I wasn't two-timing you, if that's what you mean. Me and her . . . it wasn't going to work, even without the whole distance problem. You see, the thing is . . .'

He got off the stool again and walked over to the cooker, where he picked at a bit of burnt-on egg with a fish slice.

'. . . the thing is,' he repeated, 'I know what I did with Hez, and I know I behaved like a bit of an arse at times, but I loved you; I really did. And my feelings never actually went away. If I'm being honest, it's the reason I wanted to look you up; to see if – eventually – there was a chance you would give us another go.'

Even though he'd mentioned his feelings for me in Jo's back yard, I had no idea they ran this deep. One minute I was accusing him of sleeping his way through our mutual acquaintances, the next he was professing his undying adoration.

'But – but – at Bristol – you must have at least fancied Hez?'

'Oh, bloody hell, Lucy! She was incredibly attractive and I was a twenty-three-year-old bloke. Of course I fancied her. And about half of the girls I met at college too. But that was as far as it went.'

He put the fish slice in the sink and rubbed his face with his hands.

'I probably shouldn't have said anything,' he muttered. 'In fact I think we should forget I ever opened my mouth.'

But my thoughts were wrestling with the fact that six years down the line, Jonathan still loved me; and my feelings for him ran deep too – perhaps deeper than I cared to admit. Dumping him was the hardest thing I'd ever had to do. Even though right had been on my side, I'd fallen into a black, miserable depression. I'd sniffed my way into lectures, snuffled my way through tutorials and wept alone in bed at night. Cry me a river? Pah! Cry me an estuary with a deep-water dock and a thriving ship-building industry might be nearer the mark.

Gradually, however, the Jonathan-shaped hole in my life had become less raw, and hours began to pass by without me thinking about him. Then days. Then a whole week. Then I went out with Danny. And then Richard. And then Rob. And although that Jonathan-shaped hole never actually went away, I learned to live with it and accept that it was always going to be a part of who I was and what I'd experienced. In fact, it was only Mark who had finally been able to make me see that there might be life after Jonathan.

But Mark and I were history. Weren't we?

'Are you seriously suggesting we get back together?' I asked slowly, just to make sure there was no confusion on this one.

'No. I'm apologising for my past behaviour. Pretend the rest of our conversation never happened.'

'Oh.' I felt my stomach give a little flip of disappointment.

'Why do you ask?' he said, scraping his almost untouched breakfast into the bin. 'I'm guessing that I'm the last man on earth you'd ever want to go out with; and if friends is the best we can manage, then that's all there is to it.'

Fine words indeed, but the atmosphere in the kitchen had changed. It was as if someone had thrown a set of points that would allow my life to disappear off down a track I'd previously thought was inaccessible. I had been in love with him once, the one and only time I'd succumbed to that emotion – could I feel that way again? Had I ever really stopped?

For the nano-est of nanoseconds, the thought of Mark and how much I had wanted him washed over me like a flood tide; but I made myself push the feelings away. It took every ounce of willpower in my possession but I did it – I couldn't waste any more of my life in mourning over lost relationships.

'Unless,' said Jonathan softly, 'unless you want to tell me something different?'

'Well,' I said, the whole thing feeling decidedly surreal, 'the sensible thing would be to take it a day at a time – see how we feel in a few weeks.'

I raised my eyes to meet his, and there was an unmistakable intensity in his gaze that meant we were both thinking along the same lines: something far more dangerous and explosive than mere friendship was now on the table.

'And are we going to be sensible?' He ran his finger lightly across the back of my hand as he spoke and there was a sort of hopefulness in his eyes, almost as if he couldn't quite believe his luck.

The question hovered in the air between us. I could visualise the two divergent routes in front of me, each heading towards opposite horizons. I needed to choose my road carefully. One would lead me back to Jonathan as my partner; to the familiar feel of his body, the turn of his thoughts and the well-worn path of our time together. The other veered off in a totally different direction and would carry me to a version of my life in which he might possibly feature, but never again as my boyfriend.

He had hurt me; but I had loved him. It was the known versus the unknown; the shock of the old versus the fear of the new.

'Do we *want* to be sensible?' I asked, recklessly allowing my eyes an experimental twinkle too.

'The only thing I want, Lucy,' he replied, dipping his head in towards mine, 'is you.'

Jonathan dropped me back in Muswell Hill early on Sunday evening after a very weird day indeed: following six long years of wondering what it would be like, I had finally kissed him again. In fact, I'd kissed him more than once: several times in the kitchen; once or twice in the hall; and then an awful lot more in the living room.

However, this was as far as I was willing to go. It wasn't that the experience wasn't *nice* (Jonathan remembered exactly which buttons to push); or even that it wasn't passionate (the fact that we didn't get round to finishing breakfast till half past two says it all); but when it came to moving things up the last important notch – taking us back to where we had been before that fateful night in Bristol – I found myself declining gracefully.

'Look, Jon,' I said, doing up a couple of buttons on my borrowed shirt, 'what would you say about running this slowly? I mean, it's only been just over a week since we met at the theatre and I think we need more time to get to know each other again.'

Jonathan was lying full-length on the sofa, one hand behind his head, grinning.

'What's all this, Lou? Having second thoughts already?'

'No, no, of course not.' I attempted a smile in reply. 'I just need to get used to the idea; plus I'm concerned that with everything else on my plate at the moment, I might not be able to give you the attention you deserve.'

Yes, that was it. Given the seismic events that had blown our relationship apart six years earlier, it was bound to take a while before we could get back up to speed for Round Two. And my feelings on the matter had nothing to do with Mark, I told myself. *Absolutely nothing.*

Jonathan sat up and planted another kiss on the end of my nose.

'Believe me,' he said in a low voice, 'I do want your attention. All of it.'

A little shiver went down my spine, but I wasn't entirely sure if it was pleasurable.

'Come round tomorrow and I'll cook you dinner,' he continued, trying his best to undo the buttons on my shirt again. 'I'll tell you how my television meeting went and we can see how your attention span is doing.'

'Maybe,' I replied, wriggling free of his wandering fingers. 'I'll let you know.'

Later that day – once we'd said goodbye and he'd left me standing on the pavement outside my flat – a thrill of panic about a completely different issue charged through me, pushing the problem of my feelings for Jonathan right to the bottom of the agenda: the latest Jones leaks! I'd been so wrapped up in other things (well, Jonathan's arms, actually) that I hadn't switched my phone on all day. I could have a million messages waiting on my voicemail from Guy, each one angrier than the one before. Arrgggh!

I delved into my bag and turned it on, shaking with apprehension. Would this be enough to get me fired from the case, or would a public bollocking in front of the client suffice? However, the god of Unexpected Liaisons With One's Ex-Boyfriend was obviously on my side: *You have no new messages.* Just to make sure I really was off the hook, though, I rang Guy myself; first on his mobile and then on his landline – but there was no reply. Then, once inside, I checked my landline voicemail (zilch); and finally I rang Stan, our head clerk, on his mobile and discovered that he hadn't been able to get hold of Guy all day either. Stan was also able to reassure me that nothing had come in from Sheppertons, and that in the absence of express instructions from them, there was nothing I needed to do.

I allowed my panic to subside.

Crisis over, I looked round the flat for signs of Hez. Returning home meant that sooner or later our paths were going to cross, and I could feel my stomach beginning to churn at the thought of what we were going to have to say to each other. My shock and anger at seeing her with Mark was ebbing slightly, and the odd lucid thought was starting to make its voice heard. But this was not necessarily good news. You see, the more I thought about it, the more I realised what a lose-lose situation I was in. If my interpretation of her actions did turn out to be correct, I doubted whether I would ever find it in my heart to trust her again. However, if she *was* the innocent party in all this, it meant I had behaved like a complete cow and she would be perfectly within her rights to decide she no longer wanted me as her top chum and flatmate.

My anxiety, however, turned out to be premature. A quick recce proved that I was alone, and the place remained Hez-less for the rest of the day. I suppose she must have come home at some point that night, but as there was no sign of her either when I went to bed or when my alarm went off at six the next morning, I couldn't say for sure.

I arrived at work at half-seven and went straight into Guy's room. He was already tackling a pile of paperwork that stood about six inches deep.

'I tried to ring you yesterday but your mobile was off,' I explained, just in case he thought I'd been slacking the day before.

'I know, I did get your message,' he said, shifting uneasily in his seat, 'but I was, um, otherwise engaged. Sheppertons dealt with the whole thing anyway.'

'What's the damage?'

'It's bad. And I've just had a fax from Spiggott informing me that if the leaks continue, Llew will be taking his business elsewhere. He's losing trust in his legal team and I can't say that I blame him. These leaks,' Guy continued, lowering his voice, 'you haven't spoken about the case to anyone, have you? A friend? A rival? Someone in the *media*?'

For a moment I went hot and cold with fear at the thought that he had somehow found out about my discussion with Jonathan the day before. Then I got a grip on myself. No one knew about that apart from Jon and myself, and I hadn't actually divulged anything apart from the fact that I was one of the PM's advisers. No, Guy's suspicions had to come from elsewhere. Most likely Spiggott had concocted some irrational theory about me just as he had with Hez and then mentioned his thoughts to Guy . . .

'Look,' I said as firmly as I could manage, 'this case is the most important thing in my life: my whole future is riding on it. Do you honestly think I would risk chucking all that away for a few lousy quid from the *Stoat*?'

'I'm not accusing anyone, Stephens,' he replied. 'But reputations are at stake here – and not just Llew Jones's. Just think of it as a friendly warning, that's all.'

I bit my lip in lieu of reply; there was nothing friendly in his tone of voice. Guy went on:

'Sheppertons are putting out a statement that was agreed yesterday, something about the amicability of the Joneses' separation and that all involved are hoping for a speedy resolution of the matter, yadda yadda yadda. Hopefully that will contain things for now. But if anything else goes wrong, the consequences for all of us on the team will be disastrous.'

I went back to my room, the events of the past few days running round my head. That must have been where Hez was yesterday: in at work, batting between a furious Spiggott and a grouchy Macdonald. She'd probably had to be in at ridiculous o'clock this morning as well and, given the current climate on the Jones case, wouldn't be home much before midnight.

The thought of talking to her still made me feel queasy. However, natural justice demanded that I at least hear her side of the Mark fiasco, and if I wanted to talk to her, given the hours she was putting in at the office, I was going to have to do so by phone.

I decided to get it over and done with.

I looked at my watch: it had just gone eight. With any luck, Spiggott would be on to his second breakfast of the day and too preoccupied to listen in on Hez's conversations. Not wanting her to recognise my number on her phone's display, I rang Estelle, intending to ask her to put me through.

'What is it now?' snapped Estelle. 'Oh, er, Miss Stephens, sorry about that. I thought you were Mr Spiggott. What can I do for you?'

'Can I speak to Miss Irving, please?'

'Yes, of course. I really am sorry I jumped down your throat like that. I'm not having a good day today, and certain members of staff here aren't making it any easier for me.'

I listened to the clicks as she connected me to Hez's line.

'Hez, it's me,' I said as she picked up. 'I want to talk about Saturday.'

'If you're ringing up to have another go at me, you can forget it, Lucy,' she said in a fierce whisper. 'I don't need any more hassle. Spiggott's in a foul mood and he seems to be under the impression that I'm his personal punch-bag. If this is about work, fine; if not, I don't want to know.'

'Is Spiggott playing up because of the stuff in the *Stoat on Sunday*?' I asked, playing for time in the hope she wouldn't hang up on me.

'Mmmm,' she replied in a tight little voice. 'I was in all day yesterday helping him deal with it.'

'And what's your take on it?'

'That Spiggott is a big fat git with the managerial skills of a baboon's bottom.' She paused. 'Actually, that's not fair. The managerial skills of a baboon's bottom are much more developed. Sorry. You probably couldn't care less about what I feel, but if I hadn't got that off my chest I was going to have to slap someone.'

There was a definite catch in her voice that was unusual for Hez. Normally she took as good as she got, or in the case of Spiggott (when telling him exactly where he could go and shove his affidavits would have resulted in the immediate production of her P45), she counted to ten and let it bounce harmlessly off her.

'You're okay, though, aren't you?' I said.

'Yes,' came a very small voice on the other end of the phone. 'Course I am.'

For a minute I was stunned. This was Hez – feisty, indomitable Hez, who chewed up big-name lawyers in court and then spat out the pips. Hez, who with one look could chip nail polish at a hundred paces. She didn't do upset.

'What happened?' I probed.

There was a short silence, punctuated by sounds that may or may not have been stifled sobs, then I heard Hez take a deep breath.

'ThatthemolehadtobesomeoneintheofficeandIwas undersuspicionandifhefoundoutit*was*mehe'dmakedamn sureIneverworkedagain. Ever. Anywhere.' This was followed by another gasp and a loud nose-blow.

'And what did you say?'

'He wouldn't let me say anything.' Another sob/gasp.

'When he'd finished shouting he told me to get out of his sight and sort it out or he'd be looking at my contract.'

'But he can't sack you – you haven't done anything wrong,' I protested.

'It's not,' there was a small choking sound, 'as simple as that. We all make mistakes, right?'

'Yes,' I agreed slowly.

'Well, he said if he had no proof I was the mole, he'd dredge up a whole load of little things from years back, bung them all together and boot me out. If there are any more leaks, I'm going to be the scapegoat: they'll fire me so that Llew reckons the matter has been dealt with.'

A trace of hysteria was beginning to enter her voice. She was heading for core meltdown.

'Can you say you've got a headache or something and bunk off?' I suggested.

'That'll just make it worse,' she replied. 'He'll either see it as proof positive I'm up to something or that I'm a total girlie wimp. I just can't win.'

'Miss Irving!' Spiggott's voice barked from across her office and ricocheted down the phone line, making me jump. 'Is that call to do with the case?'

She didn't miss a beat.

'Temple Buildings on the phone.'

'Very possibly,' he sneered (I began to think Hugo might be taking lessons from him). 'But is this work-related, or are you and Miss Stephens just discussing the latest handbag design?'

The bastard! How dare he. As if *I* could afford a new handbag.

'I take it from your silence that it is a social call,' Spiggott continued. 'May I remind you that using the firm's time and facilities for personal reasons is a very serious offence, and you're on dodgy ground already.'

There was a pause, presumably for some sort of evil dramatic effect, before he continued. 'One more slip, Irving, just one more slip and I'll have you out of here quicker than you can say "instant dismissal".'

I heard him stalk off back to his lair.

'Are you okay?' I asked Hez.

For what seemed like several millennia there was no response. Then a voice squeaked, 'Must go toilet.' Followed by a huge, hiccoughing gulp.

'Hez?' I said, 'Hez? Are you there?'

But the line had gone dead.

I called in at Jonathan's on the way home that evening. Although I had no intention of staying for the dinner he had suggested yesterday, I wanted to be suitably supportive over his commissioning meeting for the art and environment show, whichever way it had gone.

Even though a full twenty-four hours had now elapsed for me to become used to the possibility of us getting back together, it still felt distinctly odd to drop in on him like this. In fact, if I was being honest, the whole thing was completely bizarre – and not in a good way, either. When I'd been aware of anything other than Hez or the Jones case that day, my mind had kept wandering back to Jonathan and the suspicion that now that he was within my grasp, he wasn't what I actually wanted.

On the other hand, I reminded myself, this was *Jonathan* we were talking about. He was my *über*-ex, my Mr Big; a man so damned handsome that simply walking down the street with him meant I could feel waves of envy emanating from every woman we passed. Of *course* I would want to be with a man like that.

After much soul-searching, I concluded that I was simply expecting too much too soon – after all, we'd only bumped into each other just over a week ago, and there was probably all sorts of stuff that needed to be worked through before it felt right again. Yes, that was it. I simply needed to hang on in there and things would get better.

When I got to the flat, Jonathan was in his space-age kitchen, messing about with complicated ingredients like pine nuts and garlic.

'Pasta?' he offered, bunging a bunch of basil into a blender.

My first instinct was to decline, but then my stomach gave an ominous gurgle: I'd only had a cheese and ham sarnie at lunchtime and it had been a long day.

'Go on then,' I said, putting my bags down but adding hurriedly, 'but I can't stay long – I've got an opinion to write for tomorrow. What I really want to know is how your meeting went; are you all set for the new series?'

Jonathan whizzed up the contents of the blender into a green mush and grinned at me.

'We got the go-ahead for a pilot. I'm going to start shooting it in June, once the students have buggered off.'

'That's brilliant!' I cried.

He moved his head down to kiss me, but I turned my face away at the last moment, so his lips landed on my cheek rather than my mouth. I then wriggled free of his arms and helped myself to a glass of wine. Jonathan didn't react to this evasive action and instead concentrated on stirring pesto into the pasta pot.

'Tell me more,' I prompted, leaning against the counter and watching as he shared out pestoed penne between two white bowls.

'Nothing to tell, really; it just means masses of extra research to plough through in between lectures and tutorials next term. Actually, it wasn't till after the meeting that things got rather interesting.' He raised an eyebrow and looked at me. 'I ran into an old mate of mine from Cambridge and ended up having lunch with him. He's called Tom Gedge, and he's just been promoted to be the producer for *Hot Topics* – the trendy current-affairs programme on Saturday nights.'

I knew *Hot Topics* very well indeed. It was a sort of cross between a celebrity gossip magazine and a politics show – all the big issues being discussed by the most interesting people – and it was utterly compulsive viewing.

Jonathan passed me a bowl and rummaged around in a drawer looking for cutlery.

'His first show as the big boss is next week, and he told me they're going to be doing it as a special on the PM's divorce – is there such a thing as family values; does a divorced prime minister mean a weak prime minister and – rather importantly from your point of view – who the mystery mole is and what someone like that would have to gain from disseminating highly personal information to the media. Parmesan?'

'Does he have any idea who it might be?' I asked hopefully, declining cheese but accepting a fork.

Jonathan shook his head as he ate.

'No; although he has managed to get hold of the documents that were sent to the *Stoat*.'

With an almost audible 'ping', an idea popped into my brain.

'Your mate Tom, would he like to meet me off the record?'

'I think he would sell his grandmother six times over to talk to you; but wouldn't hobnobbing with gentlemen of the press be a bit of a dangerous thing for you to do?'

That point had not escaped my notice: if Guy found out, I'd be sacked on the spot. On the other hand, though, it might be the only chance I'd have to figure out who the leak-meister was before the PM made alternative legal arrangements . . .

'You'll have to make it clear I'm not prepared to discuss the case with him,' I said hurriedly. 'That would be like signing my own death-warrant. In fact, you'd better not mention the nature of my involvement in the matter full stop; but I'd like to see the stuff he's got from the *Stoat*, and maybe I can shed a bit of light on the mystery for him in return. Will you ring and ask him tomorrow?'

Jonathan nodded gravely. 'Consider it done. Now, speaking of having words with people, how about you? Did you sort anything out with Hez?'

'No. When I rang, she was almost in tears – Henry Spiggott had just had a go at her over the Jones thing. It wasn't the right time for us to have a no-holds-barred chat about the future of our friendship.'

'I suppose not. So what else? Mr Jones still causing trouble?'

'No, he's a sweetie. The real downer is having to deal with Spiggott on a daily basis. Have you seen today's *Standard*?'

I took it out of my bag and handed it to him. A seriously off-putting photo of Spiggott glowered out at us from the front page. Jonathan took an involuntary step back.

' "PM's Solicitor Vows Vengeance for Client",' he read out loud. 'God, he sounds scary. I wouldn't like to be in Hez's shoes if he's got it in for her. Let's hope he doesn't train his fire on you too. Now, one other thing . . .'

'The Turner exhibition?' I asked, putting my fork down. 'I'll do my best, but with the amount of work I've got on my plate at the moment, I don't know if—'

'No, not Turner; us.'

A whisper of relief wound its way through me: it sounded like he wanted to talk. He must have guessed that I was having second thoughts. Was he going to tell me it all felt weird for him too?

'What I need to know,' he said, looking down into my face and wrapping an arm tightly round my waist, 'is whether we have dessert now – or whether we take it with us into the bedroom?'

That would be a no, then.

'You know,' I said, slithering out of his grasp and heading for my bag, 'maybe we could save dessert for another time altogether?'

The next day, things didn't improve for Mr Jones. Although there were no new revelations, the papers were still full of the Divorce of the Century, the latest opinion polls were down again and Guy was starting to look increasingly despondent.

'I don't believe it,' he said as I entered his room for our now regular eight o'clock meeting. 'Twenty-five years I've been in the business and *never* has one of my clients been so publicly humiliated. First we have the melons, then Llew's so-called U-turn on the sanctity of marriage, and now all this loneliness crap!'

'And the picture of that mystery woman,' I reminded him. The fact that I still got a flicker of recognition each time I thought about it was niggling me.

Guy's eyes bulged behind his trendy specs. 'There are some things,' he said, 'about which I do not care to be reminded!'

'Sorry,' I muttered.

'The whole thing is a disaster,' he said, shaking his head. 'And for once in my life, I have no idea how to sort things out.'

'Do you know what I would like to see, Guy?' I said, suddenly remembering my conversation with Jonathan about Tom Gedge.

'An end to this ridiculous charade?'

'Apart from that. I'd like to see the Jones file from Sheppertons.'

'Why on earth would you want to do that? We have copies of the main files here in chambers.'

Guy indicated the five lever-arches.

'And the subsidiary files.'

He pointed to the four lever-arches of paperwork we'd racked up since he'd accepted the brief.

'And the back-up extra documents over there.' He pointed to a teetering pile of papers on a table in the corner of his room, all bound up with pink ribbon. 'What more could you possibly need?'

'The originals. You know, just in case there's something there to tell us who's been passing the stuff to the *Stoat*. Stuff put back in the wrong place, fax transmission numbers, that sort of thing.'

Guy pulled a thoughtful face.

'It might be worth a try, I suppose. Frankly, the whole thing is becoming hugely embarrassing. Even if we don't get the sack, I don't think I'm going to be able to show my face on *Have I Got News For You* again.'

He took off his glasses and ran a hand wearily across his face before continuing. 'I hope you realise that asking to see the originals is highly unorthodox; but as I can't come up with a better idea, I'll go along with you. Let's ask for the papers and go through them with a fine-toothed comb. Actually, why don't we get Miss Irving to bring the files over in person, then I can ask her a few questions about whether anything unusual has happened in the office without Spiggott sticking his oar in.'

I bit my lip. Spending the rest of the day with the Jones documents was one thing; being in close proximity to Hez for the duration was something else entirely. Of course it was the sensible thing to do (if anybody had picked up on any unusual activity in the matrimonial department at Sheppertons, it would have been Hez), but that wouldn't make the situation any less awkward from a personal point of view.

I went back to my room and picked up the phone to dial the Sheppertons switchboard.

'Mr Spiggott, please. It's Lucy Stephens of counsel here.'

Even after three years I still loved saying that. It made me sound like a real lawyer.

'Yes,' barked Spiggott as he picked up. 'What do you want?'

I pulled my ear away from the phone slightly. 'I'm ringing on behalf of Mr Jennings.'

'Oh, that jumped-up county-court hack,' said Spiggott with his usual bonhomie. 'What does he want now?'

'He is requesting sight of the original file of documents on the Jones case and a conference with Miss Irving,' I continued in my best telephone voice.

'Miss Irving?' He now sounded surprised as well as cantankerous. 'Why the monkey and not the organ-grinder?'

'Because the monkey knows what it's talking about.'

Was what I *didn't* say.

Instead, I replied: 'I'm afraid Mr Jennings did not make me privy to that particular piece of information. Please send the papers over with Miss Irving as soon as possible.'

'Well, you can tell Mr Jennings from me that I don't appreciate him hoicking my staff out of the office at a moment's notice, but if this is a one-off, I suppose I'll go along with it.'

And he hung up.

When the taxi finally dropped Hez and the files off, I had managed to work myself up into a state of nervous apprehension. However, as soon as I saw her, it was clear that she wasn't spoiling for a fight. Her eyes were red and she had obviously been crying again, and as I got close to her, I could hear her sniffing slightly.

'Thanks for coming,' I said. 'I guess I'm not your top choice for Person You Want to Spend Time With at the moment.'

'You'd be surprised,' she said. 'Things were getting pretty nasty in the office again today.'

'I'm sorry,' I replied. Whatever our personal differences, she didn't deserve the hassle she was getting from Spiggott.

'Don't!' she said, alarmed.

'Don't what?'

'Be nice to me – you'll just start me off again.'

'All right,' I said, hoping that if I made her laugh it might help to break the ice between us, 'I'll be horrid instead. How about "I hope Spiggott falls madly in love with you and forces you to marry him and live horribly ever after"?'

She managed a half-smile. 'I said don't make me cry, not please make me chuck.'

'Ah, ladies.' Guy opened his door and beckoned us inside. 'This way, please. Glad you could make it in person, Miss Irving.'

'So am I,' she said fervently.

He ushered us into his room and pulled up a couple of chairs, while Danny the junior clerk brought the files in.

'I'm not going to beat about the bush,' Guy announced, sitting down behind his desk. 'We are having this emergency conference session to discuss our mole. Now, since I spoke with Miss Stephens earlier this morning, I've been doing some thinking. I hate to say it, Miss Irving, but every single document that has found its way into the *Stoat*'s clutches has had your reference on it.'

'Apart from the photograph of that woman,' I added.

Guy glared at me. 'Will you *please* stop going on about that wretched picture. It is not part of the leaks and is therefore not part of our discussion. Is that clear?'

'Er, if you say so.'

What was *with* him over that photo? God, if only I could work out who I thought it was . . .

Guy flicked through the file and found the first letter that had gone *Stoat*-wards.

' "Jon/HI/ED" – is that your reference?' he asked.

Hez nodded. ' "Jon" is an abbreviation of "Jones"; "HI" are my initials, and the last two are the initials of whoever typed it. In this case it was Estelle Douglas. She's Spiggott's secretary really, but she often does my typing too.'

'And the most recent letter to be leaked has exactly the same reference,' Guy went on, flicking through the papers. 'Now, both of these were letters from us to Mrs Jones's solicitors. How did you send them?'

'The same way that we send all urgent correspondence,' Hez replied. 'First we fax it, then we put the hard copy in the document exchange to the other side. A photocopy goes by DX to you, another photocopy goes by post to the client and we retain a further photocopy for our file. So at any one time there is one original and four copies of the letter in existence.'

'Do you have records of all the faxes sent from the matrimonial department at Sheppertons?' asked Guy.

'As this was such a sensitive case, I took the precaution of monitoring the destination of every fax sent from our departmental machine,' replied Hez, handing over a large pile of computer paper.

'Good girl,' murmured Guy, running his eye down it.

'But the only numbers on the printout relating to the Jones case are your fax number, here,' Hez leaned over the desk and pointed it out, 'and Llew Jones's private fax machine, here. Spiggott has sent a couple of faxes to the Number Ten press office – but nothing confidential. I've checked to see if the *Stoat*'s numbers appear anywhere, but they don't.'

'What about other fax machines in your building?' I asked. 'Whoever's doing this might be using one in a different department to cover their tracks.'

'I thought of that,' replied Hez. 'I got Wayne in IT to cross-check the *Stoat*'s fax numbers against all the machines in the building, and there was nothing. No e-mails either. And Spiggott is so paranoid, he's checking all the outgoing snail-mail himself – there's no way anything can get out of our department without either him or me knowing about it.'

'And yet it is getting out; right under our noses,' said Guy, scratching the back of his head thoughtfully. 'Thank you for that, Miss Irving. Now, remind me, where are we with the case itself?'

'The decree nisi came through yesterday,' said Hez, 'and we're waiting to hear from Mrs Jones's solicitors in response to our counteroffer for settlement.'

'Good!' Guy nodded. 'Maybe, Miss Irving, you'd like to give Mrs Jones's solicitors a ring now and find out how close we are to an agreement. It won't hurt to chivvy them along, and I'm sure Miss Stephens won't mind you sharing her office for a bit. Whilst you're doing that, I'd like to have a good look through the papers by myself. I'll let you know when I've finished with them.'

We took this as our cue to leave.

Hez and I went to the tiny kitchen next to the clerks' room and I made us some coffee; then we walked in silence down the corridor. Hez looked at me a little nervously as we reached the top of the basement stairs.

'It's all right,' I said. 'I'm not going to start berating you about Mark – and you heard what Guy said: you need to ring the other side and find out if we can settle this case sooner rather than later.'

'Lucy,' she began, 'about Saturday – I wasn't coming on to Mark. Honestly I wasn't.'

I took a deep breath. This was it.

'Go on.'

'I was trying to talk him up a bit; you know, make him look good in comparison to Jonathan. I remember what a hard time you had getting over Jon and how much you cared about him, and, well, I was worried you might pass up the chance of being with Mark to pick things up with him again. You see, Jo and I organised that dinner party so you and Mark would see sense and get back together, and I couldn't bear the thought that Jonathan might scupper your chance to make it up with Mark.'

'And the reason I found you wrapped round him like a boa constrictor in the hall was . . . ?'

Hez shook her head and grimaced.

'He was leaving. He'd had enough and went into the hall to get his coat, and I was trying to get it off him and push him back into the living room. However, he jumped to the same conclusion you did about my, um, behaviour and gave his little speech just as you came into earshot – the timing couldn't have been worse. Lucy, I'm so sorry. I feel horribly responsible that I've wrecked things permanently for you and Mark when I was trying to make sure the exact opposite happened.'

I nodded slowly; I could tell she was genuinely sorry. Sadly, however, that wasn't the end of the matter; there were other things we needed to discuss.

'I was in the house, that night in Bristol,' I said quietly. 'I came home early. That's how I knew about you and Jon. I dumped him over it, but he obviously didn't tell you that I knew.'

Hez's face crumpled.

'Oh, Lucy. I . . . oh God.' Words failed her and she looked as if she might be about to cry again. 'What I did was hideous. You see, I had a row with Peter and got all upset; then Jonathan told me that you and he had finished the day before. I wanted to get back at Peter and I wasn't thinking straight, so I . . . You can't imagine how much I hate myself for that. I hated Jonathan too when I found out the truth. The only saving grace was that I didn't think you knew. Oh, bloody hell! Why didn't you say something at the time?'

'I blamed Jonathan. And yes, it hurt like crazy; but the bottom line was that Jonathan was expendable – you weren't. I couldn't imagine my life without you, so I tried to carry on as normal. For what it's worth, I thought it was all forgotten. I didn't come out on Saturday night with the intention of letting you have it with both barrels.'

'Well, whatever, thanks for making the effort to talk. I know it can't have been easy for you to ring me yesterday,' she said.

'I had to. I owe you an apology too, Hez. Saturday night was certainly not my finest hour.'

Hez smiled with relief; then, a moment later, looked serious again. 'Did you mean what you said about Mark, that you're never going to see him again?'

I took a sip of coffee. 'Yes. Even if he did still fancy me after my little outburst, it's just too complicated. I don't think we can ever go back.'

Even before you factor Jonathan into the situation . . .

We started to make our way down the stairs.

'What about you and me, Lou. Can we ever go back?'

'I hope so,' I replied honestly. 'But then again, I thought I'd got over the thing with you and Jon years ago – obviously it had hit me harder than I was prepared to admit. We can talk more tonight if you like.'

'I won't be in tonight,' said Hez, pulling a face. 'I've got to go to some stupid Sheppertons do at the Guildhall.' She turned round to face me. 'Lucy, please believe me when I say I'm sorry. I shouldn't have flirted with Mark; I shouldn't have been so horrible about Jonathan, and I . . .' She paused as a thought struck her. 'Where did you stay on Saturday night, by the way? I sat up waiting for you but you didn't come home.'

Er . . .

'It's a long story,' I said hurriedly. 'I'll buy you a drink sometime and tell you about it.'

Hez gave a big sniff and wiped her nose on the back of her hand.

'Sorry,' she said. 'I warned you not to be nice to me, and I used the last of my tissues in the taxi coming over here.'

'Are you still upset about Spiggott?' I asked, fishing a Kleenex out of my jacket pocket. 'Exactly how bad is it back at the office?'

'Hideous,' said Hez, taking the tissue and blowing her nose vigorously. 'The idea of going into work today was so bad, I cried in the shower.'

'Oh Hez,' I said, rubbing her arm in what I hoped was a suitably supportive manner. 'I really think the time's come for you to get out of there. I've got a copy of the *Law Society Gazette* in my room. After you've spoken to Mrs Jones's lawyers, why don't you ring up a few recruitment firms and I'll sweet-talk Jane into letting you fax your CV off on the chambers' machine?'

Hez managed a feeble smile. 'Why not?' she conceded.

'It'll be a breeze,' I said. 'You'll be free of Spiggott and probably get a big fat pay rise to boot. What's not to . . .'

My voice trailed off. I had thrown open my door – but instead of the chaotic landscape of files, papers and battered furniture that made up my lair, I was confronted by a stunned-looking Hugo popping up from behind my desk, his eyes all bulgy with surprise.

'You're in a meeting with Guy!' he squawked.

'Not any more,' I said grimly, putting my coffee cup down on a rather precarious-looking pile of lever-arch files and folding my arms. 'Hez, shut the door.'

She went one better and leaned against it to prevent Hugo making a quick dash for freedom.

'What the hell do you think you're doing?' I said, advancing towards the desk.

'I was looking for the Smithson papers.'

'Why would you need to do that? Mrs Smithson is *my* client.'

He trembled. Visibly. God, it felt good!

'I know – but there's a short hearing on it tomorrow. I'm, er, doing it instead of you because Guy's had your diary cleared for the next couple of days due to the Jones thing. And – um – and like I said, you should have been in a meeting,' he stuttered.

'So why couldn't you have waited till I got *out* of my meeting, then come and knocked politely on my door and asked me for the file?'

He tripped over a book lying on the floor and fell backwards into my chair.

'Don't sit in my seat, either!' I barked, and enjoyed the sight of Hugo leaping up in confusion and disarray.

Honestly, I could have gone on like this all day.

'And another thing,' my eye caught the label on the folder he was holding, 'if you're looking for the Smithson papers, why are you holding the D'Larney brief?'

'It just came to hand.' He hung his head.

'Give it here.' I held out my hand and he passed it across the desk. 'Now, I can't see any reason why I shouldn't just go straight to Stan and tell him I've caught you red-handed rifling through my things, can you?' I paused for effect. 'Actually, forget Stan; I think this is something that Guy should know about, especially since we have a mole on the Jones case.'

He looked absolutely petrified.

'Cat got your tongue? Right, Hugo, I'm leaving Miss Irving here on guard while I go upstairs to see Guy – and no, she doesn't fancy you and she's never, ever, *ever* going to go out with you, so don't bother asking.'

I turned on my heel and opened the door. On the other side, with her hand raised to knock, was none other than Jane.

'Miss Stephens,' she said, 'Mr Landsdown rang earlier, and when I said you were in a meeting with Mr Jennings, he asked me to get you to call him on this number. He says it's urgent.'

She handed a memo slip over to me.

'Thanks,' I replied, pocketing the slip and wondering why on earth Mark wanted to talk to me.

As soon as Jane was safely out of sight, Hugo walked calmly out of the door and into the corridor beyond.

'So our mutual friend Mark Landsdown wants you to ring him, eh?' he whispered, making sure he was out of Hez's earshot.

'None of your business, Spade,' I replied haughtily.

'Oh, I think it is,' he drawled. 'It would be a shame, wouldn't it, if the fact that you had been seeing Mark Landsdown against Guy's express wishes were to be, how shall I put it, let slip?'

I was almost, but not quite, speechless.

'You wouldn't dare,' I hissed. 'And anyway, the Jones case is almost over. Guy's not going to sack me now.'

'Maybe not,' the Slimy One continued, 'but the same doesn't go for the tenancy meeting next week, does it? You must be pretty sure you're going to win hands down if you're prepared to risk Guy voting against you. Not to mention speaking against you during the meeting and canvassing against you beforehand. Big majority in your favour, is it?'

I hesitated. And that was enough for Hugo to know that he'd won.

'All right,' I spat, 'you've got off this time, but if it ever happens again . . .'

'Rest assured it won't, Looby-Lou. Not least because by this time next week my name will be up on that lovely brass plaque by the front door and you will be unemployed.'

'Don't bank on it, Spade,' I replied and stuck out my tongue at his retreating form.

After I'd slammed the door and kicked the bin over in order to relieve some of my anti-Spade feeling, I sat down behind my desk and stabbed a pencil repeatedly into my notebook.

'He's a pig,' said Hez, after I'd told her how I'd been blackmailed.

'A git.'

'A bastard.'

'A tosser.'

'Okay, so we know we hate him – the question is, what are we going to do about it?' Hez cut to the chase.

I shrugged. 'Nothing. As per usual, he holds all the cards; I'll just have to make sure I keep my door locked in future.'

'Was he really looking for the Smithson file?'

'I have no idea. I gave up trying to figure Hugo out a long time ago.'

Hez leaned over the desk and lowered her voice. 'The Jones leaks – it couldn't be him, could it?'

I thought about it for a bit and sipped my disgustingly cold coffee.

'I'd love it to be him, but he doesn't have any motive.'

'Yes he does: the leaks will embarrass you and he stands a better chance of getting the tenancy.'

'He can do that without leaking confidential information to the press and jeopardising his own career. Every day he's alive and breathing is an embarrassment to me,' I reminded her.

Hez grinned for the first time that morning. 'Call it a hunch, but I'd keep my eye on him if I were you. Anyway, forget Hugo; what are we going to do now?'

'Well,' I said, taking another sip of disgusting coffee, 'first things first: we go and put these cups of coffee in the chambers' microwave.'

'Then?'

'You ring Mrs Jones's solicitors.'

'And then?'

'Then we get your CV in order and you prepare to enter the job market.'

If I was being honest with myself, I wasn't entirely sure why I was ringing Mark. Of course, the overt reason was because he had left a message asking me to – but as for the real *why*, I found myself at a bit of a loss. He was undoubtedly a great bloke and I'd been attracted to him like an iron filling to a particularly handsome magnet, but none of that could make up for the fact that every time we got together it all went gut-wrenchingly, heart-achingly wrong.

So, whatever the reason he had rung, I was going to have to tell him (again) that we were better off apart.

Later, while Hez trotted upstairs to draft yet another offer of settlement with Guy on the Jones case, and I'd checked Hugo was busy in a courtroom on the other side of London, I picked up my mobile and dialled Mark's number.

'Hi! Mark here. Sorry I can't take your call right now. If you'd like to leave your name . . .'

Bugger! Still, I'd leave a message and ask him to ring me at home.

'Oh, hiya, Mark. It's Lucy returning your call from earlier. Please don't ring me back on my work number. If you need to talk urgently, you can get me in Muswell Hill after—'

'Hi – Lucy?' Mark picked up. 'Thank God.'

He sounded very out of breath.

'Goodness!' I was concerned. 'What's up?'

'Lucy, I need to see you. I *have* to see you. Are you busy this afternoon?'

Oh God! The message hadn't got through on Saturday – he was obviously still hoping for a reconciliation.

'Listen, Mark,' I began slowly and gently. 'You and me – well, it always seems to go wrong between us. I think we need to be honest with ourselves and ask whether this is actually—'

'No, you don't understand!' he interrupted. 'Please, Lucy; I need you.'

'Oh Mark,' I sighed. 'I just don't know if now is—'

'Lucy,' he butted in, 'this is about Josh – not us. I don't want to have to explain it all on the phone, so can you come round? I need some advice and there isn't anyone else I can ask.'

'No,' I said firmly, hating the way I'd felt my heart sink slightly at the news that it wasn't me he was focused on. My love life was complicated enough as it was, without any feelings for Mark making their presence felt. 'If this is about Josh, there is certainly no way I can get involved. You saw how much trouble there was when I acted for Jennifer. But,' I paused as a thought struck me, 'what do you need me for anyway? You've already got a legal team – why don't you just set up a meeting with Tony?'

Tony Harding was Mark's solicitor and another friend of mine from law school. He was a kind-hearted, blokey sort of a man and I knew that he and Mark got on like a house on fire.

There was silence from the other end of the phone, then:

'He's not acting for me any more.'

'*What?*'

'We had a meeting a week ago and he reckoned it would be plain sailing from now on because things with Josh were going so smoothly.'

'So? Tell him it's all gone pear-shaped and you need him and Hugo back on the case.'

'I can't. I'm broke.'

This wasn't making any sense.

'But how ... Have you lost your job or something? I thought you just got promoted?'

'I did. But buying into the partnership cleaned me out and then there's – oh, never mind. I can't afford Tony's fees and that's all there is to it.'

It didn't sound like he had a whole lot of options, but what could I do? Basically, the whole thing was a no-go zone: if Guy ever found out I'd been advising Mark, it would be like putting a large amount of dynamite underneath my career and then pressing the 'Explode' button. And that was before you took into account the hideously complicated personal circumstances that Mark and I found ourselves in.

Or, for that matter, what a certain Jennifer Woodford would make of it all ...

'What about Jennifer?' I asked, a trace of desperation in my voice. 'If she finds out I'm helping you, she'll go into orbit.'

'Sod Jenny,' he said. 'This is all her stupid fault anyway. You are the only person who can help, Lucy; *please* say you'll come over.'

This wasn't so much a request as a howl of anguish.

'All right then. But you have to understand we keep things on a strictly professional footing from now on. I'll ring you when I'm on my way.'

'Thanks, Lucy, you have no idea how grateful I am.'

I put the phone down and slumped back in my chair. I had to be stark raving mad to agree to do this – but hearing Mark's despair, I also knew I didn't have a choice.

Ignoring the voices in my head, which were screaming at me not to get involved, I picked up the phone and dialled Jo. It would be a good idea to get some background info before I went round, and it was a racing certainty that Mark had spoken about the situation to Dave.

'Hi, Lucy.' Jo came on the line.

'Hi,' I said a bit sheepishly. We hadn't talked since Saturday, although I had texted her to tell her I was okay and to apologise for ranting at her dinner guests over the pavlova. 'How are things?'

'Yes, no need to worry. Dave and I got stuck into the leftover wine and talked properly for the first time in years. Then we went to bed and made up properly.'

'Good,' I said enthusiastically, even though this was slightly more information than I was happy to receive. 'I spoke to Mark.'

'Ah.'

'Yes, "ah" indeed. What's going on?'

'Hasn't he told you?' She sounded a little shocked. 'I said he should ring you right away and fill you in.'

'He called,' I confirmed, 'but he wouldn't give any details over the phone.'

'Well, it's about Josh.'

'That much I do know,' I replied.

'Jenny's taking him to Hong Kong.'

I actually dropped the receiver. '*Hong Kong!*' I echoed.

No wonder Mark had sounded frantic.

'She's got some shit-hot new job with her bank and they're going to pay her about a million pounds a minute to go out there. The catch is that because Josh lives with her, he's going too.'

'Bugger.'

'As you say, bugger,' confirmed Jo. 'He got the letter from her solicitors this morning and there's a thirty-minute hearing listed next week at short notice to sort out witnesses, statements and so forth.'

'No wonder he's panicking,' I said.

'Which is where you come in,' Jo replied. 'If you're

good enough for the PM, you're good enough for our Mr Landsdown.'

'How did you know I was acting for Llew Jones?' I asked, hoping Guy wasn't bugging my phone line.

'Bar grapevine, sweetie; it's common knowledge. Now, get yourself over to Mark's and sort him out. I've told him you won't be able do the hearing, but you can go through the law with him, tell him what to say and be there cheering him on from the sidelines. Let's kick some ass and keep that boy in the country.'

I put the phone back on its hook and sat back in my chair. Jo might sound upbeat, but that was because she specialised in tax and had no idea how unlikely it was that Josh would be doing anything apart from getting on a BA flight to China. You see, the law here was very clear: if the parent with whom a child is living wants to up sticks and move abroad – particularly if there is a fabby new job in the offing – the court almost never says no.

And I was going to have to explain all this to Mark; the man who, after four long years, had only just succeeded in seeing his son on a regular basis.

It was going to kill him.

I shook myself. I couldn't let this happen – I just *couldn't*. Maybe if I scoured the law reports, went through the papers with a fine-toothed comb and racked my brains, perhaps I would stumble across something we could use as leverage to put up a fight.

Because that was what Mark needed to do now: fight – like he never had before.

The rest of the day passed in something of a blur. I remember packing Hez and the Jones papers off in a taxi back to Sheppertons at about half-three (Guy had drawn a blank) and I then spent the remainder of the afternoon with my nose in a variety of law books. As soon as I had ascertained there wasn't any urgent work for me to crack on with, I scooped up as many of the books as I could physically carry and made my way to Blackfriars station.

The Mark who opened the door of his flat was not the man I had left sitting on the arm of Jo and Dave's sofa wearing a grey cashmere overcoat. That Mark had been embarrassed and twitchy, but he'd been a darn sight happier than the one now standing in front of me.

'Come in,' he said, summoning up the ghost of a smile – which seemed to be directed at the pile of volumes I had brought rather than at me. 'Cup of tea or something?'

I looked at the clock. It was seven o'clock: normally that was corkscrew time. But not tonight: tonight there was to be no room for error.

I nodded. 'Tea would be great. Now, where are the papers?'

Mark gestured to the dining table at the far end of the living room. Piled up in the middle was a mound of lever-arch files that contained virtually every detail of his private life over the past four years, probably including me. There was no way Jennifer would have been able to resist firing off a few angry letters concerning my involvement in the whole sorry affair.

I popped my portable law library on the floor next to Mark's tasteful brown leather sofa, went over to the table and started flicking through the lever-arches. Thankfully Tony was incredibly organised and everything was neatly filed according to topic, document type and chronology. Even so, the sheer volume of papers meant that getting to grips with it all would be no easy task. I took off my jacket, put the files on the floor next to my law books and prepared to wade through it all.

On the other side of the tiny hallway that bisected his flat, Mark was clattering away in the kitchen. He was filling the kettle, finding tea bags and looking for the milk: essentially going through the motions of normal life when inside he was probably scared to death that next Tuesday would effectively end his relationship with his little boy. Please God, I prayed silently, don't let this be the killer blow that lets Jennifer walk away victorious.

Mark came back into the room and handed me a mug of tea.

'How's it looking?' he asked.

I forced a sort of twisted smile.

'I haven't really got going yet,' I said, gesturing to the sea of paperwork that surrounded me on all sides. 'It'll take me a while.'

Mark regarded me with an almost inscrutable expression.

'Tony gave me a free half an hour's advice. He reckons that if the parent making the application is the one with whom the child normally lives, in the absence of extraordinary circumstances, they'll win.'

Mark didn't take his eyes off me once as he spoke; he was waiting for me to tell him Tony had it wrong.

But I couldn't; Tony had it spot on.

Except I found it impossible to make my mouth move and produce those words. So I muttered:

'Well, I'd better find you some extraordinary circumstances, hadn't I?'

Mark's eyes closed and his face relaxed momentarily. He was allowing himself the luxury of hope.

'Okay,' he said quietly, 'I'll leave you to it. You don't mind if I boot up the laptop, do you? I'm no good at sitting around waiting.'

'Be my guest,' I replied. 'We'll speak later.'

And that was how we passed the next hour. Me sitting on the floor reading; Mark staring at his computer screen and punctuating the silence with the click-click-click of his keyboard.

It didn't matter if he'd been thrilled or not the day that Jennifer had told him about the second blue line on her pregnancy test; the fact that he had four years of paperwork documenting his fight to be a part of Josh's life was testament enough to his love for his son. But it hadn't been easy for him.

Reading through the letters and affidavits, it became clear that Jennifer had used every trick in the book to try and keep Mark and Joshua apart – and had thankfully failed. Through it all, Mark had taken on the chin whatever she'd thrown at him and kept plugging away, not letting anything interfere with his ultimate goal of spending time with his son.

There were photos that managed to bring a lump to my throat, hard-bitten, cynical lawyer that I am: Mark with a smiling Josh on his shoulders; Mark at the beach teaching his son how to hold a cricket bat; and an A4-size digital print of the pair of them, their faces contorted with laughter as Josh carefully placed a big blob of blue paint on his father's nose. Mark should have been a contender for Dad of the Year; but instead here was Jennifer about to rip him apart by carting Josh off to the other side of the world.

And you know the thought that kept popping into my head? *There should be a law against it.*

I couldn't help remembering the various dads I'd encountered in my professional life: dads who didn't give a damn; dads who beat up their partners while their traumatised offspring looked on in horror; dads who would rather see their kids go hungry than hand a penny over in child support. I'd seen it all, heard every excuse under the sun and bought the T-shirt; and it threw Mark's dedication into even sharper relief.

Then, at the point where I could happily have written to the Pope nominating Mark for instant sainthood, it was time for me to read Jennifer's side of the story.

And it came as a bit of a shock.

Knowing Jennifer, I'd assumed her 'promotion' had been engineered by her purely to put as much distance between Mark and Josh as humanly possible. However, reading her court application form cast doubt on that theory. Yes – she *had* been promoted, but not merely one or two positions above her current one. This was a really big deal: she was being offered the job of running the Far East office for her bank. I whistled under my breath. From what I knew about the world of international finance, it could sometimes be pretty difficult to get on once you'd pushed out a sprog, and yet here was Jennifer – a talented, successful (although admittedly mad) individual – forging ahead.

And here was me, about to try and stop her.

Because that was what successfully challenging her application would mean: for Josh and Mark to keep on laughing and playing cricket together, Jennifer was going to lose either the job – or custody of her son.

But now was not the time for me to get maudlin, because my concern was Mark, and moreover, *I'd had an idea*. Not a cast-iron-guarantee, we-can-win-this-one-no-sweat sort of idea; it was more a glimmer of hope.

But it was worth a shot.

I snapped the file shut and Mark looked up from his laptop.

'All done?' he said.

I nodded. 'Glass of wine?' I asked tentatively. Something more than a cup of PG Tips was needed to get us through the discussion we were about to have.

It was his turn to nod. He slid off his chair and disappeared back into the kitchen. I followed. Spread out on the counter next to the hob were some estate agent's particulars. They were for a cottagey-looking white terraced house in Highgate, covered in overgrown rosebushes and with an old-fashioned front door.

'Business?' I asked. 'Or pleasure?'

Mark looked up from the drawer in which he'd been rummaging for the corkscrew.

'Pleasure,' he said. 'We're exchanging contracts on Wednesday.'

First his partnership and now this. I was seriously behind the times.

'Congratulations,' I said. 'But I thought you were broke?'

'I am,' he explained, 'in no little measure due to that place. I had to take out a loan to get the deposit and now I'm going to be mortgaged up to the hilt for the rest of eternity. But it'll be worth it once I've had all the work done.'

'It looks lovely,' I replied, fingering the brochure and wishing I was in a position to live somewhere like that.

Mark nodded. 'Decent-sized living room, a dining room/study, good bathroom – or it will be when there's actually a bath in there. Two bedrooms . . .' His voice tailed off.

'One for Josh?'

He nodded and concentrated his energy on uncorking the wine.

I didn't feel I could avoid the subject any longer.

'Even if next week doesn't go your way, you do know

you'll continue to see him, don't you? He can still have his own room in the new house.'

I almost added, 'and you'll still be his dad', but as that was both painfully obvious and also smacked of badly scripted Hollywood schmaltz, I held back.

'Lucy, be honest with me. Is it a foregone conclusion that I'll lose?' Mark said, an almost unbearable dignity in his voice.

That wasn't one I could answer with a straight 'yes' or 'no'.

'Let's go and sit down,' I said, accepting a glass of wine, 'and I'll take you through the paperwork.'

We pushed the slew of files and papers to one side and sat next to each other on the floor.

'Okay,' he said, 'shoot.'

'I'd like to get some extra information on Jennifer first,' I said, taking the lid off my pen. 'How long, exactly, have you known her?'

He furrowed his brow. 'I think we first met about seven years ago. She used to work at the same place as Dave.'

Ah, Dave. Did he introduce Mark to all his girlfriends? I wondered.

'Yes,' he went on, slightly sheepishly, 'in fact she was Dave's boss.'

'Really?' I said, making a note. 'And she's' – I scanned the court application form – 'four years older than you.'

'We got together about a year after we first met. But she was never off duty, you know? The phone, the pager, the e-mails; she didn't know how to switch off. After six months I tried to finish it, but she wouldn't take no for an answer and two months later we were back together.' He paused. 'If it happened now, I'd be changing the locks and going ex-directory, but back then I just thought it was proof of how much she felt for me; I was flattered. And we sort of kept that break-up/make-up pattern for the next two years.'

'And then?'

'Then we had one of our usual bust-ups, but this time I told her it was over for good.'

Mark took a large glug of wine and started to fiddle with one of his cufflinks.

'I'd met someone else – where I used to work – and the whole on/off thing with Jennifer was wearing a bit thin. So I took her out for a drink to explain that I meant what I said about us being over for good, and she told me she was pregnant. I felt I owed it to her – and to Josh, as it turned out – to try again, but it was a living nightmare. In the end I left. In fact, I moved out of London for a while.' He paused. 'Doesn't that sound awful?'

I shook my head. 'No,' I told him. 'You gave it your best shot and it didn't work. It happens. The grown-up thing was to hold your hands up, admit defeat and then bow out gracefully.'

Mark closed his eyes and let out a short but heartfelt sigh.

'It didn't feel like that at the time,' he admitted.

'I can understand that,' I said. 'There must have been times since when it felt as if it was taking over your life.'

Mark nodded and gave me a half-smile. 'I suppose you could say it's cramped my style on occasions.'

'I know how Jenny reacted over the girl you saw last year,' I confessed. 'That sounded particularly rough.'

'It wasn't pretty,' he admitted. 'We went through a really bad patch over it.'

It struck me then for the first time: when he spoke about Jennifer, he often made it sound as if the pair of them were still an item. How weird was that?

Mark continued in a low voice. 'She wouldn't let me see Josh if Sam – Samantha – was there. Jenny said Josh was upset at the thought of having another mummy. Not that it ever got that serious between me and Sam, of course.' He ran a hand through his hair. 'I only saw her for a couple of months, and that's far too early to start thinking in terms of . . . Well, it was with Sam, anyway.'

'But you broke up with Sam because of Jenny's reaction to her?'

'I suppose so. But who knows what would have happened in the long term? Chances are it wouldn't have worked out.'

I took a large gulp of wine to mask my reaction to his words. That was exactly the sort of thing I always said about my relationships, only coming from the mouth of a decent, successful, handsome bloke like Mark, it sounded unbearably negative. Maybe it was time for both of us to think about changing the script.

'Is that how you always feel? I asked. 'Jenny denies you the opportunity of a new relationship, and rather than fight for it, you pack up your emotional tent and walk off alone into the sunset. What about you? What about what Mark Landsdown wants? Isn't that important?'

'Of course what I want is important.' He didn't sound very convinced.

'You know you and Jenny,' I went on. 'Do you somehow feel safer going over the same old ground with her rather than giving it a go with someone like Sam?'

What I meant, of course, was 'someone like me', but Mark wasn't in the mood to decode my subtext.

'It's not as simple as that, Lucy. Unlike you, I can't afford to put myself first. I – oh, what's the point? You don't know what it's like to have a child.' He put his wine glass down and rubbed his face.

A little spark of resentment flared up in me. Whether or not I had kids had nothing to do with my ability to understand his situation, just as ultimately Josh had nothing to do with Mark's ability to find a loving relationship.

'I might not be a parent, but I've dealt with more

cases like yours than you've had hot dinners,' I said quietly. 'It may surprise you to know it, but you are not the first father – or mother, come to that – who has had to fight to see their kid. It's crap, it's ugly, but I deal with this sort of stuff day in and day out and I do know what I'm talking about, so please believe me when I say that you can't put your whole life on hold simply because you have a child. It might sound all gritty and self-sacrificing, Mark, but it's not how things should be.'

Mark was not a happy camper. 'I'm sorry, I didn't realise you were a qualified therapist as well as a lawyer. Do you do this to all your clients – dictate to them how to live their lives?'

I was so worked up, I threw the file I was leaning my notebook on down on to the floor. It emitted a sort of 'flup' noise as the lever-arch sprang open and a slew of pages slid out on to the floor.

'Bloody hell, Mark! You are *not* one of my clients.'

'Well, what am I then?'

Mark gave me a searching look, but try as I might, I could not quite read his expression.

'I don't know,' I said at last.

Mark's eyes did not leave my face for one moment; then he opened his mouth as though he were about to speak – before abruptly closing it again. I looked away, unable to bear the intensity of his gaze one second longer.

'Anyway,' I did my best to gather up the tattered remnants of my professionalism, 'it's all rather academic now, isn't it? I'm here to advise you on the best way of winning your case, and that's all that matters.' I tapped my finger on the open page of my notebook. 'Now, you're saying Jennifer's always been full on with her career?'

Mark took a large slug of wine, the moment passed and we settled back into business mode once again.

'Jennifer's career,' he said, guiding the conversation

round to a more neutral topic. 'She's frighteningly bright. Double first from Cambridge, MBA from Princeton. She always said it was her ambition to be the first female governor of the Bank of England, and I've no reason to think she won't do it.'

'And is the move out to Hong Kong pretty much what you would expect from her?'

He took a moment to consider this.

'No,' he said. 'I'd always assumed she'd stay in London. Even though she's done her level best to keep me and Josh apart, I'd always hoped that somewhere down the line she'd realise it was good for him to have me in his life. Now I'm not so sure.'

I scribbled this down.

'Okay, next question. Do you think she has been trying to scupper contact between you and Josh as payback for you leaving her, or are you charitable enough to think that she is just a control freak who finds it hard to delegate *anything*, let alone responsibility for her child?'

Mark managed a wry smile. 'Whose side are you on, Lucy?'

'If you're going to fight this, I need an honest answer. Now, you know her pretty well – which is it?'

Mark paused and furrowed his brow thoughtfully.

'I actually think it's both. She *is* frighteningly adept at control freakery, and she's used it to regulate not only my relationship with Josh, but also as much of the rest of my life as she can – hence the fuss over Sam. But why all this psychology?'

'Know your enemy, Mark: it's the first rule of battle. You learn what their weakness is and you use it against them. In this case, Jenny's is that she's very controlling – and we are going to make that work for us. From what I've just read, she's lost the battle over contact. If she continues to mess around with Josh visiting you on a Saturday, the court has said it will either send her to prison or make an order stating that Josh is to live with you. Right?'

'Right.'

'Now, unpleasant as it might be, I want you to imagine for a moment that you are Jennifer. Can you do that?'

Mark pulled a face. 'I suppose so.'

'Right then, Jennifer. You really, really want to stop Mark, that horrible ex of yours, from seeing your son, but the courts in England aren't having any of it and you don't fancy a stretch in Holloway for breaching the order that Josh sees his dad. What do you do?'

'I get a promotion, move to the other side of the planet and take Josh with me?'

'Got it in one. Now, the court appointment next Tuesday is only a short one – half an hour or so. Its purpose is to get everything set up for a full hearing in about a week's time. At that main hearing, Jennifer will be trying to convince the judge that this new job of hers is a once-in-a-lifetime, bona fide opportunity that she'd be nuts not to accept. And I have to say that from the paperwork, that is a reasonable conclusion for a judge to reach. What *you* will need to do, if you are going to have a hope in hell of stopping her, is to convince the judge that Jenny's promotion is not about her career at all, but has come about because she is hell-bent on keeping you and Josh apart. And to achieve that, you're going to have to drag up every unpleasant thing she's ever done to you and use it in evidence against her.'

Mark gave a sharp intake of breath. 'She's not going to be too happy about that.'

A tiny understatement on Mark's part. To say that Jennifer wasn't going to be too happy about it was like saying the USA entered World War Two after having a difference of opinion with Japan over the bombing of Pearl Harbor.

'I know; and if you do follow my advice, any goodwill

Jenny might feel towards you now – and I appreciate it isn't much – is likely to vanish.'

'I see.' He didn't sound very enthusiastic.

I wasn't done with the bad news yet.

'Something else you'll need to consider is what will happen if you *do* win. On a purely practical level, it will mean that either Jennifer passes up her promotion and stays in London, or Josh moves in with you but loses his mummy.'

Mark nodded thoughtfully.

'It's not going to be easy, Mark,' I said softly. 'Somewhere along the line, one of you is going to have to make a huge sacrifice; and before we set the ball rolling in terms of sworn statements and cross-examinations, you need to be one hundred per cent certain that fighting this case is actually for the best.'

'Okay,' Mark replied, 'I'll make sure I am. Believe me, the last thing I want is for any of us to go through more avoidable pain. But let me get this straight: if I do everything you've suggested, it puts me in a strong position?'

Shit. I must have sounded too positive. Putting my pen and notebook down, I swivelled round to face him.

'Tony wasn't having you on when he told you how difficult this was going to be. The route I've just described gives you nothing more than a slim chance. However, in my opinion it's the only chance you've got.'

'Right.'

He got up and walked over to the window. He stood there in silence for a minute or so, looking out over the back garden of the flat downstairs.

Right at that moment, my mobile started bleeping its *Mission: Impossible* ring tone. As musical interludes went, it seemed highly appropriate, however much the timing sucked.

'Hello?' I said, wrestling it out of my handbag and straight to my ear.

'Hi, Lucy,' came Jonathan's voice on the other end.

I leapt up and rushed into the kitchen, my palms cold and clammy and my stomach churning.

'Is this a bad time?' Jonathan asked.

'About as bad as it could be,' I said. 'What can I do for you?'

'I've just spoken to Tom. He'd love to meet you.'

'Thanks, you're a total star and I owe you. Now, are you dying?'

'No.'

'Trapped under a heavy object and in danger of being squashed to death?'

'No.'

'Stuck up Mount Everest and about to pass out from hypothermia?'

'No. Should I be?'

'Then I'm afraid I'm going to have to go. I'm dealing with a bit of a crisis.'

'Okey-dokey,' said Jonathan cheerfully. 'I'll speak to you soon.'

And we rang off.

'I am so sorry about that,' I said, re-entering the living room and chucking the phone back in my bag.

Mark hadn't moved an inch.

'Have you reached any conclusions about what you want to do?'

There was no answer.

'Look,' I said, picking up my pen and notebook and putting them in my bag, 'there's no need to make a decision today. Sleep on it and we'll talk about it again tomorrow. I'm going to run this by my old pupil master and see if he has any ideas. He's done masses of these sorts of cases and he might be able to think of some other avenue we could try.'

There was still no reaction from Mark.

I walked over to the window and stood behind him.

His fists were clenched and his breathing was fast and shallow. He lifted his right hand and then, without any warning, hit the wooden window frame as hard as he could.

'Jesus Christ, Lucy! I'm going to lose him, aren't I?'

I'd never seen him like this. In fact I don't think I'd *ever* seen anyone so eaten up with frustration and anger. It was frightening.

'No you won't, Mark,' I said as authoritatively as I could. 'Even if he moves abroad, the court will order that you see each other at least a couple of times a year. Whilst he's little, you may have to travel out to Hong Kong to visit, but as he gets older he'll be able to fly on his own and—'

'You don't get it, do you?' said Mark, glowering out across the back gardens of Dartmouth Park Road. 'There's no way Jenny's ever going to put him on a plane to see me – and even less of a chance she'll let me into her house to visit him. This is it. If I don't win this case, Josh won't have a dad any more.'

'That's not true, Mark; I can promise you—'

He shook his head angrily. 'No you can't, Lucy; you can't promise me anything. He's four years old, and if I don't see him regularly, the fact is that he'll forget me. Most of the time he doesn't have a clue what he had for breakfast – six months down the road, he's not going to remember who I am.'

He paused and took a deep breath.

'I know what it's like to grow up without a dad,' he continued, 'and I've spent the past few years trying to ensure my son doesn't do the same. Only I've failed. Look at me, Lucy; in the fatherhood stakes, I'm a complete loser.'

I opened my mouth to deny this, but there didn't seem to be any point; what he needed right then was someone in his corner. I took the two steps over to the window and slipped my hand into his. Whatever the ins and outs of our past relationship might have been, my heart was breaking for him.

I looked at him, and for the first time he dragged his gaze away from the window and met mine. His eyes were rather red and watery, and something that looked suspiciously like a tear was trying to slip out of the corner of one of them. Almost immediately, he looked away again. I lifted my hand up to his face and smudged the almost-tear away with my thumb.

'You'd better go,' he said. 'You'll be in big trouble if Guy finds out you've seen me.'

'He's not going to find out,' I replied, squeezing his hand. 'And besides, you needed me. What else was I going to do?'

I pulled him back from the window.

'Look,' I went on, taking his other hand in mine, 'I know it's easy for me to say, but try not to worry about it too much. Concentrate on making the right decision, and then, if you decide to fight, we'll give it everything we've got, right?'

There was another pause.

'Everything may not be enough, Lucy.'

Even though his voice was almost expressionless, there was still a slight catch in it. I couldn't bear it any longer and threw my arms round him.

'Please, Mark – don't do this to yourself. You've got to stay positive. Do it for Josh if you can't manage it for yourself.'

He didn't reply; instead he buried his face in my hair and held me tight.

Then the unmistakable *Mission: Impossible* theme ripped through the air again.

'Are you going to get it?' Mark asked the top of my head.

'No, it'll only be – oh, just let it ring,' I mumbled into his chest.

The phone switched on to voicemail and the bleeping stopped. Mark softly kissed my hair and then pulled away slightly.

'Thanks,' he said, smoothing away a few stray wisps from my face. 'That was just what the doctor ordered.'

'Any time.' I smiled at him.

He looked at me very intently, a finger tracing the line of my jaw from my ear to my chin.

'I wish I could take you up on that,' he murmured.

Then, before I quite knew what was happening, his lips brushed mine. And again before I was entirely sure what I was doing, my mouth opened slightly and I found myself kissing him. He tasted of tea, Chardonnay and himself and it was delicious.

With tremendous self-restraint, I pulled away. Mark looked at me, stroking my hair away from my face and tucking it behind my ears.

'Nothing happened on Saturday with Hez and me. You know that, don't you?' he said softly.

I nodded.

'In fact,' he went on, putting his hand under my chin and making me look up into his eyes, 'I think her performance was for Jonathan's benefit rather than mine.'

I froze momentarily at the mention of Jonathan's name, but Mark put his arms round me and pulled me closer, his mouth on mine, and I found myself instinctively yielding to him. This wasn't the urgent, heated snogging of our first encounter, when we'd fallen on each other the moment the front door of his flat had been closed. Or even the weirdly unsettling stuff I'd experienced with Jonathan. This was deep, eyes-closed, kiss-me-for-ever-type action, and, as always with Mark, I never wanted it to stop. I remember thinking, 'It'll all end in tears, you know'; but even as the words formed in my head, my lips were parting that little bit wider and I was sinking further into his arms.

I ran my hands over his body, feeling the movement of his back, neck and throat as his mouth pulled on mine. His shirt worked lose and I shimmied my fingers along his spine, through the slight smattering of hair on his chest and down over his stomach. The smell of his skin, the taste of his mouth, the sensation of his hands moving over me was overwhelming. The more I had of him, the more I wanted: the man was like a Class A drug.

I pulled away again. 'Look, Mark,' I said, as I caught my breath, 'should we be doing this?'

'No,' he replied. 'There are many, *many* reasons why me kissing you is a monumentally bad idea.'

As he spoke, his hand was meandering its way up my left leg. I turned my face in towards his chest and inhaled deeply, waiting for one of us to make the move and break the spell.

But instead, with Mark infiltrating and overwhelming my senses, all the tiresome irrelevancies of our situation suddenly fell away. None of it actually mattered – not Guy, not Jennifer, not our own insecurities, not even Jonathan. It was just him and me; in our own space, our own private bit of time.

'You're probably right,' I said, before taking a step back and slowly and deliberately undoing the buttons on my shirt.

I slipped it off over my shoulders and deposited it floorwards. It landed on top of a letter from Jennifer berating Mark for spending that fateful weekend with me and not answering her calls. How appropriate, I thought, as I stretched up once more to reach his lips.

Then my phone rang – *again*; but by this time, with Mark's mouth just below my ear and his fingers pulling the straps of my bra down over my shoulders, it barely registered.

'Just one more thing,' I murmured.

'Mmm?' asked Mark, transferring his lips from my ear lobe to my collar bone.

'I seem to remember that your bed is much more comfortable than your living-room floor.'

He smiled. 'I was about to make the same suggestion.'

And he took my hand and led me across the hallway.

I opened my eyes in a bleary sort of way, my brain registering the fact that it was no longer dark. Then panic gripped me like a boa constrictor and I sat up in bed with a start.

'Shit! It's six o'clock!'

Mark's arm wound its way round my waist and pulled me back down into the warm cocoon of the duvet.

'So? You never have to be in court before nine, do you?'

'I'm not in court,' I protested, struggling half-heartedly but actually enjoying it as he tightened his grip, 'but I need to be at chambers for eight.'

'That's two hours away. You've still got bags of time.'

He rolled over and spooned up against me, lazily tracing his fingers across my waist and kissing the back of my neck.

'No I haven't. I have to get home, shower, change, catch the tube—'

'Why eight?' he asked, his mouth poised above my ear lobe.

'Breakfast meeting on the Jones case,' I said, luxuriating in the warmth of his body against mine. 'Guy wants me in first thing to— Oh, rats; I shouldn't have said any of that.'

Mark, who had been in the process of running his lips from my shoulder blade up into my hair line, stopped mid-nuzzle.

'Jones? Do you mean Llewellyn Jones?'

Bugger, *bugger*!

'Uh-huh,' I admitted guiltily.

'That's your big case, isn't it?'

'The biggest ever,' I confirmed. 'And also possibly the worst-kept secret in the world.'

'Well,' he said after a pause, 'I suppose it's not everyone who gets dumped because their girlfriend has a gig as the PM's lawyer.'

'I didn't feel I had any choice,' I protested. 'It was probably the hardest decision I've ever had to make.'

'Well, for what it's worth,' Mark replied, 'I was to blame as well. Maybe if I'd shouted less, we'd have been able to work something out. Oh Lou, I really wish things hadn't turned out the way they have.'

'Me too, Mark, me too.'

He didn't reply. Instead he put all his effort into kissing my shoulders and as much of my throat as he could reach.

There was no way I was getting out of that bed.

'Please, Mark,' a thought struck me, '*please* don't tell anyone I mentioned the Jones case. It's been awful – someone's been leaking stuff to the *Stoat* and we don't know who it is, and if anyone found out I'd told you . . .'

'I promise,' he replied – and then paused, a wry smile on his face.

'The only question is,' he continued, rolling me over on to my back, 'what price my silence?'

As we climbed the hill towards Highgate in Mark's car half an hour later, I pulled my phone out of my bag.

'*You have four new messages.*'

Hmmm. I pressed the button and waited. The first one was Jonathan.

'I've had a call from Tom. Can you ring him before ten tomorrow? His mobile number is 077—'

Oh, no, *Jonathan*. I guiltily pressed the 'save' option and went on to the next message: it was Hez.

'Lou? I'm off to the Guildhall now but I'm going to try and get home as soon as I can so we can talk properly. Thanks for this morning and hope to see you back at the flat later.'

Hearing her voice perked me up a bit. Right. So I needed to call Hez, explain I'd been waylaid by Mark (ah-hem) the night before, and say that I'd see her tonight. Given the hours she'd been doing lately, she'd probably already be at her desk being shouted at by Spiggott.

The next one was from my dad.

'Lucy I need you to ring me and explain this capitalisation of maintenance thingy that my solicitor is going on about. It sounds expensive, but if it gets your mother off my back it might just be worth it. Do you know what she did on Saturday? She—'

I pressed delete. With everything else going on in my life, there was no way I had the emotional energy to get involved with the parents' squabbles. I accessed my final message. To my surprise it was another from Hez – only she sounded dreadful.

'Lou, ring me!' She was sobbing so hard she was almost incoherent. 'You have to ring me!'

'Mark!' I cried, exiting my voicemail and dialling the flat. 'Something's happened to Hez. Shit!' I exclaimed as I got through only to hear the 'beep beep beep' of the engaged tone.

'What's up?' Mark's voice was low and concerned.

'I don't know,' I said, redialling and clenching my teeth in frustration as I failed once more to get through. 'It's engaged.'

'She's probably trying to ring you,' he said.

I ended my call, and sure enough, as soon as I did so, *Mission: Impossible* filled the car.

'Hi? Hez?'

'Lou – where are you?'

'In Mark's car – we've just passed the end of Highgate Woods. What's up?'

'I don't know – I can't open my eyes.' She sounded terrified.

'We're coming,' I told her. 'Don't move.'

'What's the problem?' asked Mark.

'She can't see,' I replied. 'Step on it, Mark!'

We skooshed over the railway bridge, up the hill and on to the Broadway. Mark stopped on the double yellows outside the flat to let me out before driving round the corner to park legally, whilst I raced up the stairs and opened the front door. Hez was curled up on the sofa wearing the same clothes as the day before. Actually, that made two of us – the difference being, of course, that she hadn't spent the night in the bed of a structural engineer.

'Hez,' I panted, rushing over to the sofa and putting my arms round her, 'what the hell's happened?'

'Everything,' she said, burying her face in my shoulder and clinging on to me as if her life depended on it. 'And my eyelids are glued shut.'

Mark's footsteps pounded up the stairs and into the flat.

'Where are you?' he called. 'Is she all right?'

'In here,' I yelled.

Mark ran in and knelt down next to me, prising Hez's face away from my shoulder.

'Let me have a look,' he said calmly, taking her head in his hands and gazing intently at her face.

'I fell asleep on the sofa and now my eyes are stuck!' she wailed.

'Right!' he said, jumping up and fishing his car keys from his trouser pocket. 'Lou, put her shoes on and bring her down the stairs. I'll get the car out front.'

'Where are we going?' I asked, bewildered.

He bent down and kissed the top of my head.

'Casualty, kitten. Your learned friend here appears to have dropped off with her contact lenses still in.'

Poor Hez was in an awful state as I steered her down the stairs and into the back seat of Mark's car. I jumped in with her, put her seat belt on and held her hand as we bombed back down Muswell Hill Broadway.

'What on earth happened at the Guildhall?' I asked.

Hez shook her head sorrowfully. 'It was awful. It was the worst night of my life.'

'But you were at a client function,' I protested. 'What can go wrong at a client function?'

Hez gave a little whimper and buried her head in her hands. 'Spiggott,' she whispered.

'Hez's boss,' I translated for Mark, who had just shot me a concerned look via the rear-view mirror. 'He's a total wanker. He's got this idea in his head that she could be the source of the leaks in the Jones case.'

At the sound of the name 'Jones', Hez gave a squeal and clapped her hands across her mouth; but whether it was because it aroused unpleasant memories or because she thought I was being a blabbermouth, I'm not sure.

'It's okay,' Mark reassured her. 'Lucy did let it slip but she bought my silence pretty easily. It won't go any further.'

'You haven't – you haven't told anyone else, have you?' Hez whispered, still aghast.

'Don't be ridiculous,' I replied, rather offended. 'Anyway, I don't need to. Everybody knows already. Get a move on with your story.'

'Well, Spig was off with me all afternoon but I just kept my head down and avoided him as much as possible. When we all trooped off for this do, I did quite well steering clear of him there, too. Then he suddenly collared me and asked me if I knew anything about an article he'd been told was due to be published in the *Stoat* today – something about how the case is going to settle and with the letter Guy drafted yesterday quoted verbatim. I've never seen him so mad – he was red in the face and his eyes were popping out. He said it had to be me who leaked it because I was the one who gave the draft to Estelle for typing. Nobody else apart from Guy had seen it.'

'Don't worry,' came Mark's soothing voice from the driver's seat. 'I'm sure it's not as bad as it seems. We'll get you sorted out at the hospital, then you can go back into work and straighten things out.'

Hez shook her head violently. 'No I can't – not ever. You see, I didn't have time for any lunch yesterday and the booze at the do went straight to my head. I was so angry, I grabbed this jug of Pimm's from one of the waiters, marched over to where Spiggott was chatting with the Attorney General and emptied it over his head.'

I was torn between shock, horror and the urge to shout 'Go girl!' and pat her on the back.

'I told him he was a nasty, vengeful little shit and that I would rather have a job cleaning toilet bowls out with my tongue than work at Sheppertons. I think I shouted to the whole room that Spiggott was accusing me of being the mole in the Jones case when I wasn't, then I swiped a bottle of Bollinger from the kitchens and got a cab home. That's when I rang you the second time,' she added.

'Oh, Hez, darling,' I said.

Any animosity I felt towards her melted away. I tried to put my arms round her, but as we were both strapped in it was impossible.

'So now I'm unemployed, the laughing stock of London, I can't see and my head is going to explode with pain any second.' She slumped back into her seat and screwed up her face. 'It's awwwwwful!'

'That's right,' said Mark softly, 'have a good cry. Lucy, there's some tissues under my seat; give her one.'

I handed Hez a tissue and patted her hand while she howled. Tears ran down her face and she went all red and blotchy. But Mark knew what he was doing. As Hez's sobs gradually subsided and she blew her nose for the umpteenth time, she blinked, and first one of her eyelids unglued, then the other.

'It's a miracle!' She sniffed. 'I can see – you're all blurry and fuzzy, but I can see!'

'Yay!' I shrieked. 'You're saved!'

'We're still going to the hospital, though,' Mark the Grown-Up told us. 'You'll need your lenses removed and some sort of eye-wash thing. And besides, we're there now.'

He swung into the car park and drew up as close as he could to the main entrance. Together we manoeuvred Hez out of the car and into reception, where we left her telling her sorry tale to a sympathetic lady at the desk.

'Now, do you need me to stay or would you rather ring when you're done and I can pick you up?' Mark asked.

'I think we'll probably be okay,' I replied. 'You've got some tough decisions to make and I'm guessing this won't be the best place for you to sort your head out.'

'No,' he agreed, 'you're right.'

'As soon as I'm done here,' I continued, 'I'll take her home in a cab and then go on into chambers. I'll have a word with James my old pupil master, and phone you this afternoon. Unless you want me to drop round this evening?'

Mark pulled a face. 'I've got to fly up to Inverness this afternoon to see a man about a late-sixteenth-century fortified farmhouse – can you call before three?'

'I'll do my best. If not, ring me when you get the chance.'

'And as for last night – thanks,' he paused, 'for everything.'

'Everything?' I gave him a wry look.

'Of course,' he said, touching my cheek. 'Everything. You mean a lot to me, Lucy, but like we said, things are going to be tough for both of us for a while.' He paused as if he was collecting his thoughts. 'I was thinking, there's going to be a lot of upheaval for me over the next few weeks with Josh, the court case, the house and so on – not to mention Guy's views on you and me. Maybe it's for the best if we don't think in terms of getting back together for the foreseeable; you know, try to keep things simple.'

I looked down at the rather unpleasant lino that covered the reception area. The irony of his words wasn't wasted on me: twenty-four hours ago I would have agreed with him wholeheartedly. The problem was that last night had made me reassess what I wanted from him.

'I suppose so,' I agreed grudgingly. 'And after we've kept things simple . . . ?'

Mark put his hands on my shoulders and gave me a long, searching look. 'Let's just get through the next couple of weeks first.'

What choice did I have?

'All right. But until then, I'm here as your friend, your legal adviser and anything else you might need – okay?'

'Okay.' He smiled briefly. 'Now, I'm going home to digest your advice and make a decision about what to do for the best. I'd do anything for Josh, Lucy – *anything at all* – so maybe fighting this is a bullet I have to bite.'

He kissed me on the cheek.

'Speak to you later.'

And he walked off back to his car.

Taking a deep breath that filled my mouth and nose with the unpleasant aroma of hospital disinfectant, I went over to Hez, who was perched on a seat next to a fake potted plant.

'Where do we need to go?' I asked.

'A sort of A and E for eyes,' she explained, and we trotted off down an anonymous-looking corridor, our arms linked.

'How are you feeling?' I asked.

'Better; although I still can't see properly. But that's not what I want to talk about – I need you to tell me about you and Mr Landsdown. What happened last night? I noticed you didn't make it home.'

'Well, you know how it is,' I said. 'Gorgeous man in need of urgent legal advice and, after legal advice has been delivered, in urgent need of serious cheering up.'

'Oh God – is he in trouble?' asked Hez, the smile wiped from her face. 'Was that why he rang you yesterday?'

'Jenny wants to move to Hong Kong and take Josh. I think his only chance of stopping her – and it's a long shot – is for him to argue that she's doing this purely to frustrate his relationship with Josh; you know, play on her past form and – oh, I think we've arrived.'

Hez checked in at another reception desk whilst I grabbed us a couple of uncomfortable-looking plastic seats.

'Bloody hell!' exclaimed Hez five minutes later, as she sat down next to me and took up the thread of our conversation once more. 'And I thought *I* was having a bad time of it. But isn't it awfully high-risk? If the judge doesn't buy your version of events, Mark will look like a vengeful ex trying to sabotage Jennifer's career prospects. And as for her – she'll freak out and make his life hell.'

'I've warned him,' I replied, 'and I promised that I'll speak to James Gilleard about it.'

'Good idea,' said Hez. 'If there *is* another way, James will know about it. But getting back to the main event, does this mean that you and Mark are back together? I do hope so.'

'Things are going to be pretty tough for the next couple of weeks and he wants to keep things simple.'

Hez tried to raise an eyebrow and winced slightly.

'That would be "keep things simple" in the sense of "become emotionally and physically involved", would it?'

I scuffed the toes of my shoes along the dusty floor.

'He was upset, I hugged him and one thing sort of led to another,' I admitted.

'Oh, so it was a comfort shag?'

I cleared my throat nervously and looked the other way.

'Comfort shag*ssssss*?' hazarded Hez, trying not to laugh. 'Honestly, what are you two like? The sooner the pair of you get your act together and realise you were made for each other, the better.'

'I hope we can work something out, Hez, I really do. No matter how hard I try to shut Mark out of my life, the moment I see him I just melt.'

'I don't believe it!' Hez replied, a twinkle appearing in her red, watery eyes. 'Lucy Stephens has met the one man she can't run away from. And about time too.'

'Something like that,' I said, having the slightly uncomfortable feeling that she might just be right.

But crystallising my emotions where Mark was concerned was only part of the problem; still to be resolved was the fact that he didn't actually want a relationship at the moment. I also needed to sort out what I was going to say to Jonathan, and I felt bad – *really* bad – about that. Even though I'd been straight from the start that I wanted to take things slowly, his declaration of love had made it pretty clear that he was hoping for a full-blown loved-up reconciliation. The news that I was backing out was going to hit him hard, even before he knew about Mark's involvement in the whole thing.

'Oh, bugger,' I said, giving vent to my pent-up frustrations.

'What?' asked Hez.

I looked at her out of the corner of my eye. Should I tell her the truth, or would she blow her top once she found out I'd been halfway down the road to going back to Jonathan.

'Well . . . you see . . . you see . . .' I began.

'Not until you tell me I don't,' she replied. 'Spit it out.'

'Jonathan,' I whispered, cringing at the name. 'You wanted to know where I stayed on Saturday? Well, it was with him. And even though nothing happened that night, we sort of ended up kissing on Sunday morning – and now I've gone and slept with Mark. I've behaved like a complete slapper, and Jonathan says he loves me, and he's pulling some strings so we might find out who the mole is and – I don't know what to doooooo!'

'Lucy, are you in love with Jonathan?' Hez's voice was low and serious.

'I think I *was* in love – but with the idea of him rather than the man himself.'

'Then you need to tell him that you've thought things through and you feel it's just not working. Say you want out but you can still be friends. How about that?'

'But what if he loves me like he said? He's going to feel devastated. And how about if he asks me if there's someone else?'

'Unless you feel the same way as him it's a no-go,' she said firmly. 'You can't conduct a relationship with someone on the basis that you feel sorry for them – even you must realise that. And don't mention Mark either, just keep it about you and Jonathan.' She took a deep breath. 'Look, Lou, there's something you need to know. Back in uni, Jonathan kept trying it on – not just with other girls, but with me. Repeatedly. And that night, he didn't just tell me that you'd split up, he told me that it was me he really wanted, and I was stupid enough and upset enough to believe him. I'm sorry, Lucy, I really don't want to hurt you, but I think one of the best things you ever did was to dump him. Something tells me he's still bad news, and however much he says he's changed, I don't believe him.'

I nodded, thinking of Jonathan's protestations about his fidelity. There was no doubt in my mind as to which of them was telling the truth . . . and their name didn't begin with J.

'No, you are right. Even without what you told me, even without Mark, I need to sort it out. It'll be fine; we'll simply go back to Plan A and stay friends.'

'One other thing, though,' she said. 'If you do decide to make a go of things with Mark, make sure it's what you really want. It wouldn't be fair to bail out on him again.'

Hez reached over and squeezed my hand and we sat in silence for a moment.

'Now, what are we going to do about you?' I said at last. 'Do you want to go back to the office after the doctor's seen you?'

'No point. I've pretty much burned every single bridge where Sheppertons is concerned. I think I'll try and keep what shreds of dignity I have left intact and get another job somewhere else. I spoke to Jill at that recruitment place again and she seemed to think I wouldn't have any problem finding something – it's just the question of my references. I reckon Spiggott would rather eat roadkill than give me a good one.'

'You know,' I said, thinking that Jonathan might be a tad less enthusiastic about sharing his contacts with me once he knew the truth about my feelings for him, 'if you and I could just figure out who's actually behind the leaks, it would solve everything: you'd be home and dry and Spiggott would have no choice but to give you a cracking reference. Any ideas?'

'Well, it's not you and it's not me.'

'And it's not Mark, Jonathan or Jo – despite the fact that they all know I'm working on the case.'

'Right,' Hez considered, 'and it wouldn't be Mr J or Macdonald – they both have too much to lose.'

'Mrs J?' I suggested.

'No.' Hez shook her head. 'I know she hasn't always been helpful to us, but it's not in her interests either to be leaking away like a damaged sieve. The moment Mr J is no longer in office and earning a nice salary, her maintenance payments will go down.'

'Spiggott?' I asked. 'Blaming you as a smokescreen for his own indiscretions?'

'I *wish!*' exclaimed Hez emphatically. 'I'd take out a full-page ad in *The Times* and tell the world what a shit he's been.'

'Laura the trainee?' I asked.

Hez shook her head. 'She's leaving in two weeks to work in the company commercial department. Besides, she'd have to be mad to jeopardise her own career so early on. She'd never get another job in the law.'

'Estelle?' It was a pretty remote possibility, but I wanted to make sure we'd covered all the bases.

'I know she hates Spiggott as much as I do, but with his vice-like grip on the outgoing post, fax and e-mails, I just don't see how she could pull it off even if she wanted to. Besides, she needs her salary desperately: I helped her draft a letter to the bank yesterday about her mortgage – she was going to offer them a lump sum to hold off foreclosure.'

'A lump sum?' I was puzzled. 'But they don't have any money.'

'I know,' replied Hez. 'She said I wasn't to tell anyone in case it got back to her husband, but she's borrowed a bit from her mother; apparently he'd get upset if he knew what she was doing.'

'Honestly, men!' I shook my head. 'Right, it's not Estelle then. The person we're looking for must have both the motive and the opportunity. Someone devious and low enough to sell the client's personal details to the press and with a reason for doing it . . . Your idea that it could be Hugo trying to rubbish me is the only logical one – I just can't believe he'd stoop so low.'

'I can!' Hez cried. 'I didn't tell you, but I Googled him yesterday afternoon.'

'Really? Let me guess, you typed in "sleazeball" and it took you straight to him?'

'Not quite. But it seems his father is thinking of

running for parliament – against Llew's party – and the leaks are damaging Llew's electoral prospects, so . . .'

'It's possible, I suppose. It just doesn't seem very likely – and like Laura, he'd never get another legal job ever again.'

'I agree it would be a high-risk strategy.' Hez sighed. 'But we both know Hugo isn't a wage slave like the rest of us; even if he was uncovered and never worked again, he's hardly going to starve. Plus, snooping round your room like that, there's got to be something going on. He may not be our mole, but I reckon he still needs to be checked out.

'How?'

'Well, he's got a bit of a thing for me, hasn't he?'

'Sadly, yes,' I admitted.

'I'll ask him to take me out for dinner or something, get him hammered and see what he has to say for himself. It's worth a go, anyway.'

'You're brave.'

'I'm desperate.'

'What if he tries to kiss you or something?'

'I shall just have to do what women are biologically programmed for in such circumstances: close my eyes and think of Brad Pitt. I'll ring him when we get home.'

Hez had her eyes sorted out by a nice young doctor,
who, unfortunately, she couldn't see properly; then
I put us both in a taxi back to Muswell Hill. After I'd
changed my clothes and rung chambers to let them know
I'd had to go to hospital (I didn't tell them it wasn't for
me), I programmed Hugo's direct-dial into Hez's mobile
and looked forward to events unfolding in a satisfying
manner.

I splashed out on another cab into the Temple and
finally arrived at nine, an hour late but feeling like I'd
already done a full day's work. My plan was to check
whether or not Guy needed me to do anything on the
Jones file, have a word with James Gilleard, grab some
breakfast and, most importantly, ring Tom Gedge.

It was a great plan: it was just a shame things didn't
work out as I intended.

'Was Mr Jennings all right about me being late?' I
asked Jane as I checked in with the clerks and picked up
a couple of briefs for the next week.

'He hasn't noticed. There's nothing come in on the
Jones case today and he's booked out for a client
conference all morning on the Woodford case. I seem to
remember he'll be away for lunch as well. Do you want
me to check his diary and find out when he can see you?'

'No, it's fine, thanks. Is Mr Gilleard around?'

'He's just gone up to his room – he'll probably be

leaving for court in about half an hour, so if you want him, I'd go and see him now.'

'Thanks, Jane. I'll be up there if anyone needs me.'

Tom would have to wait; for Mark's sake I needed to speak to James ASAP.

As I wound my way up the three flights of stairs to James's attic room, my thoughts wandered in the direction of Jennifer and Guy downstairs, busy plotting Mark's downfall. Come Tuesday, Mark would be in court on his own, trying his best to argue a difficult case, whilst Jennifer would have Guy, possibly the most persuasive man on the planet, to do her dirty work for her. In all probability they were going to wipe the floor with Mark. I hoped against hope that James would have a bright idea.

James was one of my favourite people in chambers. A strikingly handsome forty-something with a brain the size of a large continental land mass, he was funny, modest and, when it suited him, adorably camp. Perched on the edge of a velvet chaise longue in a room furnished almost entirely with lovingly restored antique furniture, he listened carefully as I explained the situation, his fingers pressed together and his head slightly on one side.

'I'm sorry,' he said. 'I really wish I could tell you it was all going to go your friend's way.'

'Friend of a friend,' I corrected hastily.

'Yes, of course.' He tried to stifle a smile. 'If he does decide to use his ex-girlfriend's behaviour against her, it's a very high-risk strategy. Equally, however, it *is* the only one he's got. You advised him quite correctly.'

James paused and looked at me intently.

'You know your – your friend's friend doesn't have to do the hearing by himself; you could always offer to do it for him pro bono.'

The thought had occurred to me – there would be nothing I would have liked more than to save Mark the pain of facing Jennifer alone by being his unpaid brief – but the situation was too complicated.

I could feel myself reddening as I spoke.

'Um, I have sort of been involved in another aspect of the case already – and it wasn't on behalf of the father.'

'Ah,' said James knowledgeably, 'so this concerns Jennifer Woodford.'

My face must have been a study in horrified amazement, because he added swiftly: 'It's all right. I won't tell Jennings. I know your Mr Landsdown is forbidden fruit at the moment.'

'What – how – when . . . ?'

He gave me a large, comforting wink. 'Office gossip – and if you weren't dependent on Guy for both the Jones brief and the tenancy, I hope you'd have told him to stick it up his bum.' He grinned, and I began to relax a bit.

'And before you ask, dear girl,' he went on, 'of *course* I'm going to vote for you over that hideous oik Spade. Plus, I'm drumming up as much support for you from the rest of the tenancy committee as I can. Now, back to poor Mr Landsdown: I know you can't do his hearing, so would you like me to do it instead? No charge, naturally – I'll take the look on Jennings's face when I walk into court as payment in kind.'

'That's brilliant!' I threw my arms round him and hugged him. 'Thank you so much!'

'Anything for my favourite ex-pupil!' he said, disentangling himself. 'But go easy on the public displays of affection – I do have a reputation to keep up.'

'Can I ring Mark?'

'Be my guest. I'll take the opportunity to have a bit of a chat myself.'

I dialled his number.

'Hi, Mark, Lucy here. Listen – my colleague James Gilleard is offering to take your case on for free. This is his specialist area and . . . Great! Shall I hand you over and you can get acquainted? Not at all. Have a good trip up north.'

I handed the receiver over to James and made my way to the door, mouthing thank-yous as I did so.

What a result! She shoots – she scores!

Right! That was Mark sorted; it was now time to ring Tom Gedge and get the mole business knocked on the head too.

I pretty much skipped down the bazillion steps from James's garret to my basement slum, and as I walked along the subterranean corridor leading towards my own door, I noticed Hugo's was ajar and I heard someone speaking.

I stopped. *Was* that Hugo's voice? It sounded a *bit* like him, but there was a distinct lack of oiliness there, and my skin wasn't creeping half as much as it usually did when I was forced to listen to him droning on. I crept up as close to his door as I could to make sure I didn't miss anything.

'Well,' he was saying, 'this is, um, a bit unexpected.' There was a pause. 'No, no, of course I want to; there's nothing I'd like more.' Then he went all bashful. 'I've – er – always thought you were – ah – rather lovely actually. Do you mind me saying that?' Another pause. 'Good – because it's true. So shall we say eight o'clock? Where? The Orangery? No, I don't know it. Wonderful! I can't wait.' And he hung up.

I looked at my watch: half past nine. I had more than enough time to toy with Hugo a little before I rang Tom.

Knocking on his door and shoving my head round almost instantaneously, I cooed: 'Sounds like you've got a hot date there, Spade.'

For a split second he looked taken aback and even blushed slightly – but he soon recovered himself and was back to his old repulsive ways.

'The hottest of the lot, Stephens.' He may have rubbed his hands together in the manner of a silent movie villain at this point. 'I knew she wouldn't be able to resist me – well, she is human after all, I suppose.'

'And who is your latest victim – I mean dinner companion?' I asked innocently.

'Your mate Henrietta. She's just been on the phone, begging me to take her out. Of course I started off by playing hard to get, but she's obviously gagging for me, so what else could I do?'

I was gagging too by this time, although not in the way Hugo meant.

'And you're seeing her?'

'Friday. At the Orangery; out-of-the-way little place with a couple of Michelin stars. I know how to show girls like Irving a good time,' he assured me confidently.

'Good,' I said, stifling a smile at this barefaced lie. The Orangery was indeed supposed to be excellent: Mark had told me he had eaten there with people from work a couple of times, and raved about its intimate yet opulent style and magnificent food. 'I hope you both have – er, fun.'

I slipped back into my room and closed the door. I picked up my mobile to ring the *Hot Topic* office, but *Mission: Impossible* rang out loudly. It was Hez.

'You did it then,' I whispered down the line to Muswell Hill.

'Yeah,' came Hez's voice, 'it was almost too easy. I feel a bit sorry for him actually, he was surprisingly *sweet*.'

'You're going soft in your old age,' I warned her. 'This is Hugo, remember: the man with an attitude problem where his heart should be, and who may have inadvertently cost you your job.'

'You're right. I will show him no mercy.'

'Attagirl!' I replied.

'Now, what news from Jamie Gilleard?'

I sighed. 'Mark's got an uphill struggle – but James offered to do the hearing for him pro bono, which is good news.'

'The best. And I've got some too – I spoke to Jill at the recruitment agency before I rang Spade and she's got me an interview on Friday with Carridan and Lacey. However, I'm going to need at least two references and I don't know what to tell her.'

'It's going to be fine,' I assured her. 'By Monday morning Spiggott will be begging your forgiveness and writing you the best reference in the world.'

'Well, I hope so, otherwise I'm stuffed,' she said in a matter-of-fact way. 'Right now, though, I'm off to get some proper shut-eye before I keel over. See you later.'

It was all coming together nicely. Just one more piece needed to be slotted into the puzzle for it to be a fully productive morning, but I had to do it now. That call needed to be made before ten and it was already nine forty-two.

Once again, I was just about to punch the number into my mobile – when my desk phone rang. It was Jane.

'Mr Jennings's conference is having a bit of a break,' she announced, 'and he says he'd like to see you for a couple of minutes.'

Bugger. But there was nothing I could do – a summons from Guy had to be obeyed.

I put my phone in my bag and walked down the corridor, passing Hugo's half-open door and catching the words: 'Henrietta . . . She's the one who – yeah, that's right. I know, I can't believe it either.'

I cringed and hoped Hez knew what she was letting herself in for.

'Can I go in?' I asked Jane, jerking my thumb in the direction of Guy's door.

She nodded. 'Ms Woodford has gone for a coffee. It sounded like it was a frank exchange of views.'

'Full *and* frank,' grinned Stan over the top of his computer. 'That Mandy French has got the patience of a saint to put up with what I just heard.'

'What do you mean? Mandy wasn't there,' said Jane in puzzlement. 'I went in to see if they wanted water or anything and it was just him and her. They must be waiting for her to turn up – Guy wouldn't have a conference without the solicitor being present, would he? That would be most unethical.'

I left them arguing and knocked on Guy's door.

Guy was on his mobile. He gestured for me to sit down, but continued his call; it was obviously to his wife.

'I'm sorry, but something's come up . . . No, no, I can't rearrange . . . Well, I'm sorry, but this is business and my work has to take priority.' Pause. 'That is simply not true, Gemma; I was home before nine last Wednesday. Oh, don't nit-pick . . . All right, it wasn't last Wednesday but it was certainly the Wednesday before that.' Pause. 'Now calm down; you're just getting hysterical. I'll see you later tonight . . . I won't? Why not? All right then, be asleep!' And he hung up. 'Bloody women – oh, no offence there, Stephens.'

'None taken,' I replied as diplomatically as possible. 'You wanted to see me?'

Guy ran his hands through his hair.

'Yes, I've just had a call from Sheppertons. Mr Jones: we've got a deal.'

'Thank goodness for that!'

'It's not quite what we offered yesterday, but it's good enough for the client. Henry Spiggott is getting the court orders typed up today. The plan is to have them signed by the parties on Friday and lodged at court by this time next week. Llew will be having a short press conference on Monday to say it's all been sorted out, and a written statement containing the details of the settlement will be thrown to the slavering jaws of the press as soon as the orders themselves are stamped by a judge.'

'So what deal did they reach?'

'If it's all the same, Stephens, you'll find out next week with the rest of the world. We're keeping it under wraps for security reasons. I just wanted to let you know it looks like it's come good in the end and to thank you for your input.'

'It was my pleasure, Guy.'

'I'll be handling any loose ends that might come up on my own, so it's time for you to bundle up your copies of the papers and give them to Stan. I'll get him to invoice Sheppertons as soon as the court order is made next week and we will hopefully both be paid before the end of next month. Oh, and Stephens . . .'

'Yeeeees?'

Guy glanced down at a handwritten note in front of him on the desk and frowned. He looked distinctly uncomfortable.

'Mark Landsdown,' he said.

'He's no longer *persona non grata*?' I asked, my heart in my mouth. Obviously this was what Guy was about to tell me – the Jones case had all but finished and the embargo on us was about to be lifted . . .

Guy took off his half-moon specs and gave me a slightly apologetic look.

'Quite the reverse actually.'

My mouth flapped open and I struggled to find words – any words – in response.

'But why? What objection can you possibly have?'

'I've given it a lot of thought, and although the days are long gone when it would have been my duty as head of chambers to vet members' potential partners, I think in this case the old tradition should be resurrected. Your little interlude with Mr Landsdown gave all of us a lot of adverse publicity. In fact, Gerald Masters informs me that last week he was doing a case at Carlisle county court and some wag from the Manchester Bar was sniggering about it. I do not look kindly on my chambers being made into a laughing stock, Stephens, and I do not want word to get around that the pair of you are reunited.'

I was struggling to keep a lid on my temper. Anger was rising inside me like magma in a volcano, and it was with great difficulty that I managed to remain civil. This wasn't about me and Mark any more; it was about Guy and his self-appointed mission to run my life.

'Don't you think that as this concerns me rather closely, I deserve some say in the matter?' I said.

'Go on then.' Guy sounded unutterably bored, and I think he may actually have rolled his eyes. I prickled with resentment: this was not going to be a fair hearing.

'For starters, it's at least fifty years since a head of these chambers has interfered with anyone's private life,' I said. 'And secondly, it is absolutely none of your business whom I spend time with when I am not here. Like everyone else at the Bar I am self-employed and therefore answerable only to myself. If I choose to form a relationship with Mr Landsdown, I do not need your approval to do so.'

Guy nodded. 'Brave words, Stephens, very brave.'

I shivered slightly; and not in a pleasant way, either.

'You see,' he went on, 'even though you are indeed self-employed, I am still chairing the tenancy committee next week. It may interest you to know that Spade and yourself are running pretty much neck and neck in the polls. Wouldn't it be a shame if my vote were to go to him simply because you refused to take my advice on Mr Landsdown?'

I was livid. 'That's blackmail!'

Guy again looked uncomfortable but shook it off.

'No, Stephens; it's real life. My duty towards chambers goes beyond your personal welfare to the well-being of everybody here; and that means keeping our collective reputation intact. Now, you are popular, you've done a good job on the Jones case and you potentially have a successful career in front of you. Don't go and spoil all that because of a silly love affair.'

'It is *not* a silly love affair. I . . .'

What was the point? Unless Mark changed his mind, it was all speculative anyway.

'Whatever,' I growled, pushing my chair back and standing up. 'I'll be in my room.'

Guy smiled, and wiped a handkerchief across his forehead. 'Good girl; you know it makes sense.'

'Does it?' I replied and closed the door behind me.

I looked again at my watch: I needed to ring Tom NOW!

As I stomped through Inner Temple trying to find a private spot from which to make the call, yet again my phone went off. Checking there was no one within earshot, I ducked down a little alleyway and pulled it out of my bag.

'Hello, Tom?' I hazarded. Maybe he'd obtained my number from Jonathan and had got fed up of waiting for me to call.

'No,' came a familiar voice. 'It's me.'

'Oh, hi, Jon. How are you?' Exactly *how* guilty did I feel right now?

'Great, and I've had a call from Tom. There seems to have been a bit of a development on you-know-what and he's suggesting dinner on Friday at the Orangery. I've just booked it – had to pull a few strings, mind you – but we've got a table for eight thirty.'

Friday was Hez's big date with Hugo ... at the Orangery. Oh, bugger. Meeting Tom was risky enough by itself, without factoring in the extra complication of having Hugo on the next table ready to grass me up to Guy at the earliest opportunity.

'Friday is top; but, um, how about dining somewhere else?'

Jonathan gave a big sigh.

'Lou, I've booked it and cleared it with Tom, and I don't have time to redo all the arrangements right now. Just be there, okay?'

I hesitated. Was I worrying over nothing? After all, the chances of Hugo knowing who Tom was and what he did for a living were pretty slim. Besides, he probably wouldn't be able to drag his eyes away from Hez for long enough to focus on anybody else; and if he *did*, all he'd see was me having dinner with a couple of old friends . . .

. . . which brought me on to Problem Number Two and the issue of telling Jonathan that he'd been relegated from 'once and future lover' to the position of 'old friend'. I took a deep breath.

'All right, the Orangery it is,' I said. 'Look, Jonathan, I need to see you; there's something we have to talk about.'

'Can it wait till Friday, Lou? Something rather urgent has come along and I'm going to be tied up for a couple of days. Meet me a quarter of an hour before we're due to rendezvous with Tom and we'll go through it then.'

'I'd rather speak to you before Friday,' I said, battling on. 'Let me phone you. When would be good?'

Jonathan did a throat-clearing/coughing sort of thing. 'Phoning might be a bit tricky too – a project at work has just kicked off and I don't quite know what my movements are going to be for the next few days. Let's just say we'll see each other as arranged – okay?'

I hesitated – it was far from ideal. The last thing I wanted him to think was that I was using him purely to gain access to Tom; but if he really was tied up till then . . .

'Okay, Jon; eight fifteen.'

'Can't wait!' I could almost hear the Cheshire cat grin he must have had plastered all over his face. 'It's going to be a night to remember.'

Hopefully not for all the wrong reasons . . .

Thursday came and went. Mark rang briefly from his hotel to tell me that he was feeling a little bit more optimistic about Josh and was seeing James on Monday for a conference about the hearing.

'Guy had a word about you,' I said as casually as I could. 'Well, us really. Apparently the prospect of us being an item is an affront to the professionalism of chambers, and we are never allowed to be together – *ever*.'

'*What?*' screeched Mark, so loudly that they could probably hear him in Berwick-upon-Tweed.

'Not that it's an issue right at this moment given that we're keeping things simple,' I added, 'but I'm glad no one knows I was round at yours on Tuesday. Can you keep it to yourself?'

'Of course I will. Look, I have to go now, but I'll phone you Monday and tell you how it went with James. I've got some business to see to tomorrow night and Josh is staying over for the first time on Saturday, so I'm going to be a bit busy.' He paused. 'Lou, about Tuesday. It was great, but you and me – no promises, okay? I don't want to let you down.'

You won't let me down, Mark; this time I know you won't.

'I understand,' I said. 'No promises.'

*

Friday dawned grey and cheerless, but as the hours ticked by, a definite feeling of excitement came over me: there was something in the air, something vague and intangible but which spoke of good things.

I won my case in the morning, and after lunch, as I was reading through my papers for Monday, there was a knock on my door. It was Hez, sharp-suited and spike-heeled, fresh from her interview.

'How did it go?' I asked.

She grinned. 'Brilliant. They're speaking to Jill but want me to start as soon as poss, and they're giving me a five-grand rise on what I had at Sheppertons.'

'Yay!'

'So there's just the question of references ... I said there was a bit of an issue with one of my referees and I'd tell Jill when it was okay to contact him, but that my other one should be fine.'

'Who is it?'

'You.'

'No problem.'

'Are you all set for tonight?' she asked.

I nodded. 'I'm going to break the bad news to Jonathan before we hook up with Tom. I just hope he doesn't have a hissy fit and pull out.'

'I'm sure he won't. In fact, knowing Jonathan, he'll probably take you bailing out of the relationship as a challenge to win you back.'

That sounded about right.

At that moment, the sound of the door next to mine being unlocked floated through the air.

'Excuse me for a moment,' said Hez. 'Duty calls.'

She applied a fresh coat of lipstick, hoicked her skirt up a bit and went out into the corridor.

'Hi!' she said, slightly breathlessly. 'Long time no see.'

There was a resounding crash as Spade presumably dropped whatever he'd been carrying.

'Oh, um, Irving, I mean Henrietta, I mean . . .'

'Call me Hez,' she purred. 'All my friends do. How's it going, Hugo?'

I stuck my head round the door and saw Hez leaning nonchalantly against Hugo's door frame. There was a lot of eyelash batting going on, and it seemed to be having a devastating effect.

'Fine – er – good – wonderful. Just won a tricky little contact case, actually. Um, although when I say little, I actually mean really big and—'

'Well done,' drawled Hez with a flick of her amazing hair. 'I like that in a man: the killer instinct; the desire to win; the cut and thrust of a good argument.'

At the word 'thrust' (which Hez *did* overemphasise just a tad), there was another crashing noise that sounded like Hugo had fallen over a pile of books.

'Are you okay there?' said Hez, putting her sex-kitten voice on one side and addressing him with real concern.

'Fine, fine!' he panted above the sound of scuffling. 'Er, do you want to sit down? I can clear some space here and, um, would you like a cup of tea or something?'

'No thanks,' Hez replied, bestowing the most dazzling of smiles upon him. 'I'm having a meeting next door with my friend and esteemed colleague Miss Stephens. I just popped in to let you know how much I'm looking forward to our dinner *à deux* this evening.'

She unleashed the eyelashes once more.

'Me too,' Hugo croaked, obviously overcome with emotion – or, knowing Hugo, something less attractive. 'Can't wait.'

Hez then summoned up a smile/slight lip-licking combo that produced an involuntary whimper from her hapless victim.

'Well then,' she concluded. 'See you at eight.' And she blew him a kiss.

There was another crash, which was presumably Hugo passing out into his bookcase. Hez pulled his door to and withdrew into the safety of my room. I hastily shut my door and collapsed on the floor, literally doubled up with laughter. She punched me on the arm.

'Shut up, you wazzock, he'll hear you!' she hissed, trying (and failing) to keep a straight face herself.

'You were brilliant,' I mouthed, pulling everything out of my handbag in the hope that I might have a reasonably clean hankie in there that I could shove in my gob to soak up the laughter. 'When you said "thrust" – what happened?'

'He went as white as anything and dropped his brief,' she explained. 'He is so *easy*! It's almost unfair.'

'Bollocks to that – this is your reputation we are salvaging,' I told her sternly, wiping away the tears with the sleeve of my jacket. 'Oh, I wish I could be at your table, I really do.'

'Keep your phone on and I'll text you progress reports. Now, we need to figure out what we're wearing – although if the past five minutes is anything to go by, I could turn up in a bin-liner and he'd still end up proposing by the time our main course arrived.'

'What a horrible thought,' I replied. 'Look, I'll see you at home by half-five at the latest and we can do the wardrobe thing then.'

For Hez, we plumped for the same wrap dress and pair of dizzyingly high heels that had had the unfortunate effect on Jonathan; and for me a smart LBD that managed to be attractive and businesslike at the same time. Hez twisted up her hair and pinned it loosely, allowing a few curls to wisp round her face in an alluring manner; then we painted on a bit of make-up and were ready for the off. Hez left first.

'Wish me luck!' she trilled.

'Let me know what happens,' I implored. 'Keep slipping out to the loos to text me.'

Hez frowned. 'I don't want him to think I've got some

sort of bladder disorder, but I'll do what I can. What do I do if he asks me back for coffee?'

'Go, of course – but make sure it really is only for coffee.'

'No danger of anything else happening, matey. Even though I do feel a bit sorry for him, I'll leave all that sympathy-shag business to you and Mark. When are you next seeing him, by the way?'

'I don't know. He's got a business meeting or something tonight and Josh is staying over tomorrow. I guess I won't actually see him till after the hearing – if he still wants me, that is.'

'Of course he will,' Hez soothed. 'He's bonkers about you, Lou, you can tell from the way he looks at you. Give it time and it'll all come right; you can trust your Aunt Henrietta on this one.'

'Go on – go!' I ordered. 'You're late already.'

'All part of my master plan,' said Hez, slipping a tiny cashmere cardie thing round her shoulders. 'I'm going to whip him up into a lather of anticipation by being fifteen minutes late, throw enough booze at him to sink an elephant and then reduce him to a quivering wreck of desire. He'll be singing like a lark.'

'You know,' I said thoughtfully, 'if you don't get this job at Carridan and Lacey, you could have a very promising career with MI5, extracting state secrets from Russian agents.'

'I'll bear it in mind,' she said, and stepped out into the night.

I met Jonathan outside the Orangery about an hour later, dreading what I was going to say. The irony of the situation had not escaped me: that by sleeping with Mark, I'd committed a similar crime to the one that had made me dump Jonathan all those years ago. However, for the sake of all concerned, Mark needed to be kept firmly out of the equation. Jonathan and I weren't going to work, and that was all there was to it.

'Before we go in,' I said, evading a kiss, 'I want a quick word about you and me. Is that okay?'

'Of course,' he replied.

'The thing is,' I began, 'the thing is – I've done quite a lot of thinking about us over the past few days, and I really don't believe that we have a future together. I'm sorry, Jonathan; I know how you feel about me, and I'm conscious I've led you on to think that we could get back together properly. It would mean a lot to me if we could still remain friends, but if you want to call it a day in the friendship stakes as well, then I'll understand.'

I looked at his face, searching for some sign of disappointment, and felt slightly puzzled when I found none.

'Whatever.' He shrugged. 'In fact, it probably makes things a whole lot easier if we both know where we stand.'

I couldn't help feeling slightly put out. He'd seemed so keen about the whole thing . . . but then again, maybe he was just adept at masking his disappointment.

'If that's all,' he said, switching on the smile that had turned him into the poster-boy of Middle England (not to mention Wales, Northern Ireland and his native Scotland), 'let's go and meet Tom.'

And as far as I was concerned, that was the end of the matter.

We found Tom (as dark-haired as Jonathan, but with a wicked lopsided grin) waiting for us in the sumptuous bar area. For someone like me, who generally only got as far as the pubs of Fleet Street on a Friday night, this was a decidedly glamorous departure from the norm, and I made a mental note to move a bit more upmarket in future. There were one or two people giving Jonathan sideways don't-I-know-you-from-somewhere glances, and I suddenly felt very grown-up and important – and it was rather nice.

Anyway, Jonathan did the intros, and then Tom and I

repaired to a secluded spot behind a potted palm whilst Jon got the drinks in.

'I'll be honest with you,' Tom said, as soon as we sat down. 'I'm doing this as a personal favour for Jonathan. My cut-throat journalistic hat is at home on a peg, and anything you want to be off the record will be off the record. Jon hasn't even mentioned your name to me.'

'Good. Then you can, er, call me Hugo,' I said, mindful of the revelations Hez should at this very moment be unearthing in the restaurant.

Tom looked at me quizzically. 'Well, whatever floats your boat, *Hugo*,' he said pointedly as Jonathan put a bottle of champagne and three glasses in front of us.

'Hugo, eh?' Jonathan raised an eyebrow. 'I've always thought of you as more of a Colin myself.'

I kicked him under the table.

'I'm guessing you are somehow involved in the PM's divorce,' Tom went on, 'but I'm not sure in what capacity.'

'And I'm not going to enlighten you.' I smiled, not quite trusting his 'I've left my journalist hat at home' story. 'But I do understand you have a bit of information concerning the leaks in the case.'

'I have more than a bit,' Tom grinned back, 'including some up-to-date stuff. As we're planning to devote next week's programme entirely to Mr Jones's divorce, it's all come at quite a convenient time.'

'Come on, Tom,' said Jonathan, pouring the drinks, 'don't leave us in suspense – spill the beans.'

'Well . . .' Tom began.

Just then my mobile bleeped.

'Excuse me,' I said, pressing a couple of buttons and bringing the text up on screen.

nsty sprise in rstrnt. rng me. hxx

That didn't make any sense at all. The only nasty thing in the restaurant would be the sight of Hugo drooling over Hez, and seeing as I'd been in on the plan from the start, that wasn't going to surprise me. I texted back.

2 busy. spk soon. lx

'Sorry about that,' I said, taking a sip of the ice-cold champagne.

'Right,' continued Tom. 'I had a call on Tuesday from the *Stoat*, and—'

My phone went again.

'I do apologise,' I said, reaching for it and reading the text. It was another from Hez.

rng now! emrgncy hx

Emergency? What sort of emergency could you have in a Michelin-starred restaurant? Was the wine corked? Had the hand-baked pumpkin-seed rolls failed to materialise? Or had Hugo sussed it was all a set-up and was holding Hez hostage with a pudding fork at her throat? Still, she sounded agitated, so I texted back:

v bsy. r u ok?

Almost instantly my phone bleeped again.

im ok u may nt b

This was madness. Of *course* I was okay; why wouldn't I be? I turned my phone off and put it in my bag. I'd text her back when Tom had finished his revelations.

'No more interruptions,' I said firmly. 'Please, Tom, do go on.'

'Right. Well, my source at the *Stoat* sent this over, and I was wondering if it meant anything to you.'

He handed me a piece of paper.

I gave a sharp intake of breath: it was a photocopy of Hez's letter to Mrs Jones's solicitors; the one where we'd threatened to tell the world about the pet psychic.

'Familiar, is it?' asked Tom.

I nodded and looked again at the letter, my heart rate soaring. Even though I already knew it had been leaked and, ergo, was in the public domain, it was still a shock to see such a confidential piece of correspondence floating around in a restaurant bar.

Then I looked more closely.

It wasn't the hard copy of the letter; it was a faxed version. And running along the top were the date, time and sender's fax number. I gave another gasp: the fax number was a Sheppertons one. But not the one from the machine in the matrimonial department – and hadn't Hez said she'd double-checked the destination numbers for all the other fax machines in the building and drawn a blank? My mind was reeling. How could a fax have come from Sheppertons, but not have been sent by one of their machines? It didn't make any sense.

'And this found its way to my desk this afternoon,' Tom went on, passing another two sheets over.

The first piece of paper was a letter dated two days previously – the same day I'd had my little chat with Guy about his continuing prohibition of Mark. It had Spiggott's reference on it and it was – no! It couldn't be. *Could it?* I read it twice just to make sure.

It was the letter closing the deal on the Jones case; and again it had the untraceable fax number running across the top.

I scanned the second piece of paper. It was a Sheppertons memo sheet. On it was a typed note of a telephone conversation between Spiggot and Cameron Macdonald, outlining the details of the press conferences to be given next week. It confirmed that Mrs Jones's payment was as set out in Spiggott's letter, but that the figure to be released to the press was substantially lower. With my heart now trying to climb up my throat and out of my mouth, I read the words: 'M/Donald concerned public will balk over lump sum so we'll announce it is less.'

The implications of this memo being published flashed through my mind like a 'how to' guide on political suicide. The public might well feel that Mrs Jones didn't deserve such a huge pay-off – but what would really upset them was the fact that they had been lied to. With Mr Jones's popularity ratings already at an all-time low, this was all that was needed to finish him off.

And it was sitting in Tom's in-tray waiting for him to light the fuse.

'Did this come straight to you?' I asked quickly. 'Or has it done the rounds at the *Stoat* first?'

'The two most recent items came directly to me,' he said. 'But going by the fax numbers, the source for all three is the same.'

I nodded. 'The mole has to be at Sheppertons; but whoever they are, they're not using one of the main fax machines. Do you have any idea of their name?'

Tom shook his head. 'No, although one of my researchers has spoken to her.'

Her? For one wild, hopeful moment, I'd thought it might be Spiggott.

'She didn't trust the *Stoat* to continue to protect her identity, so she jumped ship yesterday. She told us something quite interesting.'

'Yes?'

'That she's not interested in the money any more and that's why she's come to us. Now, Hugo, I want to make it very clear that at my station we don't pay people for this sort of thing; whatever information is forthcoming is purely voluntary, so whoever is supplying it will feel very strongly about the reasons for doing so. Apparently her main objective is to show up a senior member of staff for what he really is.' Tom paused and looked me dead in the eye. 'I heard there was a bit of a rumpus at a Sheppertons function on Tuesday night. A female employee got quite upset, and I think it's her. Can you confirm that?'

'Quite the opposite,' I said. 'The person in question left the firm rather abruptly on Tuesday and wouldn't have been in a position to obtain this latest information. Your mole is obviously still *in situ*.'

'That's helpful.' Tom nodded. 'I don't suppose by any chance you are that disgruntled employee?'

I shook my head. 'No, sorry. Although the incident you described has been doing the rounds on the grapevine for the past couple of days, so I expect most people in the field are familiar with it.'

Then a thought struck me: at this very moment, the disgruntled employee Tom had spoken of was wining and dining Hideous Hugo in the belief that he might be the mole. Given what I now knew, Hugo was in the clear. I needed to get in touch with Hez and tell her. But before I could wrestle my phone out of my bag, an immaculately attired maître d' stood before us.

'Your table, Mr Gedge.'

And we rose and dutifully followed him into the restaurant.

As we entered, my eyes scanned the small, candlelit room with its white cloths, assorted greenery and expensive artwork. Ah, there they were (I breathed a sigh of relief), well over on the far side of the dining room, half hidden by a potted orange tree. But something was wrong. I blinked and looked again. Hez was leaning in over the table, as was Hugo. Her eyes were alight and her lips slightly parted as she listened with rapt attention to what he was saying. Then she smiled, blushed slightly and replied. Next, it was Hugo's turn to smile, and when he did – oh my God – it was a nice, open, *normal* sort of a smile, not his usual leer. For a second, he actually looked handsome.

Although I decided that had to be down to a trick of the candlelight.

I pulled my gaze away from the happy couple and focused on the maître d' as he wound his way through the Friday-night diners. Tom and Jonathan were a few steps ahead of me and I hurried to catch them up. It was turning out to be a brilliant night. Not only had I wriggled painlessly out of a relationship with Jonathan, but I was also getting free food at a top-notch restaurant *and* was probably about to discover the identity of the mole. That meant Hez would get her reference, Guy would be fawningly grateful and let me date Mark as well as giving me the tenancy, and Llew would probably recommend me for a knighthood.

So far, so fabulous.

The maître d' stopped by a table in the middle of the room and tucked our menus under his arm before pulling out my chair. I was just about to sit down on it when something truly unexpected swam into my field of vision.

In fact, it was so unexpected that at first my brain couldn't compute it, and when it did, I went all wobbly and hit the seat of my chair with a thud.

You see, three tables away was Mark.

And sitting opposite him, looking intently into his lovely face, was none other than Jennifer Woodford.

Hez had been spot on with her analysis. The words: '*nsty sprise in rstrnt*' just about summed it up: Mark and Jennifer, having a cosy candlelit dinner for two in a plush London eatery. Mark had said very clearly that he'd do anything for Joshua. At the time, I'd limited 'anything' to putting up a hard fight to stop the boy leaving the country; but perhaps it went further than that. Perhaps he was about to give Jennifer what she had wanted all along: himself.

Because why else would they be having a romantic meal together on a Friday night? This was, after all, the couple who had employed an army of legal advisers to sort out their differences because they couldn't manage a civil conversation between them.

I took the menu I was being offered with shaky hands and stared hard at it to try and quell the maelstrom of emotions threatening to overwhelm me. I was torn between a desire to storm right over and ask Jennifer what the hell she thought she was doing with my man, and an equally strong need to curl up into a tiny ball and hide under the table until it all went away.

'Will there be any drinks?'

'Yes please,' I heard myself saying. 'Whisky – Talisker if you've got it – double.'

'Would you like any ice or—'

'No thank you. Just as it comes.'

Jonathan nudged me under the table.

'Are you all right?' he mouthed round the side of his menu.

I shook my head. 'Mark,' I mouthed back. 'Behind you.'

Jonathan instantly turned round.

'Don't *look*,' I hissed. 'They might see you!'

Oh God – how awful was this? The last thing I wanted to be doing was talking business with a television producer while watching Mark and Jennifer in the early stages of a grand reunion. Luckily for me, the fates took pity – even if it was merely a temporary respite.

Tom suddenly clapped his hand to his chest. 'My pager's just gone off,' he said, standing up. 'If you'll both excuse me . . .'

'Who's he with?' said Jonathan as soon as Tom was out of earshot.

'Jennifer, his ex.'

'The mad one?'

'That's putting it mildly, but yes. The one I reckon would love to get back together with him just to show that she can still pull his strings.'

Jonathan frowned at me over the top of his menu. 'Look, they have a kid. They're probably just discussing who gets to go to parents' evening.'

'But they can't stand each other,' I protested. 'Why would he want to spend the whole evening with her?'

'Your whisky, madam.' A waiter appeared at my elbow with a cut-glass tumbler on a small silver tray.

'Thanks.' I threw my head back, drained the glass and replaced it on the tray.

'Will that be all, madam?'

'I hope so,' I replied, 'but I'll keep you posted.'

'Anyway,' said Jonathan, putting his menu down and folding his arms across his chest. 'What's it to you? You said on Saturday that you never wanted to see him again, and I don't blame you: apart from having the family life from hell, he was really off with me all evening. I still have no idea why.'

It did occur to me to give Jonathan an inkling of how Mark might have been feeling, but I thought better of it. Empathy had never been one of Jonathan's strong points, and besides, me and Mark was a subject I didn't want to draw his attention to. Instead, I glanced over in Mark's direction again and saw Jennifer signing a credit-card slip.

'They're paying the bill,' I whispered. 'Now they're standing up; he's helping her on with her coat and— Oh God! They're coming this way!'

I slithered down as low as possible into my chair and held my menu in front of my burning face to shield myself from recognition.

But it was all in vain.

'Oh, hello, Jonathan,' came Mark's voice. 'What are you doing here?'

'Bit of business in pleasant surroundings,' breezed Jonathan. 'And yourself?'

'Um – sort of something similar.' Mark sounded distinctly uneasy.

'Nonsense,' purred a female voice that sounded totally unlike Jennifer's but had to be. 'It's been a real treat. I think we'll be doing this more often. Oh, hello, Lucy. How are you?'

Lowering my menu, my face aflame, my eyes met Mark's, which were full of confusion. However, I was saved the bother of actually speaking, because at that moment Tom came back.

'Mark,' said Jonathan, taking control of the situation,

'I'd like you to meet Tom Gedge, a friend of mine from university. Tom, this is Mark Landsdown and Jennifer . . .'

'Woodford.' She smiled, extending an immaculate hand. 'Very pleased to meet you. I know the name – you're on the *Hot Topics* team, aren't you? I *love* your programme.'

My jaw went slack with amazement: she was completely charming. I'd only ever seen her in full-on Rottweiler mode.

'Yes.' Tom grinned back. 'Just here with Jon and – er – his friend to discuss a bit of TV-related business.'

A flicker passed across Jennifer's face, but her perfect smile didn't falter.

'Well, it's been a real pleasure to meet you, Mr Gedge,' she gushed. 'Goodbye.'

They began to walk away, and then, when they were about ten feet from our table, Jennifer stopped, placed a hand on Mark's arm, smiled and said loudly: 'I am *so* pleased you feel you want to give it another go, Mark. This means a lot to me.'

Jonathan heard her too, and shot me a look. With an enormous effort, I stapled a smile to my face, grabbed my bag and said: 'You know, I think I may need to pop to the – er.'

And I left.

I walked straight over to Hez and Hugo's table. Hugo was just in the process of pushing his plate forward so that Hez could help herself to a forkful of his grilled sea bass, or whatever it was, when I grabbed Hez by her forking arm and tugged hard.

'Toilet. Now,' I hissed, managing also to articulate: 'Good evening, Hugo,' in a semi-normal voice.

'Yes, of course,' replied Hez, without missing a beat. 'See you in a minute, Hugues.'

Hugues? Who the hell was Hugues?

'You saw him then,' said Hez when we arrived

breathless in the safety of the ladies' a few moments later. 'I tried to warn you.'

'What was he *doing*?' I gasped. 'He said I meant a lot to him, for goodness' sake. How can he be all over her three days later?'

'Oh, Lou.' Hez put her arm round me. 'Calm down. He wasn't all over her. It seemed quite dignified from what I could see.'

'But you didn't hear what she said,' I persisted, turning on a tap and letting the cold water run soothingly over my wrists. 'She was thanking him for giving something another go. She wants to reel him in one last time, just to prove she can have him if she wants to. And he told me he'd do *anything* to get Josh back – maybe that includes getting it on with her.'

'You know a lot more about their relationship than I ever will,' Hez replied, 'and maybe she *was* making a play for him, but it doesn't mean he went along with it. Before you start worrying, you need to speak to Mark himself and find out what was really happening.'

I turned off the tap, dried my hands on a fluffy towel and stared into the mirror, doing my best to get a grip. I didn't want Tom to think that panicking in the toilets was how I normally behaved during business meetings.

'All right.' I made air go in and out of my lungs in an orderly fashion. 'I'll ring him tomorrow.'

'Good,' said Hez. 'But him and Jennifer – it's bound to be nothing. We know she's a nasty piece of work, and the chances are she'd love to pay you back for the mix-up at court; she was probably saying something provocative to upset you. Now, forget her and concentrate on pumping Tom Gedge for all the information you can.'

'You're right,' I replied, blowing my nose and getting out my lipstick. 'I need to focus on the job in hand. Speaking of which, how's Hugo?'

Hez blushed slightly and fiddled with her hair.

'Really nice, actually. And I mean *really* nice. It's come as a bit of a shock.'

'But—'

'But at work he's foul to you – yes, I know. If it's any consolation, it's because he's terrified you're going to get the tenancy over him. He keeps on apologising and telling me he's not normally like that.'

She rearranged the neckline on her dress and hoicked her bra straps up a bit, while I stared at her and tried to compute this new interpretation of Hugo.

'You fancy him, don't you?' I challenged at last.

Hez pursed her lips. 'Maybe. A bit. All right then, a lot. And I can tell you, he's not the mole.'

'I know,' I replied, touching up my lipstick. 'It's someone at Sheppertons.'

Hez gave a little gasp and spun round to face me. 'Really?'

'Really. Tom Gedge has the fax number to prove it.'

'But I got Darren to check every single fax machine in the building!'

'Hez, I know you and Hugues might be at the start of a beautiful friendship and all that, but would you like to join us? I think you could add quite a lot to the discussion.'

Hez frowned for a moment.

'Well, I would have liked to have a bit more time with Hugo, but I suppose duty calls . . . Er, would it unnerve you if I invited him back for coffee?'

'Real coffee, or that other stuff that me and Mark tend to get caught up with?'

Hez giggled. 'Probably real coffee. This time at least.'

'Then no, it wouldn't unnerve me.'

'Right-oh. I'll tell him he's moving tables.'

It turned out to be one of those nights that pick your life up, shake you around a bit and then set you down on a completely different track. For starters, of course, there had been Mark. Why couldn't he have told me he was meeting up with Jennifer, rather than couching it euphemistically as 'some business'? Whilst Hez's words had been rational and soothing, part of me didn't buy into the old innocent explanation thing, and I was coming dangerously close to convincing myself that he'd said he couldn't make any promises to me because he knew he might be resurrecting his relationship with her.

Then, of course, there had been Mr Spade. With great self-control, I had managed not to utter the words: 'Who are you and what have you done with the real Hugo?' but it was touch and go on a number of occasions, not least when Hez got a bit emotional recounting her parting of the ways with Henry Spiggott and Hugo produced a large white handkerchief and proceeded to gently wipe her tears away. He and I even agreed a truce, something that had never happened before in our hate-hate relationship. Whatever Hez had done to him, it was impressive stuff.

But the biggest deal was finally cracking the identity of our mole. The five of us gathered round a single table and argued long and hard about his or her possible identity. Then, when it became clear that our presence there was no longer a thing of joy for the restaurant staff, we repaired back to Muswell Hill to carry on the discussion over numerous cups of coffee and a bottle of cognac Jonathan had thoughtfully procured from the local off-licence.

The clues so far were these: we knew it was someone at Sheppertons, and we knew that that someone was involved with the Jones case. However, because of the highly confidential nature of the work, only a limited number of people had been allowed to come into contact with the papers: namely Hez, Spiggott, Estelle and Laura the trainee who'd done all the photocopying. We again postulated the idea that it might be Laura, but as she wasn't yet qualified and therefore had even more to lose than Hez if her cover was blown, we dismissed it.

We then agreed that from the purely financial aspect of getting the *Stoat* to cough up great fat wodges of cash, Estelle would have more reason than most to throw caution to the wind and start passing letters over to the press – but we also reluctantly concluded that just because she was broke did not necessarily mean that she would put her job on the line by going to the papers. However, as we were about to move on, Hez clapped her hand across her mouth and uttered a muffled: 'Oh my God!'

'Mmmm?' I said, swilling the last of my cognac round in the bottom of my glass.

'Estelle,' said Hez, squeezing Hugo's hand excitedly, 'she was sacked.'

'She was *what*?' I stared at her. 'Why? When? Why didn't you tell me before?'

'I only found out this afternoon,' said Hez. 'I went in to clear my desk and she said that the day after I'd told Spig where to shove his job, she'd been given a month's notice because after working two weekends on the trot she'd refused to do any more of his bloody unpaid overtime. Thankfully she's found another job to go on to, but the things she said about Spig were unbelievable; I've never heard her so angry.'

'But would she leak a client's details?' asked Hugo. 'I mean, it's not as though Mr Jones ever did her any harm.'

'To be honest,' Hez replied, 'she was so short of cash and Spiggott was so horrible to her, I think Mr Jones's feelings might have been the last thing on her mind.'

Much as I hated to think of loyal, long-suffering Estelle as our mole, she was the only candidate to have a credible motive. However, the fact remained that she didn't have any real opportunity to execute her crime – and if she couldn't get the stuff out of the office, she couldn't be the source of the leaks. The really annoying thing was that we knew the answer to the whole conundrum was somehow bound up with the mystery fax number, and if we could only make sense of that, the rest of it would somehow fall into place. But despite racking our collective brains, the answer eluded us.

It wasn't until I got my laptop out to make a note of our discussion that we had a breakthrough. Or, actually, *I* had a breakthrough – which was most unexpected, given the amount of Courvoisier I'd been guzzling. I'd just booted up when my eye alighted on one of the icons at the bottom of the screen. It was a program I'd got years ago, thinking it would be tremendously useful, but as is always the way with this sort of thing, I had played around with it on a couple of occasions and then forgotten about it.

It was a fax programme.

If I wanted to send a fax, rather than print stuff out, run upstairs, fill out a cover sheet and use the machine in the clerks' room, I could simply do it straight from the laptop.

'Hez,' I said, pointing to it, 'did you ever have anything like this at Sheppertons?'

Hez took her hand off Hugo's knee and leant over to look at the screen. The 'QuickFax' icon blinked lazily at her.

'The fee-earners like me didn't,' she said at last. 'I can remember Spiggott vetoing it at a partners' meeting. He said it was beneath our dignity as professionals to send our own faxes. He reckoned it was a job for the secretaries.'

'You know,' said Tom, topping up his glass, 'the more I find out about this guy, the more intensely I dislike him, don't you, Jon?'

'A man of exceptional talents and abilities,' agreed Jonathan, 'and not a single one he can be proud of.'

'So the fax option was installed on the secretaries' computers?' I asked.

'That's right,' said Hez. 'But about two minutes after that had been done, Spiggott did a U-turn. He decided it was too much of a confidentiality risk letting the underlings fax things straight from their machines and got IT to uninstall it.'

'And they eliminated it from all the secretaries' computers?'

'I guess it's possible they missed one or two.'

'Or even,' I said, 'if someone was so inclined, they could delete the icon but keep the programme secretly installed on their hard drive. That's why the sending number didn't correspond to any of the known fax machines in the office.'

Hez then went very white.

'I know who it is,' she breathed. 'She sent a couple of faxes for me last weekend when our departmental fax machine was broken, and that must have been how she did it. It *has* to be Estelle after all. She sent the papers to the *Stoat* because she needed the money, and after she'd been sacked and she was mad as hell with Spiggott, she went all out and sent documents to a television show – including the memo, which she knew would incriminate Spiggott personally. I hope she knows what she's doing – this could all get horribly nasty.'

'Well,' said Tom, 'we don't reveal our sources, and unless

the *Stoat* have an axe to grind with her, they probably won't bother naming names. She may get away with it.'

'Even so,' Hez concluded, 'I'll contact her on Monday and tell her the game's up. If she's got any sense she'll get the hell out of Sheppertons without working her notice. I wouldn't want to be hanging around there once Spiggott knows the truth.'

The relief of solving the Riddle of the Mole meant the party broke up on a bit of a high. We decided that I would confront Guy on Monday and warn him of the coming storm over Mrs Jones's lump-sum payment, and that Hez would have the pleasure of tackling Spiggott on her own. She made Tom swear he wouldn't go issuing any 'exclusive' stories until she'd had a chance to speak to Estelle; and then made him double-swear that on no account would he let anyone know we'd been talking to him. So chuffed was I that she now had nothing to worry about re: references for her new job that I didn't even mind when Hugo disappeared into her bedroom rather than out the front door with Tom.

That left just me and Jonathan. He was loitering in the kitchen, rinsing out glasses and drinking a cup of coffee as slowly as possible.

'Thanks,' I said, handing him the last of the wine glasses. 'I owe you one. We couldn't have done that without you; Tom as well, of course, but you were the link in the chain that made it all possible.'

'All part of the service.' He grinned, drying his hands on a tea towel and walking over to me. 'And I think you'll find my terms and conditions quite reasonable.'

He reached out a hand and tucked a strand of hair behind my ear, then ran a finger along my cheekbone. I moved his hand away from my face and placed it firmly on the counter top.

'No thanks, Jonathan. I'm truly grateful for everything you've done to help, and I'm glad we can be friends, but a relationship is out of the question. I told you where you stood before we went into the restaurant.'

He rolled his eyes in mock exasperation. 'Oh come on, Lou, stop being such a prude. We weren't in a relationship on Sunday morning but that didn't stop you from throwing yourself at me.'

Despite the fact that I'd thought the throwing had been pretty much mutual, he was right; and of course I hadn't *technically* been in a relationship with Mark on Tuesday night. But my feelings where Mark was concerned were worlds away from the skin-crawling embarrassment of having spent a chunk of Sunday snogging Jonathan.

I took a step in the direction of the door and folded my arms in front of me in a *don't mess with me* pose.

'I'm being serious, Jonathan. Friends, yes; more than that, no. Not now, not in the future, not ever.'

He gave a sort of snorting laugh, as if he was indulging my stupidity at clinging on to such an absurd notion, and crossed the floor towards me. Then he reached out and took hold of the tops of my arms so forcefully it hurt, bringing his mouth down to meet mine at the same time. My stomach heaved and I wrenched my face away from his milliseconds before impact. Then I pushed him as hard as I could in the chest and broke his grip.

'I think you'd better leave, don't you?' I said, reaching along the counter for his wallet, which was sitting by the off-licence carrier bag the cognac had come in. Not wanting to put myself within mauling distance again, I flung it at him and scored a direct hit in the stomach area, causing a couple of credit cards and some papers to pop out and fall to the floor. I picked up a card and a photo that had landed at my feet and went to bung them back at him, eager to do anything that would get him out of the flat as quickly as possible. Before I did so, however, I instinctively paused to look at the photo, and what I saw made me feel physically sick.

It was a recent picture of Jonathan standing in an

exotic location with his arm round the waist of a stunningly beautiful blonde girl, obviously called something like Fifi or Jojo. He was wearing his smuggest, most self-satisfied grin; while adorning the ring finger of her left hand was a diamond the size and luminosity of a mirror ball.

The smiles on their faces said it all: they had just got engaged.

Speech being beyond me at that moment, I held the photograph aloft so that Jonathan could see it too. He stared first at the picture, then at me, then at the picture again. Finally he shrugged.

'She's away on business a lot,' he said at last, as if this was excuse enough.

'You bastard,' I hissed, furious that I was complicit in Jonathan's latest bout of infidelity. 'You complete and utter bastard.'

Then a thought struck my brain with the force of a meteor crashing into the earth's crust, and I gasped for breath.

'And that's why you wouldn't see me or let me phone you this week, isn't it – because she was back in town!'

I snatched the wallet out of his hand, ran to the front door, opened it and chucked everything down the stairwell.

'And don't you EVER come back!' I shrieked at his retreating form as he scurried down the steps in an effort to retrieve his belongings.

I slammed the door shut and stood with my back against it while I caught my breath: Jonathan Hodges was finally history, and it felt good!

By the next morning, though, I wasn't feeling quite so upbeat. Even though I was now officially an A1 mystery solver (probably even worthy of a place in the Scooby-Doo line-up) *and* had had the balls to send Love Fink Hodges packing once and for all, there was still the little matter of Mark and Jennifer to attend to. Even though it was strictly speaking none of my business who Mark went out to dinner with, I knew that for my own peace of mind I was going to have to give him a call. After my second cup of coffee, I managed to get as far as picking up my mobile and selecting his home number from my contacts list, before I bottled it and put the phone back in my bag.

I'd do it later. A lot later. Like tonight.

But the image of the pair of them leaving the restaurant together refused to vanish from my mind, and so, after moping about in my dressing gown for a bit longer, I decided to get the bus into town for a spot of window-shopping. I showered, dressed and was just slipping a jacket on when the phone rang.

'Lucy! Thank goodness!' It was Jo, and she sounded panicky.

'What's happened? Is Dave all right?'

'Dave's fine,' she replied, in a voice that indicated she'd almost rather he wasn't. 'He's asleep.'

'Well, what about you? Are you fine too?'

'I don't know. Meet me in town?'

'Okay. Where?'

Jo thought for a moment. 'Long Acre. I need to spend great fat wodges of cash. See you in half an hour.'

'Okay,' I agreed, and hurriedly left the flat for Covent Garden.

I saw Jo almost as soon as I emerged from the tube station. She looked pale, with big dark circles under her eyes; and she was leaning against the window of Hobbs, biting her nails.

'So,' I said, having played Russian roulette with the traffic before noticing that there was a zebra crossing just a few yards further up, 'what's up?'

She shrugged and tried to hide her chewed fingertips in her pockets.

'Nothing,' she replied, looking at the window display rather than me. 'Well, nothing I want to talk about.'

'Come on,' I tried again, 'something's the matter; why don't you tell me what it is?'

'Like I said, I don't want to talk about it; but what I *do* want is a stiff drink,' she announced, suddenly grabbing me by the arm and frogmarching me along the pavement and into the nearest hostelry.

'Vodka and tonic, please,' she said as soon as we were over the threshold.

The clock above the bar said it was only just midday, and Jo was not normally a daytime drinker. In fact, she rarely had more than a couple of glasses of white wine in one go; so to see her rush into a pub at lunchtime, head straight for the bar and order vodka was a first for me.

'What will you have, Lou?' she asked.

'Er, Coke, please.'

'Okay.' She turned back to the barman. 'One Coke and another vodka.' She lifted up the glass already sitting on the bar and downed the contents in one. 'No, make it a gin and tonic. A double gin and tonic.'

She thrust a twenty-pound note at him and tapped

impatiently on the counter with her fingernails whilst he prepared our order and gave her the change. Then, drinks in hand, we made our way through the bar and out through some French windows on to a sunny little patio area dotted with picnic benches. Jo parked her glass on the nearest wooden table and sat down.

'So,' I said, taking the seat opposite her, '*now* are you going to talk to me?'

Jo sipped her G and T and picked at her peeling nail polish. I decided to try another tack.

'Okay, if you *don't* honour me with your confidence, I will call Hez right now and tell her to get down here right away with the thumbscrews.'

Jo squinted up at me through the glare of the April sunlight.

'If I do, you are to swear you will not repeat a word to another living soul,' she said.

'I swear,' I agreed.

Jo diverted her gaze back to her fingers; she was twisting her wedding ring round in an agitated fashion.

'Do you think I made a mistake marrying Dave?'

'What!'

This was sacrilege. Even in with my warped world-view, I knew that Jo and Dave were soulmates. They'd been in love from the moment they clapped eyes on each other.

'I mean, we were only twenty-four when we got married, and now I'm signed up to him for the rest of my life. Look at you and Hez – you're out there meeting great new blokes, having a good time, and I'm stuck with the same one day in, day out.'

'Er, excuse me,' I interrupted, anxious to set the record straight on this rosy view of my single life. 'I have met *one* new bloke in recent months, which has resulted in nothing but confusion and chaos; I live in a rented flat; I have no job security and no money. You have a house, a great job and the man you love.' I paused and waved a wasp away from my drink. 'You do *love* him, don't you?'

'I suppose so,' Jo admitted after much thought and chewing of her gin-soaked lemon slice. 'But we had a bit of a row last night.'

'About?'

'He thinks I should give up my job when we have a baby. He's never mentioned it before, but he read something in the paper about childminders versus parents bringing up kids and started bleating on about how research shows that it's better for the child to have one parent at home and that parent ought to be the mother – just like his was. I mean, can you honestly imagine me at home with a baby, making Thomas the Tank Engine smiley faces out of carrots and broccoli? I think I'd have to kill myself.'

'Then tell Dave how much you'd like to stay on in chambers when you have a kid. I'm sure he'll come round.'

'And what if he doesn't?' persisted Jo. 'From what I've seen, it's hard enough to hold down a full-time job once you've had a baby without waging a pitched battle with your husband over childcare. I've seen how stressed some of the other women in chambers are; I *know* that there are still men around who see motherhood as a form of weakness.'

'Look,' I said, 'there's loads of stuff you could do: talk to Dave, or chat to some female barristers who have children. It's not as if you need to solve the problem right now – you could even put the idea of the baby on hold for a while; you know, till you feel more confident.'

Jo shook her head miserably. 'I can't,' she said.

'Why not?'

'I'm pregnant,' she replied and put her head in her hands. 'I did the test this morning. Dave doesn't know yet.'

I opened my mouth to say, 'But that's what you've been trying to be for the past two years,' and then closed it again, sharpish. Even though they'd been babybonking for ages, there was no law that said she had to be ecstatic when it finally became a reality.

'Does that sound awful?' she asked.

'No,' I replied. 'Babies are a big deal: it's going to change your life.'

'And as far as I can see, not in any good ways. I'm going to get fat, my brain is going to decompose, my career will stagnate and then Dave will have an affair with his secretary and run off to Kazakhstan.'

'Kazakhstan?'

'Oh, I don't know, it just sounds a depressing sort of place.'

'We'll all help out,' I said, trying to sound as cheery as possible. 'I'll babysit. If you want me to, that is – I don't actually think I've got the gene for motherhood, but if you're willing to risk it, I'm game.'

'Thanks,' said Jo, producing a thin, watery smile. 'It's not going to be easy, though.'

'I know,' I replied. 'This is new territory for all of us – but Hez and I will do what we can. We're not about to abandon you just because you're a mummy.'

Then she clapped her hand to her forehead as a thought occurred to her.

'You know, Lucy, if you got back with Mark and Mark won his case, Josh would move in with him and we'd both be in the same boat. Beginner mums together. We could swap tips.'

Whilst this realisation seemed to cheer her up, in contrast I almost sent my glass of Coke hurtling floorwards. She was right: I was one romantic reunion and one court case away from being a full-time stepmother. Because I'd been so focused on both the legal complexities of the case and the excruciating uncertainty as to whether or not Mark loved me, I'd managed to bypass the fact that there was a living, breathing child at the centre of it all. One who if the necessary (and granted, rather improbable) events came to pass would have me as the nearest thing to his real mother. Geographically speaking, of course.

How shallow, exactly, did that make me?

This was a million miles away from the Saturday footballing scenario outlined by a sozzled Hez all those weeks ago. Would Mark expect me to take time off work if Josh had chickenpox? Would my domestic commitments mean I was unable to scoot off to Newcastle County Court at the drop of a hat? Would I be able to handle the fact that a small person wanted to climb into my bed at four o'clock in the morning and poke me in the face?

I honestly didn't know.

'Lucy? Are you okay? Lucy?' Jo was patting my hand and sounding concerned.

I took a restorative sip of Coke. Well, if last night was anything to go by, the chances of me and Mark ever getting back together were thinner than a stick insect on the Atkins Diet. Perhaps I shouldn't go worrying about it just yet.

'Yes, er, thanks. I'm fine. You?' I said, draining my glass.

'A bit better.'

'Good. How about we go and get some food? I think you should soak up some of that gin you've been packing away.'

Jo pushed her glass away from her.

'No more of these for a few months, I suppose.'

'And then you need to go home to Dave and tell him the news.'

'Okay.' She nodded before a worried look clouded over her face. 'It is going to be all right, isn't it, Lucy?'

'Of course,' I replied cheerfully.

It was all going to be all right: Jonathan, Hugo, Hez, the tenancy, Mark, Joshua and Estelle. Everything was going to be tickety-boo.

I just wished I knew how.

*

Somehow I got through the rest of the day. We ate lunch, then Jo bought shoes and earrings on the basis that they would adorn two parts of her anatomy that would not be expanding over the next eight months, and finally, after supper at Pizza Express, I packed her and her shopping (including a T-shirt for Dave emblazoned with the legend 'Who's The Daddy?') off home to Vauxhall.

It was about nine thirty when I got back to Muswell Hill. I decided I couldn't put off the evil moment any longer: I had to ring Mark. Unless I was very much mistaken, Josh would have been in bed long ago and Mark should be sitting in front of some hideous reality TV show wondering why he hadn't thought to go to Blockbuster earlier in the day.

I picked up the phone and dialled.

It rang once.

My palms were sweating.

It rang twice.

I felt sick.

It rang for a third time.

Someone picked it up.

'Hello,' I began but was cut off by a strident female voice.

'Mark Landsdown's phone. Who is this?'

Fuck!!!!!!! It was Jennifer.

I slammed the phone back down. What was she doing there? At half past nine? Was there some sort of emergency? Had Josh been taken ill? She hadn't sounded panic-stricken, but then Jennifer wasn't exactly the panicking sort.

I redialled and prepared to hold my ground.

'Hello?' It was Mark's voice.

'It's me,' I said. 'What's she doing there?'

Oh, bugger. Internal monologue failure – I hadn't meant it to come out like that.

'Ah,' said Mark slowly. At least he was too busy feeling embarrassed to notice how rude I'd just been.

'Mark?' Jennifer barked from somewhere on the other side of the room. 'Whoever it is will have to ring back. I'm just dishing up supper.'

'What!' Again, I had failed to keep my thoughts to myself. What the bloody hell was she doing playing houses round at Mark's? *My* Mark's.

Well, more mine than hers, anyway.

'I've – ah – got to go,' Mark excused himself. 'I'll see you maybe Monday afternoon?'

In his dreams.

'Nope, I'm busy all day Monday,' I replied briskly. 'Busy, busy, busy. All day. No free time,' I added, just in case he was in any doubt. 'Well, can't hang around here chatting – goodbye!'

'Thanks for calling,' he said.

'My pleasure,' I lied. 'Bye.'

And I hung up.

Hez had been wrong. Very, very wrong. Despite my fears, I had fed myself the line that Mark and Jennifer *were* over; that last night at the Orangery had just been some weird bon voyage party, or that he'd been doing his best to convince her to rejoin their old lottery syndicate – or something equally banal. But this – *this*! Try as I might – and I was trying pretty bloody hard, believe me – I could not put an innocent spin on it.

Mr Mark Landsdown, you are charged with an improper association in respect of a Ms Jennifer Woodford by your putative girlfriend and sometime lover Miss Lucy Stephens. Let us examine the evidence against you:

1. You had dinner with the said Ms Woodford at the Orangery on the evening of Friday the twenty-seventh of April this year, a restaurant which is both notoriously expensive and rather posh. You

have given evidence to the effect that you are currently impecunious and Ms Woodford was witnessed paying the bill. The only conclusion that can be reached, therefore, is that you were there as her date.

2. Whilst you and the said Jennifer Woodford were leaving the restaurant, she was heard by Miss Stephens to say loudly – and I quote – 'I am so pleased you feel you want to give it another go.' Of what it was that you were so keen to re-experience, we have no direct evidence; but the number of options is extremely limited, isn't it, Mr Landsdown?

3. Miss Stephens then telephoned your residence at half past nine on the evening of Saturday the twenty-eighth of April and the call was answered by Ms Woodford. Not unsurprisingly, Miss Stephens terminated the conversation due to shock. When she rang back and spoke to yourself, not only was it apparent that Ms Woodford was still in attendance, but it became clear that she had cooked a meal for you both and was in the process of serving it up. You became rather defensive and attempted to end the telephone call as quickly as possible.

I put it to you, Mr Landsdown, that your actions can at best be described as dodgy, and at worst downright suspicious. Under the circumstances, you have given Miss Stephens no option but to conclude that you and Ms Woodford are attempting a reconciliation. That is the truth, isn't it, Mr Landsdown?

As I adjusted to what I had heard on the phone, a series of realisations clicked into place. Yes, I had had a tough time as a kid, and yes, my time with Jonathan had damaged me; but instead of letting the pain of these events heal over and then moving on, I had worn my wounds as a badge of honour and used them as justification for my avoidance of a healthy adult relationship. The only problem was that when a man turned up who had no other agenda apart from being hopelessly in love with me, I took to my heels.

I put my face in my hands. I wanted to cry. I wanted more than anything to howl at the injustice of it all and let the emptiness wash through me and out of me so that I could pick myself up and move on; but the tears wouldn't come. I knew that despite everything I'd done to try and avoid it, I had fallen in love. No, no – it was worse than that: I actually *loved* the man. For the first time since we'd met, and with a clarity that shook me to my core, I knew I didn't care whether his personal life was a war zone; or that he had a son; or even that our time together had run as smoothly as a car with no suspension and only three wheels: I loved him and I wanted to be with him.

Only it had taken until he was no longer available to make me realise quite how much.

At that moment, the phone rang. For a nanosecond my heart lifted at the thought that it might be Mark ringing back with a plausible explanation for Jennifer's presence in his flat.

But it wasn't.

It was my mother.

'Lucy?' she said. 'I really have to tell you how let down I feel by your refusal to give me your support over this maintenance row. It really is too bad, you know; after all I've done for you and your sister, the pair of you go and desert me in my hour of need—'

I cut her off. I didn't want to deal with that right now. Right now? Make that *ever*.

'Really?' I said. 'Well let me tell you something. I am fed up with playing the adult and having to mediate between my parents whilst they carry on like a couple of kids. Now, if there is any further mention of divorces, maintenance money, second spouses or anything of that sort within my earshot, I will hang up on you – or Dad if he tries it on. Here's what you are going to do: you will ring Dad; you will apologise for your behaviour to date and you will sort out the matter of the maintenance in a civilised manner. Do you understand?'

I made a mental note to call my father and force him to do some grovelling too.

There was a momentary stunned silence from the other end of the line.

'Yes. Okay. If you say so.'

'Good. I'll ring you in the week and find out how you got on, but I really can't talk at the moment.'

And I hung up.

With my body feeling like lead, I heaved myself off the sofa and rummaged around in the kitchen cupboards till I found the rest of Jonathan's cognac. Then I got into bed fully clothed, pulled the duvet up to my chin and did my best to blot out the realisation that Mark was now permanently beyond my reach.

26

Court buildings can be some of the most godforsaken places on the planet, and generally the rule is that the lower down the scale you go, the worse things will be.

Magistrates' courts, for example, are usually housed in draughty Victorian buildings that look impressive from the outside but are home to miles of dirty linoed passageways littered at intervals with nasty-looking plastic chairs bolted to the floor. There are very few areas where you can have a private conversation with your client; even fewer where you can get a cup of coffee; and the whole place seems to have been designed to make anyone who enters its door want to get out ASAP and never, ever return.

Which, I suppose, may be the point.

At the other end of the scale is the House of Lords. I was taken there to see a case as a special treat when I was James's pupil, and it was an experience to remember. We wound along panelled corridor after sumptuous staircase to the room where the hearing was to take place. Although all the barristers were bewigged and gowned, their lordships (five of them) sat in normal suits round an oval table taking copious notes. Every so often, one of them would politely interrupt the speeches to ask a question or clarify a point. There was no witness box, no cross-examination, and even though each legal team was fighting strenuously for their client, the atmosphere was one of everybody working together to try and find the best solution possible. It had given me, a cynical young trainee, a great deal of respect for the system.

Mark's case on Tuesday was due to be heard neither in the local mags nor the House of Lords, but in the Family Division of the High Court, situated at the Royal Courts of Justice in the Strand.

To get to the family courts, you need to go through the main entrance hall of the RCJ with its high, vaulted, cathedral-like ceiling, and turn left into the broad cloister of a corridor that runs along the back. Go through a little courtyard and into the modern building you see before you, and there, on the first and second floors, is court after court after court dealing with nothing but divorce, children and families.

At one forty-five on Tuesday afternoon, I found myself trudging up the steps to the entrance of the Royal Courts, putting my bag through the scanner and being checked for hidden weapons before proceeding down the maze of passageways towards the Family Division and Mark Landsdown.

The question you are probably asking yourself is 'Why?' Why would I want to be with Mark, Jennifer and Guy – all in close proximity? And the answer is twofold. Firstly, after three full days of winding myself up into a state about Jennifer and Mark, I needed to hear it from him that they were back together; and secondly (and just as importantly), I was about to show Guy that I wasn't prepared to be pushed around any longer.

So there I was.

The Guy thing came completely out of the blue. I hadn't been able to catch him on Monday because he'd been doing a case in Bath. Then, just before lunch on Tuesday, I arrived back from Kingston county court and ran into him in the clerks' room, where he was checking his pigeonhole. Before I could get a word out, he exploded at me.

'You,' he said, with a face like thunder and obviously not caring who overheard, 'had dinner at the Orangery on Friday with Tom Gedge from *Hot Topics.*'

Shit. This wasn't going the way I'd planned.

'I did,' I replied as calmly as I could, 'and there's something I need to discuss with you arising from that meeting.'

'No,' he said, lowering his voice. 'I think you'll find it's *me* who has a bone to pick with *you*. I am extremely concerned that a member of my chambers was seen gossiping with a political hack just three days before Mr Spiggott received a letter from the said hack informing him that confidential information relating to a prominent client was in the latter's possession. In fact, I am more than concerned, I am livid!'

'Don't be ridiculous, Guy,' I protested, anxious to set him straight. 'I am *not* the mole. But I can divulge who—'

His eyes flashed angrily.

'Save your breath, Stephens. I can tell you that on the evidence I have, there is no way, *no way*, you are getting the tenancy. In fact, I hereby give you a month's notice to get your act together and leave.'

'What?' I had solved the Mole Mystery, saved his client's reputation, and he had just sacked me! 'Guy, will you *listen* to what I have to say?'

My entire reputation depended on me getting him to shut up for five minutes and hear the truth.

Guy, however, was having none of it.

'I will not be drawn into a discussion over this. The subject is closed,' he growled and swept out of the room.

I should have been upset that my worst fears concerning my meeting with Tom had come to pass. I should have followed Guy into his room and shouted the odds.

But I didn't.

You see, another, more sophisticated plan was busy forming in my head. Guy had done his high-handed 'I-don't-care-what-you-have-to-say-Lucy' act once too often, and I had finally had enough. If he wouldn't listen to my side of the story voluntarily, then I was just going to have to *make* him pay attention. I was damned if I was going to roll over and let him trash my career.

Knowing that Hez had already spoken to Estelle, warned Sheppertons not to lie about the size of Mrs Jones's settlement and netted the best reference in the universe as a consequence, I went straight downstairs and dialled Cameron Macdonald's direct line.

'Mr Macdonald? Lucy Stephens of counsel here. About the mole. I had a meeting with a contact in the press on Friday, and after seeing his copy of the leaked documents, I can tell you who it is. No, not Miss Irving, although you're not a million miles away . . .'

Then, with fire in my belly, I gathered up my bag and made my way over the road to court. I was going to rub Guy's nose in it. It had to be Jennifer who'd told him about my meeting with Tom, and I wanted to see her face when he had to grovel to me big-time.

I arrived to find the courtroom where Mark's case was due to be heard locked, and none of the other players in our private drama waiting outside. Scattered along the anonymous-looking corridor with its magnolia walls and green carpet, a few worried-looking people were speaking in low voices to their clients; but none of them were Guy or James. Thankful for a few minutes of respite, I sat down and pulled out my brief for Wednesday morning and started to flick through it.

A few minutes later, I was dragged rather unwillingly back to reality by an unmistakable foghorn boom.

'What's *she* doing here?' demanded Jennifer Woodford loudly and ungraciously, as she strode towards me followed by Mandy.

'Miss Stephens is probably here on an entirely different matter,' soothed Mandy, flashing a quick smile in my direction once Jennifer's back was turned. 'Now, why don't you take a seat? I'll go and get us a cup of coffee, and Mr Jennings will be here any minute.'

Jennifer pushed the large designer sunglasses she had been wearing on to the top of her head and as she did so, a strange flicker of recognition passed through me . . .

Now, however, was not the moment to pursue such things. Instead, I put my papers away, ready to do battle with Guy the moment he stepped into the corridor, just as the lift at the far end of the corridor opened and Mark stepped out, followed by James. The pair of them hotfooted it down the corridor towards me.

I suddenly didn't feel very well and decided that seeing Mark again might perhaps not have been such a good idea; but by then it was too late. With my stomach twisting like an ice-skater going for gold, I waited for them to reach me.

'Right, Lucy,' said James, flashing a dazzling smile in my direction. 'Do you want the good news or the bad news?'

'Er, I'll take the good first, I think,' I replied. Not that there was going to be any good news. Ever again. Not unless Mark told me I'd got the wrong end of the stick where he and Jennifer where concerned.

'The good news is that it won't be a problem,' replied James.

'Excuse me?' Had I missed something? 'What won't be a problem?'

'The fact that you'll be doing the hearing for Mark.'

'But,' I stammered, 'I can't – I just can't. Jennifer hates me, she's an ex-client of mine, and Mark and I used to be an item. I'd say that fairly much rules me out of any further professional involvement in the case, wouldn't you?'

I'd intended the last bit to be less of a question and more a statement of fact, but James didn't seem at all bothered. He just aimed an even bigger grin at me.

'Like I said,' he told me, 'I don't think it's going to be a problem.'

'Well,' I wasn't giving up yet, 'how about the fact I haven't prepared the case?'

'You've read all the papers.' James dismissed my objections with a wave of his hand. 'It'll be a piece of cake. Look, one of my social services cases has gone ballistic and I'm on in the courtroom next door at two o'clock. It'll only be a short hearing, so if I'm back in time, I'll take over the reins; if not, I'll leave it in your capable hands. You'll be fabulous, darling!'

And he bestowed another smile upon me.

'Right,' he said, spotting Guy walking down the corridor, 'I'll just have a quick word with our beloved leader and leave you to it. Catch you later, kids!'

And with a waggle of his hand, he turned on the heel of his bespoke Italian leather shoes and made his way over to Guy.

'Thanks, Lucy,' said Mark. 'I do appreciate this, you know.'

'You'd bloody better had,' I replied. 'But how on earth is he going to get Jennifer to agree to me doing this? Has he got something on her?'

Mark shrugged. 'Haven't got the foggiest. She hasn't mentioned anything to me.'

'Yes,' I said, fixing him with a Paddington Bear hard stare. 'You've been seeing quite a bit of each other over recent days, haven't you?'

Mark went bright red. 'I think I need to talk to you about that,' he began, before our attention was arrested by Guy's voice saying:

'I don't think that's a good idea, Gilleard, do you?'

We watched as James, leaning nonchalantly against the wall, paused for a moment before saying something inaudible in reply. This was obviously it; the piece of super-information. Guy went white, then red, then a weird greenish-yellow, and then he appeared to choke. When he'd finished coughing and spluttering, James patted him on the back, said something that sounded like 'Good man!' and went off with a little skip into the court next to ours.

Guy, on the other hand, was not a happy camper. Giving me a frown as he passed, he went up to Jennifer, took her by the arm and pulled her over to the far corner of the corridor. There was muttering, their heads close together, and then Jennifer exclaimed:

'Bloody hell, Guy! How *could* you?'

He shushed her – a brave man in my opinion – and they muttered again for a minute or so, Jennifer obviously extremely angry. In the end, she broke away from their little huddle and called Mandy over. Mandy listened to what they had to say, frowned, looked at me and then shrugged.

'Well, if you're cool about it,' she said to Jennifer, 'that's fine by me. It's only a short hearing. I shouldn't think you'd be prejudiced by it.'

'I am *not* cool about it,' hissed Jennifer in the world's loudest stage whisper. 'I simply don't have any choice.'

And turning her back on Guy, she stomped over to her seat and sank into it, arms folded and legs crossed.

Now it was my turn to put Guy properly in his place.

I laid my notebook and pen on my chair, marched over to where Guy and Mandy still had their heads together and glowered at him.

'Mr Jennings,' I began, with a nod to Mandy in lieu of greeting.

'I have nothing further to say to you, Stephens,' he observed loftily.

'Good. Because that means you can concentrate on *listening* for a change. If you want proof that I am not the mole in the Jones case – which,' I turned to Mandy, 'Mr

Jennings has sacked me for, despite the fact that he has no substantive evidence against me – I suggest you ring either Henry Spiggott or Cameron Macdonald, who will confirm that it was Estelle Douglas, the secretary who worked for both Mr Spiggott and Miss Irving. I had dinner with Tom Gedge not to pass on information but to receive it – and thus get to the bottom of the leaks before even more damage was done. Anyhow, Guy, I will expect your profuse apologies and a retraction of your allegations after the conclusion of this case. Good day.'

He gave a sharp intake of breath and went white, and I walked off, leaving him punching Spiggott's direct-dial number into his mobile.

The judge's clerk came down the corridor clutching a Tupperware sandwich box and smiled at me.

'I got Mr Gilleard's message about the change of counsel on this case. Judge would like to know if ten minutes more with your client will be enough time, Miss Stephens?' she asked, pulling her sagging black gown back over her shoulders.

It should be dandy – all I needed to confirm with Mark was whether or not he still wanted to contest the matter.

'Yes, that should be fine.' I smiled back. 'I just need to have a quick chat with Mr Landsdown here.'

'Excellent.' The clerk nodded. 'Judge had a good look at the papers this morning and she thinks we should try and get the whole thing sorted out today. She reckons that the little boy is going to need as much time as possible to adapt to the outcome and that the case itself is pretty straightforward.'

'Right.' I nodded, trying not to be disconcerted that I now had a full hearing on my hands. 'Ten minutes then – although if it could be a long ten minutes, I think that would be helpful.'

The clerk grinned at me. 'No problem, Miss Stephens. Now, I'll just go and tell Mr Jennings the good news.'

'Mark,' I said, walking over to where he was loitering under a window, 'the clerk has informed me that the judge wants to get the whole case over and done with today.'

Mark took a deep breath.

'Fine,' he said. 'The suspense was killing me anyway.'

'Come and sit down,' I told him. 'I need you to fill me in on one or two points. Most importantly, are you still going to fight – and if so, what sort of tone do you want me to set?'

'Yes, I am going to fight.' Mark's face was pale, but his gaze was steady and determined. 'Things are better between Jennifer and me than they have been for a long while, but I can't let her get away with this.'

I focused hard on my page, trying not to let my writing go all shaky. I wished to God this man didn't have such a profound effect on me.

'Okay,' I said. 'Now, the judge will want to hear evidence from both of you. Because it is her application, Jennifer'll go in the witness box first. Guy will ask her some questions and then it's my turn. After that, you'll give your evidence: I'll help you tell your story by asking fairly open questions, then Guy will cross-examine you.'

'Oh, shit,' he muttered under his breath.

'It'll be fine,' I said firmly. I almost put my hand on his knee and gave it a comforting squeeze but decided that wouldn't be a very good idea.

'The judge isn't interested in point-scoring,' I went on. 'All she wants to know is what the best outcome is for Josh. Just remember to do three things and you'll be okay.'

'What are they?' asked Mark, as if I was offering him a life raft.

'One: answer the question head-on. If there's a "but", that's cool – but explain it *after* you've answered the question. It makes you look honest and helpful rather than evasive and dodgy. Next, always tell the truth. And finally, stay calm. Whatever she suggests, however black a picture of you she paints, don't get shouty.'

'Right,' said Mark, fiddling with his tie and making it go all skew-whiff. 'I think I've got that.'

'Now,' I continued, 'our case is that Jennifer has done everything she can to stop you and Josh having a relationship and that this is just the latest phase in her campaign.'

Mark nodded, his tie still awry. I had to fight very hard not to reach over and tweak it back into place.

'There is something else,' he said, 'something you need to know about her and me. I was going to tell you before the clerk came over.'

'Oh?' I asked, as dispassionately as possible. Whatever it was, I was pretty certain I wasn't going to like it.

'Yup.' He ran his finger round the inside of his collar and made his tie look even worse. 'I had dinner with her on Friday.'

'I was there,' I reminded him.

'Mmm.' He pulled a face. 'So we had dinner on Friday night, and—'

'And she came round to yours on Saturday?' I supplied.

'Yes, she did.'

'And did she, um, stay over?' I looked at my notebook.

'It's not as simple as that . . .' Mark began.

I snapped into barrister mode. 'Did she stay? Yes or no, Mark.'

'Yes.'

'Will she be staying again in the future?'

'We only have a short time before she leaves to make sure that—'

'Answer my question please, Mark.'

He looked at his feet. 'Yes. She'll be there this Saturday.'

'Fine.'

Actually, it was a very long way from being fine, but it was now a quarter past two and everybody who was anybody in the world of legal London seemed to be hanging around the corridor waiting for their cases to start. Now was not the best time for me to have hysterics.

'Right.' I snapped my book shut angrily. 'Let's go in, shall we?'

'But . . .' he stammered, 'I need to tell you—'

'It's not important, Mark,' I said. 'Just let me get on with my job.'

And leaving him to bring the papers and files in, I stalked through the pale wooden double doors with their blacked-out windows into the courtroom and took my seat at the front.

27

'May it please your Ladyship, I represent the applicant in this matter, Ms Jennifer Woodford, and my learned friend Miss Stephens is for the defendant, Mr Mark Landsdown. Despite the voluminous papers in this case, the matter before the court today is almost brutally straightforward: is Ms Woodford to be allowed to take Joshua, the parties' only child, with her when she begins her new job in Hong Kong in three months' time? The history of the case is rather protracted, but the seminal dates are these: the parties first met in . . .' Guy was on his feet and going great guns with his opening speech, the pleasant baritone of his voice effortlessly filling the huge space of the courtroom.

A little further along the same row of seats was yours truly, flicking through Jennifer's previous statements and planning my cross-examination questions. The judge, Geraldine Snow, beamed benevolently down on us from her boxed-in dais at the front of the court, as if it gave her particular pleasure to be involved with our case. I shot a glance over my shoulder at Mark, sitting in the row directly behind me. He met my gaze with a grimace and ran a worried hand through his hair; the state of his clothing too seemed to have degenerated even further in the past ten minutes. He looked a mess. I tore off some paper: *Your tie is crooked*, I wrote and handed it back. Mark dutifully rearranged himself.

'. . . Contact has been going well, thanks to the efforts of both parties.' Guy was coming to the end of his opening spiel. 'On Saturday, Joshua stayed overnight for the first time at the father's house. It is intended that this will be repeated this coming Saturday . . .'

Only it wasn't just Joshua, was it? I thought to myself grimly.

'Ms Woodford, if you'd like to step up into the witness box,' invited Guy.

Jennifer walked down to the front of the court and up two steps into the pulpit-like wooden witness box. The usher approached with a Bible and a large laminated sheet of card.

'Hold the Bible in your right hand and repeat what is written on the sheet, please,' he asked.

In a clear, Oscar-winning voice, Jennifer took the proffered volume and declared:

'I swear by Almighty God that the evidence I shall give shall be the truth, the whole truth and nothing but the truth.'

Guy rearranged his papers. 'Will you please tell the court your full name and occupation.'

'Jennifer Louise Woodford. Banker.'

'How would you describe your present relationship with the father?'

Oh, bloody hell, Guy – rub my nose in it, why don't you?

Jennifer shot a look across the court at Mark. It wasn't an altogether affectionate one, but then this was Jennifer. Perhaps this was her doing fully loved-up and back together.

'Things have markedly improved during the last week or so,' she said at last. 'It's important for Joshua that we try and get on as well as possible.'

Yeah, *right*!

'And how did last Saturday's overnight visit go?' Guy continued.

'It went very well. Its purpose was twofold: firstly to

make sure I was on hand if Joshua was unsettled, and secondly to spend some time with Mr Landsdown so that we could discuss the future.'

'And the rest,' I muttered to myself.

'What was that, Miss Stephens? Do you have something to add to the proceedings?' The judge raised an eyebrow and smiled at me.

Bugger! Note to self: make sure internal monologue is activated at all times.

I stood up. 'No, your Ladyship. I – er – was just clearing my throat, that's all – a bit of a tickle.'

'I'll have the usher bring you over a glass of water. Can't have a tickly throat interrupting proceedings, can we?'

'I'm grateful, your Ladyship,' I repeated automatically, as the clerk poured me a glass of water and made her way over towards me.

'Not at all. Now, please continue, Mr Jennings.'

I sat down with my heart pounding away and took a sip of water, Jennifer looking daggers at me all the while. It could have been worse, I supposed; I might have shouted, 'Hands off him, you harpy! He's mine,' and been forced to kill myself afterwards.

'And my final question, Ms Woodford: how do you see the future?'

'Well, a lot of that will depend upon my employer. Certainly, I do see myself in the Far East for the short to medium term, but I hope in a few years to move back to London. In the meanwhile, Josh will have built up a strong relationship with Mr Landsdown based on substantial, if not frequent, time spent together.' She smiled a truly frightening smile. 'Naturally, Mr Landsdown will always be welcome at my home, wherever I am in the world.'

I turned round. To my surprise, Mark was not looking ecstatic at that pronouncement. He had gone a sort of puce colour and was having difficulty swallowing. Still, he had told me he would do *anything* for Joshua . . .

'No further questions, your Ladyship.' Guy sat down.

I rearranged my papers and rose. The blood was pounding in my head. I knew it wasn't just Josh I was fighting for; it was Mark too. But as much as I tried to keep a professional head on my shoulders, it was almost impossible.

'Ms Woodford,' I began, trying to focus on the enormous coat of arms hanging on the wall above the judge's head, rather than Jennifer's face, 'you have just told the court that Mr Landsdown will always be welcome at your home, but in the history of this case, your reaction has been to try and shut him out of Joshua's life, hasn't it?'

Jennifer glared at me.

'No,' she said, slowly and deliberately, 'it has been to make sure things progressed in Josh's best interests.'

'Ah,' I said, 'Josh's best interests. And those were served by you changing your phone number on two occasions and not letting Mr Landsdown know? Or, last summer, when Mr Landsdown had arranged to take Joshua to the seaside, booking a foreign holiday on the day of his trip and only informing him when you and Josh were actually on the way to the airport?'

The judge forgot to close her mouth. Taking this as a good sign, I pressed on.

'Or perhaps Joshua's best interests were served by refusing to let him see his father for two months last year. The same two months that he was involved in a new relationship.'

Jennifer gave me a look that should have turned me to ice. Luckily I was too worked up for it to have any effect: the thought of Mark playing happy families with someone who had treated him so badly was unbearable.

'And your point is?' she replied archly.

'My point, Ms Woodford, is that you have frequently

sought to disrupt contact between Mr Landsdown and Joshua. That's the case, isn't it?'

'I've done what I saw as being in Josh's best interests.'

'Ms Woodford, please answer my question. Over the past four years you have frequently sought to disrupt contact between Joshua and Mr Landsdown: yes or no?'

There was a long pause: she was wavering.

'Mr Landsdown has previously made a number of sworn statements describing how you have prevented Joshua from seeing him,' I persisted. 'Were these statements untrue?'

'No.'

'Then I shall ask you one last time before moving on. Have you, on a number of occasions in the past, sought to prevent or otherwise hamper contact between the defendant father and Joshua?'

'Yes. But—'

'Thank you, Ms Woodford.' I leapt in before she could develop the 'but' any further.

Landsdown leads, fifteen–love.

'Now,' I went on to my next point, 'you have told the court today that you will do everything in your power to facilitate contact between Joshua and his father after your move to Hong Kong.'

Jennifer smiled sweetly at the judge and nodded. 'Naturally.'

'And what do you see that contact entailing?'

'Well, telephone calls, of course, and the odd visit.'

'Frequency?'

'The phone calls – maybe once a week; and the visits will become more frequent as Joshua gets older and is able to fly on his own. Until then, Mr Landsdown is welcome to come and stay with us – as he has already said he will.'

She smiled at Mark again, and it had a bad effect on me; my stomach did a short of nasty twisting motion and for a moment or two I felt seriously queasy. As the room swam back into focus, I realised someone was tugging at the sleeve of my jacket.

It was Mark.

'Excuse me one moment,' I gasped and turned round, glad of the distraction. 'What is it?'

'Ask her about the new relationship,' he hissed. 'She hasn't mentioned it and the judge needs to know.'

I closed my eyes and tried very hard to keep breathing.

The syllables rattled round my head like gunshots: *new relationship*. Jennifer and Mark, back together for the sake of Joshua. *Their* new relationship. I turned back and faced my witness, consciously forcing the air into my lungs.

'I am instructed to ask you, Ms Woodford, about your new relationship.'

Jennifer went quite pale and clutched the edge of the witness box. I kind of knew how she felt and was doing much the same sort of thing with the ledge in front that I was resting my books on.

Then she threw a panic-stricken look in Guy's direction and he got to his feet.

'I hesitate to rise,' he said (this is what real barristers say instead of 'Objection, your Honour!'), 'but I fail to see how this line of questioning will assist the court.'

'On the contrary, Mr Jennings, I feel it may serve to clarify matters. Please continue, Miss Stephens.'

Mark tugged at my sleeve again.

'Ask her how she expects the new relationship will affect Josh,' he insisted.

I cleared my throat and did my best to look Jennifer in the eye.

'What effect will your new relationship have on Josh?'

She eyeballed me back fearlessly. 'I expect it will be entirely positive,' she announced. 'He's getting to the age when he needs a male role model.'

'Exactly!' cried Mark, leaping to his feet. 'And it

should be me who is that role model!'

This didn't make any sense: I goggled first at Jennifer, then round at Mark, and then back to Jennifer again. They were glaring at each other across the court, and there certainly wasn't the rosy glow of love in their eyes. I didn't understand.

'It. Is. None. Of. Your. Business!' Jennifer spat, with enough venom to fuel a large nest of vipers.

'Now!' said the judge, firmly and loudly enough for us all to jump a couple of inches in the air. 'Ms Woodford – calm down; Mr Landsdown – you will have your chance to speak later. Continue please, Miss Stephens.'

'I, um, I just need a moment with my client,' I stammered. 'May I have five minutes?'

'I think a five-minute adjournment might be in everybody's interests.' The judge beamed, becoming her usual sunny self once again.

'Court rise!' commanded the clerk.

As we scrambled back into the corridor, Jennifer barged past me and almost knocked me flying. She made a beeline for Guy and dragged him a safe distance down the corridor for a confab. She was livid: she pushed her hair away from her face and bit her lip as he spoke to her, his hands at the top of her arms. Then she took a deep breath as Guy continued to talk, before finally looking down and nodding, the anger slowly ebbing out of her. The transformation was fantastic: if Guy ever had enough of running chambers, I reckoned he could always go for a job as a lion-tamer.

'Lucy?' Mark was looking at me. 'Are you okay?'

'Yes,' I said, swivelling round to face him. 'I'm fine. Now, please, *please*, whatever you do, don't shout out like that again. Judges hate it. Plus, what I'm trying to do is paint her as the villain of the piece and put you on the side of the angels – that won't work if you start heckling her.'

Mark looked as if he might be counting to ten under his breath.

'I'll do my best, Lucy, but – bloody hell! She's planning to bugger off to Hong Kong, cut me out of my son's life and then replace me with a dad substitute.'

'No, Mark,' I said very slowly and calmly, thinking that at least one of us had to get a grip. 'You and Jennifer are together, remember? For the sake of Joshua? Giving it another go?'

He looked at me as if I'd gone bonkers.

'Me?' he asked incredulously. 'Why on earth would I want to get back with her?'

'For Josh,' I protested. 'That night at the Orangery – you wanted to give it another go. And you told me you'd do anything to keep Josh in the country.'

'Anything within reason,' he protested. 'I love my son, of course I do, but I have my limits.'

'So you and her,' I was feeling a bit dim, 'you're not – um – together?'

'No, you big muppet,' he said affectionately. 'She told me on Saturday that there was someone new, and if he can get the right sort of job, he might be emigrating with her.'

Relief crashed through me like a tidal wave and I leaned against the wall for support.

'Who is he?' This seemed quite a basic bit of information.

Mark shook his head. 'She wouldn't say. But I'd put money on it he's a high-flyer – especially if he's relocating to the Far East without much difficulty. And it hasn't been going on that long: she said something about having been swept off her feet.'

'Why would she keep his identity secret?' I asked.

Mark shrugged. 'That's Jenny all over: always got to have the upper hand; always got to be in control – even if it's something like this that I'm going to find out about anyway. You know, it really gets to me sometimes, and . . .'

But I wasn't listening to him; I was watching Guy and

Jennifer. They were standing close together with their heads almost touching. She was saying something; he nodded and replied and then went to turn away. She addressed him again, and as she did so, her fingers smoothed an invisible speck of dust off his tie. It was an entirely unconscious motion, one that I'm not even sure she knew she had made.

But I'd seen it.

And I knew exactly what I was going to do with the information she had just given me.

I turned back to Mark.

'Let's go in,' I said, and opened the door for him.

'You will remember, Ms Woodford, that you are still under oath,' I said, once everybody had settled back into their places and we'd risen for the judge.

'Of course,' she snapped. 'I can hold a fact like that in my brain for longer than fifteen minutes, you know.'

'I'm sure you can,' I replied. 'Then you will recall the topic we were discussing immediately prior to our adjournment.'

'We were discussing my departure for Hong Kong in order to take up an excellent position offered to me by my employer.'

'Not exactly,' I replied. 'We were, if you will forgive me for correcting you, discussing your new relationship.'

Jennifer blushed hard and glared at me. She managed to look scary and embarrassed at the same time: no mean feat.

'You *do* have a new partner, don't you?' I probed.

'Yes,' she admitted with her eyes cast downwards in the manner of a guilty teenager who has been caught snogging in her bedroom by her mum.

'And how long, exactly, has that relationship been in existence?' I continued.

'About three weeks.'

'And in your view, is it a *serious* relationship?'

'Your Ladyship,' Guy was on his feet again, 'I really don't feel that this line of questioning is going to establish anything of use to the case.'

'On the contrary, Mr Jennings,' replied the judge with a broad smile, 'I think it is of the utmost interest.'

Hoorah!

'You were about to tell me, Ms Woodford,' I reminded her helpfully, 'whether or not you consider this to be a serious relationship.'

'Of course I do,' she snapped back. 'He wouldn't be thinking of emigrating to Hong Kong with me if it wasn't.'

'So are you planning on living together, then?'

She nodded her assent.

'And Joshua gets on well with him?'

'Yes, he does, as a matter of fact.'

'And what does he do, Ms Woodford? How does this new partner of yours earn his living?'

Guy was perpendicular again before the words had even left my lips.

'I really don't see why my client should have to answer this question – it is irrelevant to the outcome of the matter.'

'I disagree,' the judge replied. 'Please continue, Miss Stephens.'

'He's – he's,' Jennifer spluttered, 'he's a—'

'Actually, Ms Woodford,' I broke in, 'he's sitting just over there, isn't he?'

For a moment I thought she was having some sort of seizure, because she went very, very pale and very, very still. I couldn't even see her chest moving to tell whether or not she was breathing.

'It's Mr Jennings, isn't it, Ms Woodford?' I said calmly. 'Mr Jennings is your lover.'

There was a sort of clattering noise as the judge dropped her pen, followed by a scrabbling one as the clerk tried to retrieve it for her.

'You are still on oath, Ms Woodford,' I persisted. 'Please reply to my question.'

Jennifer looked at Guy, who nodded; then, in a tiny voice, she muttered: 'Yes.'

As Jennifer spoke, something else clicked into place in my brain: Guy's discomfort whenever the photograph of the mystery woman was mentioned; the familiarity of the features in the picture that had shimmered through my brain but never fully registered; the sunglasses that were still pushed up on top of Jennifer's immaculate hair . . .

'And, just for the sake of completeness, the picture that was circulating in the newspapers a week or so ago of the mysterious lady leaving Number Ten by the back door, that was you, wasn't it? You'd been to a party there with Mr Jennings.'

She nodded.

'No further questions, your Ladyship,' I said, and sat down.

For a moment or two there was complete and utter silence. I couldn't tell you what was going on in the rest of the courtroom, because at that moment I was concentrating hard on not bursting into tears. I had gone into court intending to fight for Josh on Mark's behalf, but somewhere along the line I'd allowed it to become a rather personal battle between Jennifer and myself. I was a crappy, self-indulgent lawyer who'd let her personal life get in the way of her professional duty and bullied a witness into making a highly embarrassing disclosure. Mark was next up in the witness box and Guy would undoubtedly be thinking that as I'd sown the wind, Mark should reap the whirlwind. He was going to be crucified for what I'd just done.

I sat there staring at my blue counsel's notebook with all my lovely, rational questions staring back at me; and I have no idea how much time passed or what on earth was going on around me – until I felt a kindly hand on my shoulder.

'Come on,' whispered James, 'you deserve a cup of coffee.'

With great difficulty I got to my feet and, on shaky legs, manoeuvred myself out of the courtroom and into the corridor. Mark was over by the window with two plastic cups in his hands. He held one out to me.

'You were fab,' he whispered. 'How on earth did you work that one out?'

I sipped the coffee. It tasted foul.

'I was watching them,' I said. 'It seemed obvious.'

'Well done, girlie.' James smiled at me. 'I slipped in the back and heard the last bit. I was going to offer to take over, but as you were doing so well without me . . .'

'But,' I took another gulp of the evil brown liquid swilling round my cup, 'I didn't ask half the questions I should have done.'

James shook his head. 'Doesn't matter: you've rattled them. Even if the case goes against us, the fact that Guy was shagging his client is embarrassing enough for them to be on their knees begging for decent contact between Mark and Josh.'

'Oh,' I said, taking another sip and then putting the cup down. 'I'm sorry, Mark, but the coffee's undrinkable.'

'You're right,' he agreed, putting his on the windowsill and slipping his freed-up hand into mine.

'So, what happened?' I asked James. 'After I sat down, I can't really remember anything.'

'Not a lot. Guy said he needed to speak to his client and everyone filed out.'

I looked round. Guy and Jennifer were nowhere to be seen. Mandy was on her own, loitering by the door of the court and toying with a packet of cigarettes. She smiled at me and came over.

'I'm not sure how long we've got,' she said. 'I'm dying for a ciggie but I don't want to be outside when the judge calls us back in.'

'You didn't go with them?' I was astonished. The normal rules of engagement dictate that solicitors must chaperone their client and counsel at all times. However, this case was such a muddle that the casual observer would be hard pushed to recognise which rules of professional conduct we were actually adhering to.

Mandy shook her head in reply to my question.

'Guy said it was personal and it would be better if it was just the two of them. God, how could all that have been going on under my nose and I didn't notice? I must be losing my touch.'

'I had no idea who her bloke was either,' said Mark. 'She told me there was someone new, but – Guy! Well, he's married, for a start, isn't he?'

'Yup,' I nodded, 'with kids. It's going to be one hell of a mess.'

'And the papers,' said James, with an almost gleeful glint in his eye. 'Think about what they're going to say once they get their hands on it: leading barrister carrying on with one of his clients, contemplating fleeing the country with her and allowing the PM to take the blame for having a mistress when she was Guy's all the time. I think we may be electing a new head of chambers this week.'

'Actually,' I turned to him, 'given the media interest in the story, it may be an idea if Josh comes for an extended visit to Dartmouth Park Road. At least until all the fuss has died down. I'll go and suggest it to them when they reappear.'

Hearing footsteps coming down the corridor, we looked up and saw Guy and Jenny walking towards us. She was still looking very pale, but they were both composed. I noticed that her right and his left hand were clasped together.

'We need to talk, Mark,' she said.

'We do indeed,' he replied.

I reached for my notebook and Mandy put her packet of cigarettes back in her handbag.

'No,' said Jennifer, 'just Mark and me. We brought Josh into this mess and it's up to us to get him out. I think there's been more than enough legal wrangling in this matter for now.'

'Good girl,' said James. 'As I always say, if there's anything worse than one lawyer, it's two of the buggers; and as there seem to be at least four of us tied up in this case, I think you'd be better off sorting it out by yourselves.'

Mark smiled.

'Come on, Jen,' he said, 'we'll get it straightened out.'

Jennifer nodded, mutely.

'Hey,' he said, 'it'll be okay.' He put an arm round her shoulders as they walked off up the corridor.

And you know what? For the first time in weeks, I felt he might just be right.

28

Hez was waiting for me when I got back to chambers.

'Jane said you'd gone to see Mark. How did it go?' she put down the newspaper she'd been reading and slid off my desk to help me unload the bazillion books and law reports I'd carted back with me.

'We're back at half nine tomorrow,' I said. 'Or at least James is. I've got a case in Woolwich.'

I flicked through the telephone messages I'd picked up from my pigeonhole. There was one from my dad telling me that he and my mum had gone out for a meal at the weekend (*a meal?*) and sorted out the maintenance problem. Jeez, maybe there was a God after all . . .

'So Mark didn't lose?' Hez brought me back to the here and now with a bump.

'He's having a quiet word with Jennifer to see if they can sort this out without a fight.'

'No way!' Her eyes were virtually out of their sockets.

'Way!' I was almost too tired to talk, but I needed a drink and had taken the precaution of stopping by El Vino on my way back. 'Go to my bag, get the bottle of wine out of it and see if Hugo's got a corkscrew. I'll get a couple of mugs. Meet me back here in two.'

By the time I'd dragged myself up the stairs into the kitchen, secured some clean cups and headed back down again, Hez had rustled up not only the corkscrew but some real wine glasses and Hugo, who had just got back from court himself.

'He said I couldn't have the corkscrew if I didn't invite him to the party,' said Hez, with a coy smile in Hugo's direction.

I was going to have to watch her, or they'd be jumping on the next train north to Gretna Green.

'So.' The corkscrew provider beamed. 'What are we celebrating?'

I poured three glasses of wine and told the tale – although I omitted to let on who Jennifer's new paramour was. I didn't want to be accused of spreading salacious gossip round chambers; that would happen fast enough without me.

But Hez wasn't having any of it. Putting down her wine glass, she gripped my knee with a pleading look on her face. 'Pleeeeeease tell me who it is,' she wheedled, 'please please please please please! I'll do all the washing-up for a month.'

'We have a dishwasher.'

'I'll clean the bath.'

'No.'

'And the loo. And the washbasin.'

'No.'

'For a year.'

'Our lease runs out in five months.'

She sat back in her seat with a sulky look on her face.

'You're no fun any more, Lucy Stephens.'

'Does it involve a third party?' Hugo was trying it on too.

'Perhaps.'

'And from what you've said, someone in whom the newspapers would take more than a passing interest?'

'Possibly – look, Hugo, this isn't fair and I'm *not* going to tell you, so you might as well give—'

'Well, unless it's the Prime Minister,' he shot me a

penetrating look, 'and I can see from your face that it's not, it must be – Guy!'

'Hugo!' I hissed. 'How did you guess?'

'I didn't,' he replied cheerily, 'it was a process of logical deduction. Besides, haven't you noticed he's been "working late" rather a lot recently?'

'He has been running the most important divorce case in the country,' I reminded him. 'It wasn't going to settle itself.'

'No, but he's had Jane make loads of dinner reservations – I've overheard her at least seven times – and she's ordered six bunches of flowers from that posh Stems place in his name. So either she's whooping it up with Guy's credit card, or he's busy doing a bit of mattress-surfing with someone who isn't Gemma Jennings.'

He helped himself to another glass of wine.

'Plus he went AWOL the weekend before last and not even Stan knew where he was – remember? And,' Hugo grinned at me, 'you're forgetting the complete, give-away, looking-you-in-the-face, obvious clue: that photo in the *Stoat* – it was Jennifer, wasn't it? Took me a while to realise, but there was something so scarily familiar about the mouth – and those glasses.'

I nodded. That had to have been the evidence James had used so devastatingly against Guy before the hearing.

'I can't believe it took me till today to work that one out,' I said. 'Guy's been playing a dodgy game, hasn't he? He must have known he was going to get caught out parading her around at Number Ten parties.'

Hugo shrugged. 'It was her bad luck to get papped coming out the back door. If she'd used the main entrance like everyone else, no one would have suspected a thing. Anyway, the question now is, what are you going to do about it?'

I drained my glass.

'Nothing,' I said firmly and decisively. 'Their privacy will be invaded enough over the next week or so without me sticking my oar in. Frankly, if there was anything I could do to keep this whole thing out of the papers, I would.'

'Good God, Stephens,' exclaimed Hugo, 'I'm not suggesting you blackmail Guy – I was thinking more along the lines of getting him on side.'

'Why?' I was puzzled. 'Do you mean the tenancy decision?'

'No . . . but Irving here could do with a bit of help.' He smiled affectionately in Hez's direction and squeezed her knee.

'He means,' said Hez, beaming back at him, 'that I got the job at Carridan's. I spoke to Jill at lunchtime. Only they've changed their minds about the references. They want three because of what I did to Spiggott at the Guildhall function. Now, after I spoke to him yesterday, Spig will do one, but I need two more stonkers.'

'So I think a meeting with Guy is in order, don't you?' Hugo arched an eyebrow. 'I'll just ring Jane and see if he's available.'

As Hez and I shuffled into Guy's room five minutes later, I half wished I'd brought the remains of the wine with me: if anyone had ever been in need of a restorative glass of the red stuff, that person was Guy.

'Yes,' he said, as we entered. 'What can I do for you?'

'We need to talk,' I said.

Guy glanced at Hez. 'I don't really want to discuss the matter in front of a third party,' he said. 'Too many other people are involved.'

'This isn't about what happened at court today, Guy,' I replied. 'It's about the mole.'

'Ah,' he said, gesturing to the little horseshoe of seats in front of his desk. 'You were right, Stephens, I owe you a substantial apology, and if there is anything I can do to make it up to you, I would be happy to do so.'

'Apology accepted,' I replied graciously. 'But I wasn't the only person to be wrongly accused, and if you're serious about making amends, Miss Irving here could do with your help.'

'I lost my job,' said Hez. 'The Pig – I mean Mr Spiggott – was suggesting that I was the source of the leaks. Then he threatened me with the sack if there were any further revelations – which of course there were – and the whole thing got a bit out of hand. As a consequence I now find myself unemployed and in dire need of a good reference.'

Guy nodded. 'Are we talking about the incident at the Guildhall last Tuesday?'

Hez blushed slightly at the memory.

'He humiliated me in front of some of our most important clients and I snapped, poured a jug of Pimm's over his head and told him where he could stick his job. My P45 arrived by courier the next day.'

Despite himself, a smile spread slowly over Guy's features.

'Well done!' he said. 'Spiggott's had it coming. But as neither of you was our mole, what has happened to the woman who was? Estelle Douglas, wasn't it?'

'Estelle confessed to the managing partner and left yesterday,' said Hez. 'When I warned her that the game was up, she confirmed that her original motive had been the money, but that Spiggott's treatment of all of us tipped her over the edge. The managing partner confirmed that because Spiggott had been so foul, he wouldn't be taking any further action against her – plus Spig got a written warning; so you could say that justice has been done.'

Guy pressed his fingertips together and looked intently at Hez.

'If it would be of assistance, I would be glad to stand as one of your referees, Miss Irving. I am fully aware of how much effort you put into the Jones case. Every letter, every document that I got from Sheppertons had your reference on it – and I don't imagine that's because Henry Spiggott wanted to promote your professional profile. Whom do you need me to contact?'

'Sarah Laverstock at Carridan and Lacey, please.'

'No problem. I'll get something off to her right away.' Guy smiled wistfully for a moment. 'When you say "jug of Pimm's", was it the whole strawberries and slices of cucumber version?'

'Yes,' said Hez, beginning to relax a bit, 'and he got a sprig of mint stuck behind his ear and kept on scratching at it.'

'Actually,' said Guy thoughtfully, 'have you got a moment? There's someone I think I should call.'

Hez and I looked at one another: apart from stopping Hugo from polishing off the rest of the wine, there was nothing else we needed to do that evening.

'Go ahead,' I said.

Guy dialled.

And waited.

Then smiled.

'Hi, Llew, I was wondering how things were going. Aha . . . yes . . . yes . . . really? You can't seem to get hold of her? Well, I have a bit of news for you – Henrietta Irving has left Sheppertons. No, I don't blame her either. She's going to be working at Carridan and Lacey from now on with Sarah Laverstock – excellent firm. Aha . . . yes . . . I think a phone call from yourself to Sarah insisting that Henrietta continues the excellent job she has done for you so far would be entirely appropriate. Many thanks. See you around.'

And he replaced the receiver.

'I'll give it five minutes before I ring Carridan's myself,' he said. 'I think Sarah will be tied up with a call from the Prime Minister right now.'

'Excuse me?' Hez was on the edge of her seat.

'Llew Jones is going to ring Sarah Laverstock himself

and tell her he's having all his files sent over from Sheppertons for your personal attention. It's not exactly a reference, but I hope it'll do.'

I think it was the first time in my life I'd ever seen Hez speechless.

'And you will need to liaise with Miss Stephens here, who I hope will stay on as counsel in the matter to tie up any loose ends.'

'Does that mean I'm not sacked?' I asked.

'Ultimately, your future rests with the tenancy committee tomorrow. Now, I won't be sitting on the panel because I will be handing in my resignation as head of chambers later today and it wouldn't be appropriate for me to chair the meeting under those circumstances. I will, however, be writing a report strongly recommending your candidacy.'

'Because of what happened this afternoon, or because you really mean it?'

I needed to know; if I did stay on at 3 Temple Buildings, it had to be because I'd won the job fair and square, not because it was a sop to Guy's guilty conscience.

Guy rubbed his face wearily. 'I mean it, Stephens. The work you produced for Llew Jones was of a very high calibre – and even though I hate to admit it, your performance this afternoon was also exceptional. And whilst I seem to be getting things off my chest, I need to apologise about the embargo I placed upon you and Mr Landsdown. Although I did initially fear that the gentlemen of the press might have taken an interest in the personal life of the PM's legal team, my most recent discussion with you on the subject was actually Jennifer's idea. I think she felt that with you in his corner, Mr Landsdown would put up a stronger fight over Joshua. In any event, what I did was entirely unprofessional and I should never have countenanced it.'

I opened my mouth in indignation, but before I had the chance to say anything I might have regretted, Hez leapt into the conversation.

'And you?' she asked Guy. 'What will you be doing?'

'I don't think I'm going to be here beyond the end of the month.' Guy pushed back his chair and walked over to the window, nervously jingling a bit of small change in his jacket pocket. 'Actually, I may not even be in the country by then.'

'Jenny?' I said.

'Yes. My marriage has been on the rocks for a while now,' said Guy, contemplating the BMWs and Mercedes lined up outside his window. 'I think all Jenny's done is fast-forward the process of separation. I've been offered a job working for the British Embassy in Hong Kong; and given everything that's happened today, it would probably be for the best if I took it. Anyway,' he turned round to face us and summoned up the ghost of a smile, 'I expect you girls have got better things to do than hang around here listening to my domestic plans. I think you, Miss Irving, have a new job to celebrate, and with any luck you will too, Miss Stephens. If you go to the fridge in the kitchen, you'll find a couple of bottles of Veuve Clicquot. With my compliments.'

'Thanks,' I said.

And feeling slightly dazed, we shuffled off to find our fizz.

Epilogue

The night I met Lucy had to be the maddest night of my life. I'd just moved back to London, partly for work and partly because I wanted to be near Josh, when Dave invited me along to a party to take my mind off things. What he *didn't* mention was anything about setting me up with one of Jo's mates. Good thing too, or I'd have made up some excuse and not bothered going.

I remember a sinking feeling coming over me when he said, 'There's someone I think you should meet,' and dragged me over to the other side of the room. But after that, well, what can I say? I don't really go in for all this 'our eyes met across a crowded room' bollocks, but as yet I haven't been able to come up with a better explanation, so I suppose it's going to have to do:

I met Lucy and I fell in love.

It felt weird, you know? Amazing, but definitely weird. As if I'd been plonked down in the middle of someone else's life and all the stuff about Josh and Jenny, the new job and the court case belonged to a different Mark Landsdown living unhappily somewhere in an alternative universe; all that mattered now was me and Lucy. Especially Lucy.

So here I am two years later. Sitting in the stifling heat in uncomfortable clothes in a little parish church in the south of England. It's a nice church; mainly Gothic, I think, judging by the pillars; although the east window looks a bit later – and the fan vaulting over by the side chapel is later still. I'd love to have a proper look around, but I'm not going to have time today. When the service is over, there's going to be a crush of people to contend with, then the photographs, and finally the inevitable dash across the countryside to the reception.

Josh is being unbelievably good. He's wearing one of those linen suits that are de rigueur for boys at this sort of occasion. When Lucy and I told him that he was going to have to wear special clothes, he thought we meant his England football strip. Even so, he acquiesced to being suited and booted and is now sitting very nicely beside me, reading a book about dinosaurs.

God, it's hot. But I can't take off my jacket or even loosen my tie – not that it *is* a tie; it's one of those hideous cravat things. And it's not just a jacket either, it's full morning dress with a waistcoat. I just thank God no one is expecting me to wear the hat as well. Hopefully it'll be a bit cooler at the reception. I think she said the hotel had air-conditioning.

I wonder where she's got to? I'll just have a quick look – no; no sign yet. Just more people piling into the back of the church. She can't be much longer; she's fifteen minutes late already. Still, her prerogative, I suppose.

No, I spoke too soon. Everybody's up and the music has started: Handel's 'Arrival of the Queen of Sheba'. I remember playing it in the background at my flat the night Jenny and I finally sorted everything out. After we left court, we went and had a coffee and decided that she would go to Hong Kong, leaving Josh with me. The whole thing only took an hour and was unbelievably civilised. Her solicitor drew up a court order, we signed it the next day and it was all over. I rang Lucy and some other friends to let them know, and Dave insisted on organising celebratory drinks at the pub that night. However, I soon disappeared off, leaving the others to have a couple for me. As Lucy reminds me, in her line of work there are never any winners, and I couldn't whoop it up knowing that in a matter of weeks Jenny and Josh would be facing the toughest goodbye of their lives.

Lucy slipped away too and came back to Kentish Town with me. She'd been rather subdued all evening, and she stood in the kitchen doorway fidgeting with my post while I made coffee. I couldn't stop looking at her: she was and is the most beautiful woman I have ever met. A few strands of hair had escaped from the twist she always wears it in at work, giving her a rather wanton, bed-head sort of look; and she threw me the occasional glance with her big eyes. That night, however, there was a strange atmosphere between us, something that stopped me from setting the rest of her hair free and then kissing her for as long as I could manage without drawing breath. I flicked some music on, hoping that it would magic about a change of mood, but that night not even the great G.F. Handel could lighten the proceedings.

Something was definitely UP.

'Mark,' she said at last, twisting an envelope in her hands as she spoke, 'I need to tell you something.'

Her voice was low and its tone didn't inspire much confidence that it was going to be good news.

'I know what you said about us keeping things simple for a bit, but I'm not sure that we feel the same way about each other,' she continued, fixing her eyes on the floor rather than me. 'And if that's the case, then I think we ought to be honest about it now, before one of us gets badly hurt.'

I nearly dropped the milk.

'You see,' by now she was so agitated she began tearing the envelope that contained my council tax demand into tiny little strips, 'you see, Mark – I love you. And however ridiculous it sounds, however much I try and block it out and say "it's just chemistry", or "it's just infatuation", or "it'll never last", I can't. I love you and it freaks me out.'

Just to be on the safe side, I put both the milk and the cups down on the kitchen counter. I knew I was staring at her in a way that suggested she was either mad or unstable (or possibly both), but I couldn't help it.

'Are you *sure*?' I asked, thinking I'd better check I'd heard her right. 'But we've – we've only known each other a few weeks.'

Her face fell. I was pretty sure those weren't the words she'd been hoping I'd come out with. But what if she *still* didn't want a serious relationship – or what if she was just saying she loved me as a prelude to adding that she couldn't cope with the idea and never wanted to see me again? Not that I would blame her if she did: I'd spent most of our time together giving her pretty good reasons to steer clear of me.

'Of course I'm sure.' Her face had gone a bit pale and she was dropping fragments of brown paper all over my kitchen floor. 'Do you think I'd be here making a fool of myself if I wasn't? I don't go round declaring love to all my clients, you know.'

'But love, I mean, that's quite a big deal,' I said, managing to be both unhelpful and inarticulate at the same time.

'I *know* – hence the me freaking out part.'

I continued to stare at her.

'Look,' she said, the final shreds of envelope fluttering floorwards. 'I've obviously put my foot in it again. Just tell me you don't feel the same and I'll leave.'

'I can't,' I replied, taking the bill itself out of her hands before she could destroy that. 'Because I love you too.'

I can hear the noise of silk skirts sweeping along Victorian floor tiles, which is not a sound I knew I recognised. But I'm right. Lucy and Hez float down the aisle, tiaras perched on their heads, and some make of hideously expensive shoes (I was told which, but being a bloke I forgot again quite quickly) on their feet. I catch Lou's eye and we smile, briefly. She looks amazing, she really does. She's gorgeous and clever, sexy and sophisticated, and frankly, if I wasn't in a packed church being watched by a couple of hundred people, I'd ... Well, there's always tonight. The music's stopped. There's just the obligatory clearing of throats and shuffling about before we kick off properly. I sneak a last sly look at Lucy and find she's looking back at me; we grin at each other.

The weeks after our mutual declaration of love were pretty busy. I moved house, Jennifer and Guy flew out to Hong Kong, Josh settled into life in Highgate and, seeing as Guy's resignation had left an extra vacancy, both Lucy and Hugo had been offered tenancies. In between all this, the pair of us snatched as much time together as we could. Then, one hot July night, Lucy and I were lying on the lawn trying to watch the stars come out – well, as best we could with the omnipresent orange glow of London in the background.

'There – up there!' she said. 'That's Cassiopeia. The one that looks like a W.'

'Lou,' I said, and cleared my throat a bit.

'And over there – is that Orion, or does that only come out in the winter?'

'I don't know,' I said. 'Look, Lucy—'

'There's a really bright one up here. What is it?'

'No idea. Lucy—'

'What about—'

I was beginning to learn that there is only one way out of a situation like this with Lucy Stephens. I rolled over and kissed her.

'Now that I've got your full attention,' I said, stroking her hair away from her face, 'there's something I want to ask you.'

Lucy kissed me back teasingly. 'Go on then.'

'You know I love you . . .'

She grinned at me through the half-light. 'I love you too,' she said. 'And I can now say it without panicking. Listen – IloveyouIloveyouIloveyou!'

'Good,' I said, propping myself up on my elbow so that I could look into her eyes as much as was possible given the growing darkness. 'Do you think you might love me enough to marry me?'

She glanced down and for a second I thought I'd arsed up.

'Promise me you'll think about it,' I said. 'I know it might make you feel a bit weird, but will you try?'

'I have done already,' she said, a smile stretching right across her face. 'And I think it's a top idea.'

And now here we are, standing at the front of the church with a million people staring at us. I can hear a baby crying at the back and a gentle 'flup' noise as either Jo or Dave takes the cap off a bottle of milk and plugs it into the infant's mouth. This is Imogen, baby number two; child number one, a sturdy toddler called Emily who was the cause of Jo's pregnancy angst, is wreaking havoc at the back of the church by the font. Thank God for Jo and Dave, I think to myself; or there's no way I'd be here, at a wedding in a tiny country church with the girl of my dreams.

'Out of ten?' I hear Lucy ask Hez quietly.

'Off the scale,' Hez whispers back.

Lucy takes Hez's bouquet and sits down next to me.

'Hello, gorgeous,' I whisper, kissing her just below the ear. In return, she squeezes my knee and we both look up to see Hez and Hugo beaming at each other as the vicar clears his throat and launches into his 'Dearly Beloved' bit. We're both really happy for Hez, and bizarre as it may seem, we've got used to the idea of her and Hugo: they work well together.

You're wondering about Lucy and me? Well, we're old hands at this matrimony thing. Once we'd actually decided we were going to do it, there didn't seem to be much point in waiting. So one Saturday a month after I'd proposed, and without telling them what was going on, we arranged to meet Jo, Dave, Hez and Hugo outside the registry office and did the deed, followed by an impromptu beer and ready-salted-crisp reception at the Feathers in Highgate village. Lou didn't have a proper wedding dress and I don't even think I wore a tie. But it was perfect: from the look of complete and utter astonishment on everyone's faces, to the scent of the four lilies that Jo insisted on buying Lucy in lieu of a bouquet hanging in the heavy August air – we wouldn't have changed a thing.

It was the best call either of us could ever have hoped to make.

little black dress

brings you fantastic new books like these
every month - find out more at
www.littleblackdressbooks.com

Why not link up with other devoted Little Black
Dress fans on our Facebook group? Simply type
Little Black Dress Books into Facebook to join up.

And if you want to be the first
to hear the latest news on all things
Little Black Dress, just send the details below to
littleblackdressmarketing@headline.co.uk
and we'll sign you up to our lovely email
newsletter (and we promise that we won't share
your information with anybody else!).*

Name: _____

Email Address: _____

Date of Birth: _____

Region/Country: _____

What's your favourite Little Black Dress book?

_____

How many Little Black Dress books have you read? _____

*You can be removed from the mailing list at any time

Pick up a *little black dress* – it's a girl thing.

ITALIAN FOR BEGINNERS
Kristin Harmel
PBO £5.99

Despairing of finding love, Cat Connelly takes up an invitation to go to Italy, where an unexpected friendship, a whirlwind tour of the Eternal City and a surprise encounter show her that the best things in life (and love) are always unexpected . . .

Say 'arrivederci, lonely hearts' with another fabulous page-turner from Kristin Harmel.

978 0 7553 4743 8

THE GIRL MOST LIKELY TO . . .
Susan Donovan
PBO £5.99

Years after walking out of her small town in West Virginia, Kat Cavanaugh's back and looking for apologies – especially from Riley Bohland, the man who broke her heart. But soon Kat's questioning everything she thought she knew about her past . . . and about her future.

A red-hot tale of getting mad, getting even – and getting everything you want!

978 0 7553 5144 2

You can buy any of these other
Little Black Dress titles from your
bookshop or *direct from the publisher*.

FREE P&P AND UK DELIVERY
(Overseas and Ireland £3.50 per book)

TO ORDER SIMPLY CALL THIS NUMBER

01235 400 414

or visit our website: www.headline.co.uk

Prices and availability subject to change without notice.